BETRAYAL

DAVID GILMAN

HEAD
ZEUS

An Aries Book

First published in the UK in 2022 by Head of Zeus Ltd,
part of Bloomsbury Publishing Plc
An Aries book

9 7 5 3 1 2 4 6 8

A catalogue record for this book is available from
the British Library.

ISBN (HB): 9781838931438
ISBN (XTPB): 9781838931445
ISBN (E): 9781838931469

Typeset by Divaddict Publishing Solutions Ltd

Printed and bound in Great Britain by
CPI Group (UK) Ltd, Croydon CR0 4YY

Head of Zeus Ltd
First Floor East
5–8 Hardwick Street
London EC1R 4RG

WWW.HEADOFZEUS.COM

BETRAYAL

For Mike Thyrring
Semper Fi

Each betrayal begins with trust.

Martin Luther

Prologue

Central America

The world was ablaze. Booming echoes of explosions ricocheted around the compound. Ignited fuel spewed lethal tongues of flame. The ammunition stored in the caves erupted, hurling debris and men into the air and casting fireballs into the treetops. Palm trees flared, beacons lighting the darkness. Howler monkeys bellowed as the troop attempted to escape the burning treetops, flames jumping from one to another, a chain of fire. What had been the silent depths of night now roared from one man's actions that devastated vehicles and buildings. Bodies lay strewn.

Gunfire crackled from one side of the jungle compound to the other. His assailant's blow to his head had disoriented him for vital moments and now he was dragged semi-conscious through the turmoil. The stench of fuel and death mingled with the sickly odour of seared flesh. He had barely escaped the city alive, but now, here in the jungle, death seemed certain.

Another explosion boomed, torn metal raining down. Crouching behind a wall, his captor forced a knee into his chest. This was his only chance. He bucked against the man's weight, but it wasn't enough; the man struck him hard.

As he slipped into unconsciousness, a final thought whispered. The attack had trapped the woman in the compound. She would have to face this killer alone.

1

Marseilles, France

Raglan walked along the narrow street that separated the single-storey terraced houses from the city's main railway station. Rich people didn't live on this side of the tracks. Streets were barely wide enough to manoeuvre a car through their labyrinthine one-way system, so Raglan stayed on foot. The Rue du Petit Sol lengthened behind him. Plenty of scope to watch for anyone tailing him. The call for his help had come through his former French Foreign Legion friend, Serge 'Bird' Sokol. Contacting the Russian ex-legionnaire was the only way for anyone to find Raglan. Especially when they needed help. And Jacques Allard had made the call. One veteran to another. Could Raglan meet him today?

As he walked past the only small tourist hotel in the street, he smelt the wafting temptation of a small patisserie at the end of the road. The sole shop and bakery in the area would do a steady trade. And they would know what there was to know about the locals. Better to hear if there was anyone other than Jacques in the house before he stepped through the door.

The house he sought was less than fifty paces away from

3

where the narrow street bellied out into a small square. Hardly a square. More like a lay-by which gave access to a nondescript backstreet garage workshop. The house was next to it. He feigned disinterest in the glossy, green-painted sheet of iron that served as a gate to the rundown building. His knowledge of the area told him it was likely to be only three rooms and a bathroom. He kept walking towards the bakery, keeping his peripheral vision on the house. Overgrown shrubbery clambered for daylight above the wall. A dog barked. He checked behind him. No one. It seemed that in every street of France a chained dog barked. But it wasn't in the target house. There, nothing moved. Not even a breeze to lift the torn lace curtain that he could just make out behind a cracked windowpane.

He bought a fresh croissant. The woman smiled, thanked him, wished him a pleasant day. French civility ruled.

'*Madame*,' he said, taking his change from a ten, 'I'm looking for an old friend who lives in these parts.'

'Oh, then you've come to the right place. My husband and I have run our business for over thirty years. We know all our customers.' She hesitated and took a second look at the tall, stubble-faced man dressed in jeans and a weatherproof oiled cotton jacket. 'Your accent. It's not from around here.'

'No,' Raglan answered. There was no need to tell her anything more. Fifteen years in the Foreign Legion's specialist commando unit and since then his work as a freelance asset for intelligence services could twist an accent this way and that. 'His name is Jacques Allard.'

French civility disappeared.

Her lip curled. 'You're not welcome here. You and your

kind. Get out before I call the police. We're sick of drug dealers. You shame us. Go on.'

'*Madame*, I apologize but I have nothing to do with drugs. My friend and I served in the army together,' he said to placate her. If the elderly woman was correct and Jacques was dealing or using, then he was already implicated in the woman's mind. She was a perfect police witness if trouble erupted.

She shouted after Raglan as he left the bakery: 'Soldiers! You're good for nothing! Better you should get yourselves killed than come back home and disturb decent people.'

Raglan was already out of sight. The half-eaten croissant tossed for the foraging birds. There was no other crumb of kindness to be had in these backstreets.

2

The sheet-metal gate was locked from the inside. Raglan checked over his shoulder. The street was empty. He climbed over. The broken canopy across the front of the house flapped forlornly. The old door hadn't seen a lick of paint since Napoleon Bonaparte had stopped for a mouthful of abuse at the corner bakery. Raglan wiped a layer of grime away from the frosted glass set in the door. There was no bell, no door knocker. He pressed his palm against the wood and, with little effort, felt it give. Someone had already forced the door and eased it closed behind them.

If an intruder was still inside and this was drug-related, then odds-on he was armed. Raglan reached inside his pocket and took the four two-euro coins the woman in the bakery had given him as change. Big coins. Decent weight. Pressing aside the door, he stepped into the gloom of the narrow entrance hallway. Most houses like this had a room on either side and another at the back that served as a kitchen and place to eat. The first of the two rooms had a bed and enough detritus to make it look like a squat. The second room was worse. The whole house stank.

He stepped down the passageway, rolling his feet to lessen any chance of hitting a creaking floorboard. Someone was moving in the back room. A muted grunt of exertion and then the sound of a drawer being wrenched open. There was another small door on his left at the end of the passageway, but he was too close to the intruder to open and check it. Pressing his back against the wall opposite the door, he dared a glance around the corner. A man was bent over, rummaging in a low chest of drawers. He wore a leather jacket, jeans and trainers. Dark-haired. Stocky.

Lying on a threadbare sofa, whose springs had long since gone, was Jacques Allard, wearing only a pair of boxer shorts. Impervious to the cold. Dead.

Raglan was about to step into the room when the door to his left opened. A burly man, head down, struggling with his shirt tails caught in the trouser zip.

'It doesn't flush...' he muttered, and then he looked up.

Raglan hit him in the throat. A short savage blow that crushed the man's larynx. He crashed back into the toilet. Raglan stepped into the back room as the second intruder turned on his heel and flicked open a folding knife with a curved blade, the crescent moon gap cut in its tempered steel to accommodate blood flow. He was a pro. Raglan hurled the coins into the man's face. He flailed, trying to protect himself from the metal striking his eyes. Raglan took two strides, levelled a kick at the man's leg and heard the kneecap snap. As the man yelled in pain, leg folding, Raglan blocked the knife and struck him in the temple. He collapsed like a felled ox in a slaughterhouse.

Raglan stepped over him, checked the small lean-to kitchenette, saw there was a back door and then turned his attention to his friend. Either Jacques had already been dead from the syringe in his arm or they had made it look like an overdose – which made no sense if the unconscious men had wanted something Jacques had hidden. Perhaps the ex-legionnaire had overdosed and his interrogators had arrived too late. He checked the dead men. They carried no wallet. No driving licence. No credit cards. If caught by the authorities, they couldn't be immediately identified. He turned the second man's palm over. Acid burns had taken off his fingerprints. Organized-crime hitmen? Drug enforcers? What the hell did Jacques have that had scared him enough to call for help? What could have been so important? Raglan checked the man in the toilet. His head had cracked the toilet bowl. Neck broken. He was dead.

It took only a moment for Raglan to decide that whatever information Jacques held, it had either died with him or was hidden elsewhere. Raglan jammed shut the broken front door then made his way back into the kitchenette. As with many a drug addict's home, there was little sign of food. He checked the cupboards. They revealed nothing more than a box of stale crackers and a bag of half-empty sugar. Sugar could help stave off the cravings. Maybe Jacques had been trying to get clean. There were some blackened rags dumped in a bowl. Raglan stepped back into the room and checked Jacques's hands. They had been washed clean but were still ingrained with oil. He rolled the body over and pressed his hands down the crack between the sofa's cushions. He found a small cheap mobile phone. He checked the calls and messages. There were few of them: all looked to be local. Two girls. Three or four men's names. Maybe trying to score? He pocketed the phone.

In the bedroom, Raglan saw the mechanic's oil-stained overalls. He slipped his fingers into the pockets and fished out a small key on a Foreign Legion fob. The motto was inscribed around its rim: *Legio Patria Nostra.* Damned right, Raglan thought. The Legion was their home and, for most veterans, it always would be. So many fell through the cracks after they had served their time. Indifference often replaced that camaraderie, and sometimes downright hostility. Unemployment and loneliness beckoned. The key looked as though it might fit a small padlock. There was no sign of any such lock on any of the cupboards or single wardrobe.

Raglan heaved aside the bed in case there was a loose floorboard that might hold a strongbox. There wasn't. Nor in the second room. It took time to clear away the mess and shift the bed, but once again there was no sign of anything hidden. Chances were there was only one place left to look.

Raglan checked his watch. Almost twelve. The French close shop for two hours at midday so they can enjoy lunch. Very civilized. And convenient. He heard the doors being rolled shut on the garage next door. A car started. Then it fell quiet. He waited ten minutes then went through the kitchen door. The enclosed yard's outside walls shared a common boundary with the garage. What better place was there for a mechanic to live than next to his place of work?

A raised corrugated asbestos roof, the rafters resting on the wall, allowed cool air to flow through the workshop. Raglan clambered on top of an abandoned washing machine and squeezed through the gap, dropping into the workshop. An old Renault stood over a pit, a toolbox on a workbench lay open. Everything pointed to an owner-garage that used an extra mechanic. Jacques Allard. Two lockers stood in a side room off the dingy office. Dirty tabletop, a grimy phone.

Finger-smudged papers and invoices. Raglan tried both of the padlocks. It was the second one. Inside the locker were a second pair of overalls, a pair of oil-slicked industrial shoes and a couple of photographs of when Jacques had served in the Foreign Legion's 2nd Parachute Regiment. The lean, tanned and muscled man who grinned back at him was not the same person whose shell lay dead inside the house next-door. Reverse metamorphosis. A caterpillar pupa digests itself and emerges as a thing of beauty. Jacques Allard had been consumed from within by whatever despair had seized him. The result was ugly.

Various car and men's magazines were stacked on the shelf. Raglan shuffled through pictures of aircraft and helicopters. Another photo from the past fell to the floor. A soldier mechanic stood with his arm around Jacques. Legionnaire buddies. The same man appeared in an article about an air museum in the USA in an aircraft enthusiast's magazine; the page corner had been turned down. The man had left the regiment and returned home.

Raglan searched his memory. And remembered the man's name. Rudi Charron. He tugged out the mobile phone he'd found in the sofa and scrolled down the names. But Charron wasn't listed. And then Raglan realized that neither was Serge Sokol's name. For anyone to contact Raglan, Sokol's name was essential. There was nowhere left to search. As a final thought he patted down the overalls but there was nothing in the pockets. He bent down and lifted out the mechanic's steel-capped shoes. Something black and shiny slid forwards into the toe. Raglan pulled out the second phone and switched it on. More than twenty names and faces stared back at him. This was the phone that Jacques did business with. In the time and date call list was the call made to Serge Sokol, seeking Raglan. Every legionnaire had the right to assume a new identity when he enlisted and there was a text from an American ex-legionnaire called Robert de Vere, who had been known as Rudi Charron. It was a simple message. *Find the Englishman.*

3

The headquarters of the British Secret Intelligence Service, known as MI6, stands at Vauxhall Cross fronting the River Thames. The Norman Foster-designed building is known as Legoland to those who walk through its doors, and legend has it that when the spooks were invited to watch the James Bond film *The World Is Not Enough* and saw their HQ being blown up through film wizardry, they cheered. Their response when, in *Skyfall*, it was completely destroyed is likely to have been ecstatic.

In an office overlooking the bridge and the river, a man in his fifties was reading. He did not need reading glasses: his vision was as sharp as his intellect. Once a commander of special forces, now he was a guardian of state secrets, and the discretion demanded within MI6 was second nature to him. As were the lies. Lean and fit, silver hair trimmed behind his ears, he sat behind a broad mahogany desk, his charcoal suit-jacket on a hanger next to his similarly dark overcoat. There was a snap to the air, particularly on the river. His white shirt was ironed. Crisp. Creased, military fashion. His groomed appearance contrasted sharply with how he'd looked during his days in the field as a soldier. Then he had been as bewhiskered and crumpled as any combatant spending months in a hostile environment. As success rewarded him with higher rank, and diplomacy and politics crept into his arsenal, so too did the understanding that those he briefed needed to be advised by a man who looked the part. Which he did.

He was reading a buff-covered report. On the top and bottom of each page the security clearance was typed in upper case: 'UK EYES ONLY', the top-secret classification designating information of particular sensitivity to the UK. The desk was clear save for three different pens neatly laid side by side. The first a fountain pen with red ink for marking queries in reports from field officers, and the other two black, one a 0.7-mm point for writing comments in a small, tight script in margins, the other a broader rollerball, usually 1.0-mm point for a snappy flourish across a sheet to instruct, commend or criticize.

He did not raise his head when a firm double tap on his door told him there was some urgency behind the request to enter his office.

'Yes,' he said.

A senior member of his staff entered the room, closed the door quietly and waited.

He finished the paragraph he was studying. Made a mark in the margin. Raised his eyes. He smiled. 'Jenny. Something of interest?' He knew damn well that Jennifer Armstrong, senior department coordinator for his division's SIS–CIA liaison, would not disturb him unless necessary.

'Mr Maguire, I have Lewis Culver from Langley on line one.'

'But you want to brief me before I speak to him.'

'Yes, sir.' She stepped up to the desk, opened the folder she carried and placed a single sheet of paper in front of him. 'We had this advisory from the Americans. Their passport control at Florida's Orlando International airport flagged Dan Raglan's arrival. He was accompanied by Mrs Reeve-Carter, her son Steven and daughter Melissa. There was no bar on his entry to the States; his visa was up to date. He used his own passport.'

Maguire read the single paragraph. 'Raglan has gone to Disneyland?'

'Disney World, sir. Disneyland is in California. He's in Florida.'

'Thank you, Jenny, I'm much the wiser for you telling me that. And the CIA wants to know why one of our assets is on their turf?'

'Yes, sir. And given Raglan's background, he isn't the kind of man to go to a Disney theme park' – she hesitated – 'without an ulterior motive.'

'You think he's going to kill Mickey Mouse?' said an exasperated Maguire.

Jenny Armstrong raised an eyebrow.

Maguire's quip had fallen flat. 'Raglan's obviously there to have some time with the closest thing he's got to a family, and no doubt they are still traumatized from Jeremy Carter's murder. His widow and children will still be grieving. It's not even been three years, Jenny. You don't get over something like that quickly. If ever. Is Lewis Culver seriously questioning his presence on American soil?'

Armstrong remained silent.

Maguire sighed. 'I have to give him something.'

She placed another sheet of paper in front of him. 'I checked. Amanda Reeve-Carter has a friend, Lisa Mayfield.

She and her son live in a gated community an hour from Orlando. The two women are good friends from some time back. Odds are that's where they're heading.'

Efficiency was a Jennifer Armstrong blessing. She left the room as Maguire picked up his desk phone and pressed a button on the console. The secure line between the intelligence officers on either side of the Atlantic clicked and then quietened.

'Maguire,' said Lewis Culver in a lilting South Carolina accent. Charm personified. His accent was described once as honey being poured over molasses. Lying beneath that southern charm was a man capable of incisive decision-making, unafraid to tell harsh truths to reluctant politicians, when his mellow tones would become as sharp as a stiletto slipped between the ribs.

'Lewis, good to hear from you. What can I do for you?' Maguire had no desire to prolong the niceties.

'Caught you at a bad time?'

'Head down in a report. I'm sorry, I don't have much time.'

'Understood. A quick one. One of your boys came through Orlando. Raglan. Barefaced. Used his legitimate passport. Is there anything I should know?'

'Lewis, he's a shared asset. Your people have used him before. No need to be at all concerned. He was involved in the Russian business here a while back.'

'Jeremy Carter?'

'Yes. Look, he's with Carter's widow and kids. They're staying with friends.'

'That's what I wanted to check. See if what he told passport control gels.'

'Hang on a moment, Lewis. Let me look something up. See if I can help.' Maguire tapped some random keys on his desktop keyboard, making sure the receiver picked up the sound. He put the phone back to his ear. 'I checked our records. Known associates of Amanda Reeve-Carter. I have an address in front of me. Friend's name is Mayfield, 2012 Cypress Avenue, Sunrise Lakes, Vero Beach. He's taking Carter's widow and kids to Disney. That's all there is to it.'

Lewis Culver grunted. 'That fits. OK. You're certain that's all it is? A family vacation?'

'Absolutely,' Maguire lied. Nothing was certain about Raglan. Except for Jennifer Armstrong's suspicion.

Raglan was not the kind of man to go to a theme park.

4

Raglan had a small daysack with one change of T-shirt, underwear and socks. The family had six suitcases. Once they had gone through customs and reclaimed their baggage at Orlando, Raglan stacked three cases on one trolley and three on another. He and Amanda's young teenage son Steve did the heavy lifting and guided the trolleys through the terminal. Amanda carried a large shoulder bag and held a tired Melissa's hand. The airport's vast atrium was a taste of a new, bright, shining world where the sun always seemed to hover in an azure sky. Eating and sitting areas were embellished with potted palm trees; the encircling curved corridors of the Hyatt Regency hotel in the heart of the airport embraced travellers, a welcoming port of call. Raglan settled Amanda and the sleepy child on a bench, told Steve to stay with the trolleys and went to a booth selling phones and SIM cards. Ten minutes later he returned and herded the family towards the exit.

Amanda and her friend Lisa had met at a conference years before, though Lisa Mayfield's life could not have been more different from twice-widowed Amanda's. A bio-scientist, Lisa had married a successful entrepreneur. They'd had a son and moved to Florida from New York.

Then, three years ago, when he walked out on the marriage with a woman half his wife's age, Lisa had taken him to the cleaners. The beach house with its multiple-car garage, staff quarters and short drive to the coast from the upmarket gated community became hers. So too the bastard's prized cars. Substantial alimony was the icing on the cake. Lisa was raising her son with no financial burden. She was free and happy.

Raglan spotted a trim, petite woman in the front row of the waiting crowd at Arrivals. Tanned, with silver hair cut short into the nape of her neck. White blouse, slim ankle-grazer slacks and a pair of red slip-ons. Rich friends. Always an asset in life.

'Is that her?' said Raglan.

Amanda saw where he pointed. 'God, why do so many American women always look so glamorous?' she said. 'I feel like Toad of Toad Hall. I can feel a spa treatment coming on.' She waved and called out and walked briskly towards Lisa Mayfield's shriek of joy. The two women embraced, kissed, embraced again. Lisa beamed with delight with perfect teeth and then made a beeline for Steve.

'Shit,' the young teenager muttered.

'Hang tough, mate. It's genuine,' said Raglan.

Lisa had the good sense not to embrace a teenage boy in public. She extended her hand. 'Steven, Stevie or Steve? What do you prefer?'

'Steve,' he said, taking her hand.

'Then welcome to Florida, Steve. You and my son will get along just fine. I know you will.' She turned to Raglan. 'And you are... Raglan.'

'Yes.'

'Just Raglan?'

'It's usually enough for people to remember.'

She placed her palm over Raglan's fist curled on the trolley handle. Her exuberance eased momentarily. Her voice lowered. 'Thank you for bringing her here. I shall make certain she and the children have a wonderful time.' There was a heartfelt note of gratitude for whatever Raglan had done for her friend. She turned on her heel. 'Come along, then. Let's get you home and settled.'

Lisa Mayfield hooked her arm through Amanda's and guided her towards the car-parking area.

Steve looked up at Raglan.

'Your mum needs this.'

Steve nodded. 'I know. But I'm not so sure I do.'

The kingfisher-blue Chrysler Pacifica minivan purred along the expressway. Amanda sat in the front talking animatedly with her friend. Raglan figured they had analyzed and embraced every breathing moment since they had last met. Except for Jeremy Carter's abduction and murder in 2019. Raglan sat at an angle so he could see the Pacifica's wing mirrors. Lisa was barely a couple of miles per hour over the speed limit as they drove the 528 Expressway east. They slowed to pay the fifty-cent toll. Raglan expected to pick up a tail sooner rather than later but as far as he could see no one was following yet. He would have been flagged at passport control and that would have been passed through to the designated agency deemed responsible. In Raglan's case that would be the CIA. He had shared missions with Agency field officers and was listed as an asset. It would take a few hours, maybe even a day before they requested the FBI to set up a surveillance team on him. It was what he wanted. Let them waste a couple of days trailing behind a man taking his family around the sights on vacation. The moment the watchers signed off on him and reported that his behaviour was not suspicious, he would be gone. Lisa Mayfield turned the Pacifica south on to the I-95 towards Vero Beach. The vehicle's mirrors still revealed nothing suspicious behind them. Not even a Highway Patrol. An hour and a half after leaving the airport they drove through the security-manned gates of the luxury community called Sunrise Lakes. Tomorrow the Feds would be on him.

And he would lead them on a wild goose chase.

5

FBI Special Agent Jenna Voss closed another bulky report folder, signed off the checklist and placed it on top of the half-dozen case files she had already studied since arriving at the Miami Field Office. The vast glass structure of the FBI building made her feel as if she were sitting in a goldfish bowl, letting the whole world see her failure every second of every day. They couldn't of course, but that didn't help ease the pain and guilt. And shame, yes, shame wrapped its damp, depressing blanket around her as surely as an east coast winter's fog. It erased any sense of warmth from the Sunshine State.

Twelve months earlier she had been riding the curve of the wave. Success in the Washington DC office had seen her promoted to Miami, where she commanded their elite Hostage Rescue Team. Nothing in her twelve years at the Bureau had made her feel more fulfilled. She was lauded for the work she did and the team she led. It seemed nothing could stop her rising even more rapidly. And then Lennie Elliot came into her life.

Lennie was an informer. And he was nurtured because he unpeeled, layer by layer, an international money-laundering cartel in Florida with suspected links to US government corruption. After a year of surveillance and raids the big prize was within sight. The man behind the operation was slipping out of the country and Lennie Elliot had given Jenna Voss the location where the big shot was going to be, and the time. After the operation Lennie was going to be well rewarded and put into witness protection. Jenna checked and double-checked. Her oversight reports went all the way to the director himself. And then she got the go. She planned the operation, led in her team and two members of the HRT were killed and three wounded.

It had been a well-planned set-up from the beginning. Lennie Elliot had played an ambitious federal agent. Perhaps, she had told herself after the failed mission, she had been blinded by previous success. It was not one piece of incorrect information but a series of small inconsistencies in Lennie's story that she had missed. The money-laundering cartel had set Lennie up as an informer, sacrificed some small-time operations and lured the Feds into a kill zone. Lennie and his masters were long gone. So too the laundered money. And Jenna Voss was held responsible.

The Bureau's internal investigation could have finished her career there and then, but the chain of command, all the way to the director, had read the reports, heard the wire-taps and ticked the go box. She was reprimanded, demoted and pushed behind a desk to do grunt work until she could be transferred out of Miami. That was her punishment. That and the searing guilt of two team-members' deaths.

She opened her desk drawer, searching for a marker pen, and saw her old insignia from the HRT mocking her. *Servare Vitas*. To Save Lives.

'Voss?'

She looked up to see the special agent who ran the Miami office standing in front of her desk. Brad Sheldon held two sheets of paper bearing the Bureau's official letterhead. 'Your transfer date's come through. Within seventy-two hours – sooner if possible. Make sure your desk is cleared.'

'Where?'

'Back to DC.' He saw the glimmer of hope in her eyes. And enjoyed extinguishing it. 'Not the Field Office. CJIS.' He handed her the sheet of paper.

She looked at her transfer details and nodded. No point in whining. They were pushing her out into West Virginia, away from the DC Field Office. The Criminal Justice Information Services Division was an electronic clearing house for data that any law-enforcement agency could tap into. It meant no field work. Just information. The DNA of fighting crime today.

'Something else,' said Sheldon, handing her the second sheet. 'I can't spare anyone else for this, so I'm sending you and Diaz.'

Voss groaned inwardly. Ronaldo Diaz was a month away from retirement, with no ambition beyond going fishing. He had been a desk jockey for the last three years. His paternal concern for her after the failed mission was well intentioned. Rather than soothe, it grated.

'Anything to get away from these,' she said, touching the stacked folders.

'Don't count on it. It's a routine surveillance. Diaz has the details. It's grunt work for the Agency. Three days tops. Stay in a motel then get back here. Call it in when the subject's on the move. The quicker I can put this to bed the sooner you can get back to these reports and clear your desk.'

He turned away. Voss looked at the scanned photo on the page with the description and name of the man on the person-of-interest sheet. It was an Englishman.

Raglan.

6

Lisa Mayfield's home gave everyone the space they needed. The pool was heated, the games room had toys for big kids and little kids, and Raglan's room over the vast garage felt large enough to host a convention. Too big. There was a huge bed in the middle of the room and a 65-inch television on the opposite wall. She had pressed the keys into his hand and told him the comforters – and then corrected herself in case the Englishman didn't know she was referring to what Europeans called duvets – were new, no one had slept under them, but there were lightweight blankets in the cupboard if he preferred. He did. Raglan tested the bed. It was too soft. Pulling the bedding on to the oak floor, he folded the feather-filled duvets to make a mattress. After showering, he stripped, switched off the air conditioning, opened the windows and slipped under a cotton throw.

The Florida dawn was too good to miss. Checking in on Steve to see if he wanted to run, he saw the boy sprawled in bed, still fast asleep. Raglan let himself out of the kitchen door and jogged along one of the roadways that looped around the estate. Within fifteen minutes he had passed two crimson lakes where egrets glared into the still waters for their breakfast as slow-flying pelicans made their unhurried way to a favoured haunt. Sunrise Lakes lived up to its name. The gated community clearly had rules. Lawns were trimmed, no behemoth RVs sat on driveways, no tarp-covered boats. In fact, there were no boats. Clean, uncluttered living. Designed for those wealthy enough to live an aesthetic life without the detritus of modern life cluttering their eyeline. Which is why the car parked beneath a palm tree in a driveway on one of the other streets a half-mile away was so out of place. The silhouette of the person behind the wheel was no romantic dawn-watcher witnessing the sun rise.

The Feds were up early.

Lisa Mayfield gave Raglan a choice of cars. He and Steve stood in front of the pristine vehicles. A classic Ferrari shared the space with other status-rich bedmates in a wealthy man's garage. Lisa knew what they were worth but good manners prevailed; she merely let slip that the convertible 1966 Bentley S3 was one of the least expensive. That probably only meant it was in the quarter-of-a-million-dollar range because the other classic cars were rock-star standard.

'You any good with cars?' said Raglan.

'Dad had a company Jag.' Steve shrugged. That was just about the extent of his interest in cars.

'Me too,' said Raglan. 'You choose.'

'This,' said Steve, laying a hand on a Land Rover Defender V8 open top.

'Good choice,' said Raglan.

Ronaldo Diaz scratched the stubble on his face. The hard motel bed had kept him up most of the night, and after he had finally dropped off, he had slept so deeply that he had awoken late for Voss's pick-up time. He had also missed breakfast. Voss knew the big man needed fuel for the day. She handed him a coffee and an assortment of pastries.

'You been up a while?' he asked.

She nodded as she kept the black-gloss Defender in sight. It was going to be a long, ass-aching day.

'Going south,' said Diaz, watching the vehicle ahead.

'Really? You know that for sure?' she said.

'Sarcasm is the lowest form of wit. Did you know that?'

'You read a book sometime in your life, Ronnie?'

'It was in a Christmas cracker. What's south of here?'

'How about Miami?'

'He's not straying from home. What's around here that's of interest to a tourist? And one who's got a teenage kid in tow? Fishing, you think? If they go out on a boat, we'll be sitting on a dock on the bay.'

'Watching the tide roll away.'

'You're gonna miss me. Admit it,' said Diaz.

'I'll miss not having your food crumbs everywhere. There he goes,' she said.

Raglan's Defender had swung towards the ocean across the Fort Pierce Inlet's causeway.

Voss sighed when she saw the sign. 'Should've known.'

*

Raglan took Steve into the cool interior of the National Navy SEAL Museum. A dozen tourists were already inside the building. It would be a slow hour or so while Raglan spoke knowledgeably about the special-ops weapons and equipment on display. The heat outside would beat down on the two FBI agents. He would let them stew awhile and then take them on a tourist route north. By nightfall Raglan would have spent the hours of daylight doing what any enthusiastic visitor might do, but he would also have contacted the man who had sent the message to the dead legionnaire in France.

In the gloom a couple of other tourists whispered reverentially as if they were in a place of worship, which, to many, this place was. Light caught glass as the front door opened. Raglan manoeuvred Steve in front of a weapons cabinet which listed a special-operations combat assault rifle's specification and saw the reflection of the woman as she half turned away from them, as if she was interested in the information being related in the brochure she held.

After Raglan and Steve had spent the best part of an hour looking at all the exhibits, Steve stopped in front of one and looked up guiltily at the man he idolized. 'I don't really like seeing all of this stuff,' he said.

'Oh? I didn't know,' said Raglan, concerned.

Steve winced. 'Just makes me think of all the violence that's around. I can't imagine you being a part of anything like this and it makes me think of Dad being killed. Just doesn't feel right.'

'I'm sorry,' said Raglan. 'It was thoughtless of me bringing you here.'

'It's like you're part of something I can't ever understand,' said the teenager, eyes scanning the weapon case. His voice dropped to a whisper. 'That you kill people.'

Raglan put a hand on the boy's shoulder. 'I don't wake up in the morning with that thought in my head, you know.'

Steve nodded. 'I'm sorry.'

'Don't be. It's understandable. Killing is never something you forget. Sometimes, though, it's necessary.'

'Like the man you killed who murdered Dad?'

'Yes. That was necessary. Things have to be made right.'

'Could you have brought him back for a trial?'

'No. There's a time when a simpler justice needs to be meted out. How about we move on? There's a place down the road I think you'll like.'

'OK,' said Steve.

'I want to check on something first so while I do that head over to that corner of the museum.'

'What am I looking for?'

'Remember the film *Captain Phillips*?' said Raglan.

'He wasn't in the SEALs,' said Steve, moving along the cabinets.

'No, but he was rescued by them and the lifeboat he was in is over there. You're allowed to sit inside.'

The boy turned to where Raglan pointed at the hard-shell-encased lifeboat. Guiding the boy allowed Raglan to step behind him and see the woman in his peripheral vision by one of the glass cabinets. She dipped her head to look at the brochure again.

*

Voss groaned inwardly. She raised her eyes and stared at her reflection. If this person of interest to the CIA was connected to the intelligence world he might have seen her. She abandoned the charade and went back to where Diaz sat waiting. He had stayed in the car which allowed him to remove his jacket without anyone seeing his sidearm. The window was down, the tie loosened, the sunglasses glimmered as she walked back to him.

'And?' he said, lifting a chilled can of drink to his lips.

'Nothing. Just a walk-through.'

'He's in no hurry,' said Diaz. 'Now that's what I call a fishing boat,' he added. He raised the camera and snapped a succession of photos of the effective-looking special-operation craft on display.

Voss leant on the car next to the open window and raised a hand across her eyes to shield the glare. 'You know that's eighty feet long and near enough eighteen high. Those boats carried sixteen SEALs plus crew. It was armed to the teeth and could do fifty knots.'

Diaz pushed the sunglasses up from his face. 'Hey, when did you get to be an expert on special ops?'

'About five minutes ago.' She tossed the brochure into his lap and relieved him of the drink can.

They followed Raglan north on the I-95.

'I staked out the house at four this morning,' said Voss.

Diaz dipped into the pastry box again and ate hungrily.

'Jenna, he's a nobody. You have no idea how many times the Agency screws up. He's low priority.'

It was not in Voss's nature, or training, to treat anyone flagged by the Agency or Bureau as low priority. Ronnie Diaz had done more than his share of dangerous investigations and arrests. He had received commendations for valour. No one questioned his years of service. But he was mentally at the end of a fishing rod. Voss might have screwed up on the money-laundering operation but she was still sharp.

'He's fit. He ran for an hour before breakfast. Not jogging, Ronnie. He ran hard.'

'He see you?' said Diaz through the Danish.

She shook her head. 'I was parked up in a driveway. Security at the gate told me the owners were away. He wouldn't have noticed. He's a visitor here, why would he think a parked vehicle outside a house meant anything?'

Diaz wiped his moustache with the paper napkin. 'OK. Your instincts are good. I know that. Mine are so out of shape they need a panel shop. We stay with him a couple of days and report back to Sheldon. As ordered. Then, job done. Yeah?'

'Yes.' Voss kept the Defender in sight. Do as Ronnie says, said the voice in her head. It's a straightforward surveillance. Probably her last considering where she was going. But she had seen Raglan pound the winding tracks through the estate. He had been focused. He had pushed past the pain barriers. She knew what that meant from her own training. But watching the man run she'd realized he had not even hit his stride. Part of her wished he would turn out to be something more than a man on vacation with a family.

And if he was?

One last chance to be involved in something that might put her back on the front line.

Redemption.

7

Raglan and Steve walked through the turnstiles into the rocket garden of the Kennedy Space Centre at Cape Canaveral and, awestruck, made their way through the various exhibitions showing the ingenuity and courage of those who had flung themselves into space riding a high-octane rocket. The time eased by as Steve relaxed, spoke more of his late stepfather and warmed to the expansiveness of the American way of life.

'It's amazing. Dad would have loved this,' he said, his pace quickening. The boy's enthusiasm was reward enough for Raglan, who made sure they wound their way from one end of the centre to the other. He gave the teenager free rein as Steve clambered through space modules and then strapped himself into the shuttle launch simulator, and all the time Raglan was keeping watch for those who followed him. He recognized the woman from the SEAL museum behind him again. She was too well-dressed to be a tourist. Her smart two-piece suit and pressed white shirt didn't fit with the casually dressed crowds. She was a long way back and if he hadn't been looking hard he would have missed her. It took him another half-hour to spot the man he thought to be with her. They had worked the crowds and bracketed his movements. Not difficult, considering he was not trying to evade them. The overweight man carried a space centre pamphlet. Raglan guided Steve straight towards him. The man put on a lost air, like any member of the public, then raised his chin, made it seem as though he had decided where he was going and walked away – he had no choice. By the time Raglan and Steve found themselves at the nose cone of the space shuttle *Atlantis* in the vast indoor hangar, Raglan had located the woman again. She was taking advantage of the shadows and low lighting, but when she stepped across a backlit doorway her silhouette matched the image Raglan held in his mind's eye. By now the older man would be footsore and no doubt hungry. Also by now they would know Raglan was nothing more than a tourist. He had bought the time he needed.

He ushered Steve away from the wonders of the space centre and swung the Defender back on to the I-95. A dozen cars back, the same dark blue sedan dipped its nose out once to check where he was. Raglan felt the temptation to give the V8 its head and power away, but he held the urge in check. The real reason for his visit was only fifteen minutes away.

The Valiant Air Command Warbird Museum was set up nearly half a century ago by volunteers determined to restore military planes used in conflict. There were over forty combat aircraft on display inside a vast hangar and on the apron beyond. Steve gaped and insisted Raglan take his photo in front of the huge Stars and Stripes that hung alongside a Grumman F11 Tiger with its painted shark-toothed nosecone. It took less than ten minutes for Raglan to find the man he wanted. Steve needed no persuading to go and explore the sleek hunter–killer lines of the jet fighters as Raglan approached the mechanic working on the C-47 transport plane. He feigned interest in reading the plaque giving the aircraft's history of carrying paratroopers across the English Channel back in 1944. An engine cowling had been removed and the mechanic stood on a raised platform working on the entwined cables and manifolds.

'Sturdy plane,' said Raglan, gazing up at the mechanic's efforts.

'Sure is. Workhorse of the Army Air Corps and more. And still flying,' said the mechanic without shifting attention from his work.

Raglan glanced around. There were few people in the vast hangar. He had deliberately arrived near closing time for that very reason. The woman and the older man had not followed him inside. He stared up at the front-of-cockpit artwork. A sultry pose from a woman with great legs and a loose-fitting, thigh-revealing blue dress. She was the original forties plane emblem: *Tico Belle*.

'*J'ai reçu ton message*, Rudi.'

Robert de Vere, the former legionnaire known as Rudi Charron, turned quickly, dropping the wrench. Raglan snatched it before it hit the ground.

The mechanic stared open-mouthed for a couple of seconds, wiped his hands on a rag then clambered down, eyes scanning the hangar. Old habits died hard. He made no attempt to embrace his old comrade in case they were being watched; instead, he turned past Raglan and climbed up the low steps into the aircraft's belly. Raglan followed. They squatted on the military benches running each side of the ribbed fuselage.

'Christ, Raglan, you made it here. I didn't think Jacques had got hold of you,' he said, voice lowered.

'He didn't.' Raglan remembered the gaunt former legionnaire lying dead in the rundown house in the side streets of Marseilles. 'I found his phone. Saw your message.'

'They killed him?' said the American.

'Who's they?'

'I dunno. There's something big going on and that's why I got the call to find you.'

'Who asked?'

'Remember Casey Zeller?'

Raglan pictured the face behind the name. At any given time there was never more than a handful of Americans serving in the French Foreign Legion. 'Yes. Kept his own name. Tried for my unit but got injured. I came across him in Central America a few years back when he was at the embassy in Venezuela. Did he contact you?'

'His wife.'

'Didn't know he was married.'

'It was a while after he came home.'

'Why would she call you?'

De Vere glanced warily beyond the aircraft's door. 'She was frightened. Still is, I'll bet. Said he told her that if he ever went AWOL that she was to find you because when you left the Legion you did intelligence work. All Casey had to give her was my name and number. All I had was Jacques.'

'You think there's a connection between him going missing and Jacques's death?'

The mechanic shrugged. 'I've never believed in coincidences.'

Raglan studied the man for a moment. He had put on the pounds since Legion days and there were flecks of grey in his dark hair but there was still enough core muscle for him to look after himself. Yet he was nervous.

'Bob, what is it? Something's spooked you. I can see that.'

De Vere sighed and needlessly wiped the wrench with the rag. 'She called me on my landline. At home. I tried phoning Jacques but got no answer. After that I felt damned sure the line was compromised.'

'Someone wiretapped your phone?'

'Dunno. Don't see who. But last I heard, Casey Zeller was at the Pentagon. Defense Intelligence. Does that ring alarm bells or what? You need a judge to give permission to wiretap. But no one has any beef with me. Anyway, that's why I used my cell to text Jacques.' He looked sheepish. 'I might be blowing things out of proportion but I swear that after I sent the text I thought I was being tailed.' He grimaced. 'Now you tell me he's dead.'

'He had a drug problem.'

'Then maybe I'm imagining things.'

'Maybe not. There were two men in his house when I got there. He had OD'd, or they had made it look that way. They were searching for something. His cell perhaps.'

'Nothing on there except the message.'

'No trouble since?'

De Vere shook his head.

'Then you're out of the loop. If there's trouble it's further up the line. Give me Zeller's address. No point phoning her.'

'Just in case?'

'Just in case.'

★

Raglan parted company with his former comrade, the reason he had created this whole charade of a trip. Those following him looked every inch FBI agents. Tasked by someone at the CIA who was concerned at his arrival. If legitimate government agencies had been spooked by his presence and a surveillance team had been put on him, that made sense. What did not yet make sense was a missing ex-legionnaire, and his distraught wife reaching out for help. De Vere was a robust, capable but nervous contact, someone who had known enough danger in his life not to be easily put on edge, yet whose instincts told him he was being followed and his phone tapped. These threads needed to be combined with the two men in France who might have killed Jacques Allard.

Raglan saw no sign of the dark sedan when he drove out of the Warbird's Museum car park but picked it up half a mile down the I-95 as they slid in behind him in traffic. He would give them one more day and one more reason to quit their surveillance and report back that he was a man on vacation. Nothing more.

It was time for him to disappear.

8

Next morning Voss and Diaz repeated their early start
and waited in a cutting across from the gated entrance to
Sunrise Lakes. Traffic was sparse. There had been no sign
of anyone from Lisa Mayfield's house leaving the gated
community. Voss had gone without coffee except for what
she had drunk at breakfast. Sitting out here on the lip of the
road gave her no opportunity to relieve herself as easily as
Diaz. She wasn't shy about walking twenty yards back into
scrubland and squatting but the thought that Raglan might
slip away from her while she was doing so would have been
a professional embarrassment too far.

It was after midday and Vero Beach would have their
diners sitting in the warmth of the late-winter sun, sipping
margaritas, making sure there was a designated driver
among them. Vero Beach Police Department and the Brevard
County Sheriff's patrol officers liked to wait in cuttings like
the one where the two special agents were parked. The cops
would spot-check drivers coming from the seafront bars
and restaurants. Occasional checks. Not too often. Nothing
regular. No pattern or timetable. There was no way those
enjoying themselves could predetermine whether a cop
lurked in the bushes on the side of the road like these two.

The Brevard County patrol officer had received a call from his despatcher. A concerned citizen from Sunrise Lakes had phoned in. It was an Englishman's voice, said the operator, a tourist concerned about his family and two people parked-up near the gated community's gates. Guy sounded really paranoid about it. Scared for the family driving about in a strange country. The cop had noticed the parked car when he passed the Sunrise Lakes entrance. He went another half-mile, spun the wheel on his Crown Vic and crossed over the median. The patrol car glided effortlessly in behind Voss and Diaz's car, pulling up ten yards short of the cutting so he could not be seen. Easing his sidearm loose he stepped cautiously up behind the two occupants.

His raised weapon and his challenge roused the two agents from their surveillance stupor. They cursed. Kept their hands where the officer could see them and obeyed his instruction to get out of the car. They asked permission to show their badges. Once satisfied he holstered his weapon and glanced across towards the entrance.

'You have someone of interest in there?' the patrol officer said.

'None of your business,' said Voss dismissively, climbing back in the car.

'Thank you, officer,' said Diaz in a more conciliatory manner as he joined his partner.

The patrol officer shrugged. Two dickhead Feds sitting on the side of the highway, their car pushed back into the bushes, were so out of place it would take a visually impaired robot not to spot them, never mind a nervous tourist.

For good measure he hit his siren when he peeled away.

Across the road Raglan moved away from the bushes that concealed him. He had confirmed it was the same surveillance team that had been following him the previous day. Had there been more than one team in place then that would indicate a higher priority had been placed on his presence. These two were routine.

Voss and Diaz's cover was blown. Cars had exited the gated community during the confrontation. People had stared. The patrolman would have logged who it was he had questioned. The 911 operator would see it on her screen and go back to assure the caller it was a police matter and there was no need for concern.

After the encounter with the Highway Patrol the Feds might as well hire a light aircraft and tow a banner telling Raglan they were watching him. They had a choice now. Report back to the Field Office, request a replacement team and face their fellow agents' scorn and insults no matter how light-hearted they might be. Or change location and spend a long afternoon and evening in a less obvious location until they crawled back to the motel.

The problem was solved for them when Lisa Mayfield's Mercedes swung out of the gates. She checked the road for traffic, appeared not to even notice them and turned the sleek Merc south.

'Ronnie, that's the friend,' said Voss.

'If she's playing any kinda game Raglan could be in the trunk of that Merc,' Diaz said.

'Or she's a decoy,' Voss suggested.

It was a no-win situation. Follow the Mercedes or hope

the man they had been following was still inside the gated community. Just how important was this Raglan character? They hesitated long enough for the blue Pacifica to turn out of the gate and head in the opposite direction from Mayfield's car. Amanda Reeve-Carter was behind the wheel, three youngsters in the back and the Englishman riding passenger.

'Going north for the I-95.'

'Be nice if he was just on vacation after all,' said Diaz, 'and that they're heading for Epcot.'

Voss swung their car into the light traffic. If the man they were watching really was nothing more than a tourist taking his family to Disney World, then they would know in an hour and a half when he turned on to the expressway. And then they could go home and file a final report that any suspicions the Agency had about Raglan's arrival were a false alarm.

The traffic on the I-95 was light so Voss kept the car as far back from Raglan's vehicle as possible without losing sight of the sleek blue people carrier. For the past hour Amanda Reeve-Carter had religiously stayed at the speed limit. They were in no hurry.

Diaz yawned. 'We can't do no more of this,' said Diaz. 'When my kids were growin' they got one Saturday in four. This guy is getting more done in a day than I used to in a month. I'm growing old tailing this Englishman.'

Voss shrugged and cast a glance his way. 'We're the bag carriers on this one, Ronnie. As soon as he's with Mickey Mouse, we call it in. All he's done so far is do what any family would do. They're turning.' She directed his attention to the road.

The Pacifica eased westward on to the 528, and once again, the two federal agents settled back for the long, slow journey. Thirty minutes later Voss saw Raglan's vehicle swing right on to the I-4 East.

'No Mickey Mouse today,' said Diaz. 'Sea World. Has to be.' The Disney Sea World theme park was north of Disney World.

'Never liked it,' said Voss.

'Why's that?'

She shrugged. 'Wild creatures should be in the ocean. Swimming free. Dolphins shouldn't be behaving like tame dogs, jumping through hoops.' She looked at her partner. 'Just like us.'

When they reached the theme park, they pulled over a safe distance from the Pacifica and waited patiently as Raglan and Amanda ushered the youngsters through the entrance.

'It's done,' said Voss. 'Happy families. Let's get back. I know I'll get stuck with paperwork.'

'It's what you're good at,' said Diaz.

A passing eighteen-wheeler's air horn blanked out Voss's expletive.

Amanda Reeve-Carter held Melissa's hand as Steve walked ahead with Lisa's son. She held her phone to her ear, waiting as Raglan covered the entrance area.

He nodded.

'It's clear,' she said and ended the call.

'You and Lisa don't have to say anything to anyone about me not being around for a few days. Likelihood is they've already lost interest. If I'm not back by the time you're due to fly out, go home without me. OK?'

She nodded but Raglan saw she wasn't happy.

'It's all right. I'm here to help a friend.'

'When you helped us in London, people died. You came close yourself.' She glanced to where her son was checking out the Sea World attractions. 'You know Steve would be devastated if anything happened to you. That would be a death too far.'

'I told him I was going off for a few days. He's OK – those two boys are getting on well together. He has enough distractions.' He lifted Melissa in his arms. 'I'm not getting into any trouble. You had better look after yourself. There's a seventy-mile-an-hour hypercoaster ride here.'

'My feet will not be leaving terra firma. And if he thinks he's going on it he has another think coming.'

'Let him take the ride. The adrenaline kick will be good for him.' He kissed Melissa's cheek. 'Are you going to see the dolphins?' he asked the excited child.

Melissa nodded. 'And the penguins. And I want to see them feeding the octopus.'

'Well, you'd better not keep them waiting.' He eased her down and touched the face of the woman who was as much a sister to him as any blood relative. When a young teenage Raglan had been orphaned and it looked as though he was going off the rails Amanda's parents had taken him in. The bond between the two was strong. It was Raglan who had hunted down her late husband's killer in Russia. She never asked if Raglan had killed him. She didn't have to. Raglan stroked the child's hair in a tender gesture of farewell and strode away to where Lisa Mayfield's Mercedes was waiting.

Thirty-three minutes later she pulled up alongside a row of palm trees next to a company logo showing a greyhound at full stretch. Passengers at the North John Young Parkway bus station waited beneath the slanted corrugated iron canopy that ran along the outside of the low-level terminus.

'It's a long ride. Are you sure you don't want to take one of the cars?' Lisa said.

'If anyone is interested in where I might be going, taking the Greyhound gives me a head start. They'd check to see if any of your cars were missing, then hire companies and airports. This is my best bet. Thanks for doing this and not asking any questions.'

Lisa had a sense of what Raglan had done for Amanda when her husband Jeremy had been murdered in London. She knew Raglan had been wounded, but Amanda had said nothing more about the circumstances of his injuries. A tight-lipped intelligence officer's widow. Lisa Mayfield looked across to the people queueing for their bus. A few unsavoury-looking characters mingled with ordinary folk. She thought of earlier days after graduating and falling in love and of how many times she and her ex-husband had caught a Greyhound because they were broke.

She turned back to face Raglan. As the question of where he was going left her lips, the car door closed.

The Englishman was gone.

Raglan found the dead zone from the security cameras in the building and settled down until the day began its descent into night. Low light outside the bus station would help to obscure his image on any security cameras when he boarded. There were fifty-six seats on the bus. First come, first served. No prebooking. Military personnel were given priority boarding but there were only two PFC women soldiers, so the boarding quickly took on a steady shuffle forwards. He keyed in Maguire's private number. If he was getting involved with US intelligence agencies because of a missing friend, odds were he would need backup. The call was brief. A missing Pentagon intelligence officer was of interest to MI6. Raglan, though, was unofficial. As always.

'We had a call from Lewis Culver at the Agency,' Maguire told him.

'I expected as much. They put a couple of FBI agents on my tail.'

'Still?'

'No. I'm on my way to DC.'

'Culver was on edge. Coincidence, do you think?'

'We'll find out,' said Raglan and hung up.

Raglan watched passengers file on. Some jostled as they pressed down the bus. Raglan took a seat two-thirds along. Far enough back to check who got on and off the bus at its designated stops. He preferred the aisle seat. Easy access. The twenty-three-hour journey meant other passengers would board further along the route. The window seat would stay empty at least until then. Raglan had no desire for a travelling companion. People can't help themselves. Their phones or tablets would be pinging away as they texted or browsed, attention spans tested beyond a few seconds, each key stroke noisily clicking away because they were too dumb to mute the device or they needed to hear

the keystroke being registered. Tactile comfort. Intrusive.
Greyhound travel: cheap, ideal for the budget-conscious,
necessary for those on limited income. And, for Raglan,
essential to buy time. He needed the hours the journey
would take to slip off anyone's radar. The couple of local
Feds shadowing him would have quit now they thought he
was doing nothing more than vacationing with his family.
Or maybe not. How nervous might they be? Wary enough
to have tracked him here? Had he missed a tail?

A varied mix of passengers boarded the bus. Black
and Hispanic, white and Asian. Some passengers shoved
overstuffed bags into the overhead lockers; hard, bigger
cases were in the hold. Teenagers, students by the look of
them, making their way home. Older couple, a man and
wife, the husband helping her secure her walking stick by the
window seat. They were followed by an African-American
man in a faded grey suit. About five ten, slight build. He
wore a pale blue shirt and as his coat jacket swung open, it
exposed a navy blue tight-knit sleeveless cardigan. He was
of an age. Seventy maybe. He looked in decent shape, a
slight paunch the only concession made to his senior years.
Stomach muscles were always the first to go. He wore a
veteran's cap. Raglan leant out and glanced down the aisle.
The man's shoes were worn from years of use but they were
polished, and there were creases ironed into his trousers.
Old guard. Someone who took pride in how he looked and
what he represented. He squeezed into the window seat on
the opposite side six seats away from Raglan.

Two ragged-arsed, down-at-heel characters wearing torn
jeans and sneakers that had seen better days shuffled in
behind him. Mid-twenties, wearing nylon jackets. Padded.

Zipped. Hoods up. A uniform by any other name. Cowled peaks of their baseball hats curved over their eyes. They grabbed the two seats behind the veteran, swinging their weight against the back of the seats in front, causing the elderly man to bob forward. He ignored them. They pushed in ear buds. Raglan saw their heads dipping in rhythm with their music.

The bus was only half full when the time came for it to leave. The doors hissed closed. Raglan glanced at the two drifters. The one on the aisle unzipped his jacket, reached in and then dipped his head and lifted the brown-bagged bottle to his lips. He concealed it as quickly as he had put it to his lips. The young black woman on the seat across the aisle glanced disapprovingly but the hard-eyed challenging stare she got in return needed no explanation. The bus rolled away; the woman got up, held on to the back of her seat to steady herself, eased down her bag and moved further along the bus past Raglan. The secret drinker's eyes followed her. They caught Raglan's. For a moment it seemed the man would raise an eyebrow, or curl a lip. A challenge. Raglan stared back with a disinterest easily interpreted as contempt. The cowled baseball cap turned away.

Raglan eased himself as comfortably as he could in his seat.

Next stop, Jacksonville, four hours north.

9

The low Miami sun had eased warmth into Robert de Vere's back muscles. The hours spent maintaining the aircraft in the Warbird Museum were gratifying but tiring. And he wasn't getting any younger. He wasn't due at the museum for another hour so had taken himself down to the coast. Seeing Raglan after all these years had triggered a wave of nostalgia and he regretted not extending an invitation to have a beer at least and catch up down on the waterfront at the Sebastian lagoon. But Raglan had been a man in a hurry.

'All right, Bob?' said the waitress. 'Finished?'

De Vere raised his eyes. He had been watching diners throw bread into the lagoon. Dolphin fins cut through the still surface, ignoring the offerings. It was the catfish that snapped at the morsels and without fail drew appreciative sounds from those who watched. 'Oh, yeah. Thanks,' he said. The waitresses here weren't lithe young women, tanned to perfection, a surfboard strapped to their pickups for when they finished their shift. These women were more matronly; you could imagine them laying down a Sunday roast for a family, kids, grandkids even.

The waitress hovered with a coffee jug. 'I'm good thanks,' said de Vere.

'The Maui fish sandwich was good?' she asked.

'More than. Never fails.'

She gestured with the coffee jug. 'You sure?'

'Yep. I'm good.'

His gaze lingered on the setting sun. He would work an hour at the museum before it closed then when everyone was gone have the place to himself. He liked that. No tourists asking questions as he laboured on his beloved engines. He had kept the Legion's helicopters flying in Africa where the pellet-hard dust was always a problem for man and machine: here, working in the vast cool hangar was easy, aching muscles or not. He eased away from the table and stepped out on to the fifty-foot dock that connected the Squid Lips restaurant to the shore. It was a favoured haunt of the locals; he knew many of them by name, others by sight. Not that many tourists were around. The regulars' cars and trucks were scattered across the parking area. He settled into his truck, glancing to the far side of the parking area as a sedan slowly reversed, wheels turning, ready to go in the same direction. He paid no attention. It had Miami plates; he thought that it might be a rental. No one around here had city plates and not many would drive the couple of hours north to have a Maui fish sandwich no matter how damned good they were. By the time he had dismissed the car from his mind he was already swinging on to the interstate. He would usually take the coast road before joining the I-5, keeping the ocean in sight as long as possible, but there was construction further up the road near the main turn-off so better to get on to the interstate and be at the Warbird in under an hour.

The ocean was turning a deep purple. A lone fin scythed

the lagoon. The dolphin jumped, splashed and was gone. A final farewell.

A fitting end to a beautiful day.

Two hours later the sun was long-gone. The handful of tourists had already been ushered out of the museum. De Vere raised a hand in farewell as the last of the staff left, and he felt the stillness and the tangible comfort of the beasts of war settle over him. He walked across to the control switches and turned off the large spotlights that highlighted every aircraft. He left a cone of light illuminating the C-47 where there was still work to be done. She would be flying off the local strip in a month. He edged around his work platform towards the nose of the *Tico Belle*. He could not help but feel a sense of pride and achievement in his part of its ongoing maintenance. She was his mistress. He hammered free a stubborn bolt, the metallic clanging echoing around the vast hangar. Such was his concentration he missed the first warning sign of an intruder. The door leading to the restrooms clicked open. It was barely audible, but had he not been focused on the problem to hand he would have heard it. Then came the sound of a footfall. Nothing more than a scuff, but enough to catch his attention. He lowered his tools and gazed across the fighter planes. The grinning shark teeth of the Grumman fighter looked more deadly in the half-light.

'Someone there?' he called. His voice bounced around the steel walls.

Silence answered. He cast his eyes around again. He thought he saw a barely perceptible shift of light over by the Phantom fighter-bomber. But then he caught a reflection of movement in the burnished skin of the A-7A Corsair and its gaping maw. His heart gave an extra beat.

'Hey. We're closed,' he called out to anyone who might still be inside the hangar.

Something else caught his eye. The Stars and Stripes crinkled. Instinct took his eyes to a fanlight. He snorted. Dumb bastard. Damned night breeze must have caught the flag is all. Jesus, Bob, spooked by the wind. He shook his head in disbelief at his own nervousness and returned to the task at hand. Seconds later a searing hot pain caught him behind his leg. His mind couldn't compute what had happened. The leg wouldn't bear his weight. He gripped the engine cowling, cursing as the hammer fell from his hand. As he hopped in pain, he felt the warmth run down his leg. He looked down at the slash across the back of his leg and the flowing blood. Gazing up at him was a woman. Immediate thoughts were she was like one of those athletic types who ran down at the beach. Slim, dressed in body-hugging black. Red running shoes. A black peaked cap obscuring half her face as she watched him, her blonde ponytail tucked in neatly at the back. None of this made sense. The pain intensified. She was holding something in her hand and below it a small oil slick of blood formed on the polished concrete floor.

His weight forced him to loosen his grip. He grappled with the work platform, slid down; his good leg failed to take the strain and he fell badly, the damaged leg taking the full brunt of the impact. He cursed through clenched teeth. Eyes screwed in pain, his mind still couldn't make any sense of what was happening.

'Help me,' he said, looking up at the lithe woman who watched disinterestedly.

She went down on one knee. Her eyes were still shadowed by the cap's peak.

'Jesus, lady... what... what's happenin' here? Call 911.'

'Raglan isn't around to help you. You know that.'

'Raglan?' De Vere winced, one hand gripping his severed hamstring. His mind swirled. 'Raglan? I don't know anyone called that.'

She took a moment, watching his pain. 'A man shouldn't die with a lie on his lips. You don't have to protect him. I know where he's gone.'

Her hand whipped across his neck. That same razor heat tore across his throat. He choked, hands gripping the gaping slash. He was drowning in his own blood. The woman stepped away. The last thing Robert de Vere saw was the curved beauty painted on the *Tico Belle*. And her come-on smile.

10

The Jacksonville stop was a leg-stretcher. Several passengers disembarked, and another dozen boarded. The veteran walked to the restrooms as Raglan bought himself a soft drink. The two young black men who had sat behind the older man smoked, shoulders hunched, heads down, folded in on their own narrow world as they leant on the depot's hoarding. The empty bottle had been dropped in the trash. Raglan noticed their eyes. They looked glazed. Booze and something else. They shuffled back on board, took the same seats behind the quiet man. The ruction started two hours later when the bus was halfway to Savannah.

The two men were curled back in their seats, hoods pulled low. Ear buds shutting out the wheels' humming traction on the road surface. Their voices had become louder, increasing in volume the longer the bus rolled onward. Exclamations of satisfaction with their music were punctuated with occasional expletives. The bus driver switched on his mic, asked over the tannoy for the language to be kept down. That worked for another twenty miles, then their bent knees pressing into the back of the vet's seat became too much for the old soldier. He half stood, twisted so he could speak to them and asked politely for them to stop rocking his seat.

He was met with grunts. Was that an acknowledgement or disrespect? Raglan saw the badge on the man's cap. He was an Airborne veteran: 101st. The legendary Screaming Eagles. Likely to have been in Vietnam, looking at his age. He didn't budge. He stared the punks down until the one on the aisle raised his face and smirked.

'Fuck you, old man,' said the younger man.

The vet appeared to take no offence. He nodded, leant forward and said calmly, 'Son, if you two keep annoying me the way you have been these past few hours then I will be happy to give you a lesson in good manners.'

By now the younger man's travelling companion was sitting upright. The two of them stared at the old man who gazed down at them. The one on the aisle eased out of his seat. He had a couple of inches in height and fifty pounds on the grey-suited veteran.

'Old man, you wanna walk off this bus on your own two legs you'd better shut the fuck up. Fuckin' baby-killers like you don' get no free pass here.'

'Well, then perhaps I should ask the driver to pull over and put you off the bus,' said the veteran, his voice still reasonable. And without smiling added, 'Before you get hurt.'

That's when the punk made his first mistake. By now the old man was in the aisle facing him and backtracking a couple of paces; maybe the kid thought he was going to complain to the driver. Raglan saw it for what it was. The veteran was giving himself room to move.

The kid made his second mistake. He poked a finger in the veteran's chest. Once. Twice. Fuck you. And fuck you again. He jabbed a third time. It was what the old man wanted. He had drawn him in. Empty seats either side. His hand shot out, grabbed the kid's wrist, twisted, used his own momentum to overcome the aggressor's weight advantage, threw him off balance, and hit him hard. A double tap with his left fist. Temple and throat. Stunned and choking, the man fell into the empty seats. The veteran was facing the front now, back turned as he twisted and held the flailing man's wrist. Swan-necked. Classic self-defence manoeuvre. Cops use it all the time. That's when the victim's companion swung himself free of the seat; his right hand came out of his pocket with a knife. He was concentrating on the old man's turned back, ready to ram the blade in, but he had the instincts of an alley cat and sensed the new threat behind him. He spun around and slashed wildly. The knife caught Raglan's coat sleeve as he stepped into the aisle to save the older man from having the blade stuck in him.

The man screamed as pain ricocheted up his arm into his neck and back: Raglan had gripped his bicep, fingers digging beneath his muscle into the arm's deep-seated nerve, its origin in the spinal nerve roots. The knife dropped; he went down on his knees, mouth gaping from the blinding hurt. The vet looked over his shoulder, saw what had happened.

The veteran nodded his thanks.

'No problem,' said Raglan.

By then the driver had pulled the bus over. Air brakes hissed. He was a big man in his own right. He saw what had happened.

'I'll call the cops,' he said.

'No need for that,' said Raglan.

The old man looked hard at Raglan. Natural thing to do would be to have these two hauled away. But he understood.

Cops could complicate this man's life. The man who had saved him.

'That's right,' said the vet to the driver. 'No need for cops. That would hold up these good folks on the bus and make a dent in your schedule.'

The driver nodded. The less complicated the better. He turned away, hit the door release. The doors hissed open. The driver, the vet and Raglan bundled the troublemakers off the bus on to the verge.

A minute later the driver engaged gear and eased the Greyhound away. He made a brief announcement about abusive, drunk passengers, relayed a set-piece comment on company rules and assured everyone the disturbance had been dealt with in an appropriate manner and that they would still arrive in Savannah and all points north in good time.

The veteran eased himself down into the opposite aisle seat to Raglan's. Close enough without either man feeling crowded. He extended his hand. Raglan took it. There was strength in the man's grip. Not to impress, just inherent firmness.

'I owe you my thanks. He'd have shanked me.'

Raglan dismissed the man's gratitude with a compliment. 'You'd have seen him out of the corner of your eye. You didn't really need my help. Besides, it livened up a boring journey.'

'Sorry about your jacket.'

'No matter. It's been around the block a few times.'

'You're English.'

'I am.'

'TJ Jones,' said the vet, offering his hand.

'Raglan.'

The Airborne veteran nodded. 'Then my thanks again, Mr Raglan.'

'Just Raglan is fine, Mr Jones.'

'TJ.'

'TJ,' said Raglan, reflecting the man's smile.

11

As the Greyhound passed through Savannah, Georgia, then rolled across into South Carolina and northward to its sister state North Carolina, TJ and Raglan settled into easy conversation. It was sparse at first. Neither man was in a habit of social chit-chat. Little mention of sport; less still of the weather, which became wetter and colder the further north they travelled from Florida's sunshine. A common bond emerged over the miles when they discovered a shared love for books. It allowed both men to avoid becoming too personally involved with a stranger but eased the strictures of formality. Slowly each man began to give a little more of himself. Not much – just enough to engender companionship on the journey north.

The passenger manifest slimmed down after Fayetteville. It made sense. The warmth was south; the cold that scratched the skin could already be felt when they crossed the state line into Virginia. By then enough had passed between the two men for each to know a little of the other. Raglan was going to DC to find a friend who might be in trouble. TJ had been in Orlando at a veterans' reunion. And former master sergeant Titus Jackson Jones was old enough and wise enough to sense that the Englishman sitting opposite him was not the kind of man who needed any free advice. But he was going to give it anyway.

The older man had waited a few hours, gauging when to ask the question that needed to be asked. 'Now, I don't want to cause offence to a man who saved me from having a blade stuck in my back, but when the driver was going to call the police about those two misguided members of society, you were keen that he did not, so I ask: are you in trouble with the law?'

'Because then you might be guilty by association.'

'Self-preservation is something I have learnt over the years.'

'I'm not in trouble with the law. I'm a tourist, so I didn't want to get drawn in. These things have a way of worming their way on to future visa applications. Like I said, I'm here to find someone.'

'You know DC?' said the veteran.

'No.'

'Friend, being a stranger in a city like DC means there are places you should not go.' He raised a hand to stop Raglan's response. 'I know. You can handle yourself. That's a given. All I am saying is that it'd be good to know your ground.'

Raglan studied the older man's face. He was offering the hand of friendship and with that came free advice that could prove valuable. He remained silent. A signal for the veteran to keep talking.

'Like you would want to know where you would patrol if you had ever been in the army or suchlike.'

'Or suchlike.'

'Right. You'd want to know where your enemy might be.'

'It would be helpful,' said Raglan. Now the man knew Raglan had served in someone's armed forces.

'Good thing would be to base yourself in or near the centre because DC spirals out into suburbs, so good access in and out, but you need deep pockets to stay in the city. Now, I would like to extend my appreciation for what you did back there and draw you the no-go zones on a map when we get to DC.'

'That would be helpful.'

'It would,' said TJ, 'because, son, you look like the kind of man who might want to go where the trouble is.'

TJ nudged Raglan awake when the Greyhound reached Dupont Circle bus stop in Washington DC. Raglan followed the veteran, taking in his surroundings at what looked to be the capital's downtown area. He fell in alongside the veteran's easy stride.

'Plenty of hotels in this neck of the woods. Expensive for the likes of me, mind,' said the vet. He gave an enquiring look at the athletic man at his side.

'I don't want anything fancy. A room, a shower. Somewhere to eat. I'd be obliged if you pointed me in the right direction.'

'Oh, I can do one better than that. I happen to be going right past a place that might just suit you. Twenty-minute walk OK?'

Raglan checked the street signs. They were heading south.

TJ skirted the busy traffic on New Hampshire Avenue, which looked to Raglan as if it fed traffic north and south. His companion pointed out places. This hotel, that deli, there's Pennsylvania Avenue, home to the White House. Metro's there. Foggy Bottom station in that direction. 'That building peeking over the skyline is the George Washington University Hospital. I can attest to their skill,' said Raglan's companion without further explanation.

Raglan thought it none of his business to enquire further. He listened and looked. TJ was like a reconnaissance patrol leader pointing out the lie of the land. Three side streets and a couple of half-turns later, a quieter street presented itself. Old-fashioned, low-rise apartment blocks that had escaped the developers' bulldozers.

'This is the place that might suit you. I know the owner. He's not always agreeable to having people lodge with him but if you were thinking of an Airbnb around these parts you might as well pay a hundred and fifty a night in a hotel. You picked an expensive place to do your visiting, my friend.'

Raglan followed him through a narrow entrance into a modest quadrant of lawn and shrubbery, a few flower beds lying dormant waiting for the warmer weather. At first glance the three-storey walk-up had a couple of dozen apartments. The entrance vestibule was pure forties. A bygone era. Highly polished tiled floor and painted walls in cream and brown. No graffiti. No scuff marks. No noise.

'Mostly retired folk here,' the vet told him. 'Fixed rentals for life. Otherwise none of the residents could get within a snake's spit of the place.'

He opened the first door on the left and ushered in his travelling companion. The dark herringbone, polished-wood flooring was original. The lampshades too by the look of it. The only nod towards the modern world seemed to be the modestly sized flat-screen television in the lounge corner beyond the entrance hall and coat rack. It was not a large apartment, but it felt right. A bookcase displayed well-worn books. Fiction separated from non-fiction. They all looked as though they had been read more than once. The window overlooked the quadrant.

'This is your place,' said Raglan.

'That it is,' said TJ, shrugging out of his jacket, hooking that and his veteran's cap on to a coat stand. 'I'm the superintendent here. For which I am paid a modest stipend and have use of this apartment. It is a happy relationship I've had for more than twenty years.' He pointed beyond the bathroom. 'There's a small spare room back there. A cot and a couple of hooks for clothes behind the door. It was my son's room when he was home on leave. Figured you don't have too many suits to hang up. I have food in the freezer. I'll rustle up a bite to eat while you take a shower.'

Raglan knew it was an offer too good to refuse.

12

The table was just big enough for two to sit without banging heads when each man dipped forward to spoon the food into their mouths.

'I sure hope you like chilli beans,' said Raglan's host as he placed two steaming bowls on the table. Bread and condiments were laid out on a freshly unfolded tablecloth. The man had probably spent years in the military and, like others who suffered hardship and deprivation in the line of duty, would have eaten food from a tin, flies and all. Once home, a crisp tablecloth and clean cutlery made a man feel human.

Raglan had seen only two framed photographs on the room's mantel. One was of a young black man and his bride. A woman shorter than her husband by a good six inches. Her eyes sparkled and her arm was wrapped around the man she loved, the man who now sat opposite him. It looked to date from the 1970s. The other photograph was a three-quarter shot of a fresh-faced lieutenant sporting a maroon Airborne beret. Like father, like son, Raglan guessed. They ate in silence for a couple of minutes. The beans were good, the warmth corrugating the back of the throat. Raglan sipped the bottle of chilled beer.

'You married, Raglan?'

'No.'

'Not even close?'

Raglan shook his head and spooned in the beans.

'I recommend it. It has its benefits. For a start you get to eat better than this.'

'This is good,' said Raglan, sipping again.

'Well, it's what's available right now until I get across to the whole food store. But the positive thing about being married is that the right woman keeps you on the straight and narrow. Keeps you from doing dumb things.' He paused in his eating and looked at Raglan. 'Saved me, for sure. I came out of Nam with a mess of squirming snakes in my head. I was ready to take on anyone. Look at me the wrong way and one of us was going down in the dirt.' He gave a nod in the direction of the mantel. 'She saw me through it. The bad nights. The nightmares. She gave me purpose. She's been gone fourteen years now,' he said matter-of-factly. 'There isn't a waking minute in every God-given day I don't think of her. We had insurance back then and that hospital I showed you, they did what they could. Her heart just didn't want to beat any more. I wonder if I hadn't broken it.'

'I'm sorry,' said Raglan.

TJ shook his head. Memories of war never left men like him and Raglan. 'Oh, it's not sympathy I'm after, it's a sharing with someone who I think might have a few of the same issues I had back then.' He saw Raglan's hand falter with his spoon. 'Now, I don't mean to offend but you were mumbling in French when you slept on the bus. Seemed you had a bit of a tussle going on inside. You being an Englishman, I'm guessing you served in the Legion at some point. That where you did your soldiering? The French Foreign Legion?'

'Fifteen years,' admitted Raglan.

TJ Jones gave that a moment's thought. It told him a damned sight more about Raglan than most else he could have said. He eyed his guest. 'The paratroopers?'

Raglan nodded.

'I'll be damned. The airborne brotherhood is alive and well. And your Legion had its own misery in Indochina as they called it back in the fifties, long before you were born. I'll wager you know your history about the Legion and how your people kept sending in their airborne at Dien Bien Phu no matter how bad it was. My friend, that history repeated itself.' He laid down his cutlery and rested his elbows, hands clasped. 'Fifty-odd years ago I was a know-it-all kid from the bad part of town with a chip on my shoulder bigger than the Empire State. I was a tunnel rat. I went underground and I dug out the VC with knife and pistol. But then in March 1970 they sent my regiment up to the A Shau Valley to rebuild and man Fire Support Base Ripcord. You heard of that?'

Raglan shook his head.

'Not many have. With good reason. It was a focal point for the North Vietnamese Army. We were going to hit their supply lines. They were damned good fighters. Crazy to die. Had more courage than a junk-yard dog let off its chain. We had some of that ourselves. Ripcord was to be the jump-off point for the covert sweep into Cambodia. I tell you, they came at us with every damned piece of firepower they had. For months. And then they got real serious. The big hit came on the first of July and they kept that up for twenty-two days.' He eased the plate of food away. His voice softened further. 'We lost two hundred and forty-eight dead on that hill and it was hushed up because the government didn't want any more bad publicity about the war.' He paused again and put the beer bottle to his lips. 'I still hear the explosions and screams to this day.'

Raglan felt the man's eyes searching his own. He shook his head. 'I never fought in any war like that.'

The Vietnam veteran gave an almost imperceptible shrug. 'But you know the shit-scared heat of battle. That's all it takes for the past to stay at your shoulder.'

'I left the Legion before it got too bad.'

'Well, I stayed on. Nothing was the same after Ripcord. It made me so damned hard and bitter. I went up a few steps and earned me some rank. Day came when I was about to put a bullet in a major's head because he was a goddamned medal-hungry, desk-jockey SOB. My young lieutenant saved me and him. I left soon after. Some of the best decisions were made by the non-coms and junior officers. Most had a way back to civilian life. They didn't have to worry about the greasy pole. Didn't think of their own careers. Their men came first. First and always.' He paused, his eyes flitting quickly towards the photograph. 'That's what I drilled into my boy. And I think he took that on board.'

'My commando unit worked with your special forces in Afghanistan. They were hard days.'

'Then you'll understand when I tell you that my boy clawed his men out of an ambush.' He sipped beer. 'He didn't make it, though. I guess he took my advice to heart.'

Raglan recognized the quiet dignity of the man sitting

opposite. The burden of war and personal loss had not diminished him. A part of Raglan hoped he might display the same poise when, and if, he reached the same age. He, like TJ, often heard ghostly cries demanding that he remember. He could lock them out and find sleep.

What haunted him were the eyes of the dead.

13

Raglan was up early. He walked barefoot through to the kitchen, wary of waking his host. He needn't have worried. He saw TJ through the window, dressed in a tracksuit, doing exercises. For once Raglan felt positively slovenly. The veteran saw the movement behind his kitchen window, gave a brief acknowledgement and dropped out of sight to do press-ups.

By the time Raglan had fried a couple of eggs and the toast had popped, a breathless TJ was just coming back inside.

'You said to help myself,' said Raglan.

'Glad you did. Sleep well?'

'Good firm bed, thanks. Shall I rustle up some breakfast for you?'

'No. Just coffee. I take a break about eleven and head down to a diner. Get to my age and you pile on the pounds, then the damned joints get worse, and next thing you know they're feeding you through a straw.' He reached on top of the refrigerator and took down a map of DC and environs; easing aside the tabasco sauce on the table, he unfolded it. Raglan finished the last mouthful of the eggs and toast and moved the plate so the map could be spread out fully.

'I marked this up for you last night. Pretty basic but will give you an idea. I use paper not digital. You OK with that?'

'Perfect.' Raglan looked at the marked-up areas. Like many American cities, Washington was laid out in grids. Easy to follow as, other than named avenues, the streets were alphabetical like K Street, L Street and so on.

TJ's finger pressed at a point on the street map. 'There's Dupont Circle, there's the hospital, you're here. Metroline there. That's a short walk. Bridges across the Potomac here and here. Roosevelt Island, that's a good place for a run. Gets you off the streets. Be careful, though, if you run from here on the bridge, the sidewalk's narrow so you're close to heavy traffic. Early morning you'll be OK.' His finger moved on. 'Happy Families suburbs where people feel safe are here: West End, Capitol Hill, Georgetown, Woodley Park. No undesirables around there except for bankers and politicians.' He tugged the map down a fraction. 'Now here, this is where you will draw attention to yourself and the locals might not be so friendly. Highlands Bellevue, not recommended. North of Massachusetts Avenue, some good places to eat but don't take a wrong turn. Columbia Heights, then Brentwood, plenty of gunfire up there. You don't need me to give you the grand tour. If it's marked in red, that's the hot zone.'

'Thanks, TJ.'

'Stay here long as you want, Raglan. I don't mind some company. There's a spare key on the hook by the door.' He pointed to his son's room. 'You'll need a coat. I gave yours to a woman upstairs to stitch.'

'I'm qualified with needle and thread,' said Raglan.

'I know. We all are, brother, but it's kind of a community

here, we look out for each other. Favours asked, favours given. Gives some of these elderly folk a sense of being useful. Sad but true. My son was about your size. Take one of his.'

'That's thoughtful of you, thanks. Point me to a store and I'll bring in some groceries.'

'No need yet. OK, so where are you heading?'

'Where's Stafford? There's a woman lives there I need to meet.'

The veteran sighed. 'Well… I dunno. It's a way out. I don't think there's a bus and the Metro goes as far… Hang on a second. I don't travel out of town much. I know someone in the building who used to.'

He picked up his phone and punched in a number. Raglan heard the ring tone and then a muted voice answering.

'Beth Ann, it's TJ… Oh, fine, fine, thanks. Beth Ann, how do you get out to Stafford? No, not for me, a friend. The one whose coat I gave you.' He listened. 'OK, that's good, thanks. Yes, drop it down when you're ready. Then I'll catch up at the monthly meeting.' He replaced the phone and smiled. 'We get together once a month in the diner I told you about. We have coffee and waffles. That way I get to hear any problems without us getting bogged down in paperwork. She's a kinda sounding board for everyone here. OK. Stafford. You take the Blue Line from the Metro station down the road as far as Franconia–Springfield – that's a half-hour. After that it's a cab or thumb a ride I guess. Might be a car-hire place there.'

Raglan folded the map. 'Thanks, TJ. I won't outstay my welcome. As soon as I've sorted a few things out I'll leave you in peace.'

'Trust me, I have enough peace and quiet. Like I said, there's a key on the hook.'

Raglan spent the morning and half the afternoon walking the surrounding streets familiarizing himself with his location. Streets were easy enough to navigate. Landmarks simple to identify. Points of reference should he need to use them in an extreme case. The darkening sky threatened rain and low light. He headed for the Metroline. Below ground it was architecturally ugly. Brutal with its vast, bunker-like slabs of overhead concrete. Perhaps, Raglan thought, a bunker might have been its purpose. Neuroses born of old Cold War cabin fever in the Capitol. Compared to the Moscow underground transit system, which was a place of beauty, this harsh environment offered no visual stimuli to the commuters who went down its gullet, soon to be regurgitated elsewhere. The crowds thinned at each stop along the way. Many of the passengers alighted at the Pentagon, a similar number at the Pentagon City station. He guessed there was some kind of shopping mall there from what he overheard of the conversation between two women passengers.

By the time they left the Regan Airport stop, the train was pretty much empty, and when they halted at Franconia–Springfield, barely a handful remained. The cab company wanted seventy dollars to drive him one way. A local car rental wanted a third of that for the day. No brainer. Raglan paid the cab. He wasn't yet ready to lay a trail in DC with his driver's licence. The time would come soon enough when he would want the right people to know where he was, and if the wrong people were looking, then he would draw them to him only when he was ready.

A half-hour later the cab swung past a sport and leisure centre and then followed the road leading into a modern housing estate. The scraped landscape was still being built on. Work in progress. Two- and three-storey houses nestled side by side, fenced yards at the rear, concrete drives leading to garages up front. Raglan gave the driver instructions to drive around the dozen looping streets.

The driver eyed his passenger in his rear-view. 'Mostly retired military. Officer types. This might be a new neighbourhood but they won't take to no stranger wandering around their streets. Cops are sharp to respond around here. Know what I mean?'

'I know what you mean.'

'You want I should take you to the address?'

'Go around again.' He knew the street he wanted and if the woman who had called for help was home, he wanted to check the surrounding area. Raglan had given the driver a different house number than the one he wanted, which was five doors down. Other than construction workers on various builds there was no sign of anyone watching the house. 'Pull over there,' he told the driver. 'Behind that grader.'

The driver made an easy turn and came up alongside the parked machine, its bulk obscuring the cab. Raglan keyed in the phone number he had memorized. It rang. He half expected voicemail but a woman answered. Nervously. An edge to her voice that said she was frightened of bad news arriving down a phone line.

'Mrs Zeller?'

'Yes?'

She hadn't asked who had called.

'I'm a friend. You sent a message.'

He heard her intake of breath. 'Oh,' she said. 'I see.'

She was being cagey. That meant she thought others might be listening.

'Is there a place we could have a coffee? Somewhere nearby?'

He heard the sense of relief in her voice. She gave him the name and address of a pancake and coffee house.

'Did you hear that?' he asked the driver.

The man's eyes locked more warily at his passenger through the mirror. 'Mister, I don't want to get involved in anything illegal here.'

'You're not. She thinks her husband is having an affair so she sent for me to investigate. I'm from out of town. Makes it easier,' Raglan lied convincingly.

'Oh. Oh, OK. You don't look like a PI.'

'That's the idea.'

The cab driver grinned sheepishly. 'I guess.' He pulled away and headed for the pancake house.

When they swung off the highway Raglan had him drive around the back of the brick-faced building. There were few people inside. He paid and gave a good tip.

'I'm here to help, not cause harm. Her husband isn't. Anyone asks, don't put her life in danger.'

Raglan's solemn tone did not sound like a request.

'Hey, I'm off my usual route. I was never here.'

Raglan waited on the opposite corner. He had already made a note of the security cameras. They were basic. One at the far side of the front of the building, the second inside the front door. He saw a compact pull up, and a petite, worried-looking woman got out, clutching her shoulder bag close to her hip; she pinged the car's remote and, looking around, went inside. She checked for anyone who might have been Raglan, failed to find him, and sat at a booth. Raglan waited another three minutes until two women drove up and walked across to the front door. He strode over to the coffee house, pushed through the door ahead of the women, turning his head as he held the door open for them. The gesture obscured his face from the camera. He went straight to her table.

She looked alarmed at the tall, rough-looking stranger, then calmed at his smile. She saw a kindness in his eyes.

'I'm Raglan,' he said.

14

Anne Zeller had the maturity and grit that befitted a woman who had married a Marine Corps officer. Her resilience shone through but so did her fearfulness as to the fate of her husband. The fear that had been strong enough for her to send word to a stranger for help.

'I didn't serve directly with your husband, Mrs Zeller – '

'Anne,' she interrupted. She raised her coffee cup, peering over its rim at the man opposite her. She knew now she had made the right call. Raglan had not tried to impress her, had not spoken of unofficial exploits. He had said very little other than to introduce himself and express his concern. He had not asked for money. He was everything she had hoped he would be.

'Anne, how long has Casey been missing?'

'Nine days and...' She glanced at the coffee house wall clock. 'Eighteen hours.'

He liked her precision.

'And before you ask, Mr Raglan, I have been questioned on three separate occasions by the police. He was not in financial difficulties. He was not suffering from any mental illness. He went out for his evening run one night and never returned.'

Raglan saw her hand tremble. She fussed in her purse and pulled free a photograph of a handsome man with greying hair, cut short. The strong features and smile of the soldier Raglan remembered.

She tucked the photograph away. 'Casey did his time in the Legion and then came home to serve ten years in the Fifth Marine Division before transferring to the First. He retired with the rank of major. I met and married him soon after he came back to the States. I was raised on army bases.' She smiled. 'He was a marine but he never held that against me.'

Raglan sat with his back against the wall, facing Anne Zeller and the rest of the coffee-house and with an unobstructed view through the large plate-glass window of the streets outside. 'There were never more than a few Americans serving with us. I know there's always a daisy chain of men who stay in touch. Can you tell me how you came to reach out to me?'

She hesitated. Raglan saw her lips tighten. She glanced nervously out of the window and then looked at the man who had come to help her. 'I knew Casey had friends from the Corps and his Legion days but I didn't know who they were. He never went to reunions, never really spoke about his past. One night, a month before he went missing, Casey sat me down and told me that he was working on something of national importance. I was scared to death right there and then. God help me, I had waited around like any other military wife while her husband went to war but this was different. This was peacetime.' She took a slow, deep breath. 'He calmed me down and said that whatever happened he would make sure I was safe, and if he had to leave without telling me it would be because he needed time to evaluate the information he was investigating but I wasn't to tell anyone that. Why? Why couldn't I explain to anyone who asked, who wanted to find him?' She shook her head at the memory. 'He made me promise.' She dabbed a napkin to her lip. A small gesture, buying time to focus her thoughts. 'How was I supposed to live with that? The not knowing. Every day wondering if he was coming back from the office.' She paused. 'I hated him for telling me. Then, when he didn't come home, those feelings made me feel guilty. I trust my husband. And I have to be strong for him. I waited all that night and then I phoned the man in Florida.'

'So Casey gave you de Vere's name and number?'

'Yes. Because he said that word would reach you and that you would come. So he had enormous faith in you.'

'And how soon was it that Casey's people at work got in touch?'

'The next morning. As soon as I reported him missing to the Sheriff's department. Casey's boss was worried. He asked me if I knew anything. I played dumb. I knew I couldn't say anything about reaching out to an old contact of Casey's. That's all.'

'Nothing else happened?'

'Like what?'

'Was there anything else that seemed out of place?'

'No. Well, he got a phone call late one night a week or so before he disappeared. We were in bed. I was half-asleep. He told the person who phoned they shouldn't have used his home number and how the hell did they get it? He was upset. He didn't speak to them and when I asked him about it he said it was a nosey journalist looking for a story.'

'Did he say what about?'

'No.'

'Did you mention that to whoever questioned you?'

'Yes... I... think so.'

Raglan backtracked, figuring out who knew what and when. 'So you spoke to Bob de Vere in Florida?'

She nodded. 'I spoke to him a couple of times. It was a bad line. He said he would reach out, that you weren't easy to get hold of. Then he phoned me back a while later and said he had found a contact for you in France and to stay put and say nothing.'

'Who's Casey's boss?'

'Jack Swain.'

Raglan knew the name. Swain had served with the Defense Intelligence Agency as a liaison officer when the Foreign Legion and American special forces were operating in Afghanistan. Their paths had crossed on a couple of occasions when Raglan became an asset for the British and American intelligence services. 'Anything more than him being Casey's boss?'

'They were running partners. He used to come around the house for the occasional beer. The two of them would hunker down in the den and watch a game, have a beer. Nothing more than that. I never got close to him.'

Intelligence communities function on connectivity, and there was little doubt that the poor telephone connection Anne Zeller and Bob de Vere had experienced meant Zeller's phone had been tapped from the moment he went missing. Perhaps even earlier. Court orders could be circumvented and the likes of Jack Swain had people he could use to bug a line unofficially. The DIA was located south of DC in its own headquarters but there was always a DIA presence at many levels in the Pentagon: if Jack Swain was still with that agency was he tasked with a specific brief? It seemed to Raglan that the two men were more closely connected than the missing man's wife knew. He decided to test her further.

'When Casey retired from the Corps, did he go to work at the Pentagon straight away?'

Anne Zeller shook her head. 'Not right away; we did two years at the embassy in Venezuela first. It was a terrible time. Their president had kicked out our ambassador. There was the whole anti-US feeling. Casey organized the logistics for the staff and the Marine Corps protection unit. Then we came back and he went to the Pentagon.' She sighed and sipped her coffee. 'Thank God. It got very messy there.'

'Did he talk about his work? Was he serving with the DIA? Were you ever briefed by them? Told what they expected from an agent's wife?'

It was a quick test to see if Zeller's wife was part of the intelligence fraternity. It might be a commonly held belief that US embassy attachés were mostly DIA agents, but it was little known that their wives were always briefed as to what was expected of them.

She shook her head. 'We led a very quiet life. He was in an office. Nine to five. Said he'd had enough excitement in his life.'

Raglan was satisfied that she was innocent of her husband's involvement, if he *had* been working for the DIA. 'Anne, Casey and I served in the Legion, as you know, but I caught up with him a few years ago when he was in

Venezuela. I was doing a private job rescuing an American woman who was being held and ransomed by FARC.'

Anne Zeller looked startled. 'The revolutionary people? The terrorists?'

'Yes. We nearly didn't make it out. I heard there was a former legionnaire in the embassy. I reached out; it was Casey. It wasn't a social call. I didn't know he'd married. He pulled strings for me. I'm guessing that he needed some kind of clearance and that he vouched for me with someone in Defense or CIA. I'm not sure who that would have been but it would make sense if it was Jack Swain, because we had bumped into each other years before.'

'I didn't know any of that. Casey never mentioned it.' She hesitated. 'But then he wouldn't, would he?'

'What agencies questioned you? Tell me, step by step, who arrived and in what order.' There would be more than one law-enforcement outfit interested in a missing Pentagon employee.

She sighed and nodded. 'I waited until late next morning then filed a missing person's report with the Stafford County Sheriff's department. Once they knew where he worked and that he might have been involved in national security, they called in the FBI because Casey had access to sensitive material and... and he might have been kidnapped.' She faltered and drank thirstily from the glass of iced water on the table. She composed herself quickly. 'They did the first search of the house and they notified DIA Counter-Intelligence who did forensics on all the computers in the house, his classified safe at the office, looking for anything out of place. They didn't find anything suspicious.'

'And part of all this was the obvious question of whether

you knew where Casey could have gone? To be out of sight for a while?'

'Yes. I didn't tell them what Casey had said to me.'

'And he did that for a reason. If he's gone voluntarily, then he knew his absence would trigger an investigation, and that might uncover information he wanted discovered.'

'But it hasn't.'

'No, not yet, but if there's something he wants found then it might still be,' said Raglan. 'Casey might be protecting you.'

'How?'

'If he's uncovered something important then he wouldn't risk being taken by those who want to find out what it is, because then they could use you against him.' Raglan also knew if her husband's absence was not voluntary and there had been no threat against Anne Zeller, then that evidence might have gone with him. Perhaps even to the grave. 'So, no cabin, no motorhome parked up somewhere?' he said.

'No.' She held his gaze. There was another question written all over Raglan's face. 'And he wasn't having an affair,' she insisted.

'You're sure? Wives are the last to know.'

She pushed the coffee cup away and eased back into her seat, ready to stand and leave. His hand reached out and covered hers.

'Anne, everything has to be considered. No matter how painful. And I'll bet every suit who's walked through your door has asked the same hurtful question.' He let her take the deep breath everyone must take when they think of their loved one betraying them.

She settled. 'Yes, they asked and I told them what I told you. Casey was my rock.' She nearly crumpled then. She bowed her head. Then courage lifted her. 'Casey would not do anything to hurt me,' said Anne Zeller.

'Then I'll do whatever I can to find the answer for you.'

She nodded in gratitude, before frowning. 'You know, there were nights I thought someone was in the house. After I went to bed, I mean.'

'You think there was an intruder?'

She shook her head. 'No, the house is alarmed, but it was just a... a feeling, I guess.' She smiled bravely. 'Nerves, I reckon. Probably me wishing he'd come home.'

She turned her head away, looking beyond the cars and the trees, not seeing what was right outside the windows. 'There was something...' she murmured. 'I've just realized.' She turned to look directly at Raglan. 'I never thought it important, but once or twice a month on his day off, Casey visited a sergeant who had served with him in the Corps.'

'And you didn't mention this to anyone?'

'No. Like I said, I didn't see any connection. I don't know why I've thought of it now.'

'Do you know the name of this man?'

'Esposito. Izan Esposito.'

'Is he still in the Corps?'

She shook her head. 'He's a civilian.'

'You have an address?'

'Yes, the District of Columbia prison.'

15

Raglan suggested he return home with her so he could look through her husband's study. He suspected there wouldn't be anything of importance after the FBI and the Pentagon's own people had done their search, but it would help him get the measure of the man he knew thirteen years before.

'Go around the block,' he told her. She glanced uncertainly at him. 'To see if anyone is watching the house,' he said.

'You think they've got a surveillance team watching me? Why?'

'They might think Casey has a reason to go missing. That his motive might compromise national security. They might also think that you have had a hand in his disappearance.'

'What?' She swerved.

Raglan reached out and nudged the steering wheel away from the kerb. 'You know how it works. Everyone is under suspicion. If they are watching, they'll want to know who I am.' Raglan's eyes followed the circuitous interconnecting streets. There were few places a surveillance car could park and watch the Zellers' house. 'Do you know your neighbours?'

'Well, at the moment we only have the Campbells next door. He's a retired navy pilot. The other houses, as you can see, are still being built. Most of the neighbours we know are in other streets. A few work in administrative offices like Casey; our friends are retired military.'

'And they've been around to see you since Casey went missing?'

She looked uncertain. 'Well, no... I mean, a couple of my friends phoned.'

'They don't want to get involved. Not yet. They're waiting for the green light. Once Casey is cleared of any wrongdoing or of compromising national security, that's when your friends will come back.'

The realization dawned on her. 'Guilt by association.'

'Yes.'

Anne Zeller's knuckles turned white on the steering wheel. 'Then I don't need friends like that.'

Raglan eased her sense of betrayal. 'People get frightened. You have to allow them that. The state is powerful and intimidating when it perceives a threat.'

'My husband is no threat. He's a patriot who serves this country.'

'So was Benedict Arnold until he switched sides and fought for the British.' His smile softened the teasing comment.

She relaxed. 'Since when do you know so much about our history?'

'Since I used to get drunk with the likes of your husband.'

They turned into her street. There were times FBI or agency people preferred to be seen. It was a twofold exercise. One, let the target know you're watching them, then if they are guilty they'll make a mistake because the awareness of your presence will force their hand. Two, if the missing man's wife is consumed with the sick fear of not knowing what has happened to her husband then seeing two suits in a government car would offer assurance. Raglan was satisfied there was no one watching. That meant either they had no concerns about Casey Zeller being a security risk or they didn't give a damn about his wife. Or he'd missed something.

'Reverse into the garage,' he told her. She didn't question him; she pressed the garage door remote and backed in. Raglan kept his eyes on the street. The garage was large enough for two vehicles. The second was a black Honda SUV. Raglan guessed it was Casey's. So he had walked out of the house and been swallowed by the darkness. A rendezvous with someone close enough to meet on foot. Then a car journey somewhere. Perhaps.

Once the electric door closed, Anne went through the utility room into the house and pressed the code into the alarm box. Raglan glanced around the garage. There was the faint imprint of a patterned boot near the driver's door of the Honda. An old oil stain held the impression. There was clay in the footprint. That would have been made after the FBI investigated and searched the house. Had it been there when they entered the house they would have photographed and likely tried to lift the mould. If Anne Zeller's feeling of someone being in the house was correct, then someone had gained access through the rear door into the utility room and bypassed the alarm.

He followed her inside. It was bright and spacious, a comfortably furnished two-storey house. Looked to be only a couple of years old. Dark wooden floors set off woven rugs. A nod perhaps to Zeller's time spent in Africa and the Middle East. A few photographs: sailing boats, holidays, skiing and beaches. Some art prints. No children in any photograph. Also nothing to suggest Casey Zeller had spent time in any man's military.

'May I ask if you have any family you can turn to?' Raglan asked.

Anne Zeller dropped her coat and bag. 'No. Casey and I couldn't have children.' He followed her into the sitting room.

'Then you do what? Charity work? You have your own career? said Raglan.

Anne Zeller was weary of being questioned by the outsiders who had come into her life, but she smiled at the tall, tough-looking man who stood in her sitting room. 'Mr Raglan, you're very direct.'

'Just Raglan is fine.'

'I'm a retired nurse and I volunteer at a local hospice.'

Raglan looked beyond the room. 'May I?'

She nodded, pointing across the house. 'Casey's study is off the hall and the den is downstairs.'

'Does Casey have any weapons in the house?'

'There's a gun cabinet.'

'Rifles, semi-automatics or handguns?'

'Hunting rifles. The FBI had a specialist open the safe. Everything was there. They removed them.'

'And no dog that I can see.'

'No.'

She followed him as he walked into the kitchen. The rear yard was fenced. The skeleton of another building loomed behind it. Urban spread was a lucrative business, especially selling to current and former government employees. Raglan checked his watch. The construction workers had gone home.

The study was little more than a small room with a desk, bookshelves, phone and internet connection. Wires lay across the desk's surface. No computer attached. Raglan did a cursory search. The gun safe was open and empty. Books had been pulled out, rifled through and rammed back on the shelves. There was no point in further searching. Others had done that already. What were they looking for? If Zeller was an administrative officer he had no connection to top-secret classified material.

The basement den leading on to the backyard yielded more of the man. A baseball bat and glove rested below a picture of Casey Zeller. Raglan hefted the bat, feeling its weight and balance. There was an inscription – *Home Run* – scrawled across the image of the smiling man in cleats and baseball shirt. Along the wall were a half-dozen photographs of his time in the Legion. Raglan was not in any of his group shots as Zeller had been in a different unit. Then pictures of his squad in the Marine Corps, framed citations, a row of medals. Zeller was not a man to run. He had faced danger on too many occasions. Was he battle scarred? Had PTSD overtaken him? Doubtful. He had worked at the Pentagon. He would have had psych tests. Any hint of PTSD and they would have offered counselling.

Raglan considered the man's disappearance. He had thought only two options were valid. Death or disgrace. What if there was a third? Desperation? If he had something so explosive, so toxic that it could bring down others, which meant that he had to run into deep cover. To a place where he could not be found and his wife's life used as a bargaining chip. It was an option. But not a bad one. He heard the house phone ring. Anne Zeller answered.

'Hello...? Hello...? Is there anybody there? Hello?'

Raglan took the stairs three at a time. He came face to face with Casey's wife as she replaced the handset in its cradle.

'Must have been a wrong number,' she said.

'What did you hear?'

'Well... nothing. The line clicked a few times and then went dead.'

Raglan remembered what Bob de Vere had told him. How he'd thought his phone was tapped. Natural enough now that a Pentagon employee was missing. He stood back from the window to give himself an unrestricted view of the street and the unfinished house opposite. That and the one behind Zeller's offered the perfect approach for anyone wanting to break in and cause harm. Why Casey Zeller's wife should be a target made no sense, but most things don't until motives are unravelled after the fact.

He saw a change in light. Nothing much. Just a movement in the dark shadows of the unfinished timber-frame house opposite.

'Pack a small bag,' he said quietly. 'Do it now. Do it fast. And then find the furthest room in the house, get into the closet and wait for me. Understand?'

Panic flitted across her face. She cast it aside, nodded and pounded up the stairs. Casey Zeller would be proud of his wife's determination.

If he was still alive.

16

Whoever they were, they would come front and back. Raglan followed a simple philosophy. Control the fight. Attack through an ambush. Outflank and surprise your enemy. Right now he needed to divide and conquer. He stepped back into the utility room and pressed the button releasing the garage door. Inviting them in. If they thought the woman inside was alone, then they might think she was leaving. That would prompt them to seize the moment. Get inside. Find your quarry.

One man walked casually across the unlit street. A professional. An unhurried approach would draw no undue attention. He wore jeans, sneakers and open jacket, loose enough to conceal a weapon. Mid-thirties, lean and fit. His unbuttoned shirt covered a black T-shirt. Raglan watched as he reached behind his waistband. He wore gloves. He was soon inside the garage. The intruder would have no choice but to walk through the utility room. He would be cautious. Slow was good.

The door into the hall eased open. The black silencer nosed through the doorway first, then the man's forearm appeared, his double grip on the Glock edging forward. A second later the killer's torso would step through the frame.

There was enough space for Raglan to swing the 31-inch baseball bat. His timing was sweet. The bat struck the man's face. The crunch of bone was the only sound other than the clatter of the full weight of his body and the weapon hitting the floor. Raglan scooped up the 9 mm, checked the man was going to stay down. Looking at his battered skull, it seemed unlikely he would ever get up again. Raglan checked the intruder's pockets. He carried no identification, no wallet, no car keys. If time had been on Raglan's side, he would have checked for labels on the man's clothes. He was betting there weren't any.

He stepped away from the body and listened for the creak of floorboards or the easing of the glass sliding doors downstairs in the den. There was no sound for half a minute. Thirty seconds of quiet except for the breeze pushing against the windowpanes. Then the unmistakable sound of the door being lifted from its track and slid open. Raglan waited at the top of the stairs to the den, knowing the second man would be at a disadvantage as he made his way up. There was no movement. A faint almost inaudible sound alerted Raglan. He looked at the body. Too late, he saw the tiny transmitter bud in the man's ear. He leant forwards and snatched at the T-shirt. There was a hidden wire loop on the man's chest. The door downstairs was yanked open. The second man had received no answer from his partner and was making his escape. Raglan pounded down the stairs. The dark-clad figure, already halfway across the backyard, turned and fired twice. The silenced weapon gave out a spitting sound. It was well aimed through the open glass door of the den. As the gunman had pivoted Raglan had seen the line of fire and thrown himself to one side. Where he had been a moment before there were now two puncture marks in the wall.

He rolled to his feet. The gunman was out of sight. Raglan went as far as the fence, took a different angle, hit it running and hauled himself up. There was no one in sight. The priority now was to get Anne Zeller to safety. He headed back.

'Anne?' he called into the house. There was no reply. His mind raced as he ran up the stairs. Another scenario flashed through his thoughts. He had come to the house to check up more on Casey Zeller. No inkling that his wife might be in such extreme danger as the past few minutes had shown. He knew what he would have done if he'd been attempting a killing. Send two gunmen into the house downstairs but have one already in the house. Upstairs.

'Anne!'

He checked the master bedroom; then he saw a door at the end of the hall. A flight of stairs went steeply into an attic storage space. The hatch above was closed. When he saw the small door beneath the boxed stairway he tapped on it. 'Anne, it's Raglan. You're safe.'

The door opened. Raglan extended his hand to the woman who came out of the crawl space. She trembled with fright.

'It's all right,' he assured her.

She nodded.

'We need to leave,' he said.

'Where?'

'Do you have anyone out of state you can go to?'

She frowned. 'Yes, I think so. One of the nurses I worked with. She was widowed a couple of years ago. We phoned a few times.'

'No good. If the wrong people are looking for you, they can track your phone traffic.'

'Then there's no one else, I don't think.' She hesitated. 'Well. Yes, I think there might be. We send each other a card every Christmas.'

'Where is that?'

'Stroudsburg, Pennsylvania.'

'You trust this person?'

'Yes. No reason not to. She's someone I knew before I married Casey. She's on her own. Yes, I trust her.'

'Then we drive to the nearest mall, you buy a pre-paid phone. You give me that number. No one else. Ever.'

Fear is a leech that sucks the life blood and Anne Zeller looked as though she had aged a dozen years. 'What's happened? Downstairs.'

'You finish packing and then come down.'

'Has he gone?'

'He won't cause any more trouble.'

She looked uncertainly at him.

Raglan smiled. 'I scared him off. Stay calm. Stay positive. If what's happened here is reported on the TV news, ignore it. Don't be drawn back or think you should contact the police or the DIA. No one. Tough it out, Anne. I'm on your side and I'll protect you. Don't do anything until you hear from me.'

'All right. I can do that. Thank you.'

Raglan returned to where the gunman lay. What blood there was had congealed in his nose and mouth. The floor showed no sign of blood splatter, and even if there were any, by the time the police checked, he and Anne Zeller would be long-gone. Dragging the man to the top of the stairs leading to the den, he threw down the Glock and then pushed him head-first after it. He made no sound. The dead don't complain.

17

Anne Zeller dug deep after Raglan insisted she drive to the mall and negotiate the busy road. She faced five hours on the road ahead to Stroudsburg and he wanted to see that the trauma at the house had not unnerved her to the point where she couldn't concentrate on the interstate. The last thing he wanted was for her to have an accident or to be pulled over by a patrol officer because it might be an emotional tipping point that made her relate everything. And if that happened then Raglan's presence and involvement would create an interest that he did not yet want.

He made sure she had enough fuel, was sufficiently calm and had a bag of groceries to take along to her friend's house. He sat with her as she set up the pre-paid phone and then used his to call her friend, who told her she would be welcome. Raglan memorized her new phone number. He knew he couldn't get her to hand over her usual phone – it was her lifeline to her missing husband – but he convinced her that the only time she should answer was if Casey got in touch.

By the time she dropped him at the Metro station Raglan was certain they had not been followed. The train stopped at the Pentagon but he was not yet ready to speak to the

DIA director, Jack Swain. That would come after he had got to Casey Zeller's man in prison.

'Jeez, I don't know,' said TJ the following morning, shovelling eggs from the pan on to a plate for Raglan. 'Visiting times are controlled pretty tight at the DC Jail. You'd have to book in, and you're no relative of this character. Usually they make you have a video call; they have a place set up for that.'

Raglan knew he needed to bring TJ into his confidence now. He told the unflappable veteran that the woman he had visited was searching for her missing husband and the incarcerated man might have vital information. 'That's where I was yesterday, out at Stafford. So whatever help I can get is for her. I need a face-to-face at the prison,' he said.

TJ squeezed tomato sauce on to his eggs, thoughtful. 'He was a marine, you say?'

'He went private, but yes, must have served a good few years.'

'Well, there might be a way.' He checked his watch. 'Finish up and I'll walk you across town. There's a man who might know how to help.'

An hour later TJ Jones pressed the entry button on a small apartment block.

'What?' A gruff voice on the intercom.

'Frank, it's TJ. Get your skivvies on, I have a friend with me who needs help.'

The door buzzed open. TJ led Raglan up two flights

of stairs. The door to 2C was already ajar. TJ knocked anyway and walked into a small apartment where a short, stocky man with cropped hair and a pugilist face was pulling on a pair of sharply creased grey trousers over an equally well-pressed shirt. He was as old as TJ Jones. Another veteran. Raglan took the room in. Bare except for various memorabilia of a life spent serving his country. The bemedalled tunic on the hanger told the same story. Raglan felt the disapproving stare of the Master Gunnery Sergeant. Compared to the marine, Raglan looked like a bar-room brawler.

'Uh-huh,' said the man as he knotted his tie. 'You're up early, TJ. Must be a first for the Airborne.'

'Frank, we were behind enemy lines before you even got your feet wet on the beach.'

'Uh-huh,' he said again. 'And your friend? Have you just bailed him? I don't do charity work, TJ.'

TJ turned to Raglan and smiled. 'Raglan, meet the grimmest Master Guns who ever served in the 3rd Marine Division. This web-footed beach-hopper has seen more action than a fly on horse dung. And Frank O'Hara does more charity work than Mother Theresa.'

'She's dead, TJ. Keep up, for God's sake. You're getting so damned senile you don't know what day it is. And you're gonna make me late for work.'

TJ explained as O'Hara pulled on a blue blazer. 'Frank and me, we're volunteers at Arlington Cemetery when he's not acting doorman at the Marine Museum. They put him front and centre to scare the visitors so they don't quibble about which way round to go.'

Frank O'Hara looked at Raglan. 'Son, if you're hooked

up with this old fool you had better know that only two things fall out the sky: bird shit and paratroopers.'

'And chicken shit stays on the ground,' said TJ.

O'Hara reached a stubby, broken-knuckled hand to Raglan. 'If you're a friend of his, you're welcome. Raglan, is it? Irish?'

'My great-grandfather,' said Raglan, feeling the older man's strength in his grip.

'Good enough.' He straightened his tie and brushed imaginary lint off the blazer. 'How can I help?'

'You know people at the jail?' said TJ.

'A couple of guys. They used to serve.'

'OK, now Raglan here is...' He turned to Raglan. 'You tell him.'

'I'm here to help find a friend who's gone missing. His wife is in danger from I don't know who yet, but there's a man in the DC Jail who might have some information. He served in the First Marine Division.'

'Jesus on the cross. Hollywood Marines. The only reason they crowd together in a bar is to form a brain.'

'Hollywood Marines?' The reference meant nothing to Raglan.

TJ sighed and explained. 'Inter-service rivalry and downright contempt. Their First Marine Division is based at Camp Pendleton in California. LA to the north, San Diego to the south. Sunshine and beaches. The likes of Master Gunnery Sergeant O'Hara here was at Camp Lejeune, a swamp-rat base in North Carolina. Now that's a shit-hole posting if ever there was one.'

'The man's name?' said O'Hara.

'Esposito. He was a sergeant.'

'Esposito, huh?' The way O'Hara said it didn't come across as complimentary. 'What's he, a damned drug smuggler?'

TJ raised a hand. 'Frank, let's not pigeonhole the man. We don't know anything about him or why he's inside. Raglan needs a face-to-face.'

'Uh huh.' O'Hara picked up a fixed-line phone receiver from its cradle. Punched in a number and waited, cradling the headset as he fussed his shirt cuffs. 'You serve, son?'

'I did.'

'Any outfit I might have heard of?'

'I don't know, Gunny.'

TJ grinned and cocked a thumb in Raglan's direction. 'French Foreign Legion. Paratrooper and special forces.'

'Might have known,' growled O'Hara. 'Like attracts like.'

TJ's smile never faded.

Finally the phone number was answered. 'Yes, Officer Tommy Parker please... Frank O'Hara.' He glanced at Raglan as he waited to be connected. 'Anything illegal going on here?'

'Quite the opposite.'

There was no time for Raglan to find out if his answer was acceptable as O'Hara spoke into the phone. 'Tommy. A favour. I have someone who needs a face-to-face with one of your inmates. Esposito.' He looked at Raglan. 'First name?'

'Izan.'

'Izan. God knows what kind of damned name that is but it's what his mother gave him if he had one. Tommy, he was in the Corps. You know him? Uh-huh. OK. That's all good then.' He looked again at Raglan. 'In an hour?'

Raglan nodded.

'His name's Raglan. I'll vouch for him, Tommy. OK. Good. You too. Thanks.' O'Hara replaced the phone and turned to Raglan. 'TJ will tell you how to get there. Your boy's a model prisoner. So far no trouble. Says he's on a firearm rap. Unlicensed. Has some prior so it's a felony. They're transferring him out in a day or two.'

TJ extended his hand. 'Thanks, Frank. I owe you.'

'Damned right.'

Raglan shook his hand in turn. 'The man who's gone missing and who I think is in danger, he was ten years in the First Marine Division. A major.'

O'Hara finished buttoning his blazer. 'Like I said. Shit for brains.'

18

The rented apartment was furnished with the basic require-
ments for transient occupation. Jenna Voss wasn't planning
on staying for long at the FBI outpost in West Virginia. The
Field Office in DC was a four-hour drive away, and she
planned to make her case to be reinstated for field work
rather than sit in front of a computer screen all day. Muscle
memory driven by rocket-fuel adrenaline had set in years
before when she had completed vigorous selection for the
Hostage Rescue Team. Being deskbound made for a body–
mind conflict.

She had been introduced to the team, memorized their
names. Mostly geeks: high priests of technology enthralled
by talk of algorithms and blockchains, hyperautomation and
quantum computing. Their language had all the religious
fervour of medieval mystics: intense and excited conversations
when they took their break in the cafeteria. Jenna was
tone-deaf to it all. She understood criminals. Those who
encroached into society and corrupted it. Saving lives was
what she did, not collating crime records for various law-
enforcement agencies. Except for the one time she hadn't.
And now she was paying the price. Thirst for justice for her
dead friends was what drove her to get back in the field.

She turned her back to the low, honey-coloured building, the Criminal Justice Information Services, nestled in its rolling landscaped grounds. She was momentarily transfixed by West Virginia's beautiful landscape, now bathed in winter sunshine. Yellow forsythia brightened the fringes of birch and oak trees tentatively unfurling their leaves. Willows showed their first flush of dusky orange; crocuses pushed through the ground, reaching for the warmth and light. Birds regaled the woodlands with song, announcing a fresh and cheerful start to the new season about to reach the thousand acres at Clarksburg that surrounded the state-of-the-art electronic hub which supplied information for law enforcement. Birdcalls and the sweet smell of meadow grass and blossoms drifted through the warming air.

It made her ache for a city's filthy backstreets and dark underbelly of violent organized crime.

'Jenna? How's Audubon's world of birds and nature working out?' said Diaz down the phone line.

'Enough colour and birdsong for a lifetime. I sleep better with the sound of sirens rather than the dawn chorus. Is this a social call?'

'I've almost cleared my desk.'

'A fond farewell?'

'Soon enough. Our man went missing.'

'The Englishman?'

'Yeah. After we stopped following him and you packed your bags, there was a development down here.'

Voss rolled back her office chair, glancing around to make sure none of her co-workers concentrating on their computer screens were showing any interest in her conversation. This was the FBI systems network division: being nosey was in their job description. She worried a pencil, tapping out an erratic rhythm on her knee.

'Oh yeah?'

'I guess you are part of the herd now, huh? Can't talk?'

'Listening.'

'Good. Now get this. Remember when we followed the Englishman to the Warbird Museum?'

'What did he do, steal a plane?'

'A mechanic was murdered.'

Ronaldo Diaz had caught her interest, he knew, as surely as baiting and reeling in a bluefin. She dropped the pencil on her desk and sat upright. 'Jesus, Ronnie, while we were outside?'

'The night we went back to Miami after leaving him at Sea World. Whoever killed him was a pro. Used the shadows. Figured where the security cameras were. We pulled a faint image of someone coming out of a service-entrance door. Vero Beach detectives asked us to enhance it but there's nothing there.'

'No alarm?'

'Hadn't been set. The mechanic was working late. Seems he did that a lot.'

'Motive?'

'None that the cops can see. Me neither. Nothing stolen except there was no sign of his phone – that's about the only thing the killer took, unless the mechanic left it somewhere.'

'So perhaps there was something on it they wanted. Maybe whoever killed him had their name on his contacts list.'

'Who knows? He was working on a platform; killer slashed his hamstring, disabled him then cut his throat. He was found next morning.'

'And the Brit?'

'Sheldon wanted us to dot the i's and cross the t's. I did a follow-up with the family. The guy's gone off to see friends.'

'Was he there the night of the killing?'

'Not sure. No evidence either way. The boss washed his hands of it. It's a murder case for the PD. He doesn't want us involved. It was a CIA surveillance favour, nothing more. We checked car hire and flights. I figure he hitched a lift.'

'That or bus or train.'

Ronnie Diaz fell silent.

'Ronnie, you didn't check?'

'Jenna, we're not involved. It's a murder. Let the cops do their job.'

'Sure.'

Diaz knew that tone of voice. 'It's not our case.'

'No. Still… we were watching him,' she said.

'I bought a new carbon rod today. I won't tell you what it cost. But the wild blue beckons. Care to join me?'

She smiled down the phone. She was a lousy sailor. Any time she tried going on a boat, she vomited for the nation. 'I've got some fishing of my own to do.'

'That's what I figured,' said Diaz.

19

TJ Jones pointed Raglan to the Metro station he needed and then returned to his caretaker duties. Thirty minutes later Raglan stepped back into daylight and after a five-minute walk stood in front of the imposing correctional facility at 1901 D Street SE. Correctional Officer Parker, O'Hara's contact, guided him through to the visitors' centre. The room had rows of metal seats either side of a wire mesh screen. All the seats were empty except for one. The man wore the standard orange prison jump suit. He turned his head when the guard brought Raglan in.

'Ten minutes. This is a favour,' the prison guard told Raglan. 'I'm here at the door.'

Raglan had already been briefed on the protocol of visiting a prisoner by the guard. 'Thank you.' He walked to where Esposito waited and sat down opposite him. Whatever mental picture the retired master gunnery sergeant may have had of this prisoner, Raglan made a bet that the two did not match. Izan Esposito was slimly built. His features could be described as delicate. He was a good few inches shorter than Raglan. O'Hara may have derided the men of the 1st Marine Division as Hollywood Marines but in this case he wouldn't be far wrong. Former Marine Sergeant Esposito had movie-star looks.

There was no animosity in his voice when he addressed the stranger who sat down opposite him. 'I don't know you, sir.'

'My name is Raglan. A friend who served with me some years ago has been visiting you. His name is Casey Zeller.'

'You're a Brit.'

'Yes. We didn't serve in the Corps together. Somewhere else.'

Esposito nodded. 'I know the skipper's background. Sounds as though you've come a long way.'

'It's what I do.'

'You're right, the major has been coming here. A couple of times a month.' There was no hint of suspicion in his voice. The intonation was one of cooperation. He was playing the game correctly. Good behaviour gets privileges in prison. 'So why are you here? This isn't even official visiting hours.'

'I need your help. He's gone missing,' Raglan said.

Esposito leant back away from the mesh screen. The news silenced him. Raglan watched his reaction. Esposito blinked rapidly. Synapses firing and thoughts zipping through his brain as he figured out what, if anything, to say next.

Raglan decided to help him. 'Intruders broke into his house last night. They were armed. I stopped them. Now his wife is in hiding.' Raglan paused. The additional information made Esposito nod. It had been expected. But he remained stubbornly silent.

'I'm not the law,' said Raglan. 'So I'm not here to judge anybody or to make their life any worse than it is. I need information.'

Esposito's hands clenched together. He was locking down. Raglan had to prise him open.

'A retired major in the US Marine Corps does not necessarily travel an hour plus each way on his day off to sit and hold a former sergeant's hand. Why would he do that? Not when his sergeant left the Corps and went private three years ago.' Raglan studied the man's face. 'I think you contacted him. Why?'

The Hollywood Marine shrugged. The glance he gave the guard against the far wall was discreet enough not to be noticed. His voice remained calm, but Raglan sensed the edge of anxiety lying beneath the words. 'I needed help. It's not difficult getting into trouble in my old neighbourhood. I went to see old friends. People I grew up with. Some of my family still live in a bad part of town. You heard of Brentwood? No, guess you wouldn't. That's not exactly on anyone's tourist itinerary. A friend was getting into trouble with the gangs. I tried to help; I got hold of a handgun. Just for protection. Just to help him. One way and another it went wrong. Cops cornered me. I didn't resist. I'm proud of my service. I didn't want it to go so bad that they painted me as another gun-happy marine. The Corps is what saved me from those streets. Turned me around.'

He glanced up at Raglan. His eyes dipped back down. The story gelled from what information had been passed down the phone line to O'Hara. But the man was a poor liar when it came to divulging the real reason Casey Zeller had spent so much time with him.

'I'm facing five years without parole. The skipper offered to help me before sentencing was passed.'

'I ask again. Why? There are plenty of ex-service personnel who hit bad times. Why you? Did you save his life in combat?'

'No. He saved mine. And I was trying to save his.' He clammed up again.

Raglan glanced at the guard. 'Save it how?'

Esposito sighed. Whatever information he had was still bottled inside.

'Sergeant, time is running out. I won't be able to visit you when they ship you out to a state prison miles away. He's missing. His wife is frantic. And someone wanted to cause her harm.' He paused and then threw in his ace card. 'And somewhere in the background is the Defense Intelligence Agency. You care anything for this man, tell me what you know.'

Esposito grimaced. 'What I tell you, you don't repeat. Not to anyone. You do not reveal me as your source. I don't have much but my family has even less. I tell you the rest, I need some assurances.'

'I never met you. I was never here.'

There was a final brief hesitation but Raglan knew Esposito had already decided to share what he knew. 'I was a private contractor for three years. So I did work here and there. Mostly in the Middle East and Central America. I took time out six months ago and went back on the block. Keeping eyes on the young kids. Trying to make sure they didn't get drawn into gangs and drugs. I did some outreach stuff. The more time I spent on the streets the more I heard things. I made my own contacts. I got my friend off the streets and in return I got information.' He licked his lips. 'It was a damned minefield of violence going on. But it shifted emphasis. Different players moved in. A whole new dynamic. I knew Major Zeller was at the Pentagon. Hell, that's HQ for the whole damned defence force. It's the beating heart. He'd know stuff. When I got arrested, I thought I might be able to trade my way out of the corner I was in.'

Raglan sensed he was finally getting to the truth. 'What do you want?'

'I have payment from a job I did. A private job. I want my family protected. I need a courier.'

'You want me to get it to them?'

'No. There's a man. He's connected. I tell you where I stashed it, you get it, then you hand it over to him. I'm in here and these people might see I don't come out. You do that for me. Pay him off so my family will be safe and I give you what I have.'

'Understood.'

Esposito whispered an address and where he had hidden the package.

'How do you know I won't just take the money? Your family means nothing to me.'

'You ever taken a risk with someone? You're all I got. You came all this way to help an old friend. That says something.'

'All right. I'll find a way.'

'Then I'll make the call, so my family will expect you. Their name is Mendoza.'

'I'll get the money. You have my word. Now you tell me about Casey Zeller.'

Esposito leant forward. 'I saw people I worked with as a

corporate contractor meeting up with those who run drugs up here from Central America and back down. I know guys who were involved and they gave me the heads up, said I could earn good money again. Then my sister's husband came to me. Said he'd overheard talk. That's what prompted me to call the skipper, to have him check it out. He did. He uncovered stuff.'

'Like what,' said Raglan.

'Military hardware is being siphoned off. The drug runners are the conduit. They have the means. They go right under the noses of the Border Patrol, Homeland Security, any agency you can think about. Do you have any idea how many agencies we have in this country? And do any of them talk to each other? You want to know about turf wars, look no further than the great USA intelligence community. I asked myself who's getting the military hardware and how. I couldn't answer that. The cartels don't need it, they're armed to the teeth.'

'Why would they run the extra risk?'

'How would I know? But there's a lot of money changing hands and it's a one-way street. Know what I think? Wash the drug runners' money. Then they do what you want.'

Raglan had fought the drug trade in Africa when he served in the Legion. Official corruption was not confined to Third World countries. 'And Casey Zeller was running an investigation into this?'

Esposito shrugged. 'All I did was give him the information I had. The things I heard and saw on the street. He scraped ice off the tip of an iceberg. My sister's husband was killed.' Esposito shook his head. 'If the skipper is missing' – he looked deflated – 'odds are he's dead. This is a bad place for someone like you, Raglan. You don't know the ground you have to fight on. These gangs, they have a simple plan. Kill, rape and control. Unless you can match that, you're out of their league.'

'I can do two out of the three.'

The prison guard tapped his knuckles against the metal door. Time was up. Esposito got to his manacled feet. 'Here's the name I gave the major. A big player. Connected in Washington. Lives in Georgetown. He's on a downward spiral. He fucked up. I don't know how or why. But he's important to these people. His name is Luis Reyes. He's dangerous. He's the one you pay off for my family. If he's not taking his own product, he's a reasonably functioning human being. If he's on it, he's as unpredictable as a rabid dog. You came here to help find Major Zeller. I hope you do. He's a good man. I owe him big time. But you've just walked into a kill zone and stepped on an anti-personnel mine. You take one more step, Raglan, and it'll kill you. Truth is, I reckon you're already a dead man. Good luck.'

20

Esposito's warning and TJ's map both said the same thing. The ex-marine's family lived in a no-go zone. But if he was to make contact with a kingpin gangster connected to what Casey Zeller was investigating, then he needed to make the cash delivery. He'd figure out how later.

The Pentagon Metro station terminus broadened out from the tracks, revealing up and down escalators. He raised his face to the approaching sunlight and saw a gathering of drab brown uniforms standing in a disorderly group at the top of the steps. The glass doors to the Pentagon side entrance were closed.

'This the way in?' he asked a US Army colonel standing with other ranks, a scuffed leather briefcase in his hand.

He nodded. 'Doing a security sweep. Happens every so often. The dogs give the place the once-over, make sure no explosives ever get inside.'

Raglan thanked him. Given that a hijacked airline had ploughed into the Pentagon on 9/11 it was a wonder everyone wasn't strip-searched. He waited as patiently as the others. Everyone but him was in uniform. Mostly army, ready for their work behind closed doors. Bureaucracy loomed large in the Department of Defense encased in the five-sided building, five storeys high, five ring corridors to each floor. The doors swung open and the government employees were quickly swept away. Raglan went into the metal barrier lanes, waited until summoned by one of several window clerks and strode up to the glass.

'Identification?'

Raglan slid his passport through.

'What is the reason for your visit today?'

'I have an appointment with Jack Swain.'

The clerk took his eyes off his screen only to glance up from passport to bearer. He studied his screen. 'I don't have you listed.'

'He sent me an email asking me to come by at this time,' Raglan lied. 'It should be there.'

The clerk searched. 'No. You're not listed.'

'Then can you phone him? Let him know I am here?' That bluff should be enough to get Raglan past the first hurdle.

The clerk slid the passport back and pointed. 'Through security, go to the reception desk. They'll phone him.'

Raglan thanked him and stepped through to the security area. The uniformed officers sported a Pentagon Force Protection Agency badge on their sleeves. He stripped off his belt, boots and wristwatch, placed them in the tray and stepped through the scanner. Once he had pulled on his boots again the security guard gave him a chit and gestured through a door into a large reception area. Twenty or so permanent seats faced a long counter. High above it was a large flat screen with a list of names. The half-dozen people seated in the area glanced up at his arrival and then let their gaze wander around what to them was the pulsing heart of their nation's military establishment. Raglan stepped up to the desk, delivered the security chit, repeated his lie, showed his ID again and was told to take a seat.

Over his shoulder the double escalator ferried badged employees up and down. The main entrance led outside to the parking lots. Raglan's name appeared on the screen. He waited. Five minutes later a marine corporal stepped out of a side door carrying a clipboard and summoned those of Raglan's fellow visitors who had booked the Pentagon tour. They would get the basic look-see. There was no way members of the public were going to enter the inner sanctum or get to the double underground basements, the holy of holies where all the intelligence computers were located. Another five minutes passed. Raglan wondered whether Jack Swain was even in the building.

His name was swiped from the screen once the tall man in a grey suit approached the desk. He took a visitor's security badge, turned and smiled.

'Raglan. You got here. I thought you might.' He extended his hand. Raglan shook it then accepted the visitor's tag and clipped it to his jacket. He followed Swain to the escalator; another Pentagon Police Officer checked the tag. No one got inside the heart of the United States military complex without being checked, checked again, and then tagged by security. Twenty-seven thousand military and civilian personnel worked in the Pentagon, and stray visitors, like stray dogs, were not welcome. At the top of the escalator they stepped into an open area much like a small shopping mall. Restaurants and food courts were full of employees, shopping was in full swing; it was a strange mix of faux civilian life mingling with those in uniform who scurried back and forth carrying folders.

Raglan guessed Jack Swain must have been close to fifty-five years old. He could have been the Marlboro Man in the now-banned advertisements. He made small talk as they wound their way through the broad corridors. 'Been here before?'

'No,' said Raglan, though he knew enough about the labyrinthine building from Defense and Agency personnel he had worked with in the past.

'I can give you the five-cent tour if you like.'

'Another time.' Raglan had done the groundwork, spoken to Zeller's wife and contact, now he needed to hear what the DIA man had to say.

They turned a corner and the corridor crossed over an outside service passage. 'For what's it's worth, you're standing where the tail of American Airlines Flight 77 hit. Punched its way right through here.' He glanced at Raglan walking alongside him. 'Know how damned lucky we were? They hit the west wall that had just been rebuilt so not many of us had returned to our offices. If we hadn't done the construction work thousands would have died. Same if they had ploughed into any other wall.' He opened a door. 'Hell of a mess. Like the one we're in now. In here.'

Raglan noticed that Swain's office was only a few doors away from that of the Joint Chiefs of Staff; such proximity seemed to show he had the ear and confidence of the top military officials. Raglan waited. Swain indicated he should sit in the chair on the opposite side of the desk. A framed photograph of the President hung on the wall behind Swain's chair. Locked cabinets lined the walls. A single computer monitor and keyboard took up one corner of the broad mahogany desk. It was a place of order. Swain pressed a cartridge into his coffee machine, made two cups, fixed one with sugar. Short and sweet. Just the way Raglan liked it. Memories of the fragrant souk. Except he was drinking this coffee in an American walled fortress not a walled city in North Africa. Raglan sipped the coffee and asked himself how Swain knew he liked it that way.

'This is completely unofficial,' said Swain.

'The coffee's not legitimate?' said Raglan. 'You're stealing from the supply cupboard, Jack?'

Swain didn't smile. 'Someone is.'

21

Raglan looked out on to the grounds boxed in by the fortress walls. Question was: how many secrets held here could be kept safe? Security was in the hands of the nearly thirty thousand who worked here.

'One of the tribe right here? I'm surprised you don't have your own passports. The Land of the Pentagonese. So at what point did you tap Zeller's phone? Did you suspect he had his hand in the biscuit tin?'

'We call it a cookie jar.'

'I know what it's called. And you tapped Zeller's phone because that's the only way you would know that I was being contacted, why you've been expecting me.'

'When the DIA set up its Defense Clandestine Service they decided it wasn't a great idea to pick up a phone and call direct. Obviously Zeller had reached out through his wife and I let her. It made sense having a trusted outsider, someone I had worked with before, someone who tracked down a Russian killer. Someone I thought I could trust. Trump called Washington the swamp – well, he wasn't far wrong. There's a lot of slithering goes on around here, and some of the inhabitants give a downright nasty bite. So, yeah, a poisonous atmosphere all round.'

'Jack, you're part of a network of intelligence agencies. I don't have enough fingers to count them on. And if your man has gone walkabout with a suitcase of spook secrets, then you'd have the FBI out on the streets.'

Swain's face soured. 'The Feds? Those idiots? I let them in on this and I'll be drowning in tons of paper. They're so far up their own rear ends they'd need a hundred agents just to start checking Zeller's background and they'll only bring in a task force when they've researched what he did on his tenth birthday. The last thing we want is to involve the FBI. If it doesn't begin with their investigation, when another agency asks for their help, they either kill it stone-dead or turn it into a circus. They follow so many procedures we'd have the Second Coming before they hit first base.' He tossed his pen on to the desk in frustration, and raised a hand in surrender. 'I cannot allow anyone else in at this stage, not until I know where Casey is and what he discovered. And if he's still alive. And if he's dead, does another interested party in any other government department have the information that he had?'

'Zeller worked in government contract and procurement. He vetted businesses bidding for government contracts. What else?' Raglan said.

'I put him there two years ago. He's clandestine. Has been since day one. Casey picked up on a hundred pieces of information a month just by being part of the procurement team and then he zoned in. Weapons and armaments have been disappearing through shell companies. He identified the bogus companies and we shut them down, but if you want a conspiracy theory, there's a supply chain of weapons leaving the country and we think other agencies are involved. Maybe even people in my own. I trust no one. And neither did Casey.' Swain paused. 'Once our suspicions become known, then I lose any headway, no matter how minimal, we have made.'

He opened a desk drawer and slid across a slim, buff folder. Raglan opened it. A dozen sheets of paper, each with the name of a company on it. He raised his eyes.

'That's what Casey gleaned from hundreds of bids. These twelve are shell companies within shell companies, layered documents spanning across the world. They all look legitimate, which means they can bid for government contracts to distribute components of military hardware. Casey traced them all. Took him months. Hidden behind every one of those companies are names of former intelligence officers. In those companies are the twelve disciples. Covert task-force directors. Retired, but with a keen interest in this country's influence overseas. We've tagged them as the Council. The one company that stands out is EDM. Executive Decision Management. Hardly a name to draw attention. Sounds like a Washington lobby firm. It's run by a former CIA section chief for the Middle East and employs a dozen former Special Activities operatives. At least a dozen. Most we can't trace.'

Raglan remembered coming across the CIA's Special Activities men in Afghanistan. They supplied and fought alongside tribesmen.

'The CIA doesn't need a shell company to sell arms or equip dissidents, Jack. They've done it for years, usually with government blessing. Are you saying EDM and companies like them are actually a cover for illegal CIA activity?'

Jack Swain leant back in his chair and raised his hands. 'Can't say. Can't prove it. Not yet. I'm on eggshells here.'

'This could be your people looking for shadows where there aren't any. It's not unusual for retired military and government personnel to throw their expertise into business ventures when they retire. All of this could be legit.'

Swain shook his head. 'We look for military threats abroad. Where the next conflict will arise. The CIA look for the next terror attack. We don't like or trust each other – that's true enough. When the DIA proposed a clandestine service of our own they tried to block it. Went all the way to the top. Officially our Director of Operations works in conjunction with their Director of Operations. But we all know that's a crock, because if they start supplying arms to clandestine armies again – and we all have long memories – then we could get dragged into a military conflict.'

'I'm in the heart of the whore, Jack. Even your Senate Armed Services Committee put the boot into your initial DIA plan to go clandestine. Your eyes are still watering from the kicking. They didn't want any more spooks. DIA and CIA are in a knife fight with each other and I don't want to be in the middle. I'm off the books but known to British and American intelligence and if it comes out that I'm working for you then the protocol between the UK and here is up the creek. Paddles not supplied. Our governments have a classified agreement: we don't poach on each other's territory.' Raglan knew the answer he would get, but it had to be said.

Swain's voice lowered. He was relaxed. 'Which is why I'm pleased Casey reached out to you. You're an asset,

Raglan. Ghost soldiers like you step in and out of our lives, shadows following the sun. I couldn't go to MI6, of course I couldn't. I'm grateful that Casey gave me the means to let you in.' He placed the palms of his hands flat on the shiny desk. 'Besides, it's not a poacher I need. It's a hunter.'

Raglan waited. So far, no mention of Esposito. It seemed Swain did not know of Zeller's contact with the former marine, and if Zeller's wife had not told him, as she said she had not, then this one link in the chain was known only to Raglan.

'Who's in play?' said Raglan. Would Jack Swain mention Luis Reyes? Did he know there might be a connection between this high roller and whoever was buying and selling arms?

'No one's in play. That's why I'd welcome your involvement. I can't even trust people around me. Outside of this room you don't even whisper about me and this office.'

Raglan prodded again. 'You must know if Casey had reached out to anyone else.'

'I don't have any evidence that he did. He was following a paper trail and, like I said, flushing out dubious and false companies bidding for government arms contracts and who was behind them.'

So, Raglan thought, Casey Zeller went missing before passing on the information from Esposito. Or had chosen not to tell. If so, why? Raglan was reminded of the old British intelligence saying: *Two people can keep a secret if one of them is dead.*

'I need to know if Zeller's alive or dead,' Jack Swain went

on. 'If he's alive, where is he? We've had no demands made so I'm assuming that if he's been kidnapped then whoever has him might know what he's discovered. Which is more information than I have. And I must discover if he has hidden evidence somewhere.' Swain reached for the folder, slid it back across the desk and locked it in the drawer again. 'I'm working blind on this, Raglan. All I know is this: Zeller had a lead. A senator who was determined to slam down the lid on this mess before it escalates.'

'Who?'

Jack Swain grimaced. 'That I *don't* know. He said he had spoken to a senator who was well positioned to open doors if they need to be opened. He and only he knows that Casey has dug the dirt on the so-called Council. I'm looking hard, using what contacts I have in Congress. Whoever it is, he or she is keeping their head down. Maybe that's because Zeller has gone missing and they're fearful that they have already been dragged into what might be a helluva conspiracy.'

Raglan pushed back the chair. 'If the wrong people learn I'm involved, then they'll try to stop me. If I get blown then you have to pull strings. Not publicly, I know you can't do that. But you need to cover for me.' He knew it was an impossible request but Swain's response would be telling. If he promised to look after Raglan no matter what, then he was lying through his teeth and Raglan might as well leave this theme park and get back to the other Disney World.

Jack Swain showed no emotion. 'You're expendable. If I did put my agents on this and lost any of them, then I'd have to explain their deaths. Next thing I know I'm in front of a Senate Select Committee and obliged to tell them everything. Raglan, you're on your own.'

Right answer.

In London, five hours ahead of DC time, Maguire took the lift down to the ground floor, passed the armed guards and exited the MI6 headquarters at Vauxhall Cross through one of the airlock tubes at the main entrance. The busy roads streamed with traffic and deafening noise. A sharp reminder of the ongoing chaos in the world outside the sterile place of secrets. It was a world he sought to keep safe. Usually, he admitted to himself, at great danger to others, who put their lives in harm's way. He was heading for a favoured watering hole. Then, after a bite to eat, he would return to the office and work late into the night.

His phone rang. He did not identify himself. The voice on the other end was familiar.

'I'm in,' said Raglan.

'Who knew Zeller had reached out to you? Langley or Pentagon?'

'Pentagon.'

'Right, well, let's see who makes a play. Watch your back. You'll be treading on someone's toes. They'll come for you now.'

The line went dead. Maguire's spirits lifted. Raglan had told him about Zeller's disappearance. And when an intelligence officer at the Pentagon went missing then Maguire allowed Raglan to follow his instincts. To see where it led. Unofficially. Now his man was getting in deep. Now Maguire had skin in the game.

22

Raglan returned to TJ's apartment. Time was running out for Casey Zeller. There had been no demand from any kidnappers so the FBI had not been brought into the case. A missing person is a police matter and in Zeller's case a federal matter. Was it possible Zeller had peeled back layers of corruption involving former CIA members still connected to the political establishment? That government officials were involved? Somewhere there would be evidence. Raglan needed to find this Luis Reyes character. If Zeller had made progress by tracking Reyes's connection to the arms smuggling, then he was the next link in the chain.

Heavy rain clouds swept up the Potomac, hugging the choppy waters as they headed into Virginia. The capital was in for a soaking: it was likely roads would be closed for a brief time and if he was going to venture into what promised to be enemy territory, then a violent storm might prove effective cover.

TJ Jones came into the sitting room, having cleaned up from his day's work. He pulled open the old refrigerator and uncapped two beers, handed one to Raglan who nodded his thanks, then slumped and put his feet up on the coffee table.

'No point trying to work in this weather. So, other than the storm, went the day well?'

Raglan raised an eyebrow at the mention of what to many was a long-forgotten title. 'Story or film?'

TJ smiled. 'Y'know, I read the original short story when I was stuck in a Saigon hospital getting put back together by a cigar-smoking, mostly drunken, army surgeon. There was little to read except some women's magazines sent to the nurses, a few horror novels, which weren't to my taste, and if you could get out of bed to scramble for the book trolley, you might snag a Leon Uris, or a Harold Robbins. But I was stitched so tight I couldn't break wind without tearing open my wounds. So the drunken medic gave me what no one else wanted. After that I read the best I could find.'

'Good choice,' said Raglan. 'I was scrambling through caves and over mountains for more years than I can remember. In the early days I took the heftiest book I could find with me. *War and Peace.*'

'And added a couple of pounds to an already heavy load.'

'Never finished it. Always meant to.'

'Too difficult?'

'Lost it in a swamp. Sank like a stone.'

'So are we gonna sit here slurping and talking books or are you going to tell me what's causing the wrinkles on your brow? Did you find out what you wanted at the jail?'

'A little. I made a promise to help the man. His family need a favour.'

'How many families are you planning to help on this vacation of yours?'

Raglan swilled the beer. 'It was a deal. He gave me

information and I'll find a man who might be part of my friend's disappearance.'

TJ waited. 'I'm off the clock, friend. I can get another bottle if it helps?'

'Brentwood. I have to get to a house there.'

TJ nearly choked. Froth spilled down his chin. 'Didn't you check that map I gave you?'

'I did.'

'And what colour shading did I give Brentwood?' He didn't wait for Raglan's answer. 'Red. Not amber or green, or a whiter shade of pale. Crimson red. Dammit, son, doing what you used to do is fine, up to a point, but those people don't just carry knives and guns, they use machetes to make their point. NOMA is the ringed area I made. That stands for North of Massachusetts Avenue but it might as well mean No Man's Land where you're concerned.'

'I can run fast when I have to.'

TJ sighed and shook his head. 'Raglan, sometimes a deal isn't a deal, it's a death wish. What did that guy in prison have that's so important for you to walk into a Latino-gang-run neighbourhood?'

'I promised him I'd make a payment to a drug dealer or a gangster or whatever he is. It's not clear. He's connected in the Capitol, though, which means he's running his protection rackets from a townhouse a few blocks from here. Apparently he's a legit businessman. Which, with clever accountants and lawyers, is how most of these people avoid prosecution. I traded a payoff for Esposito's family for the information he gave me. The man I make the payment to has information or is somehow connected. I don't know which yet.'

Swirling rain beat against the windows. 'I'm coming with you. You can't go wandering around Indian country on your own. They scalp the likes of you. Me, I'm an old Buffalo Soldier. They don't want an ancient black relic's topknot.'

'No. This isn't your business, TJ.'

'You will have a better chance of doing what you have to if a senior citizen like me plays running block while you run with the ball. Damn, I can't hold my own much in a dogfight but I can run off at the mouth long enough to put Grandma in her grave.'

He swung his feet down and turned for his room. 'Brentwood,' he sighed. 'This storm'll pass in a while but you'd better grab a coat.'

'TJ,' said Raglan. 'No.'

The veteran stopped. 'You're telling me what I can and can't do in my own house? You think I'm gonna let a guest get himself chopped into dog meat?'

'Think about it. I'm a white guy in the wrong neighbourhood.'

''S what I said!'

Raglan understood that his intentions would cause the older man grief and seemed reckless. 'See it for what it is. You and me, we'd look right out of place if we go together. Me, I'm a white guy looking to score. Drugs or women. I'm no threat. I'm not local. They can hear my accent. I'm buying what they have.'

TJ saw there was a counter-intuitive logic to what he said. He was about to argue but Raglan's look told him all he needed to know. The decision was made. TJ surrendered.

'All right. Then I'll help you another way because I do not want to see you hurt or worse. If you get cornered, you won't make the Metro and if you got that lucky they'd have you well and truly boxed. By the time you reached the next station they'd have more killers getting on board. You go on these people's turf and they'll cut you off like a pack of wolves. And I don't care how tough you are, Raglan. More than a handful of those scum come at you and you'll get chopped.' He lifted a rain jacket from the hook. 'Grab your coat and come with me.'

They dodged the sweeping rain. The sky was clearing in the south but the air still bit and scratched. They ducked into a doorway not fifty yards from the apartment. 'Wait a second. That rain'll sweep down the alley where we're heading like a stream in flood.'

They hunched. Both men watched the malevolent cloud. Neither spoke. Minutes later, when the wind had kicked the tumbleweed cloud across the river, TJ set off again, walked twenty yards, turned down an alley and unlocked a padlocked garage door. It was narrow and gave a false impression of what lay beyond. TJ threw a light switch.

'This is where I get to keep all the stuff I need for the apartments.'

It was a garage space big enough to hold all his janitorial tools. Ladders, cans of detergent, paint, brushes, rollers. Shelves ran along one wall. Boxed items the other. The concrete floor was covered in old pieces of carpet which Raglan figured probably came from those apartments that had been refurbished over the years. In the middle of the floor was a dust-sheet-clad shape. TJ hauled the drape free. He bundled up the dust sheet and put it aside.

'This was my son's. I start it up every once in a while. I even take it out for a spin come summer. Mind you, I'm no speed freak these days. But,' he said with a hint of nostalgia, 'it surely can fly if you let it.'

Raglan stepped closer to the motorcycle. Its elliptical tank was burnished in emerald green, the chrome trims and rack at the back of the deep, black single rider's seat gleamed. The fat black white-walled tyres were scrubbed clean.

TJ caressed the handlebars. 'I clean it most weeks. Takes me a step closer to who he was.' He licked a finger and rubbed a speck of dirt off the windshield above the flared handlebars. 'It's a 2000 Harley Road King classic, green over black. Seven hundred and sixty pounds of pure beef. Fifteen hundred cc, fuel injected. Air-cooled. You can do whatever with this machine. Hard to say what it is, in truth. It's a sport bike that likes fast curves and a tourist bike that loves long trips.' He glanced at Raglan. 'You take it. It'll get you out of a tight spot in a hurry.'

'TJ, I can't do that.'

'My son and I shared the same spirit of adventure. It's what took us where we went in life. Same thing for you, I'll bet. Right now there's no one else it's better suited for. He'd have agreed. Trust me, I know my son.'

The memory had softened TJ's voice. He snapped out of it and tossed the key on its Airborne-badged fob. 'There's only one thing. When you bring it back, you clean it.'

23

Jenna Voss ignored the splattering rain against the large glass windows. The view was just as dramatic as before but the streaked glass distorted what lay beyond. No different from her frustrated squinting at the three computer screens in front of her, trying to see through the veil of information that she knew obscured the answers she sought. She was multi-tasking, wanting to find Raglan, keep up to date with the crime reports being bounced between the various law-enforcement agencies and scrutinizing security-video footage from the Orlando bus station. The more she searched the more she was convinced the Englishman had boarded the bus at another stop or had purposefully avoided the cameras. Where was he and why had he slipped away? And if he was guilty of the mechanic's murder then it was another blot on her career. Trouble was, she had no authority to be searching for him.

Other agents would soon be taking over her shift and she did not want to lose any ground she might have gained. An hour ago she'd had a break. It was a maybe, but her gut told her it was significant. All she had to do was track it down. Step by step. And that's what she was good at. She had tracked all the Greyhound bus routes out of Orlando, had searched their ticket databases and had come up with nothing. If her suspicion was correct that he had caught a Greyhound he must have paid cash for his ticket. If he hadn't travelled away from Florida she had wasted precious hours. But she asked herself the classic question: what would she have done if she wanted to evade being recognized even if only for a few hours? And the answer was: slip into the crowd at a mass-transit bus station.

Rolling crime reports on the CJIS servers and Jacksonville PD had flagged the arrest of two men on the interstate saying they had been hitch hiking. A patrolman's instinct had told him differently. He checked and found they were wanted for cheque fraud in two states. After more questioning he learnt they had been kicked off a Greyhound bus. Greyhound drivers logged anything inappropriate on their journeys. Drunk passengers, abusive behaviour, racial antagonism: if it was out of the ordinary it was logged. Most passengers were peaceful citizens going from point A to point B. Jacksonville PD had no further interest in the fracas on the bus. Voss got into the Greyhound system, scanned the reports, highlighted their buses travelling on that route on the day in question. Narrowing it down to the time frame of when the men were arrested she found low-definition black-and-white video footage from one bus's security camera of two men being restrained. The camera lens's high angle and the men's action blurred the images further. She saw that one man was African American. His face was mostly obscured but she could tell he was an older man as he dealt with a young, aggressive black man with braided hair whose image fitted that of the police report photographs. The blurred action also involved a second man whose face turned to camera, eyes and mouth open in a scream. Voss froze the frame. There was a white man behind him and it looked as though he was the cause of the man's distress. She couldn't make him out. She zoomed in as much as the frame allowed but the action was too indistinct. But if the African American was dealing with the first aggressor, then the man sorting out the second might be his travelling companion. She chose a different tack and brought up the older man's face. He was wearing a veteran's cap. That meant he would have had a discounted bus fare, either for vets or seniors – or maybe both; she didn't know, she hadn't ever taken a Greyhound anywhere in her thirty-three years. And if a discount had been given, then identification would have been presented. And that's where her search faltered. Data security did not list discounted bus fares or who had applied for them. She would have to phone.

She punched in the number.

The recorded voice sweetly thanked her for contacting Greyhound but because of demand there would be a delay before being connected.

She was on hold.

Seven minutes and forty-eight seconds later, according to Voss's screen clock, her call was answered. She asked to speak to the regional operations manager for Florida or DC.

'What is the nature of your enquiry?' said the customer service representative.

'That's something I need to discuss with them. Can you put me through? This is Special Agent Voss at the FBI.'

'Can you identify yourself in any other manner, ma'am? We have a lot of people who phone and tell us they are law-enforcement officers but their intention is to make a complaint and by lying they think they can get through to someone in authority. We had one person phone on a daily basis about a blocked toilet on a—'

Voss quickly interrupted. 'I'm not interested in your complaints procedure or blocked toilets. This is an FBI matter regarding an incident on one of your buses.'

'Well, I'm sorry, but we have no record of any incident that's showing on my screen right now. And I do not have the authority to—'

'Put me through or I'll have you charged with obstruction.'

'Ma'am, if any of our staff receive threatening behaviour we will terminate the call.'

Voss drew air deep into her chest and blew a quiet stream of frustration. 'I have no means of identifying myself other than to tell you I have seen video footage of an assault taking place a few days ago on a bus from Orlando to DC. Can you at least see that incident report?'

'Anything recorded on our buses is privately held by our company. May I ask how you came by that footage?'

Because I'm the fucking FBI! she wanted to scream. Instead, she maintained her calm insistence. 'The FBI is investigating the arrest of two of your passengers for cheque fraud by the Jacksonville Police Department. I need further information about other passengers involved in a violent incident on that bus. So does that sound as though I am some creep in my basement hacking into your system? Kindly put me through.'

There was a pause. 'Ma'am, I can detect anxiety in your tone. Please hold.'

'Fuck!' Voss spat. Agents swivelled their necks. They knew Voss had been at the sharp end with Hostage Rescue. She might as well have thrown her chair through the large glass window, given their concerned looks. If her shift supervisor called her in, then that too could go on her file. She glared at the rubberneckers. 'There's a short on this terminal. Damned near electrocuted myself.'

The agent sitting closest to her reached for his desk phone, 'Jenna, I'll get maintenance down.'

She smiled her best smile. 'Thanks, Ted. Appreciate it.'

Ted was flattered.

A voice in her ear introduced himself as the Florida regional operations manager. Voss was all sweetness and light. She went through her gambit again and explained that the two fraudsters might have tried to con the African-American veteran. If he could supply the name and address noted on the discounted ticket, she would ensure a police or federal agent would interview him. Senior citizens are a target for these people. Oh, yes, he agreed. His own parents were forever getting cold calls.

'You know we can help you with that,' she said. 'If your parents are being harassed by cold callers, then you let me know and I will have someone chase that down for you.'

The man thanked her effusively. His was a thankless job, keeping a massive fleet of buses running smoothly, probably from a windowless office in some nondescript building, and his gratitude was clearly genuine. He offered to do all that he could to assist her. She gave him the CJIS general switchboard number, which he could check as being genuine, and said that when he had the information, he should ask for her by name. She rang off.

'Jenna,' said Ted awkwardly, 'you know we don't do that kind of thing here.'

'I know, Ted, but he doesn't.'

24

Raglan opened the throttle on the Harley; its engine's twin-cam power hummed through his body as it cruised effortlessly north-east along New York Avenue. It was a well-balanced bike with good cornering ability. The rain stopped and the road spray slicked away from the windshield. Twenty minutes later he swung north, passing the vast Amtrak marshalling yards facility, and rode through the industrial area. The address was fixed like a compass point in his mind after he had logged it on his phone and checked the best route in and out. He needed a fast turnaround before any locals took too much interest. The pretence of buying drugs would likely only take him so far before he was cornered by the local wildlife. Brentwood might be a bad area but good people also lived there and Esposito's family was one of many who had no choice but to live where gangs controlled neighbourhoods. No different from the bad areas of Marseilles. Guns, knives or machetes terrorized the residents. For Raglan it was business as usual.

He drove parallel to the marshalling yards, where the mighty diesel-engined beasts corralled freight wagons. He had decided to avoid the main streets and, with luck, the corner drug dealers and those who ran them. He eased the

Harley down a narrow lane, wide enough for a car, which was the rear entrance to the low-rise terraced houses. Some houses had older model cars parked on their backyard between the lane and the house's rear door. Fences separated the properties from each other and the road. There were no house numbers on the rear of the buildings but he had counted the houses when he'd brought up the digital map. There were nine houses to pass before he could get inside the one he needed to retrieve the cash payment.

Esposito's family's house was like its neighbours, the same brick structure weathered from who knew how many years since being built. Maybe this had once been a blue-collar area for workers in the marshalling yards or local industry. Then immigrants would have sought out cheap housing. Was this where unskilled labour lived now, amid the drug pushers and gang violence? People who travelled into the city and cleaned the Georgetown mansions or swept the corridors of power. The rear of the house lay behind a half-broken wire-mesh gate hanging from its hinges. A rusting washing machine lay half on its side in a corner. He kicked free the flimsy gate and eased the motorcycle closer to the raised back porch. After turning the Harley to face the lane, he tugged free the tarp that covered an old sofa and dragged it over. As far as he could see there was no one around either side or opposite, despite the chained dog barking in the next yard. He took the shallow stairs three at a time and gave a rapid few taps on the back door. Then he stood aside. If the wrong people were in the house and felt threatened, a shotgun blast through the flimsy door might be their response.

A woman's voice answered quietly. '¿Sí?'

'Mrs Mendoza?'

'Yes?'

'Izan sent me,' Raglan said, staying back from the door.

There was no reply but he heard hurried whispers. A chain and then a bolt slid free; the door opened a crack revealing a woman who looked to be in her thirties.

She glanced nervously around. 'He said you would come.'

'The longer I stand out here the sooner someone will notice.'

The woman stood aside and let Raglan in. It was a simple house. Plastic covered the only sofa, clearly the replacement for the one in the yard; two chairs had seen better days. The linoleum floors were clean and there was the pungent smell of food being cooked. Three children squatted on the floor between the furniture; an old television set ran an old cop show dubbed in Spanish.

'Who else is here?' said Raglan.

'My mother and my cousin.'

'Show me.'

The woman stepped into the living area and turned into a narrow corridor. She knocked on a door and waited until a frail voice answered. The open door revealed an elderly, bedridden woman who looked alarmed when she saw the tall white man looming over her daughter.

'Tell her I apologize for intruding and that I am here to help her family.' Raglan knew enough Spanish to make his own apology but there were times when it was beneficial to appear ignorant. That way information could be gleaned.

The rapid Spanish brought a smile to the old woman's creased features; she nodded. Mrs Mendoza had said nothing more than Raglan had asked her to. The door closed and the woman pointed to another room. 'My cousin is in there but I don't want to wake him.'

'It's late in the day to be sleeping,' Raglan said, wary of her reluctance.

'He is sick.'

'Be quiet but open the door.'

She did as she was bid and eased the door open to reveal a man in his twenties lying in bed, his laboured breathing enough to confirm he was seriously ill. Raglan eased his head into the room and checked behind the door. It was empty except for a couple of posters on the wall and scattered clothing on the floor. He closed the door.

'We have no insurance. He will die soon,' said Mrs Mendoza.

'Izan has money. That's why I'm here. Why not use that?'

'It is too late for him but me, my mother and the children, he said that is what the money is for, so that is why we must pay Reyes. So that we may live. Izan said he would find a way to get the money to him.'

'Is this your house?'

'It's a rental.'

'And you have nowhere else to go? To get away from the neighbourhood and the threat against your family?'

'Where would I go without money? No, those who control the streets, they have us trapped.'

'The same people who killed your husband?'

She nodded. Raglan had touched the raw nerve of grief.

'And Luis Reyes controls this neighbourhood?'

She wiped her tears. 'He is invisible to us. He has people on his payroll everywhere.'

He stayed with Mrs Mendoza in the corridor, keeping his voice low in case the children overheard. They would be the first to be questioned if the gangs learnt he had been there. 'Izan said Reyes was an important man in the city.'

'He controls many of the districts but he is getting more dangerous. Izan said he is...' She muttered to herself in Spanish and then found the words in English. 'He is connected.' She looked at Raglan, confirming she had chosen the correct vocabulary. 'And protected.'

'Does Izan know who protects him?'

She shook her head.

'But if I pay him the money that Izan has hidden then you'll be safe here?'

'Yes.'

Raglan looked at the house, heard the children and the muted Spanish coming from the old television set. 'Why are you in danger?'

'Someone thought my husband was talking to the police about what he knew.'

'Was he?'

The woman bit her lip and tears welled in her eyes. 'Raúl feared God. He spoke to our priest, who said he should remain silent for the sake of his family. For us.'

'So he *was* talking to the police?'

She nodded rapidly and dried her eyes. 'This country gave us a new life. We thought we had escaped the danger at home. We are not illegal people. We have the proper papers now. Every night when we thanked God for the food on our table, my husband offered thanks to this country for saving us all. He loved America. And then he told Izan what he knew because he thought Raúl a brave man and he would go to the authorities but he said no, just like the priest. Izan told him to stay silent. No one had the courage that was needed so my husband said it was his duty and that the police would protect us. He said this was not the same as home.'

It was taking too long. If anyone had seen him drive down the back lane they would be alerted. He hadn't planned on being in the house this length of time. 'What did he tell them?'

'I don't know much. Raúl worked as a gardener in the city. He said he saw important people there and overheard them saying that they and my husband's boss were buying guns but that his boss was losing control because he was taking drugs.'

It wasn't much information but enough to get her husband murdered. 'Do you know where he worked?'

She nodded and whispered the address.

'And you know the name of the man he worked for?'

'It was Luis Reyes.'

25

Luis Reyes had come a long way from the Congress projects south-east of the city. The illiterate child had educated himself by watching old movies where actors' diction was clear and concise – unlike so many of today's mumbling efforts, which caused Reyes to shout at the screen in his private auditorium. Reyes knew instinctively that to move up in the world took more than hard work. Fine clothes, beautiful women and the power to influence others, with violence if necessary, were the key to success, especially in a political town like DC. Now, thirty years after leaving the crime-ridden projects, his control of the major districts ruled by Central American gangs was close to being absolute. Pitting gangs like 18th Street against MS-13 took no effort because of their traditional turf wars and inherent hatred for each other. Mexican against El Salvadorian. Divide and rule. He had learnt that from the movies as well. The original artwork of Al Pacino in *Carlito's Way* held pride of place in his twelve-bedroom house on 30 Street NW, in the heart of Georgetown. The expansive landscaped gardens behind high security gates and walls offered privacy and space, more than most in the city, and its current value of $17 million was not only a good return on investment but added more prestige to a low-life gangster who had eventually clawed his way up through the rigid DC society. And he had learnt from other successful businessmen and showbiz personalities that supporting and starting charities placed him on the side of the righteous in the eyes of God.

The money had come quickly in those early days, thanks to his roots in Honduras and the secret routes he established for shipping drugs, but the style and acceptance he craved was slow in arriving. Before he ever dreamt of spending nine thousand dollars on a walnut and smoked-glass coffee table, it was Charlene Ortez who made Reyes realize he was capable of greater things than smuggling drugs. Charlene was unobtainable. Like any potential princess-to-be, she played hard to get. She hovered. Came and went. Lived across the river but not for long because Charlene, like Luis, was ambitious and she had talent-spotted the big man early on. No one knew much about her but word had it she was a heart- and a ball-breaker. Daddy was serving life down in Florida and Charlene had grown up as tough and mean as she was beautiful. Reyes loved her and played it just the way she liked: with respect. It was Charlene who had the connections – she never said how – and introduced him to the important people working in business who knew what corners needed to be cut in order to increase profits and to those in government who had influence. When the day came that she saw he didn't need her any more, she left him. Said an ex-husband was on her trail. Time, she said, for Reyes to find himself a nice white girl. He needed glamour now. Arm candy. Reyes made a play at begging her to stay but even he knew she could see it was a sham. Reyes was on his way up.

What Reyes never knew was that the irresistible, bright, intelligent, streetwise tough girl worked for people with lifelong connections to a government agency. Reyes was being groomed for when they needed him and his distribution network from Central America. They were playing a low-key role because if their connections were discovered the consequences would light a fire under the FBI and lives would be ruined by the ensuing investigation. By this time Luis Reyes's image of a successful established businessman, especially in the gentrification of the run-down areas he controlled, put him at arm's length from any violence. When aspiring politicians turned to him for help in their wards, he would arrange an increase in gang violence and that gave harsher law-and-order policies more attention and traction. It made little difference to police efforts because when drug-related murders were investigated in one precinct the perpetrators moved to another and sought sanctuary with local gang members. It was an unspoken understanding among those who turned to Reyes for favours that he was not personally involved in any wrongdoing. Of course he wasn't. How else could they allow themselves to be in his sphere of influence?

His 30 Street house had twenty-three cars in its vast underground garage. His day-to-day vehicles, the white Suburban and Mercedes S500, were the same paint shade as the women he chose to bring into his life. He was cool. Well-dressed, spoke convincingly on a range of matters and was rich enough to buy whatever he desired. It was a good life.

Luis Reyes still had enough rough edges to keep him interesting to those who had been born and educated with a degree of privilege. Invitations to uptown parties were common. No one said a word about the tall Latino dating beautiful white girls who looked as though they graced the cover of fashion magazines, not in this town where race meant nothing and success, influence and power everything. Besides, if anyone ever had such unwholesome thoughts they were wise enough to keep them to themselves. They had their own street smarts. They knew a dangerous man when they saw one. Reyes's money was clean by the time he bought the various businesses he owned. Accountants made sure the banks did not question any large amounts of cash going into his legitimate accounts and the rest went offshore. It was a sweet deal for everyone involved. He let his distribution routes be used and in turn his money was laundered by people who had the influence and expertise to do it.

Then Luis Reyes did something stupid. Drawn by the sweet smell of fresh baking after a long night partying and drinking, he got into an argument with a no-account kid outside a bakery at four in the morning. The two traded words and insults, and the booze and drugs in Reyes's body meant disrespect could be dealt with in only one way. He shot the kid twice in the head.

Reyes's life unravelled quickly. His use of his own product increased. He threatened the woman he was with. Scared to death, she stayed silent but made sure she got out of his life. The killing was never proved, but it got around that, after all, Luis Reyes wasn't the kind of person you wanted sitting in your Georgetown drawing room sipping 25-year-old malt. The invitations dried up. The 30 Street house fell quiet. And word reached the cops from someone who worked for him, one of his gardeners, that he was using his distribution network for more than drugs. Arms shipments were finding their way south. A contact in the police department tipped him off before it could be put into the hands of the FBI. That's when Luis Reyes butchered Raúl Mendoza.

26

Raglan told Mendoza's widow to go back to her children and her cooking. He went into the bathroom, checked the ceiling boards and climbed on top of the toilet pan. He had no difficulty in lifting the lightweight panel, and his fingers found the package exactly where Esposito said he'd hidden it. Replacing the panel, he blew the dust off a fat, brick-sized envelope. Peeling it open, he spilled out two blocks of tightly packed 100-dollar bills. Benjamin Franklin's benign expression gazed back at him. An address in Georgetown was written across the old man's forehead. Raglan thumbed the notes. At a rough guess there were $50,000. Twenty-five thousand in each pack. Raglan's instinct was to peel off ten thousand and give it to the family. How would that play? If Reyes had demanded fifty thousand, then being ten light would leave the family exposed. He pushed the money back into the envelope.

Mrs Mendoza stood back from the man who filled the doorframe of her house. She did not know or care who he was; she was just grateful that he had come from her brother. Two brave men who had risked themselves for her and her family.

Raglan handed her his phone. 'Please put your number in there for me.'

She hesitated, suddenly alarmed. 'Why would you wish to have my number?'

'I want to tell you when I have delivered the money and that you're safe.'

She nodded guiltily. She knew he would have seen the sudden jolt from gratitude to fear and distrust. She keyed in her number. 'I am sorry, I am afraid all the time.'

'I'll do what I can to ease that,' he told her.

Raglan left the house and secured the money brick in the leather pannier; then he rolled the Harley back on to the lane. If he turned back the way he'd come he'd hit a one-way system, turn right and be riding through some tightly packed streets, but if trouble flared the Harley would get him past any street-corner gangs or dealers. He needed to get out of the area before someone somewhere clocked his presence in the backstreets. He twisted the accelerator and turned right. The traffic was in sight at the end of the lane. Another five hundred yards and he'd be clear. He was halfway there when his luck ran out. Three men stepped out of their backyard. They tossed aside their cigarette butts and casually blocked the narrow passage. Raglan pulled up the Harley ten feet from where they stood. The slightly built men swaggered. They had to have the walk. All the tough guys on the block needed a bad-ass walk. And accompanying bad teeth. If they didn't like what you said they would quickly overwhelm you and twenty-four hours later your body would be found on the side of the highway with multiple stab wounds.

'Nice bike,' said their leader. He had sinewed muscle coiled like steel hawsers. He would be the first and hardest man to bring down. It would have to be quick. The others were less of a threat. Too much beer. Pot bellies sagging over torn jeans and padded jackets. All three had tatts.

A rider can look small on a hefty bike like a Harley because of its low-slung design. It gave the troublemakers a false sense of superiority. Raglan switched off the ignition and dropped the bike on to its side stand. He took a few paces away. He didn't want to risk splattering the bike with their blood. Now the men's chins tilted upwards as they were forced to look up at him. He stood unmoving. Waiting. The balls of his feet felt the grip of the road beneath him. Stable. And ready.

'It's a great bike,' said Raglan.

'Hey, you're not from here,' said the second man, bad teeth grinning. Their accents were Central American, probably El Salvador or Guatemala. That wasn't a deduction made from recognizing dialects but from knowing where the gangs had gravitated from into neighbourhoods such as this.

'I'm English,' said Raglan.

'You come here as a tourist? You wanna sell it?' said the third runt.

'It's not for sale and there's no point in you drooling over it because it's too heavy for you. You'd fall over and then your mother would have to come and lift it off you.'

The man scowled and took a threatening step forward. '*Te corto los cojones*,' he spat, a hand already reaching behind his belt for the knife he undoubtedly had in his waistband.

But the one in charge extended his arm and stopped him. And then he laughed. 'You don't cut no one's balls today. He wants something.'

Raglan stayed rooted. Stance wide enough and balanced, ready to move either right or left if they came for him. And they would.

'Whadda you doin' here?' said their leader.

'I heard this is where I come for quality goods. Real quality.'

They came a few paces closer but they weren't sure about the man in the police-style crash helmet who looked unwaveringly at them. 'You come from the city? Shit you buy on H Street or 7th. Dupont Circle is for the likes of you, not here.'

'I don't want to be entrapped. Cops in DC get high on buy-and-bust deals. I'm on a visa. I get arrested, I lose my chance of ever coming back and I have a woman here.'

The three men had not encountered a foreigner coming so brazenly into their neighbourhood before. It was a unique experience in their limited lives. Every block had their own dealers. Was this their lucky day or was the big man trouble? There were three of them. More could be summoned. The one in charge glanced left and right over his shoulder. Was he checking if anyone peered out of windows? Would it have made any difference? If they were intent on inflicting violence, witnesses were hardly going to step up to the plate and give a statement to the police. Raglan knew the leader was looking for support. They were nervous of him. That was good. The advantage was already his. Had been from the beginning because he was not on a street corner: there would be no witnesses, no matter what happened, and no cavalry nearby.

'I can go to your competition on the next corner,' he said.

They shuffled closer still. 'No, no,' said their front man. 'We got whatever you need at the right price. You got the cash?' He grinned. 'We don't take cards.'

'Really? You people are slow. I use my cash card all the time in other places.'

'They got terminals?' the second man said. It had thrown them.

'Sure. You have rock candy?'

They grinned. 'You want *topo*? We got that. We got everything. You know what speedballs are where you come from?'

'I'll take some of those as well.'

'Yeah, but first we need to see if you can pay for it,' said the wiry man.

He had the look of a raptor focusing on its prey.

Raglan tugged a roll of bank notes out of his jacket pocket. It was a thick roll held with an elastic band. The three men came closer, drawn by the tempting bundle. They were almost within arm's reach. Street-smart eyes knowing the man from the city was a fool for showing them the thousands he carried.

'We take that now,' said their leader as he and the man on his right pulled knives. The gang member on his left tried to draw a machete from inside his coat. It was a dumb move. He was right-handed and the muscled man got in his way.

The attack was sudden but not unexpected. A close encounter with extreme violence creates a surge in the limbic and temporal lobes of the brain. The brain presses the accelerator on the adrenal medulla, heightening strength and perception. Raglan always experienced that same sense of calm and heightened alertness when extreme danger threatened. Time was distorted. Everything was vivid. A bird landed on a corrugated tin roof, its claws scratching the surface as it tried to gain purchase. The sound overwhelmed everything else. The pockmarks on the face of the man in front of him became craters of the moon, distinct ragged pits that ate into the tattoo that crawled from his neck. Flecks of white spittle clung to the corners of his mouth like caterpillar froth on a leaf. Raglan had no concern about the outcome. Psychologists explain this sense of detachment as depersonalization, normally a troubling personality disorder, but in a life-or-death situation it's the mark of a survivor.

Raglan casually tossed the roll at the front man, who fumbled as he snatched at it. Raglan took an extra stride and rammed the heel of his hand beneath his chin. His neck snapped a moment after his crumbling teeth bit through his tongue. The man on Raglan's right had no room to manoeuvre and could only lunge with the machete blade but Raglan was already three strides away as his momentum carried him forward towards the man on his left, who had his knife gripped low. He met Raglan halfway, his knife curving upwards in a wicked disembowelling strike. It was a mistake. Raglan sidestepped, let the knife arc past him and then jabbed two fingers in the man's eyes. The man cried out and threw up his hands, dropping the knife. It was a temporary feint from Raglan. He needed time to face the third man who now had room to swing the machete. Raglan stepped inside the attack, blocked the man's arm and drove a fist an inch below the skinny man's sternum. It was a killing blow, severe enough to rupture internal organs and tear the abdominal aorta, the largest blood vessel in the human body. The skinny man fell forward. The blinded knifeman had stumbled and collapsed on to the ground, writhing from the blinding pain of crushed optical nerves. Raglan reached down and punched him once in the forehead. He stopped writhing, with a low hiss of fetid breath. His last. Raglan retrieved the roll of money and peeled off the single 100-dollar bill, then tossed the remaining cut paper over the gang members. A curtain twitched. A woman's face appeared. She nodded and smiled and was gone. Raglan settled back on the Harley and drove its 760 pounds forward without avoiding the gang leader's body.

He'd chalk the brief meeting down to community service.

27

Raglan headed back to the city. Once he got to Georgetown, pretty much the heart of the capital as far as town living went, he turned the Harley along a tree-lined street. Three-storey red-brick shuttered houses faced each other from either side. There was a zoned two-hour parking limit on the streets. He turned west, following the grid pattern, making sure he wasn't being tailed. Being cautious was never a bad habit. Several streets later the expensive houses kept showing how grand they were. Each clearly cost millions, in sharp contrast to the backstreets of Brentwood. No different than anywhere else in the world between haves and have nots. Raglan drove past Reyes's house on 30th Street North West, checking the security. Now that the storm had passed he could see two gardeners bent over their work through the fancy ironwork gates. There was no sign of security guards or dogs but there would be cameras.

He pulled the motorcycle into a space thirty yards down the street and walked to the gate. He pressed the intercom button, but without any response. He gave a low whistle. One of the gardeners raised his head, nervously checked the house, and then looked at the man beckoning him at the gate. Raglan lifted the envelope so he could see it. The old man held his hoe like a stave across the front of his body.

He reached the gate and studied Raglan. 'Yes, sir?' He looked and sounded no different from the people in Brentwood.

'I have a delivery for Señor Reyes.' He turned the bulky envelope, making sure the man could see it.

'You have to press the button on the intercom, sir.'

'I tried. It doesn't work,' Raglan said. 'It's an important package. Is he inside?'

'Yes, he is here. I do not know if he is receiving guests.' The man paused, his voice lowered. 'He is not always very well these days.'

'If I could get this to him, it would help the Mendoza family stay safe.'

The old man's eyes widened. He made the sign of the cross and then turned and summoned the other gardener. They were of similar age. Weather- and life-beaten, two old men grateful to have paying work. The first recounted in Spanish what Raglan had said. When the name Mendoza was mentioned, the other gardener also crossed himself. Fear ruled. Salvation not yet found.

'Do you carry a gun, *señor*?'

'No.' Raglan pulled aside his jacket and turned around so they could see nothing in his waistband.

The two men conferred again. Both shook their heads. They faced Raglan. 'We dare not let you in without talking to him first. You understand?'

'Of course. Will you go up to the house and ask him to see me? You know what happened to Raúl Mendoza. I am a friend of the family.'

'Sir, I do know but wish I did not. I will ask the housekeeper if he will see you.'

The gardener made his way towards the house; the other man returned to his work. Raglan had time to study the layout of the house and grounds. There were security cameras either side of the house and down the one wall leading to the back of the property. They covered everyone who entered or left. Raglan had covered the small lens on the intercom at the gate with his hand. Reyes would not have a security firm monitor his cameras – that would be bad for business. But somewhere in the house would be a record of who had visited.

Minutes later the gardener came down the steps and pressed the gate's release button. 'Come inside, sir. He will see you. Follow me.'

'There's no need,' he told the breathless older man. 'I can find my way.'

'Thank you. The door is at the top of the steps. Please ring the bell and someone will come.' He coughed phlegm and spat to one side. His breathing eased. He pulled a sweat rag from his pocket and made a pretence of wiping his nose. 'Be careful,' he whispered. 'He is not that well today.'

'Are there men in the house?'

The gardener shook his head. 'No more. Once, yes, Señor Reyes always had his own kind around him. Now, those men have gone.' The old man paused. 'There have been others. White men.' He lowered his voice. 'We hear them shouting. They were unhappy about him taking so many drugs. Now, there is only a maid and a cook.'

Raglan thanked him and took his time climbing the curved steps leading up to the house. The higher he went the more he could see of the grounds and the breadth and size of the building; the door to the underground garage also became visible. As he approached the house and the closed front door he skirted left along the side of the building towards the rear garden. Raglan opened a decorative wrought-iron gate. The grounds were large enough for a full-length pool and sitting area and the extended lawns and planting were surrounded by a high brick wall softened with tall trees. Reyes liked his privacy. Raglan backtracked, peered into the windows, saw little of interest. The windows belonged to expensively furnished rooms. His fingers traced the frames. Barely noticeable wires were concealed in the gap between window and frame. The alarm system would cover the whole house. He reached the front door, pressed the bell and a moment later a maid opened the door. She remained silent, stepped back from the door and ushered Raglan inside.

The vast expanse of white marble flooring would have blinded an Arctic explorer if the sun caught it. The sweeping staircase would not have looked out of place in *Gone with the Wind*. He followed the maid through to an equally impressive lounge of marble flooring scattered with animal skins. By then Raglan realized that the movie posters on the walls were not prints but originals. The man was a movie buff. He wondered if Dorothy's red slippers were under his bed. Reyes looked to be already halfway down the Yellow Brick Road.

The maid left Raglan twenty feet from Luis Reyes. He wore a white and gold tracksuit and gold trainers with turquoise stones embedded along their side. There was no point trying to gauge the cost of the encrusted watch hanging loosely on his wrist. Four thirty-two-inch television screens sat on a sideboard across the room. Surely too small for a man with Reyes's taste to watch films on? Raglan saw a dozen framed photographs of a well-dressed, elegant-looking man, someone you might mistake for a movie star. Good teeth, lithe body, a bright-eyed smile, with one gorgeous woman after another clinging to his arm in every picture. A different image of the man sitting opposite him. He looked wrecked.

Reyes sat on the edge of a white sofa large enough for the whole Washington football team, offence and defence, to relax and watch a game. Scattered food crumbs lay messily around a plate bearing the remains of cupcakes. The kind with the sprinkles on top. Different colours. It looked as though Luis Reyes, drug dealer, gangster and killer, preferred the pink ones. The opened patisserie box bore the name of a deli and coffee shop on M Street. So the man craved sugar and texture. There was also a bottle of whiskey, half empty, the glass next to it half full. A nickel-plated semi-automatic sat near to hand on the glass coffee table, a guardian to several lines of cocaine. Booze and coke. If the man didn't overdose or have a heart attack, he'd be lucky. Reyes might as well sign himself in for a liver transplant now.

Half of the coke had seemingly already travelled up Reyes's nostrils. He was edgy, his right hand reaching out, laying his palm over the handgun. Then back to his thigh, which he scratched. Raglan held his gaze as long as seemed sensible. Stare at a dog long enough and it sees a challenge. Luis Reyes looked as though he would bite.

'Who the fuck are you and why are you in my house?'

he said, then bent his head to inhale another line of powder with a whiskey chaser.

Raglan reckoned Reyes'd had a long session. Cocaine gives you a thirty-minute high and to keep the euphoria going you need to keep taking more. The man had obviously taken much more. And when he came down he'd take something else because of the deep depression. Raglan's risk heightened if paranoia kicked in. Raglan glanced at the fireplace – more marble – and the looming picture of a drug-crazed Al Pacino. Hero worship.

'Izan Esposito asked me to make a delivery for him.'

'Who?' Reyes said, trying to find the name in his damaged memory bank.

'Esposito. On behalf of the Mendoza family.'

Reyes glared, but then nodded. 'Oh yeah. The snitch. Yeah. You have it?'

Raglan stepped closer; Reyes's hand touched the gun. 'Close enough. On the table.'

Raglan bent and put the package on the glass surface and shoved it across. Reyes tore open the envelope and let the cash tumble out. He fingered the two bricks. Looked at Raglan, put the bound dollar bills to his ear; his thumb rifled the banknotes. He grinned. 'Yeah, it's all there.'

It was a showbiz gesture. Raglan figured Reyes had seen it in a film.

'OK. You can go.'

'I'd like to know the Mendoza family are safe now.'

Reyes swallowed a mouthful of drink. He winced. Something like acid had hit his gut. He held a fist there for a moment. 'What do you care?'

'You made a deal with the family.'

Reyes shrugged. 'Fifty K. I should have asked for more. It's loose change to me.'

'It's more than they'll see in their lifetime. Be good to know that they will have a life.'

It looked as though Reyes was going to snap. His lip curled. Raglan had the moves ready. A firm kick against the table would trap the man, another three strides and the nickel-plated weapon would carve a furrow across the man's tightly styled hair.

Reyes shrugged again and put the gun back on to the glass. He dipped a finger in the coke and rubbed it on his gums.

'Yeah. I don' care 'bout them. The snitch is dead.' He stared at Raglan again. 'Who'd you say you were?'

'A friend of Casey Zeller,' Raglan said, chancing the man's name.

There wasn't much reaching the inner workings of Reyes's mind. He shook his head and stared with dilated pupils at the far wall as if God might hand down the tablets with the information. His gut spasmed. He clutched at his midriff. It looked as though he was about to vomit. He pressed his forearm across his mouth and staggered to his feet. He looked at Raglan again. 'Go ahead,' he said, pointing to the lines of white powder. Grabbing the gun, he staggered from the room. Raglan waited a couple of seconds. He heard a door bang open and the sound of retching. Raglan went to the four television screens, thumbed the remote and watched as the four security cameras at the front of the house came to life. He found a replay button and ran back the recorded images, going past the mail man, the food delivery, the gardeners and what looked like a daily image of Reyes returning on foot with one, sometimes two, patisserie boxes. Not as bad a habit as coke and booze but it told Raglan he went out to the same place regularly and M Street was only a few minutes' walk. Then other faces appeared. The driveway gates swung open. Men got out of their car. They climbed the steps. Raglan froze the frame and took out his phone and photographed the men. The sound of retching continued, interspersed with groans.

He heard a footfall, spun around and saw the maid standing in the doorway. She looked from him to the screens and back. Her expression was noncommittal. She turned and left. If she wanted to raise the alarm, she could have done it there and then. Perhaps, Raglan thought, Raúl Mendoza's death had given them all something to think about. Raglan ran the hard drive further back. The same men appeared again, sometimes two of them, accompanied by well-muscled, bearded heavies who might as well have had special ops tattooed on their foreheads.

A toilet flushed. Raglan ran the images forward again until his own came on screen: him coming up the front steps. His head was down. His features unidentifiable. Raglan closed the screens and went back to where he was standing when Reyes left the room. When he returned, he looked to be more sober. He waved the gun. 'I don't know no Zeller. That what you asked?'

'Casey Zeller. Yes.'

Reyes slumped, laid his head on the back of the sofa. 'Why would I know him?'

'He was interested in supplying products to friends,' said Raglan, taking the chance that the half-cocked Reyes wouldn't shoot him there and then. The man had contacts in the DC police. If he shot Raglan and claimed he was an intruder, who would say otherwise? Not the people who worked in the house.

Reyes levelled his head and stared at him. 'Supply of what?' he said. Alarm bells must have been ringing through the empty corridors in his head.

'Guns,' said Raglan simply.

Reyes averted his eyes and poured another whiskey. Raglan saw his thumb press the safety catch.

'Not my line of work,' said Reyes calmly.

'Then I misunderstood. I apologize.'

Reyes looked at him. Nodded. Sipped the whiskey.

'Then are we OK about the payment for the Mendoza family?' Raglan said.

'It's over with. What had to be done is done. It's settled.'

'Thank you,' Raglan said.

Reyes got to his feet and stepped closer. The gun was at his hip aiming at Raglan's stomach. 'You're not a cop, are you? Someone I don't know. You don't sound like a cop.'

'I'm not a cop,' said Raglan but made no move to step away. He could have disarmed Reyes before the man blinked.

Reyes reached out his hand and pressed his palm against Raglan's chest.

'And I'm not wearing a wire.'

Reyes stepped back. 'You can't be too careful.'

'No, you can't. Thank you for your time, Mr Reyes.'

It was time to go. He got halfway to the door.

'You an Englishman?' said Reyes.

Raglan turned. 'Yes.'

'What are you doing here?'

'I'm on holiday with my family. We're going to Disney World.'

Raglan walked away and left without further comment from the drug dealer. There was hardly likely to be one. Reyes was still trying to compute what he'd just been told. You couldn't make that up. Maybe he was hallucinating more than he knew.

28

Raglan went past the gardener who had let him in. Establishing Reyes's routine would be helpful. If Raglan had a chance he would try to get back into the house, and if Reyes travelled to meet his contacts, then he could follow him.

'Does your boss sleep late?'

The man shrugged. 'I cannot say. Me and my friend, we arrive for work. We don't always see him. The women in the house, well I think... you know... they don't like it but they cannot refuse his demands.'

'He doesn't have women of his own?'

'No. Not any more. Once, yes. Now, people, they stay away from him.'

'Hookers?'

'Yes. Sometimes. Not so often these days.' The man glanced nervously towards the house as if he might be overheard. 'You know, all that drink and drugs – I think it has taken away his manhood. So I guess that if the maid and the cook go to his bed, they feed him burritos.' He grinned. 'He's trapped in the house. He goes nowhere. Once a day he walks and buys those fancy cakes but after that... *nada*.'

'What time does he go out?' he asked.

'In the morning. Coffee time.'

'Thanks,' said Raglan.

'Sir, you have done a kindness to the Mendoza family. It is remembered.'

'I was the messenger. The man you must thank is Izan Esposito.'

'Even so, a messenger places his life in the hands of others.' He studied Raglan for a moment longer. 'Though I think he was more frightened of you than you were of him.'

Raglan waited across the street, out of sight of the men working in the garden and beyond the range of the security cameras. He pretended to fuss with the bike in case a nervous resident called the police about a roughly dressed man loitering in such a wealthy neighbourhood. He gave it an hour and with no movement in or out of the house knew the pretence would hold no longer. He sent the photograph of the men on Reyes's security camera to Maguire in London and 'Bird' Sokol in France. If they were military or assets being used by those involved in the arms deals, then they might know.

TJ Jones was in his work clothes in the garage decanting disinfectant into his cleaning bucket. The Harley's purr was as welcome a sound as a cat wrapping itself around his leg and expressing its pleasure at being home. 'It went OK?' he said as Raglan switched off the ignition and pulled it on to its stand.

'Perfect,' said Raglan.

TJ wiped his hands on a rag. 'It's what it needed, a good run. Did you open it up?'

'A little.'

'Yeah, I bet,' said TJ with a grin. 'Hell, even I gave it a blowout. I'm finishing up in an hour. Oh, and Beth Ann finished your jacket. I'd like to say it's as good as new, but it never was new by the look of it. It's on the hook.'

'Thanks, it's a favourite.'

'You mean it's the only one you got,' said TJ.

Raglan smiled and took some cartons out of the pannier. 'I brought takeaway and beer.'

'Couldn't be better.'

Raglan went down the alley and into the building. An elderly woman peering through thick spectacle lenses stared closely at the papers she had retrieved from her mailbox. Mostly fliers and discount shopping coupons. Probably all she got these days.

'Excuse me? Can I help you?' she said, peering at the stranger 'This is a private residence.' What the woman lacked in height she made up for in confidence despite her poor eyesight.

'I'm a friend of TJ Jones. I'm visiting for a while.'

'Oh.' She looked past him to the front door. 'You're not from around here.'

'No.' Raglan smiled and walked on.

'Young man, we don't like strangers walking into our building.'

Raglan was saved from further explanation by TJ coming into the entrance hall with his mop and bucket. 'Beth Ann, he's a friend. Don't you worry none.'

The elderly woman beamed. 'Oh, TJ, that's all right then. You know how nervous we get when people buzz us and try and cold call.'

TJ's smile eased the old woman's fear. He gave a quick nod to Raglan, who walked on without another word. TJ was smart enough to know that nosey neighbours were not something either of them wanted to indulge. He heard him remind the elderly woman that it was Raglan's jacket that she had repaired. Raglan let himself into the apartment, laid out the food and put the beer into the refrigerator. He washed, checked a tear in his T-shirt that must have happened when he hit one of the drug dealers.

He pulled on his spare and dropped the old one in the garbage. He'd buy another to replace it when he went back into Georgetown to keep tabs on Reyes. Once he had freshened up, he pulled up on his phone the photos of the men he had taken from Reyes's security camera. He sent them through to Jack Swain with a brief message asking if they could be identified. The fragments of information were a jigsaw and the picture did not yet fit together because he did not have all the pieces. Casey Zeller had visited Esposito in jail and that had been a lead Zeller must have been following in his own investigation of military weapons going missing through fake procurement companies. Had Esposito been right? That drug money was being washed so that Reyes's supply route could be used to get weapons out of the States? White men and their heavyweight companions had visited Reyes and the gardener had said that they had threatened him because he was spiralling out of control on his own drugs. Were these men the same whose images he had copied from the security hard drives?

Raglan clicked on the television, flipped through channels until the local rolling news came on. The weather was going to be changeable. Rain had caused some roads to be closed. The breaking news ribbon at the bottom of the screen listed a robbery, a car crash and the death of three men in a suspected gang-related killing in Brentwood. He muted the sound and keyed in the Mendozas's number on his phone. After a few short rings the woman answered.

'Mrs Mendoza, I came to see you this morning. Remember?'

He could hear the nervousness in her voice. 'There was a killing here today. Near our house. Three drug dealers.'

'Yes, I saw that on the news,' he said evenly.

She fell silent. He pictured the house and the conditions inside. Her young son and daughter gazed up at him from where they sat on the floor watching the television. He'd barely given them a thought then but now he recalled the expression in the olive-skinned boy's brown eyes. Uncertain whether the man who gazed back would cause them harm. *No harm*, a voice said. His own. *Too late for some*, it went on. Years before, in a cave when he was hunting terrorists in West Africa, he had killed a child no older than those in the Mendozas's house. That boy had tried to kill him in the shadows and paid with his life. And his disbelieving stare still haunted the man who killed him.

'Hello? Yes. I am here,' said Mrs Mendoza.

Raglan wiped away the image. 'I wanted to assure you that the debt has been paid. You and your family are safe.'

She did not answer right away. He heard her sigh. Then, 'Thank you, sir. Thank you.' Her voice broke. She recovered. 'It is strange, is it not, that we have had to pay the man who murdered my husband?'

*

TJ washed and changed as Raglan laid out the cutlery. He popped a couple of the beers as TJ placed a small pocket radio on the sideboard, slid open a drawer, took out some triple A batteries and replaced those failing in his radio. 'My old radio lasts a damn sight longer than these modern digital ones. I like to have it with me when I'm doing work like swabbing the floors. There are times I wonder if I've made any progress in my life. Spent years as a kid sweeping out the corner store for pocket money, then in the army swabbed more latrine and barrack floors than I can remember. Boy, was I glad to go to war.'

Raglan handed him a beer.

'I swear DC is becoming more violent every day. Know what I heard on the news today?'

'That three men were killed in Brentwood?' said a stony-faced Raglan.

TJ settled himself at the feast before him. He lifted a carton. 'Whole Foods market. This is a real treat. Yes, three drug dealers. Better that these people kill each other than hurt innocent people.'

'That's what I thought,' said Raglan, disinterested.

TJ forked the food out on to his plate and sipped the beer. 'That woman in the hall, her name is Beth Ann. Don't worry about her; I made everything right. She's just an old woman who lives alone. You get old, you get scared. That's the truth for most old folks. Hard not to be with what's happening out there on the streets. Worse if you live in bad neighbourhoods, like Brentwood, and vulnerable people there, well, I guess that every day they live their lives in fear. Day in, day out. Times I wish I could shed twenty or thirty years, then damned if I wouldn't become a vigilante myself.' He spooned food into his mouth. 'No bad thing killing scum.'

The two men ate in silence. Both knowing each had done enough killing between them to fill a graveyard.

There was always room for three more.

29

The next morning Raglan rode along M Street, found a TK Maxx store to buy a replacement dark blue T-shirt. He only ever wore dark blue. There was an offer available. Buy one, get the other half price. An ebullient young man with the name tag Russell pinned to his chest explained the shirt Raglan wanted could not be split from its garish red partner with a graffiti-style logo splashed across its front. Time was ticking away. Raglan did not want to risk missing Reyes. He only had use for one spare T-shirt, he explained again. The illogical contest could not be solved because of the way the checkout till was programmed. Raglan bought the two items, put one in the bag and gifted the other to Russell. Raglan wasn't sure whether the shop assistant was thrilled or appalled.

Once back on M Street he drove down to the deli and patisserie where Reyes bought his cakes. It was an opportunity to get the dealer away from the cameras and press him further about anyone connected with Zeller. And with luck his brain would be less addled. If what the gardener had said was reliable, then the man's cake fix meant he would walk the few hundred yards from his house to the deli at about this time. Raglan secured the bike in a small parking lot reserved for customers and made his way to the storefront.

The deli set out its wares to entice visitors, and Raglan passed by a cornucopia of foodstuffs, rich in colour, varied in choice and with prices to match, and found a stand-up table in the coffee shop at the back. He needed a view of the entrance. Then he checked what was on offer behind the counter. There was a choice of forty varieties of beverages. He ordered a 12-oz coffee and a *pain au chocolat*. The server looked blank. Correcting himself, Raglan reverted to English and requested a chocolate croissant.

Next to the ice cream and yoghurt counter a door led out into a side passage where a glass atrium would shelter coffee-drinkers and cake-eaters from inclement weather. Raglan waited. Customers, clearly regulars, came and went with their standard orders for takeaway food and drink. After a caffeine-fuelled hour of three more 12-oz cups, Raglan was about to leave when a shambling figure came in through the front door.

It was Reyes. From what Raglan could see, the gangster was ordering a selection of cakes but changing his mind when he saw something more enticing. Like a kid in a sweet shop. He was looking this way and that, furtive glances that didn't reach Raglan sitting at the rear. It was doubtful he could focus clearly enough to see him.

Reyes kept encouraging the woman serving him to add more of this and that. She must have said something that triggered Reyes's temper. His voice rose over the hubbub of the other customers. Some turned. Checked the loudmouth and quickly turned away. Reyes wasn't the kind of man to reproach.

Raglan was about to show himself but stopped when a Metro cop came in the side entrance, waved a cheery hand at one of the counter staff and ordered the 20-oz takeout coffee. Twice. Reyes was thirty feet away at the front entrance side counter and hadn't seen him. Raglan watched. Two coffees meant there was another uniform somewhere. The Metro cop wore a wedding ring. He had two chevrons on his sleeve. A master patrol officer. Experienced. He sported a silver MPD badge. Next step up the ranks would be sergeant. A leather-holstered Glock 19 hung on his belt and sunglasses were tucked into his shirt's breast pocket. He ordered a Danish maple twist and then added any cop's favourite, a chocolate doughnut. All good. No problem. Then the situation worsened. Badly. The cop didn't take his coffee and food back out through the side entrance. One fist clamped on the food package, the other carrying the cardboard coffee-cup holder, he went for the front door as his partner drew up in their patrol cruiser.

The cop stopped and told Reyes to keep his voice down. Was Reyes so far out of it that he hadn't seen the cop in his peripheral vision? The man's voice wasn't threatening. It was calming. Meant to ease an agitated man in a public place. Reyes's eyes saucered. His mouth gaped. And then he swivelled, saw the prowler and in his disjointed mind must have thought the cops were there for him. He fired three fast shots from the concealed nickel-plated semi-automatic in his waistband. The coffee sprayed, absorbed like the bloodstains on the cop's dark blue uniform. It was the white tiled floor and glass counter that splattered red. The cop was dead before he hit the floor. Reyes turned and elbowed his way past shock-stricken customers. The prowler's driver was half out of the car, weapon drawn. Reyes kept firing. Raglan was twenty feet behind the killer. The patrol officer went down. Reyes ran. Raglan ignored the panic and screams and pounded into the street. He checked the patrol officer. A bullet had ricocheted off the prowler's roof and torn into the driver's neck. The man writhed. Raglan shouted at a dumbstruck pedestrian to call it in. Officer down. Panic would still be gripping those in the food hall. If luck was on the cop's side someone in the building was already dialling 911. But better to be sure.

He grabbed the wounded man's hand and pressed it against the wound. The cop mouthed something. Raglan heard the word 'wife'. Ignoring what was probably a plea to tell his loved one, he folded the newly bought T-shirt into a pressure dressing. He pulled the man's bloodstained hand away, slapped the cloth on to the wound and then pushed the cop's hand back to keep on the pressure. Raglan hauled him up into a sitting position, squaring the man's shoulders against the side of the car. 'Stay still. Don't move. Blood flow will slow if you're sitting upright. OK?'

The man's eyes locked on Raglan. Shock was setting in. He murmured, 'Got it.'

Shoppers were still crouching on the sidewalk; no one was sure what to do or where the gunman was. Traffic slowed. Drivers who didn't know what had happened hooted. Raglan saw a familiar shape approaching on the other side of the street, heading downtown. He pointed at a beefy-looking young man. Maybe military on leave. Maybe a gym nut. 'You! Stop that ambulance!'

The dazed man dragged his eyes away from the wounded

cop, then switched his brain into gear. He ran out into the street, dodging cars, waving his arms to stop the ambulance. George Washington Hospital was a five-minute drive away.

Raglan reached for the man's fallen weapon. He showed the wounded cop. 'I'm gonna need this.'

The cop tried to grab it with his free hand but had no chance. Raglan eased down the man's wrist. Raglan tucked the Glock out of sight. Its fifteen-round magazine would be enough for a short sharp fight. Beyond that he would need heavier firepower but he had no intention of getting into a bullet storm with Reyes's crew if they had been summoned. He ran in the direction the cop-killer had taken. Sirens wailed. Two cops down. One dead. One lucky. One widow. One happy wife. Tough call.

30

Reyes's panic turned the alcohol and drugs in his body into rocket fuel. He ran like a dog with a firework tied to its tail. And he went the wrong way. Instead of running towards home he turned left and left again and was heading south down a narrow brick-paved lane between historic terraced townhouses and the canal reconstruction. He flailed like a windmill and when he hit the canal's towpath he careered into a cyclist, tripped and sprawled. The white-silk tracksuit and stone-encrusted trainers were not designed for effort and sweat. The material on one leg tore down its flimsy seam, and his hands and knees were grazed, but despite the pain a primordial instinct clenched his fists so that he kept the semi-automatic in one hand and his phone in the other. Man the hunter was now man the hunted, and these twenty-first-century weapons were all that stood between him and the ravening wolf that, in his mind, gave chase.

The body-toned millennial on his three-thousand-dollar mountain bike rolled clear unhurt and made the adrenaline-fuelled mistake of cursing and striding threateningly towards Reyes who fired two shots. One missed; the other tore across the cyclist's Lycra-clad thigh. He was lucky the drug lord didn't finish him there and then but Reyes's own survival instinct drove him to pound up the next narrow street, at last heading for home.

Sirens wailed in the distance as Raglan ran at a fast steady pace; workmen stepped aside as he approached. The man chasing the crazed gunman who had passed a minute before looked to be an undercover cop.

Contrasting images of urban domestic life blurred as he ran. Windowsills sported plant pots of colourful flowers; a small dog confined behind a window barked. Raglan hit the towpath, saw the cyclist, who was hunched over, pressing bloodied hands against his wound. He was angry enough to shout at Raglan through his pain.

'Up there!' he called, nodding to a broad area of ground cleared for reconstruction. Raglan didn't break stride; he turned and ran hard. The open ground skirted the back of buildings; a way ahead gave access to 30th Street. Reyes had found his homing signal. There was no sign of him. Raglan slowed. If Reyes was behind any of the parked vehicles, Raglan would be an easy target. He kept moving, sidestepped every few yards, edging quickly ahead, weapon at the ready. A burly figure strolled into view from the entrance to the street. He looked brawny enough to be a construction worker. He stopped when he saw Raglan with the gun, then raised his hands as any fearful citizen would. He was thirty yards away.

Raglan lowered the Glock. 'It's all right. A cop-shooter came through here. Did he pass you?'

The bearded man lowered his arms, half turned to point in the direction of the access on to the main street, but his eyes stayed on Raglan. It was an unnatural thing to do. In that second Raglan knew he had seen the man before and his half-turn was the sign of a professional. Distract, draw and shoot. Raglan moved side on, presenting a narrower target to the man whose pistol now looked small in his meaty hand. He fired in an instant. Raglan felt one bullet snag his jacket; the other cut air and whirred past his ear. Had Raglan remained in a square stance the shot would have killed him. The big-chested man reeled back, arms thrown wide as Raglan's two shots punctured his heart. His body thudded like a fallen tree. Raglan stepped forwards, kicked the man's gun further away. Half-sleepy eyes looked back at him through heavy eyelids. Death had come too quickly to be a surprise. Blood trickled into his beard. It was one of the heavies Raglan had seen on Reyes's security cameras. The men who were dealing with Reyes must have been sufficiently concerned at his behaviour to have him shadowed. That or Reyes had pressed a fast call button on his phone to get help. And if the dead man was part of a security team, then Raglan thought it likely that they had been in a car and that Reyes had already been scooped up and taken to safety while this man had been sent to stop him.

He bent and looked at the tattoo peeking out below the half-rolled shirt on his forearm. He'd seen that design before, years ago when he fought alongside American special forces. He searched the dead man's pockets but there was no wallet bearing a driver's licence. Nothing to identify him. Raglan pulled free his phone and photographed him. He picked up the shooter's gun and tucked it in the small of the man's back, then half twisted his arm as if he had fallen that way. That at least might stop anyone passing stealing the weapon before the police arrived. Raglan tucked his Glock into his waistband and jogged on to the two-way street. There was no sign of police or of Reyes. Three hundred yards away a woman stood leaning against a wall, an office worker enjoying a smoke break. Raglan interrupted her.

'Call the police. There's been a shooting back there. In the clearing.'

She looked dazed.

'Do it,' he said.

The woman stumbled her apologies to whoever was on the other end of her call. By the time Raglan was a hundred yards away, crossing M Street again, she had made the call. Less than ten minutes later he reached Reyes's house. There was no sign of the gardeners. He clambered over the gate and took the steps three at a time. The front door was open. Raglan held the Glock ready and edged inside. There was no sign of the house staff. He quickly checked the kitchen and the rooms off the hall.

He called out. 'Hello? Anyone here?'

Silence.

'Police!' he called again, hoping to draw out anyone fearful in hiding.

The house was empty – unless Reyes was upstairs in one of the twelve bedrooms. A door opened along the corridor. Raglan raised his gun. The gardener stepped out with hands raised. Raglan gestured him out. The second gardener followed, shepherding out the cook and the maid.

'Where is Reyes?'

The terrified women shook their heads and when Raglan lowered his gun and beckoned them to lower their arms, the four staff embraced each other. The old man who had spoken to Raglan before stepped forward. 'He is gone, sir. He was in distress. A car brought him. Señor Reyes, he ran inside. Men went with him. He came out wearing different clothes. The men put him in the car and they left. It was very quick. What has happened?'

'Your boss shot and killed a police officer and wounded two other people. The police will be here soon enough. Just tell them what happened, all right?'

The nervous staff nodded.

'You should all go in the kitchen and get some food and coffee. The police will ask a lot of questions.'

The old gardener muttered something in Spanish to the others and herded them away. He looked back. 'Sir, I hope they catch this man. He is a murderer. I cannot prove it but I believe he killed Raúl Mendoza. We are free of him now. Before we could not leave because we feared what he might do to us. I wish him dead.'

Raglan went through to the sitting room. The coffee table looked as untidy as when he last saw it. There were still two lines of coke in danger of mixing with cake crumbs. A second empty bottle of whiskey lay on its side. Reyes had clearly stopped his house staff from cleaning up his mess. He was like a pig in a trough. The four security screens remained on. He spun the hard drive back as he had done before and saw the same men pull up and a dishevelled Reyes run into the house with the men following him. Eleven minutes later they left. Raglan could not see the car's number plate. It seemed obvious that whoever these people were, they were protecting a valuable asset. No one rids themselves of a troublesome collaborator before time. Reyes would end up dead the moment they had everything they needed from him and when someone else was able to control his supply line. Raglan repeated the same operation as he had before and wiped the image of himself entering the house, then killed the feed.

As he turned back he saw the envelope stuffed with dollar bills was still shoved down the side of the couch. He tugged it free and checked the two bundles. It looked untouched. Reyes must have been so far out of it he had forgotten to put it in his safe, wherever that might be. He went into the kitchen where the gardeners and two women sat around the table with food on plates in front of them. They stood when he entered. He waved them back down. 'Where is his office?'

The old man turned to one of the women. 'Show him, Carla.'

The maid wiped her hands. Raglan followed her. She opened a door and stood back. There was an antique walnut desk and bookshelves and a glass-fronted cabinet. Every surface was bare.

'He never came in here, *señor*. He did his business on his phone. There is nothing here.'

'He must have a safe,' said Raglan.

'No, *señor*, he has not. He was always afraid of the authorities raiding the house. His phone, it was his office.'

'Is there a phone directory in the house?'

Her look said, 'Whoever uses a phone book?' but then after a moment's thought she nodded, went to one of the cabinets and pulled out a DC phone book. Raglan thanked her. Sirens drew closer. The gardener appeared. 'The police. There is another way out for you. Yes?'

'Yes,' said Raglan. 'Thank you.' He found the page he

wanted, tore it out and followed the gardener, who led him through the kitchen and into a small elevator that took them into the basement garage. A side entrance through a pedestrian gate ran off it. No one could gain access without a key. The kind of key the gardener had in his hand. As the gate closed behind Raglan he walked alongside the car-parking entrance obscured by walls and hedging. He heard car doors slamming and police shouting instructions to each other. He reached the street and checked himself, holding back until he had a clear exit. The cops were concentrating on setting up a roadblock and breaking down the entrance gate. It was enough of a distraction for Raglan to casually stroll out and join the gathering onlookers. Once he reached the opposite side of the street he took out the Glock, wiped it clean and edged towards a police patrol car. Its window was down; its driver was in the street on the other side of the car, stopping and directing traffic coming from the side street. Raglan dropped the weapon into the footwell. Better the gun was returned to its rightful owner in due course. There was nothing worse in the manual of uniformed life than to have your weapon stolen.

He mentally wished good luck to the wounded officer.

Raglan retrieved the Harley at the rear of the coffee shop as a news helicopter's blades beat the air with thudding monotony. One traffic lane was still closed by emergency services outside the deli. The scene of crime was taped off, the dead officer's body covered by a shroud. The coroner's van waited, rear doors open, ready to take him to the mortuary once the forensic investigators had finished.

Uniformed officers were taking statements. Raglan keyed in the number from the ripped directory page, and then, satisfied with his plan, turned the bike and followed the building to the rear loading bays and out on to an access road.

The traffic was as heavy as usual but the Harley made short work of the lumbering cars and within half an hour Raglan had driven into the Mendoza yard, checked the street was clear and knocked on the door. Mrs Mendoza peered out. Raglan checked his watch as a private ambulance squeezed down the narrow back lane. Raglan signalled it and pushed the mesh gate wider to allow the two paramedics with a stretcher to follow him inside. After taking all the necessary particulars of the ill man and Mrs Mendoza's details they carried her cousin into the ambulance. As it edged away Raglan went into the house and took the worried-looking woman by the arm and guided her to the corridor.

'The hospice will take care of him, Mrs Mendoza. I spoke to them and told them that you will go down and settle the payment. Can your mother stay alone for a while?'

'Yes. And after you phoned I arranged someone to come and watch the children.'

Raglan pulled the envelope from his jacket. 'Reyes is on the run; he won't cause you or your family any harm. This is Izan's money. It's for your family now. Break it up into small amounts. Hide it. Don't draw attention to it. I'm sure you know your cousin is seriously ill.'

She nodded, sadness etched on her face. 'I know he is dying. I understand that.'

Raglan lowered his voice respectfully. 'When he dies,

then you leave. Take your mother and children and go to another state. This money will give you a head start.'

She gripped the money and then kissed it. 'I will do as you say.' Tears welled in her eyes.

'Stay strong for your family. Tell Izan where you're going. He's a good man; he'll protect you when he comes out of jail. Until then, choose where you want to be and start a new life.'

'I do not know how to thank you,' she said.

Raglan looked past her to where her son stood watching. He smiled at Raglan.

'There's no need,' he said.

31

Jenna Voss eventually got the address of the Vietnam War veteran who had travelled from Orlando to Washington DC on the Greyhound bus. There had been a number of senior and retired military discounts processed that day and it had taken time for him to be identified. What held her attention on her computer monitor now was a crime report from the Metropolitan PD. She pulled on headphones and listened to the commentator spieling on about the incident in a Georgetown coffee shop while watching the aftermath of the shooting. It was shown from various angles taken by the news crews on the ground and in the air. As always, people nearby had taken photos with their phones, and these were interspersed between the news footage. One shot caught her attention. A man had helped a wounded police officer. He was pointing off camera. The commentator said the Good Samaritan had taken control of a chaotic situation and staunched the officer's wounds. Just as this photograph was taken he had ordered a member of the public to run across the traffic and halt a passing ambulance. The man's identity was unknown, but he had taken the officer's sidearm and given chase to the assailant, who was alleged to be the formerly prominent DC businessman Luis Reyes.

The scene cut to another camera shot, showing the figure of a second man lying sprawled in a cleared lot with the commentary that this murder had occurred a few minutes away from the original crime scene. Police and paramedics were in attendance. The camera crew were waved away from the scene by the police officers as the area was being taped off. The camera angle didn't allow a clear shot of the dead man's face: all Jenna could see was that it was bearded. The screen changed back to the still picture of the man who had helped the fallen officer. Unfortunately, this man's face was nothing more than a reflected beam of sunlight from the police car which had completely obscured his features in the camera lens. Voss zoomed in on the man's jacket; it looked similar to the one worn by the man on the Greyhound.

If this man was Raglan and he had helped save the officer's life and then gone in pursuit of the shooter with his weapon, it was a hell of a coincidence that another man lay dead a few hundred yards away. Raglan had travelled on the Greyhound to DC; he had helped an old guy with two thugs; now there was an image of a man wearing a short waxed jacket giving orders to a civilian while he assisted a wounded cop. Was this the same Good Samaritan as on the bus? And if it was, what was it that had spooked the spooks in the first place? Why had the CIA asked her Miami Field Office to tail him? And again, if this was the same man, what the hell was he doing in DC? The heart of government. CIA HQ at Langley was across the river, a – what? – ten-, fifteen-minute drive from the city?

She swung the screen round towards her fellow analyst. 'Ted, you see this?'

DAVID GILMAN

'I heard. Two cops down. They're looking for a guy named Reyes. Used to be a big shot in DC.'

She tapped the screen with her pen. 'This guy's face, do you think our tech guys could pull back that glare and give me a reveal?'

'You're interested in him?'

'Just a hunch about a couple of things.'

'If you're working a case while you're here then you'd need to get the OK from the boss.'

'I know that, Ted, but could they pull back the image, do you think?'

Ted studied the blurred sheen. 'It's in the lens. There is no image to pull back.'

'You know the tech guys. Could they at least try for me?'

'Jenna, you have something that needs their help, then file it with him,' he said, nodding to the glass-walled office of the supervising agent in charge. 'That way no one gets into trouble.'

She pushed back her chair and made her way to the supervising agent's office. This wouldn't be the first time she'd lied to follow a hunch. She would say all she needed was some downtime to get her things out of storage in DC from when she was at the capital's Field Office. That's what she'd tell him. Something simple and reasonable. Not that she had anything in storage. Then, with luck, she could get away in the early hours. That way the crime scene might still be intact and the police officers' reports still being typed up.

The senior special agent looked up from his desk as she knocked on his open door. To lie to a superior or not, that was the question. None of this is your business, Jenna, said the critical voice in her head. Too late now. If Raglan was involved in that shooting she was going to make it her business. First, she had to get time off and then drive the four hours from Clarksburg to DC. There was one man who might know more. Titus Jackson Jones.

32

Raglan rolled the heavy bike into TJ's garage as the older man pulled the doors closed behind him.

'Good timing. The beer's chilled and I-am-done-for-the-day,' he said, shrugging out of his overalls.' He glanced at Raglan who laid an appreciative hand on the Harley's metallic green tank. 'You look as though you've had a day and a half. Bike still good?'

'Better than,' said Raglan.

'Then I suggest we retire to the comfort of the executive lounge, kick off our boots and find a game to watch.'

He ushered Raglan out of the garage-cum-storeroom and down the side street to the apartment. 'There's something I need to check with you first,' said Raglan when TJ shut the door.

'Can it wait at least until I have a cold one in my hand?' Raglan nodded.

'Damned if my life doesn't feel a helluva lot more interesting since I met you on that bus,' said TJ. 'But there's a time when a man needs to draw breath and settle his bones into his favourite chair.' He handed Raglan a beer. 'All right, the game can wait. What is it?'

Raglan showed him the picture of the dead man's tattoo.

There was no doubt in Raglan's mind what military unit used the stylized shield quartered in green and blue with a lighting flash between the symbol of the sun and a star. TJ looked from the photograph to Raglan. And then glanced at his late son's picture on the sideboard.

'That's Army Rangers.' He eased back into his chair. 'And if you took that picture then I'm thinking the man who had the tattoo is dead,' he said cautiously. 'Those guys don't like anybody snooping with a lens.'

Raglan nodded. The Rangers were the army's large-scale special-operations force. 'There was a shooting in the city. He was killed.'

The bottle of beer hovered next to TJ's lips. 'I don't think I'll ask too many questions. Dead people appear on a regular basis when you're around.' The cold liquid slid down his throat. He saw Raglan's thoughts were elsewhere. 'Am I going to see this on the news?'

'Some of it,' said Raglan.

'Does this have something to do with those three dead drug dealers?'

'I'm not sure.'

TJ had finished the bottle of beer before he had realized it. He looked ruefully at the empty bottle. 'You know, I might treat that as a starter.' He got to his feet and went to the refrigerator. 'You?'

'I'm OK.'

He helped himself to another bottle. 'They're based at Fort Benning, down in Georgia. I did my time there; my son as well. Airborne Rangers are hard nuts to crack but I'm guessing the man who owned that tattoo wasn't a serving soldier. Men like that, they get sucked into corporate work.

They're an asset. In fact, I'm damned sure we have more of these private mercenaries – let's call them what they are – than most countries have in their own army. Contracting out war is something our government does a lot of. Saves money and saves face when it goes down the pan.' He sipped. Raglan had still not taken a drink from his bottle. 'You going down there? To Georgia?'

'No need. He's not important enough but I'll find out what I can about him.'

'Son, there's nobody in this man's army is going to talk to a civilian about one of their own.'

'I know someone who might.'

Raglan finished his beer and then showered. He needed a fresh T-shirt but his latest purchase had been put to better use. Once they had eaten TJ found a game to watch while Raglan went into his room to make the call that might help to put another piece in the jigsaw. He phoned the Airborne and Ranger base. His delay in calling was deliberate. It was now after office hours so any administrative office would be closed and the person he wanted to speak to would be in his private quarters and able to speak more freely. A male voice answered from the base's switchboard. Raglan spoke in French. His request was a simple one but he hoped, if he spoke quickly, the soldier on switchboard duty would not understand.

'Bonjour, je voudrais parler à l'agent de liaison. C'est important. Le colonel, est-il dans son bureau?'

The rapidity of his speech caused an immediate faltering from the operator who stumbled in his response. 'Sir, I'm sorry, I don't speak French. Can you please repeat that in English?'

Raglan slowed his request enough for the man's ear to pick up the word colonel. '*Si je savais parler anglais, je le ferais, mais ce n'est pas nécessaire. Le colonel, s'il vous plaît. Puis-je parler au colonel?*'

'Er, OK, sir. You want to speak to the colonel, yes? Is that the French colonel? Our liaison officer?'

'*Oui, le colonel de liaison.*'

He heard the relief in the man's voice, pleased that he had figured out that the one senior officer on the base who spoke French was the liaison officer. Raglan waited as a couple of clicks came down the line and then a ringtone. The one certainty was that a Foreign Legion colonel was always on rotation from the 2e Régiment étranger de parachutistes, Raglan's first unit when he joined the Legion. The airborne and specialist units at Fort Benning had always had close links with the Legion, just as American officers would spend time at the paratroopers' base in Corsica. He heard an accented voice answer.

'Colonel Paviot.'

'Colonel, sir, this is the switchboard. I have a French-speaking gentleman on the line and as far as I can make out he wants to speak to you. Can I put him through?'

'All right.'

'Hello, caller, I'm connecting you now.'

Raglan waited until he heard the switchboard disconnect. He quickly introduced himself in French, giving details of his time in the Legion, his rank, naming senior officers he had served with, and asked that Colonel Paviot make the necessary phone calls to his contacts to verify Raglan's identity. Then, if he was satisfied with the information, to return his call on the number he gave him. He ended the call with a terse comment: 'Colonel, one of ours is missing and I am here to find him. I need your help.'

Colonel Paviot was no stranger to making snap judgements. He had served as a field officer in some of the worst trouble spots in the world, when success or failure hinged on such decision making and the lives of his men were at stake. He hung up without another word. Raglan knew he would be checked. There were people in the intelligence community who would vouch for him but Paviot's calls would be to the officers Raglan had named. The Legion was like any other private club. People knew whom to trust and of whom to ask the awkward questions. An hour later the phone rang.

'Raglan?' said Colonel Paviot.

'Yes.'

The conversation switched immediately to French. 'I had to get people out of bed and they did the same to others. How can I help?'

'We're secure?'

'We are. This is my personal phone.'

'A former legionnaire was killed in Marseilles and because of him I came here to find another who's gone missing. The DIA is in the background. I've already had a meeting with them. I was involved in a shooting today and the man I killed had a Ranger's tattoo. I want to try and identify him, and hoped to see if Fort Benning's records have anything that could help me. I thought you might be able access his file.'

Paviot did not hesitate. 'Is what you are involved in likely to cause any diplomatic tension between France and the United States?'

'None, colonel. I'm hunting those who have seized an American intelligence officer who once served in my old unit. I believe he's uncovered some kind of conspiracy within the intelligence community here. I want to send you the dead man's picture and that of a tattoo he had on his arm in the hope you can identify him and what his records might indicate.' He paused. 'Unofficially.'

The line went quiet for a few seconds. He was putting the colonel in a difficult situation. If he had to make a clandestine search of personal data then he was putting himself at risk. 'I can find a way,' said Paviot. 'Send me the picture. I will call you tomorrow.'

The line went dead.

The Legion was family.

33

At 3.47 a.m. Raglan felt rather than heard the vibration of his muted phone. He was instantly awake. He picked up.

'Raglan?'

It was Paviot.

'Yes.'

'I got into the archives. The army here is no different than our own. They have paper records. Your man's name is Josh Hamner. Thirty-eight years old. Stationed here at Benning. Served with distinction for twelve years. The tattoo was a help. Personnel haven't been allowed to have them for several years so I knew he was a regular of long standing. He did three tours of Afghanistan. He left the army four years ago. He was helped by the army's Transition Assistance Program who put together a workplace résumé for him. He applied to three different management companies as an interpreter and analyst for Middle East risk assessment. The army recommended him to two major banks as such. But it looks as though a desk job didn't suit him. He was signed by Executive Decision Management.'

It was a connection Raglan half expected. That was the same management company that Jack Swain had mentioned in Casey Zeller's investigation. A company that employed ex-special forces and highly qualified former army personnel such as Hamner and that had been formed and was run by a former Central Intelligence Agency section chief.

Paviot continued. 'There is nothing more in his file other than his qualifications, which as you can imagine are comprehensive. He was a skilled and intelligent man, Raglan. A pity you killed him; perhaps he could have given you the information you need.'

'There was no time for a conversation, colonel. My thanks.'

'I understand. The mission is sacred. I wish you good luck.'

The call ended as abruptly as it had started. It now seemed more definite that the drug dealer Luis Reyes was working with Executive Decision Management, who were bidding for military hardware contracts from the Pentagon. Raglan's thoughts ran to the man he had killed. Josh Hamner had intimate knowledge of the Middle East, so why was he playing watchdog to a drug dealer whose supply line was from Central America? If he was more than a hired gun his expertise was needed elsewhere. Raglan's instincts told him he would have been invaluable as a training asset for any of the factions in Iraq or Afghanistan. Central American drug-running did not fit the man or why he was employed by EDM. Raglan pressed a speed dial. The insistent ringtone was finally answered.

'Swain,' said a groggy voice.

'It's Raglan.'

'It's four in the morning.' Jack Swain sounded flustered.

'I sent you the photo of the man shot dead. Have you ID'd him?' Raglan had to know whether the Defense Clandestine Service Deputy Director had run the dead man's face through their database.

'You phone me for that?'

'It's important.'

'No, no, we haven't got anything back yet.'

'No name? No reference? Nothing?'

'Nothing. Jesus, Raglan, I'll check when I'm at my desk.'

'But you've run it?'

'Yes! If I get something I'll tell you.' Swain's exasperation simmered down. 'Raglan, OK, what's this really about?'

Raglan saw Swain in his mind's eye. He'd be propped on one elbow looking at the glow of his bedside clock, now fully awake and realizing that there had to be some urgency behind the call. Raglan needed to know that if a colonel at Fort Benning, Georgia, could access Hamner's file so quickly, why hadn't the Pentagon's DIA system flagged him within minutes? Or sooner. The subterranean rooms at the Pentagon were packed with enough sophisticated technology to find a black cat hiding down a storm drain on a rain-soaked night. Very little escaped those prying eyes. If they were looking. Was that the problem? Had Casey Zeller unearthed something so important that it had scared his masters and made them turn their faces to the wall? Was Jack Swain genuinely trying to unearth the truth? If not, then why bring Raglan into play? Raglan's thoughts doubled back on themselves. If Swain's search had not yet turned up anything then it was doubtful it had anything to do with the Pentagon; it would be because there was nothing to find. Josh Hamner had been wiped from every computer in the Defense establishment. Somewhere, someone had the means to digitally wipe away a man's life. What they had not done was go into a filing cabinet on an army base and yank a brown government issue folder with the dead man's military history neatly typed in single-spaced 10-point standard-issue font.

'His name is Josh Hamner,' said Raglan. 'He worked for EDM.'

'How the hell did you find that out?'

'Keep digging, will you? Ignore the obvious. He's not going to be on a database and if that's where you've looked then someone's blocked you. And he's only a small player in this. Whoever has the means to blank him out will have more than a firewall in front of the big players.'

'All right. I'll do that myself. Where are you?'

'In the city.'

'Stay close. I might have something for you soon on that senator I mentioned.'

Raglan killed the call.

He lay back, trying to find anything he might have missed that could lead to the whereabouts of Casey Zeller. If he was being held captive he'd be tough enough to hang on for a few days if whoever had him wasn't hurting him too severely. If he had been killed that first night he'd gone missing then his body most likely wouldn't be found. Raglan felt the irritating rise of frustration. Time and again he had gone over every event since being summoned to the backstreets of Marseilles. The fragments did not fit. He must have missed something at Zeller's house. He checked his watch. It was after five. Too early to call Zeller's wife. He pulled on a pair of running shorts out of his day sack and tugged on his T-shirt. He'd run in his boots.

Slipping out of the apartment, he headed towards the river and Theodore Roosevelt Island park. The light rain came and went, swirling on the breeze, fogging the street lamps in the ghostly city. He ran hard over the bridge, then once across the river curved right towards the island. The tracks and boarded walkways were popular with those runners who lived and worked in the city. It was barely light but a handful of diehards and city professionals were already out. Some had dogs on leads. The handful of joggers were easily absorbed in the tree-rich parkland. The river's reflection heralded the arrival of dawn. By the time Raglan had pounded out several miles the city was already being awoken by invading traffic. He took stock of the view. It had been only a few days since leaving his family in Vero Beach. Days that felt like weeks.

A woman in her forties jogged past with her teenage son. She berated him for being too slow. The tiger mom was behaving like a drill sergeant. It was too early in the day to be scolded. The boy glanced at Raglan as he staggered past and grinned. He was being deliberately slow just to wind up his over-achieving mother. The youngster reminded Raglan of Steve and the thought was like being prodded by a sharp stick. He dialled Amanda's number. After a while her sleepy voice answered.

'Thought you might have been out with the boys for a run,' said Raglan.

She sighed. The hint of irritation impossible to conceal. 'You think this is a good time for a social call?'

'Sorry. It's been full on my end. Just wanted to check you and the kids were OK.'

He heard her settle down on to a chair, or bed; either way she took comfort from it. Her voice settled. 'We're fine. I never thought a holiday could be so exhausting.'

'No problems?' he asked, wary that he had absconded with the help of her friend.

'Problems? With you in our life? Jesus, Dan, of course there are problems. We had the FBI knocking on our door the day after you jumped ship.'

Raglan knew there was no firm reason why they should go to the house. He knew he had been followed. 'What did they say?'

'Nothing. They just wanted to know if you were around. I told them you have a lot of friends in the States and that you had gone off to see them. They didn't get pushy. In truth it felt as though they weren't that interested. I say "they"; it was one agent. A man on his own. I thought it might have had something to do with the murder but he didn't mention it.'

'Who was killed?' said Raglan.

'Steve said you'd taken him to some plane museum after the space centre.'

Raglan already knew what she was going to say next and felt that twist in the gut you always get when bad news arrives unexpectedly. 'What happened?'

'Oh, some intruder killed a mechanic. Local news said nothing was stolen. Might have been someone out of their head on drugs and he challenged them. Who knows? Anyway, the poor man's dead. The museum's been closed since.' She yawned. 'So, are we going to see you?'

'A few more days. At least,' he added, knowing she'd understand.

'That's what I thought.' Then she hesitated, fearful of asking the question that would bring more grief into her life after the torture and death of her husband. 'Are you safe? Not hurt?'

'No, no, I'm absolutely OK. Having a bit of a vacation myself. Staying with a guy I met. Good man. We get on.'

'Who says miracles don't happen.'

'OK, look, I'm out on a run and... well, like I said, it's been a fairly busy time. I'd better get back. Is Steve all right?'

'Having fun. Wish we'd done this sooner. It was a good idea.'

'Say hi for me.'

'I will.'

Raglan ended the call and tried to get online to see what the Miami papers or news channels might have archived about Bob de Vere's murder. The connection had been good enough for a call but he couldn't reach the heavy content on the paper's website. Even though it would be close to midnight there, he keyed in a number in Castelnaudary in the south of France, the home of the Legion's induction and training camp. Like many ex-service personnel in many armies around the world, those who have retired from the Legion often choose to live in close proximity to the place they consider in their heart-of-hearts to be home. Serge Sokol was Raglan's friend and the man who had served the longest during Raglan's time in the Legion. The hawk-nosed Russian was the only contact for anyone who needed to get in touch with him. Sokol lived above a *tabac* down a narrow, cobbled street in the old town. Raglan pictured the man's tall, lean frame and close-cropped hair and his raptor's glare that put a chill in many an enemy's gut. If anyone could find out who the men were that Raglan had culled from Luis Reyes's security cameras, it would be Sokol. He attached the photos and added a brief note about the dead mechanic in Florida, using his nom de guerre. *Rudi Charron killed.* Once the images had gone through he turned back for the apartment.

He hit a fast stride. By the time he had covered the two and a half miles back he was convinced there was a kill team in play. France, Florida and Zeller's house in Stafford. Men had come to kill. Was he the target or were they shadowing him until he led them to Casey Zeller? He couldn't see how anyone could have followed him to DC or discovered where he was, but there was one way to find out. Offer himself up as bait.

34

Raglan showered and dressed as TJ tugged on his jacket and reached for his veteran's cap on the hall stand.

'Good run?'

'Yes. I'm going to be away for today. Might even stay the night. Out at Stafford. Mind if I use the Harley?'

'Course not. I'm pleased it's getting some road time. Listen, I have my weekly breakfast with Beth Ann. Remember I told you? We sort out this and that. Diner's a couple of blocks away. Good ham and eggs. Why don't you join us?'

'I need to get somewhere that has a computer. Is there a library or an internet cafe nearby?'

'I've no idea about internet cafes. The library's a short way east on K Street, but it won't open until after nine.' TJ saw his friend was in a hurry. 'By the time you get out to Stafford theirs will be open for sure.'

'Thanks. I'll make a call then get on my way.'

TJ pulled on his hat. 'You change your mind about breakfast, me and Beth Ann are a block north and then hang a right. You'll smell the ham and eggs. It's called the Corner Booth Diner, given as it's on the street corner and they have booths. It's a real friendly place.'

When TJ left Raglan poured the brewed coffee and

phoned the pre-paid number Anne Zeller had bought at his insistence.

She answered quickly. 'Raglan? Have you heard something?'

'Anne, I'm sorry. I am still trying to track down Casey's contacts. The man he visited in prison gave me some information but it hasn't yet given me any idea where Casey is. And I had a meeting with Jack Swain. Casey was into something important.'

He heard the edge in her voice. 'Dangerous?'

'He was looking into government contracts. There's no way we can know the full extent of what he found.'

'He's dead, isn't he?' She said the words matter-of-factly.

'Anne, don't give up. If Casey is in trouble, he of all people will know how to get through it.'

'Then why hasn't he got in touch?' Her tone was tipping into anguish now. She was a tough woman, but this kind of not-knowing would burn through steel.

'My guess is he can't or he's protecting you. Trust me, the moment I have any idea at all of where he is, I'll call you.'

There was a pause. She drew in breath and more courage. 'I know. Thank you.'

'Are you OK with your friend?'

'Yes. There's no problem here.'

'Good. I want to go back to your house, maybe spend a day, maybe stay overnight. Can I do that?'

'In case you missed something?'

'Yes.'

'There's a spare key hidden near the back door. I made a small rockery in the yard; it's in a conch shell Casey and

I brought back from Hawaii one year. The guest room is where you saw it. Back of the house is alarmed: 09-07-03 is the code. It's random, no significance. Casey changed it every month.'

'I don't need a bed. Is there any camera surveillance in the house?'

'No. Just the alarm.'

'What about the neighbours?'

'Bob and Claire Campbell hightail it to Florida this time of year. Until they finish building the houses around us there's no one else. I've phoned a few people who might have come to visit and told them I was taking a vacation, and before you ask, no, I didn't say where.'

'Then I'll see if I missed anything.' He wanted to give her more than he had. Hope was what flickered in the darkness. It was the sticking plaster over the gaping abyss. 'Anne, Casey is a tough, resourceful man. Survival is in his DNA. I will find him. No matter what. I promise.'

Raglan pulled into the Stafford library. It was too early for the lonely ones who came to sit in front of a computer terminal for the day, just to be where other people were. He keyed in the *Miami Herald* for the day after he'd left on the Greyhound. There was no mention of Bob de Vere's death. Being two hours from Miami pushed Vero Beach into outlander territory. Orlando was closer by an hour and its *Sentinel* carried a photograph of de Vere on page four with a brief description of his murder, saying the mechanic had died of stab wounds. The local Vero Beach paper had the killing as its banner headline. It made half a page that included a brief résumé of de Vere's life, his love of aircraft and glowing sentiments from the staff at the Warbird Museum. They were fluff pieces with no hard evidence: if the journalists hadn't been given anything of real interest by their insider informants in the police department then they had nothing more to pass on to their readers.

Raglan shut down the screen. Bob de Vere had been killed for a reason and that reason was to do with Casey Zeller. De Vere's death brought the tally of deaths associated with Zeller to five since Raglan had first stopped at the small backstreet bakery in France. Add the collateral damage of Raúl Mendoza because he blew the whistle on Luis Reyes. Six. The body count was rising. There would be more.

He checked for any mention of the invasion of the Zellers' house. There had been no coverage of the killing at the house in any news bulletins or even local news media. If it had gone undiscovered then the pungent stench from the corpse would cling to the house. Nothing could mask it. The rank odour of death clawed at the back of the throat.

He cruised around the Stafford housing estate. Construction workers busied themselves at the southern side of the building project. The fact that street lights had not yet been installed would be a bonus if he stayed the night. The forecast was for intermittent rain and the clouds were already darkening. He looked at the threatening sky and knew there would soon be a cold front and snow. He could smell it on the wind.

Raglan drove the Harley on to the hardstanding outside the garage and then eased it down the side passage out of sight. The house key was exactly where Anne Zeller said it would be. He went through the back door and cleared the beeping alarm box.

The air was a little musty, but nothing unusual for a closed-up house.

Raglan checked the stairs down into the basement den. There was no body. If there had been blood splatters he had missed then they too had been removed. A clean-up crew had bypassed the alarm and removed the body. Electronic jamming devices were easy enough to get hold of to gain entry without setting off the alarm, but it would take a parked van and a crew to make things right. Professionals. Spooks or someone just as organized. It would have been done at night. And if they knew the house was empty then they had eyes on it. Or in it. He opened the electric garage doors and put the Harley next to the Honda SUV. He grabbed a toolbox off the bench and, once the door closed again, went into the house as he had first done with Anne Zeller.

Most people leave their Wi-Fi router on 24/7. If any surveillance devices had been hidden in the house, odds were it was run through remote Wi-Fi. There were enough apps on a mobile phone to track hidden cameras and listening devices but nothing was perfect. Raglan wanted to do it the old, slow, sure way. He switched the router off. If anyone was watching they were now blind.

He stripped off his jacket and began a fingertip search, starting in the basement den where he had pushed the dead man down the stairs. He dismantled the light fittings but found nothing. He put everything back in place as he went along. Anne Zeller would see little change to her house when she returned.

He unscrewed every electrical wall plate but found no extra wiring. He moved upstairs. Raglan dropped the blinds and pulled the curtains. took a flashlight out of the toolbox and began a slow, careful sweep of the walls and fittings. Only a pinprick hole was needed for a surveillance camera but if the house was bugged then any device was likely to be in some attachment like a smoke detector or light fitting, quick and easy to conceal, no structural damage. An experienced crew could be in and out of the house in minutes.

Raglan went into every room and painstakingly repeated the operation, painting the beam across each wall. Left to right, right to left just in case they had managed to use pinhole cameras. No reflection from any hidden lens. He progressed through the ground-floor living rooms and found the first devices in the passageway. The torch beam glinted against the first and last of the four LED downlighters. He popped them out: each had the same minute lens in it, the size of a small fingernail. The lenses' field of view covered the kitchen, the utility door into the garage and the sitting room. He replaced them intact. There was one more in the smoke detector, another in the CO_2 alarm. He had covered every room except Casey Zeller's study.

It was as he remembered. The computer had been removed, the bookshelves emptied and books put back untidily. The desk drawers were unlocked. He checked the pendant light, the desk lamp and the infrared eye on the television set on the wall opposite the desk. No sign of cameras. Raglan wondered if whoever had planted those he had found was only interested in knowing who was home and when. But it didn't make sense to cover the main living rooms and not the study. He stood and looked from wall to wall, staring long and hard at the objects remaining in the room. Desk, chair, desk lamp, bookcase.

He sat in Zeller's chair, to see the room from his point of view. Everything was as it should be, except for the large framed painting on the wall depicting a log cabin in the woods nestled by the side of a lake. The ornate carved frame had a smudge on the bottom left corner almost concealed in the curlicued folds. Raglan stepped up to the frame and peered closely. Someone had dabbed wood filler on it, in a close match to the frame's colour. With his fingernail he scraped the filler off the small drilled hole. The tiny pinprick of light was the lens he was searching for. Had Casey Zeller realized he was under surveillance and thought he had obscured the lens, or had those who had planted it not been as neat and tidy as they ought in their drilling through an old wooden frame?

Raglan tipped the desk over and checked underneath in case there was anything taped below. Nothing. Same with the desk drawers. He pulled each one out, checked underneath and then in the cavity itself. Zeller would have known that these were the obvious places to be searched if anything happened to him.

No one had tried to lever the built-in bookcases away from the wall, obviously thinking a book search was enough. Raglan pulled the books off the shelves and then one by one took the shelves off their supports. He settled the light again. He was down to waist height on the third fixed bookshelf when he saw what he was searching for. A small brass screw had been drilled into the bookshelf's backing and hidden behind the thickness of the shelf. He checked the other side. Another screw. The bottom shelf revealed the same thing. Zeller's battery drill was flat so Raglan used a star-headed screwdriver and undid all four screws. The wooden panel back plate came away. There was a cavity in the dry walling. Lined and damp proof.

Raglan played the light on a pile of brown government folders. He lifted the top one and opened it. A photograph of a man stared back at him. It looked as though the picture had been taken from a distance with a telephoto lens. A sheet of paper was attached showing the man's biography. Raglan lifted the files out of their hiding place, put them on Zeller's desk and opened each one. Every file had a photograph and an individual biography. Most of the men, for they were all men, predominately white except for two African Americans and a Hispanic, were serving or retired officers of various intelligence agencies, including the DIA. Jack Swain had every reason not to trust anyone at his shoulder. Whatever Casey Zeller had uncovered, the conspiracy was widespread.

The final folder had no photograph, just a list of names. More than thirty perhaps: most were unknown to Raglan. A couple of them were senators. Twelve of the names had a handwritten notation and a question mark next to them. Executive Decision Management? The Council?

Who would Zeller have trusted with this information? Impossible to guess. High-ranking officials, both current and retired, were the underlying power in Zeller's world. Jack Swain had told Raglan that a group referred to as the Council was involved. Might that Council be the retired CIA chiefs in this group of men in the folders?

Raglan started reading closely, memorizing the names and areas of expertise that Zeller had queried in his notations.

Most were Middle East or Central and South American experts. Every one of them had a circle of influence and contacts invaluable for carrying out or supporting illegal activities. Zeller must have spent months, probably longer pulling this information together from his resources. How much had he told Swain? Enough for the clandestine chief to feel the cold chill of betrayal around him. What he had not told his boss was how widespread his suspicions were and where he had hidden the additional information on those he suspected. And Swain knew nothing about Izan Esposito or his information about Luis Reyes. Zeller had kept that to himself. Why? Raglan put the files back into the wall cavity and felt around inside. His fingers touched plastic. He tugged free a zip bag with a flash drive inside. Raglan screwed the back plate in place and re-assembled the shelving and books, keeping the zip bag at his side.

Raglan gave Casey Zeller full marks for his diligence; he also sensed the man's uncertainty. And fear. Who was there to trust? Not even, it would seem, his boss.

35

Fifteen minutes later Raglan gazed at the same documents on a computer screen in the Stafford library. Casey Zeller had done everything he could to secure his evidence. Raglan slipped the flash drive back into its protective bag. There was one place he knew it would be safe other than the wall cavity in Zeller's study. For now he zipped the bag into his inside pocket.

There was a diner next to the pancake house where he had met Anne Zeller. It was homely, creased vinyl seating in the booths attesting to its popularity, and staffed by waitresses with worry lines and tired bodies from hard lives and low incomes, but whose eyes still sparked with good humour and generosity.

'Hon, you sit wherever you like. We're not exactly burstin' at the seams like me in this damned uniform, now are we?' said the waitress. Her smile and the coffee pot she carried would have lifted the weariest of traveller's spirits.

'Can I still get breakfast?' asked Raglan, taking note of her name tag.

'All day and most of the night,' she said, turning over his chunky white mug and pouring the steaming coffee. 'The special's good.'

'I'll have that, thanks, Roz.'

'An easy man to please. You're God's gift, sweetheart.'

She turned and called out Raglan's order to the cook.

Raglan's seat gave him a clear view of the passing traffic on the main road and the turning that brought patrons into the diner. The handful of older people reading a paper, sipping coffee or eating were likely to be regulars and locals. The cars in the parking lot were mostly ten years old or more. The younger crowd, those who lived in the neighbourhood, would be in the city or the Pentagon, at their place of work, or shopping in the Pentagon's nearby mall

In contrast to those in the diner were two younger men who had just pulled up in a pickup truck two hundred yards away. They were dressed casually, jeans and padded plaid shirts over white T-shirts. Their boots had the tan scuffed look of construction workers. They wouldn't normally merit a second glance. Raglan gave them one. They leant against their truck, lifted a cold can from an ice chest in the back and casually drank. Two men with no particular place to go. So why stop in a tree-lined side street? Why park a couple of hundred yards away? Why not pull in nearer where the parking bays were clearly marked? They were heavyset. Raglan noted they wore no belts, while construction workers tended to wear their toolbelts as a badge of honour, like modern-day gunslingers.

The waitress put the plate of food down. 'There you go, hon. Enjoy.'

Raglan thanked her.

'You're welcome.' She turned as one of the regulars raised an arm. More coffee on its way.

Raglan worked through the food. There was plenty of it.

He wiped the plate with the last piece of bread and drained his coffee to the bottom of the mug. The men's pickup had gone. The waitress had already seen Raglan's empty plate.

'That was good, thank you.'

She poured again. 'It's real hot. Be careful.'

'I like it hot,' he said.

'I bet you do. You're English.'

He nodded.

'I thought so. I have a soft spot for Brits.'

'That's good to know.'

'My husband was a Brit.' She loitered at the table. 'You know something? He was illegal. Outstayed his visa. This was years ago. Way way back. Worked here and there. Cashed his cheques where he could. Worked mostly for cash. Know what he did?' She didn't wait for an answer. 'He joined the LAPD. Yeah, I was surprised when he told me as well. That's when I met him – when he was a patrolman. He was a good man. Made me laugh. All the time. No matter what.' She rested one hand on the booth back and tipped more coffee into Raglan's mug. 'I miss that. Know what happened?'

'I don't.'

'He got shot. Shot and killed by a kid out of his head on who-knows-what. Thought the kid needed help. Bang. A sucker punch. Or shot. Whatever.' She shrugged. Cast a glance towards the cook. Nodded. A plate was ready. 'LAPD called him a hero. Everyone is a damned hero these days. You put on a uniform, you're a hero. He went to save a kid from a gang. Fought them off, the department said. Fought half a dozen punks and the one he went to help killed him. So he qualified.'

Raglan thought she looked as if she could have happily slipped into the booth and taken the load off her feet. How many jobs did people like her have to make ends meet? Or at least get close?

'Know what they did?' she said. 'The Police Department? They took his pension away. Said they found out that eighteen years earlier he was illegal. He was a decorated cop. How's that for saving money?' She shrugged. 'I came back here from LA. No kids, thank God. A mother. She's gone now. And a job. That's what I got left from loving a Brit. A guy who could talk his way into the LAPD and my heart.'

'I'm sorry.'

'Don't be. I'm not.'

She leant across him to wipe the table. So close he could smell the harsh peroxide in her hair. 'Two guys just come in. They're watching you. Be careful.' She stood upright. 'I like Englishmen.'

Raglan waited until the waitress was a few feet away and then called to her so that the two men who had entered the diner would hear him.

'Excuse me, where are the toilets?'

She pointed through the door at the end of the diner. 'The restrooms are outside, around the corner.'

Raglan slid out of the booth and made his way towards the door. Its glass panel reflected one of the men getting out of his seat and following him. Raglan pushed through the door and turned the corner, following the signs for the restrooms. One door showed the symbol for the male toilet and the second female. Raglan stepped into the women's toilet and waited. Twenty seconds later he heard the man open the men's room door. He had one arm raised, pushing it open, while his right hand nestled under his shirt at the back of his waistband. That's when Raglan punched the back of his neck. The man sprawled. He was big enough to smother the confined space on the floor. He had slammed into the tiles face down but was tough enough to try and get up again. Raglan pressed his foot into the man's back, jamming him between the toilet bowl and wall. The big man was helpless. He spat blood as he tried to breathe.

Raglan threw the man's weapon into the toilet pan. 'Who are you?'

Choking, the man raised his hands in surrender. 'Swain sent us. To cover your back,' he gasped. 'ID back pocket.'

Raglan eased the pressure, tugged the man's wallet out. He flipped it open and saw the government identity card. DIA. Pentagon. The man twisted, but stayed down, wiping his arm across his bloodied mouth. Raglan tossed his ID back at him.

'Swain sent you? To cover my back? Are you kidding me? How did you know where to find me?'

The beaten man spat phlegm and blood. He made no move to get his feet. He had the good sense to know that if he did Raglan would see it as an aggressive move. 'I didn't know where you were. I figured sooner or later you'd show up at Zeller's house. I got lucky. That's all.'

'Lucky is right. I could have killed you.'

Raglan glanced outside the door to see if the man's companion had followed him. 'Tell Jack Swain I don't need his kind of help. Count to sixty slowly. Can you do that? Can you count past fifty?'

'Screw you, Raglan. You've got no chance out here on your own.'

'Better than even odds without your help. Now count to sixty slowly and then rejoin your friend.' Raglan waited. Humiliation hurt the man more than the beating.

'One, two, three, four...' he snarled. 'You're in over your head, you dumb bastard.'

'Five comes next,' said Raglan.

Raglan pushed through the door and re-entered the diner. Jack Swain's other man had stayed in his seat, watching the Harley in case Raglan made a run for it out the back. Raglan held his startled gaze as he dropped money on the table for his meal along with a healthy tip.

'Your friend had trouble with his zip. I think he pissed himself.'

As Raglan reached the door, the DIA agent hurried towards the far end of the diner. Raglan cut through one of their tyre valves with the knife he had taken from the table. He tossed it in a refuse bin and fired up the Harley. As he opened the throttle and headed back to the city, two questions nagged at him. Why had Jack Swain put two of his heavies on his back? And why hadn't Swain told him?

36

TJ Jones stood at his sink, hands plunged into the hot soapy water. Washing dishes was as much a ritual as getting dressed and polishing shoes. Two plates, a pan and coffee cup, if left lying in the sink, denoted a slovenly mind to his way of thinking. It was the same when he made his bed every morning. How in God's name anyone could leave an unmade bed all day and then simply climb back in at night confounded him. The one thing the military taught was self-respect. When the bed is made that's the first accomplishment of the day. Rituals were important. More so the older a man got.

He rinsed and stacked the clean dishes in the wire rack and then turned to lift the drying cloth from its hook. A shadow flitted across his kitchen window. He paused. No one in the building ever walked past his apartment: they would take the corridor on the other side of the small garden. Raglan wasn't due back. Not yet. He listened. There was no obvious threat, but old skills were deeply embedded, instincts honed. As a tunnel rat he had squirmed underground in complete darkness, only his hearing and senses to tell him when an enemy was near. Close enough even to touch.

TJ wiped his hands dry and stepped further into the room. Another brief flicker of light. Someone had moved towards the front door and the movement from the far window had been caught in the darkened television screen. He closed his eyes, letting his concentration search out anything untoward. Petty thieves had tried to burgle him once or twice but they were usually kids, too clumsy not to be caught. This was something else.

The faintest of creaks alerted him. Someone had put pressure on the front door. Testing. The door handle had not moved and the chain and lock would hold unless a determined hit was made. Something like a police door ram being smashed against the lock. Was it the cops? Raglan was shy of the law.

He edged to a window and without showing himself angled his head so he could look along the passageway. It was quiet. No residents coming or going. A grey, barely distinguishable shadow was being cast from around the corner near his front door. Someone was there. Standing silently. He stepped quietly to where his work jacket hung and eased out a switchblade. A knife kept handy for undoing shrink-wrapped products delivered for his caretaker duties. He did not press the release button so that the blade snapped open – that would have alerted an enemy. Enemy? He checked himself. It could be someone lost out there. Someone wanting to know if there were any vacancies. But if so, why hadn't they rung the bell?

He pressed the catch and eased the blade open with the palm of his hand. Then, curling his fist, he turned the knife so that it was out of sight. He stepped to the door and put his eye to the peephole. As he did the young woman who stood outside knocked on the door. A quick urgent rap. He whipped his head back in surprise.

'Hello?' the young woman called out. 'Sorry, I tried your bell but I don't think it's working.'

A wave of uncertainty. He had not expected a woman. Still, he was cautious. There was no trouble with the bell as far as he knew.

'How can I help you, miss?'

'Raglan told me to meet him here. I'm sorry if this is the wrong address. Do you know him?'

TJ stood motionless. The young woman knew Raglan was here. How could she if the Englishman had not told her himself? He had gone to Stafford to see a woman. Was this her?

'Could you tell me what this is about?' he said, face close to the door.

'I'm sorry, sir, Raglan told me not to talk to anyone. He's here to help me. I think he asked me to come here because…' Her voice faltered. '… because it was safe.'

It seemed convincing, but still he hesitated. A woman in trouble, in need of help, but he was damned if he could ignore the gnawing in his gut. 'Describe him to me, so that I'm sure we're talking about the same man?' She might know his name but that didn't amount to a hill of beans if she wasn't who she said she was.

The woman described Raglan. Right down to the kind of jacket he wore. 'All I know about him really is that he was a special-forces commando in the Foreign Legion's parachute regiment. That's where my husband served with him. That's why he came here. To help me find him.'

TJ sighed. She knew. It fit. He closed the blade and

dropped the knife into his pocket. 'Just a minute, lady,' he said as he eased the chain and turned the security bolt. He opened the door. The young woman was more attractive than the distorted peephole lens had showed him. She wore tight black pants and top with a loose jacket and a shoulder bag. Beneath the peaked cap her blonde hair was tied in a ponytail. She stood respectfully back from the flyscreen door.

'You'd better come in, miss.'

She looked left and right, as if checking whether anyone had seen her.

'It's all right,' he assured her. 'There's no one around. You'll be OK in here. Raglan will be back in a couple of hours or so, I guess.'

She stepped past him. TJ glanced outside just in case. There was always a 'just in case'. That's what kept you alive. He closed the door and turned to face her. She stood looking nervous and uncertain, a guest in a stranger's house.

'Now you take a seat through there and I'll rustle up some coffee. How's that?'

'That's very kind of you, Mr Jones, thank you.'

So she knew his name. Another piece of her story that made sense. But then his initials and surname were listed in the apartment's entrance hall. She sat down on the chair, eased her bag down but kept her peaked cap on.

It was customary in TJ Jones's canon of good behaviour to remove your hat in someone's house, but he decided that, being young, certain basic principles of good behaviour were missing from her upbringing, like many others of her generation. Let it be, he told himself. Stop being such a goddamned grouch. He turned to fill the kettle, placed it on the stove and reached for the coffee jar.

'It'll have to be instant,' he said without turning as he lifted down two mugs.

'That's fine, thank you.'

'Did Raglan say how we met?'

'No. He just said for me to meet him here. Said that Tommy Jones would understand.'

He froze. She had taken a chance with his first name. Applied a better than even chance that the T stood for Thomas. It was a careless slip. Why? She didn't have to take the chance. So it was deliberate. Shock tactics, to catch him off guard. The thoughts flashed fast and hard.

He spun around but she was already only two strides away. Eyes intent. Hand gripping a knife. She had been damned near silent. Age slowed him but his reflexes were sharp enough to fling the mug in his hand into her face. She blocked it, already pivoting to strike. Rather than retreat he barged into her, attempting to smother the knife thrust. It ripped across his side but missed anything vital. The stinging cut pumped even more adrenaline and he swung a punch. She dipped her head; the blow caught her shoulder. He saw it hurt her but she ignored the pain. He was overextended and she rammed the blade up and behind his shoulder. Where once there had been packed muscle was now flabby and he felt its vicious bite. He cried out, stumbling away. He reached into his pocket and the knife clicked free its wicked blade. She was lithe. Cat-like. Eyes never leaving his as she dipped and feinted. But TJ stood his ground. All he needed was one well-aimed thrust and he would finish the bitch. She had come to kill Raglan and, whoever she was, she was a pro.

Knife fighters know one bare truth. If it comes to it: stop

an attack by taking the blade through your hand and then kill with the other. TJ half stepped forward, threw out his free hand despite the agony from his shoulder wound. She slashed upwards as he readied himself to let it pierce his palm. His own knife was low at his hip: he could jab or slash into her belly and then drive it up below her chest. Strange disconnected thoughts intruded. Her hands were covered in tight-fitting black gloves. Why had he not noticed her hands before now? The upward slash did not connect with his flattened palm. She knew what he had tried to do. Her wrist twisted and the blade cut into his. Its sting made him wince. He was wrong-footed. She had expected his upward thrust and blocked his strike. He was off balance and almost fell into her. No sooner had she attacked than she stepped back. Barely a second after he felt pain in his groin and flooding wetness down his leg. For a confused second, he thought he had pissed himself. Strength seeped from the leg. His muscles failed and he pressed back against the wall. He realized what she had done. She had cut his femoral artery. A killing wound. He had done it himself to others. Once severed, the artery snaps back into the pelvic wall. It needs fast, skilled medical help to get a pair of forceps in and clamp it off. TJ knew there were barely minutes left before he bled out. Adrenaline wasn't enough now. The violence that shadowed men like TJ came when beckoned. The kill instinct once again second nature.

She thought him finished. He charged like a bull, enveloped her with his increasingly useless arm, ready to use the last of his failing strength to reach behind her to snatch the ponytail, yank back her head and stick the knife into her neck. He knew she would ram her blade into him repeatedly but it made no difference. She had to go down with him.

He damned near pulled it off, but he slipped in his own blood and his leg gave way. Then searing pain beyond anything he had ever experienced surged from his chest to his brain. His heart was torn apart. He went down on his knees, one arm wrapped around her waist. At that final moment, he smelt her fragrance. She pulled free the knife from his chest. He did not feel the impact as the back of his head hit the floor.

The Airborne veteran had fought to the end.

37

Raglan locked the storeroom after giving the Harley a wipe-down. The rain had started again and he didn't want TJ to be concerned about mottled spots left behind when the rain splatters dried. By the time he hung out the microfibre cloths to dry it was near enough a half-hour later. He walked through the light rain, collar up, unconcerned about the rivulets running down his face and neck. A hot brew and a shower would be welcome.

His key turned in the lock, and the moment he opened the door he knew the worst had happened. The old man was on his back, a dark pool of blood around him. Raglan cursed involuntarily, but at the same moment instinctively crouched, looking and listening for an intruder. He moved quickly, stepping around TJ and his congealing blood, checked the two bedrooms and bathroom. The apartment was clear. He looked outside the windows and closed the blinds.

He felt TJ's neck pulse, a reflex almost, a gesture. He knew TJ was dead. The heating was on in the room and the body showed little sign of rigor mortis. It was the small muscle groups in the hands and face that stiffened first. Three to four hours was the usual length of time for a body to become rigid. Raglan realized his friend must have been murdered while he was on the road back from Stafford. He cursed himself, silently this time, but no less vehemently. Had he not stopped to eat and then deal with Jack Swain's goons he might have been here to stop the killing. Regrets were useless but the drive to avenge the good man lying butchered on the floor of his home was not.

His presence had caused this brave and dignified man's death. He laid his hand over TJ's. There was a soft, barely discernible stroke across his palm, like the brush of an eyelash. Whatever it was, it lay curled in TJ's fist.

Raglan raised his friend's clasped fingers and looked closely. He had snatched blonde hairs from his assailant. From a man or a woman? If the police did their job right then they would see the few strands and bag them for DNA. Those who understood the killing business knew that more than half known assassins were women. Raglan looked carefully around the room. There was no other clue as to who might have been there.

He stood over the dead man. Saw how he must have tried to defend himself. The open blade at his side and the skid marks in the blood told their own story. The old warrior had taken the fight to his enemy. Raglan went into his room, dropped his toothbrush and razor, the extra pair of socks and underwear into his day sack and then wiped over most of the surfaces; he took the beer bottles out of the garbage pail and wiped them clean too. Impossible to erase his presence completely though: the cops would gather enough evidence that he had been staying there. It would soon be dark and it was unlikely that any of the elderly residents would be out and about to notice that TJ's lights had not been switched on. Discovery would come in the morning when he did not follow his usual routine. Disciplined habits died hard. As did the man.

Rain splattered against the windowpanes. Raglan lifted a waxed cotton cap from TJ's coat rack, less to shelter him from the rain than to disguise his features. With a final glance at the dead veteran, Raglan closed the door. Life was as simple or as complicated as you made it. Kill or be killed was the very basis of existence in a violent world. And it made no difference whether the person who killed TJ was male or female. If Raglan found them he would kill them.

The rain fell as light drizzle now, but it was getting colder and the forecast had warned of a drop in the temperature and the possibility of snow. By the time he turned the Harley through the commuter traffic towards Zeller's house, he was soaked.

He checked the house front and back. There was no sign of anyone in the area who shouldn't be there and as the wind whipped the rain he saw that there were fewer construction men working. The house was cold. He flicked on the heating, closed the curtains and blinds, switched on side lamps and threw some bedding from the guest room on to the couch. He would stay the night. Jack Swain's men had staked out the house long enough to see him return once before; it was doubtful they would do so again now that he had blown their cover. And he had not phoned Swain to rub salt in his wounds. The man would know exactly what Raglan thought of his attempt to shadow him. Raglan's silence would enforce his discomfort because it signalled contempt.

He spent an hour cleaning and polishing TJ's pride and joy, the distraction letting him try and figure out who had sent the killers stalking him and why. He was a legitimate target for whoever he posed a threat to, but why kill Bob de Vere and now TJ, a complete stranger, someone with no connection to why Raglan was in America? Were the killers catching up with where he had been? Did they hope those they threatened and then killed would give them information about him? What might TJ have said before he died? Nothing, Raglan suspected. But there were no answers. Not yet.

The Harley was now in the same condition as when he had first seen it and would stay locked away in Zeller's garage. Raglan didn't need it any more, especially with the weather closing in, and if anyone noticed the bike was missing from TJ's garage then cops would soon be looking for it. He found the keys to Casey Zeller's Honda tucked behind the visor, turned the engine on and saw it had a full tank. He felt the need to move on, but experience taught him to be patient. How many hours had he spent lying camouflaged out of sight watching an enemy's movement? Days of isolation, barely moving, until the time came to strike. The house would serve him well for a few more hours. Anne Zeller was far enough away and the house next door was empty.

He stripped and showered in the Zeller's spare room and then clicked through local television channels until he found one of the stations covering Washington. There was no mention of TJ's death. He kept the TV on in the sitting room and the kitchen as he raided Anne Zeller's cupboards. There were enough tins, frozen items and just-past-sell-by-date fresh food to rustle up a good meal. He kept it simple: chickpeas and vegetables in the pan over rice. One pot cooking. Field rations.

While the food simmered, he reopened Casey Zeller's hidey-hole and pulled out the files again, then sat at the kitchen island sipping a bottle of his absent host's beer as he studied the documents. The more he read the more convinced he was that Zeller was in over his head. These were powerful men of influence he had investigated. He glanced up. The news was ending. Still nothing about his friend TJ's death.

An hour later, Raglan ladled the slow-simmering stew into a deep spaghetti dish. Home comforts, for a while. After he'd eaten, he studied the folders again, searching for anything he might have missed before. Zeller had been concise. And Raglan had missed nothing.

He kept half an eye on the news and then, using the couch for a bed, slept lightly, on and off through the night, half aware of the sounds made by the house. Shifting wind and rain rocking him to sleep, as if in a creaking boat.

Raglan stood at the window watching the construction workers arrive, seeing them stamping against the cold and showing no sign of interest in who might be living in the Zeller house. The cold had started to bite and if snow fell or the light rain froze they would abandon their work platforms due to health-and-safety regulations and then the area would be quiet.

Raglan went to check the Honda's satnav. There were no routes shown going into the city. Zeller would have known those. One southerly route went to an auto-repair shop specializing in Hondas; two more routes were logged showing restaurants, again out of town. It struck him that someone of Zeller's capabilities didn't need directions to travel within a couple of miles from home. Yet there were a dozen journeys logged. And one keyed in by zip code that had a no-name destination north of the city on the Virginia side of the Potomac.

He heard the news channel in the kitchen mention TJ's death. He went through and saw shaky footage from a hand-held camera fed into the news bulletin of the cops arriving and putting up their cordon. The story of what was so far known unfolded. An elderly veteran stabbed to death during a home invasion. A man believed to have been taken in by the Airborne veteran was the main suspect. The police issued an inconclusive description of Raglan; it could have fitted most white men of his age. They were more precise about the missing Harley.

Raglan picked up his day sack. It would be good to get into the crowd at the murder scene and see if he recognized any of those he had seen in the security footage at Luis Reyes's house. He had killed one of them, but what if the others had somehow tracked him down and come looking for him? He tugged TJ's peaked cap down low and drove the SUV out of Stafford, heading back into the city.

38

Jenna Voss pulled over her old dark red Acura outside the address she had gleaned from the Greyhound passenger list. She was obliged to park a hundred yards down the street because police cars blocked the apartment's access. Blue-uniformed cops were keeping a crowd back and moving people along. Commuters shuffled from one side of the road to the next; cars trying to get through were turned back. There were already three or four freelancers filming either with their phones or small high-definition cameras. Back in the day, when newsmen wore a trilby with a press card tucked into the hat band and lugged a Graflex Speed Graphic camera, they were called news hounds. Light bulbs sizzled and popped and then the news hounds would run for the nearest payphone to log their story. Now it was every creep with any lens trying to make a buck with the rolling news channels. She doubted any of those gathered here even read a newspaper. Not in this day and age.

'Hey,' she said to the duty cop who saw her pull aside her coat and reveal the badge on her belt. 'What's going on?'

He didn't ask questions. She was trouble for the suits inside. 'Ground-floor apartment. Super's place. He got stiffed.'

*

Raglan had scanned the crowd when he arrived and saw no sign of any of Reyes's men. He moved left and right, staying back three-deep in the gaggle of rubberneckers so he could see those who were watching. And then he saw Voss arrive. What was Miami FBI doing in Washington if it was not connected to him? He pinpointed where she had walked from and shouldered his way through the crowd to the Honda. If she was tracking him, then he needed to learn more about her.

Jenna Voss ducked under the tape, went past another cop at the entrance, was waved through and walked down the passage between the gardens and the building. A cluster of cops were taking statements from what were obviously residents. She eased past them into TJ's apartment. A young female patrol officer handed out a pair of shoe covers. Voss slipped them on. Two detectives, a black man and a Latina woman, were checking the apartment as forensics examined and photographed the body. One of them used tweezers to pull something from between the man's fingers and then placed his find in an evidence bag. The detectives turned as she stood in the doorway.

'Can I help you?' said the woman. Voss glanced from one to the other. Was she the lead on the case or was it her partner, the tall black man? She ignored the attractive Latina who looked as though she could take apart a drug den single-handedly. She was tough, no doubt about it. Aggressive too. She wanted answers even before questions had been asked. Voss ignored her and looked directly at the tall man. She showed her badge.

'Special Agent Voss,' she said.

'You have business here, Agent Voss?' said the male detective.

He was definitely the senior. 'No.'

'Then unless a federal crime has been committed I suggest you leave my crime scene.'

'I'm not here to interfere, Detective...?' She let the question hang.

He answered politely. 'Delaney. And this is Detective Medina.'

Detective Medina had an expression that Voss had seen a thousand times when federal agents got involved in a police investigation. Like when you walked barefoot on the beach and trod in dogshit.

'Can you tell me if this man's name is Jones? Titus Jackson Jones?'

That made an impression. They looked more alert and less aggressive.

'So you do have an interest in him?'

'No, not really, I'm following another lead but his name cropped up during my search.'

The two detectives were cagey. If the Feds had any part of this, even peripherally, then they both knew they could be sidelined. Voss second-guessed them. 'I'm not here to get involved. I came looking for another man. If you can help with that then I'm on my way and out of your hair.'

The two cops looked at each other.

'What kind of man?' said Medina.

'White, late thirties.'

They glanced at each other. So her surmise might be right, from the look that passed between them.

'What do you know about this man?' said Delaney.

'Nothing really. I might be on a wild goose chase,' she said, playing down her desire to hope against hope that it was definitely Raglan. If it was, this was the second death she knew of that was linked to the Englishman.

Detective Delaney was more forthcoming. 'One of the neighbours saw a tall, rough-looking man in the lobby the other day. Said he had a strange accent. Mr Jones' – he gave a nod to the dead man – 'told her he had a friend staying with him. Now, it wouldn't be the first time that a Good Samaritan had taken in a panhandler out of the goodness of their heart and had violence inflicted on them.'

'You think this man is responsible?'

'There's a Harley Davidson motorcycle gone missing that belonged to Mr Jones's deceased son,' said Medina. 'Worth a few thousand dollars. Open-and-shut case. Murder and robbery.'

'You have any better description?'

'Well, an old lady with failing eyesight isn't much help.' They looked intently at Voss. 'Do you know who this man is or what he looks like?'

She shook her head. 'No. OK, thanks for sharing.'

Delaney stepped forward, extending his card. He had the look of a cop who knew when he was being brushed off. 'You think of anything that might help us, you be sure to get in touch.'

'I will. Thank you.'

Voss turned and made for the door. She felt the daggers

pierce her back. And the surge of adrenaline that told her she was just one step behind the mysterious Englishman.

Voss drove due south a few blocks, unaware of the black Honda tailing her four cars back. She turned on to the one-way H Street NW. Washington's FBI Field Office was a fifteen-minute drive away on F Street. It was a part of the world that had been her second home until she had transferred to Miami. It was always hell trying to find parking near the National Museum and it took another ten minutes to find a space two blocks away. Raglan faced the same problem and wished he was still on the Harley. He had no choice but to drive slowly, following her as she walked. It was another fifty yards until a parking angel raised her arm as a large Suburban SUV hauled itself clear of the kerb. Raglan eased his smaller vehicle in, gave the woman a generous ten dollars and followed Voss.

She pressed a speed-dial number on her phone.

'Jenna?' a voice answered after only three rings. Voss smiled: her old friend and former colleague was as prompt as ever. The special agent in charge of counter-intelligence at the DC Field Office was soon to be made Deputy Assistant Director of the Intelligence Operations Branch at the FBI's Directorate of Intelligence, whose headquarters were within walking distance of her office. It was a big promotion and if anyone could get information denied Voss then it would be Kim Burton. She was older and more senior by ten years and had proved her worth to the Bureau when she was liaison agent at the CIA.

'Kim, good to know you still have me on your phone.'

'Well, this is a surprise. It's been a while. How are you?'

'I'm good. I'm in town.'

'Here?'

'Yes. I need to talk.'

'You want to come to the office?'

'No.'

Kim Burton hesitated just long enough to compute that either Voss did not wish to visit the DC Field Office so as not to see her former colleagues, or there was something that could not be discussed in her office. Something personal.

'Where?'

'The museum?'

'Give me ten minutes to finish up. I'll meet you at the fountain.'

Voss was already halfway there. She hunched and shivered against the biting cold; the north wind was showing its teeth. But it was more than that. She felt a sense of trepidation at meeting Burton. Everyone at the Field Office and the FBI HQ a few blocks away knew of the disastrous HRT raid in Miami and the death of two agents, and for Voss to even show her face in town was a step too far in the eyes of many.

Once inside the red-brick museum Voss waited by one of the towering Corinthian marble pillars that bracketed the fountain in the Great Hall. A few minutes later she watched as Burton strode into the building. Even her walk proclaimed her sense of purpose. She was as tall as a model, and the fitted grey business suit beneath her wool coat was a statement that the elegant African-American woman was a power player. Voss cringed inwardly at her own downbeat clothing. She felt more comfortable in combat boots and fatigues with a Kevlar vest and assault rifle in her hands.

Kim Burton's five-inch heels and grey-streaked hair, flared cheek bones and sheer elegance made for a Washington-PR-dream poster. Voss saw her stop, look around, check her watch, and wait. Voss skirted the fountain and positioned herself in a side cloister so that she was directly in Burton's line of sight. Burton saw her. Voss turned and walked along the cloister, found a bench and waited, standing, ready to embrace her old mentor and friend. Kim Burton extended her manicured hand. Formal, all of a sudden. Cool, even.

'So, how's CJIS? I bet the blossoms will be popping in another month. Virginia always kick-starts spring before us. How long have you been there now?'

Kim must know it had only been a matter of days, Voss thought, feeling an awkward flush rise, hoping it didn't show. 'Not long. It's fine. It's a beautiful place. Lots of birdsong and the countryside, well... it's... stunning. No other word for it,' she lied. She had a lot of other words for it, none of which she would say out loud now.

They sat on one of the benches. Kim Burton smiled. It seemed genuine enough, but Voss sensed a touch of unease there too. 'I'm pleased for you. It will be a good place to let the dust settle.'

'Kim, let's be clear. The operation I led was given the green light all the way up to the top at the Miami office. What happened was a trap. A well-planned and elaborate trap, carefully set up. They knew we were closing in on a major drug-money-laundering operation. If it had come off, if the source hadn't been a plant, then we would have shut down a major supply route both in and out of the country.' She winced. Her sudden volley sounded exactly what it was: self-justification.

Burton looked down at her hands, twirled her wedding ring and then looked back at Voss. 'I know, Jenna. I read your reports and the disciplinary adjudication. You know how it is. Two men died; others wounded. It takes a while for the stain to wash out.' It was said with empathy.

Voss shook her head. 'I'm sorry. It's something that will stay with me forever. I didn't mean to…' She faltered.

Kim Burton reached and covered Voss's hand with her own. 'I know,' she interrupted. 'So, here you are. It's a long drive from Clarksburg. What brings you to DC?'

'Oh, I've got things to sort out. I still have bits and pieces in storage from before I went to Miami.' She was lying again, now not quite sure why. Her sixth sense had kicked in. Kim Burton was on the way up and any association with Voss, the team leader who blew an operation, was not a recommendation. A bad judgement call on Kim's part. Voss pressed on, still uneasy. 'Before I came up to CJIS we had a request from the Agency's Miami office to set up surveillance on an Englishman who arrived with his family at Orlando. My partner and I tailed him for a couple of days. It looked all OK. He seemed nothing more than a tourist. We called it off and then I left for Clarksburg. Then he went missing, and the same night a mechanic at one of the tourist sites he had visited was murdered. My partner followed up just in case we…' She hesitated, knowing what she was about to say resonated with previous failure. 'Just in case we screwed up. The Englishman's family said he'd gone off to visit friends but they didn't know where. I tracked him down and found he had travelled on a Greyhound from Orlando to here. There was a fight on the bus; our man helped another fight off a couple of lowlifes. Then he went off radar again. I traced the older man he helped on the bus to an address in town. He worked as a janitor in an apartment block and when I got there this morning the Metro police were in attendance. The old man had been murdered.'

Kim Burton showed no emotion as Voss spilt out her story. 'And why are you telling me this?'

'Kim, if this Englishman is associated with the CIA and we already have two murders—'

Burton interrupted. 'You think he's responsible?'

'Not sure about the first killing, but I think he might have been staying with the old man who was murdered. The cops think it's an open-and-shut case.'

'If that's what they think and the evidence points to that, then it's a police matter.'

'It just doesn't gel with me. My instinct tells me there's more to it.'

'And again, why are you telling me?'

'Because you have contacts at the Agency. Can you find out anything? His name is Raglan.'

Burton frowned. 'Have you discussed this with anyone else?'

'No.'

'So you haven't spoken to anyone in the Bureau?'

'Uh-uh.'

'Then why are you pursuing this?'

'Because I have a strong feeling about it.'

'Feeling? No evidence? *A feeling*?' Within seconds Kim Burton had gone from empathetic friend to ice maiden. 'You come here to ask me to use my hard-won and respected contacts at the Agency, people who trust me – and God knows it has taken a long time to forge any kind of credibility between them and the Bureau after 9/11 – but it's taken personal sacrifices and commitment at every level and I'm not about to jeopardize all of that now. Certainly not for anyone's unfounded hunch.' She stood up, even straighter than before. 'Jenna, go back to Clarksburg and let go of this nonsense. You've been given a second chance. That's the best advice any friend could give you. Look what your instinct did for you down in Miami.'

She stepped away from her old friend, but then turned and glanced back at Voss who stood there dumbstruck at the sudden switch. 'You've spent too long in Florida, Jenna. The weather's cold up here. Get yourself a better coat.'

39

Raglan moved quietly around the museum's fountain, photographing the two women from a discreet distance. When the older one walked away he watched the other stay unmoving for a couple of minutes. She looked as though she had received bad news. She slumped forwards, elbows on knees. Raglan remained where he was and sent the photograph of the more senior woman to Maguire in London with a brief request: *Who is she?* Then he followed Voss as she made for the exit. Once on the busy street he altered his position every fifty yards. The woman ahead had no reason to suspect she was being followed. The fact she was using her own car and not one from the FBI pool suggested she was on her own time. Raglan tugged down the peaked cap, hailed a cab and told the driver to follow the Acura. The driver glanced at the rear-view. He was going to ask why but what he could see of the man's unsmiling glare told him to concentrate on his driving. They drove north-west for twenty minutes until the Acura pulled into a small motel. It looked a budget motel by DC's standard. Modest but clean. No litter. No street-corner activity. A basic tourist motel ideal for those visiting the city and wanting to be within a couple of miles of the sights. Raglan paid the driver and told him he would want to be taken back to the city. There was no reason why the cab driver wouldn't wait. A double fare back to town was easy money and the meter was running.

Raglan skirted the motel's small gardens, staying out of sight as Voss checked in with a small backpack, took a key, was given directions by the woman at reception and walked along a companionway to a room on the ground floor. Raglan followed and checked the room number. He walked to the reception area and on the outside wall saw the fire-evacuation plan for residents. The L-shaped building had room numbers 1 to 10 on the one side, then the reception office in the middle of the dogleg, and beyond that the numbers continued 11 to 20. The upper floor mirrored the lower. Numbers 21 to 30 and then 31 to 40. Voss was on the far side, middle lower floor, room 14. Raglan went into the office. A bright-eyed woman, mid-fifties he guessed, pink cardigan over a paler pink shirt, smiled and put aside the magazine she was reading. Raglan saw the key hooks on the wall behind her. The empty key hooks told him most of the occupancy was on the upper floor. Rooms 5, 6 and 7, among others, were unoccupied.

'Hi,' said Raglan. 'I'd like a room. I was here last year and I liked room five. It let me see the parking lot across the garden. I'm driving my brother's car so thought I'd better keep an eye on it.'

'Oh, sure, we haven't kicked off the season yet. Sorry I didn't recognize you, Mr...'

'Harrison. No problem. I don't remember seeing you back then.'

She fussed at the keyboard on the computer, her

attention focused on booking him in. She had barely made eye contact. He was just another tourist, another interstate driver passing through, another job hunter looking for a place to stay. 'Must have been on my vacation. It was probably Steve covering for me. Tall guy with a ponytail.'

'I didn't know his name. I might need to stay longer than a night because the car's giving trouble. I'll pay for two nights.'

She smiled again. Business was slow and she was grateful to have the place a third full. And even though there were enough parking spaces available she charged the usual for reserving a bay. She swivelled her chair to retrieve the booking printout from the printer on the sideboard behind her. Raglan reached across to the lower counter and took two large thick-wired paper clips from the middle of a pile of invoices. She turned back; he paid in cash and took the key. An old-fashioned small wooden slab with the room number embossed above the motel's telephone number and address with the invitation to return the key if found. Room 5 gave him a perfect view across the dogleg to Voss's room. The bed was firm. The room clean. It smelled fresh. There was soap and a bottle of cheap body wash in the shower with one large and one small set of towels. For eighty-five dollars a night it was a decent deal. He closed the door and returned to the taxi.

'Stop off at an ATM before we get back to town,' he told the driver.

Five minutes later the cabbie pulled into the kerbside next to a bank. Raglan used an untraceable credit card in a different name to his own and replenished his dwindling dollars. By the time the driver dropped his fare at the

Honda, Raglan had made one more stop and bought a takeaway meal and bottled water. He gave the driver a modest tip. He didn't want to be remembered as a big spender.

Raglan parked the Honda at the furthest point away from Voss's Acura. Several vehicles were parked in-between. It was more important that he could see her car easily than his own. Raglan rummaged in Casey Zeller's toolbox in the back of the Honda and found what he was looking for. Back in his room he sat in a chair at the window behind the slatted blinds and watched and waited. It wasn't yet dark but the street lights flickered on. The sky was leaden and snow threatened. He unfolded one paper clip and bent the one curved end, making a finger-thumb grip; then he clipped a third off its length using a pair of pliers. He made the same grip on the second but kept its length, bending the end into a small swan neck. The thin wire needed to be strengthened. Laying the bent end on the cheap carpet bonded to the concrete floor, he hammered it flat.

Voss came out of her room dressed for a run with her phone strapped to her arm over a sweat top, ear buds in place, peaked black cap holding back her blonde hair, the ponytail pulled through the cap's size band at the back. She checked her watch, pressed a button and ran into the city streets. Raglan gave her ten minutes. Leaving his room in darkness he slipped out on to the dull walkway whose lights gave a soft glow along the building. There were no security cameras beyond the office. He checked around him. No car headlights could reach him outside Voss's room, and if a door opened anywhere he would have time to carry on walking. It was quiet except for a television in a room a few doors further on. Light from a side lamp seeped through the slatted blinds.

Raglan eased the first paper clip into the lock, tensioned it inside the mechanism and then fitted the flattened swan neck into the tumblers. It took twenty-three seconds to open. He closed the door and relocked it and immediately smelled her fragrance. She was untidy. The contents of her valise had been spilt out on her bed, as though she had reached in and tossed her clothes there haphazardly. The formal suit and shirt were on a hanger. The rest were casual. Her weapon would be in the safe but her wallet and badge were on the dresser. He opened it. Saw her name, checked her driver's license, which still had her Miami address. There were four credit cards. Plus or minus fifty dollars of mixed denominations. He pulled free a calling card, the kind handed out to witnesses. It bore her name and phone number. There was another from a DC detective named Delaney. He tucked Voss's card into his pocket. The bathroom yielded nothing of interest. A bottle of vitamin pills stood on the shelf next to her toothpaste. He used the freebie motel pen to poke around her washbag. There was a prescription bottle of tablets in a brown-tinted plastic tube. He checked the label. A. J. Myers MD had prescribed Duloxetine antidepressants several months ago. The tamper-proof cap was intact; the bottle had never been opened. An expensive natural bristle hairbrush held a web of blonde hair. He ran his hand across the nest and remembered TJ's valiant effort to leave a clue about his killer. Was it Voss? She had come a long way since he first spotted her in Vero Beach where Bob de Vere had been murdered, and then she had showed up at TJ's apartment. If she was the killer she had planned it carefully. If there were DNA traces or fingerprints inside the apartment she had compromised the crime scene by her presence. Raglan turned for the door. There was nothing more to be gleaned here.

Gentle shadows backlit by street lights fluttered across the window.

It was snowing.

40

He waited until she returned an hour later. A layer of snowflakes smothered her back. She showed no suspicion that the door had been tampered with as she went inside. Raglan finished his takeaway. There was still time for him to drive out and see who lived on the banks of the Potomac at the location registered on Casey Zeller's satnav.

His phone rang. He recognized the number. 'We secure?' he asked.

'No, I thought I'd use the phone in my mother's care home.'

'You don't have a mother, Maguire, you were abandoned at birth. What do you have for me?'

'The older woman in the photograph is Kim Burton,' said Maguire. 'We ran her through our system. She's being promoted. She was counter-intelligence at the FBI's DC Field Office but not for much longer. She's going across town to the Directorate of Intelligence at FBI Headquarters.'

'As what?' said Raglan, already suspecting the link between Voss and the woman she met and the CIA.

'Deputy Assistant Director of the Intelligence Operations Branch.'

'Then she has a strong relationship with Langley,' said Raglan.

'She mended bridges all right. The other woman in the frame is Special Agent Jenna Voss,' said Maguire, confirming what Raglan had already discovered. 'She was HRT in Miami until a few months back. A raid went wrong. Two of her people killed.'

That explained the antidepressants, Raglan realized, but not why she was on his tail. 'There's been another killing. I don't know if she is involved. But this Kim Burton has a line to Langley. If the CIA is running a covert operation then they might be using the FBI as their smokescreen. Letting them do the legwork. I'm getting closer. I found a dozen files on various people: senators, government officials. I haven't made a connection yet between them and the half-dozen retired CIA officials who set up shell companies.'

'Anything else I can do?'

'Those photos I took of the men from a security camera at Luis Reyes's house. Anything?'

'Sorry it's taken so long but they are not in our system. Watch your back.'

Raglan ended the call. A part of him wanted to confront Voss, but that would have to wait. He pulled on TJ's cap and shrugged into his jacket, turned up his collar and stepped into the white.

DC at night with snow falling after the commuter rush hour was eerily quiet. The snowflakes came thick and fast as the

Honda's wipers sluiced them from the windscreen. The suburbs fell away as Raglan followed the satnav north-west. Dark areas of forest buffeted the river indicating another wealthy and exclusive area of individual properties whose acreage flanked the Potomac. It took forty-five minutes, given the slow driving conditions, until he turned off the highway down towards the water, following a narrow road. A few inches of snow had settled by now and Raglan eased the Honda without haste as the road twisted and turned for half a mile. There appeared to be at least one house further down the road although there was no way of telling how close or far it was. Given the exclusivity of the area he supposed it would be a mile or so further on. The panhandle approach road bellied out into a turning circle. The woman's enticing voice from the console told him he had arrived at his destination.

Raglan turned off the car's lights. Ahead of him a stone-built wall curved each side of pillars supporting two wrought-iron gates. On each pillar a lit coach lamp cast its soft glow across the threshold. Beyond the gates a driveway led to a double-storey house, fronted by ornate gardens and flanked by tall trees. There were lights on in the house. Large glass windows on the front façade were covered with opaque window coverings. A silhouette moved across one of the rooms. And then the electric gates opened. Someone in the house had let him in. There were no tracks from other vehicles so whoever was inside had been home before the storm broke. As he approached the house, he studied its design: a habit of target appreciation when leading an assault against an enemy stronghold.

There would be views of the Potomac River during

daylight hours from one of the terraces and more windows than Raglan could count at a glance. A five-car garage and expansive deck was visible on the furthest part of the building, with what must have been a fifty-foot swimming pool. The main house had extensions going off at angles. Raglan felt like a pauper visiting the king's palace. He pulled up alongside a dozen broad steps that led to the front door. There were no footprints. The door opened. A man in his late sixties stood waiting, his grey hair brushed neatly back; he wore slacks, shirt and a thick knitted cardigan. Raglan looked around. There was no sign of anyone else but the shadow that had passed the window was taller than the man in the door. There was at least one younger man inside, more upright, shoulders less stooped from age. He opened the car door and crunched through the snow.

'Come in,' said the man, stepping aside, allowing Raglan to wipe his feet and remove his cap, shaking the snow on to the broad door mat. 'Please,' said the man, extending his arm, guiding Raglan into an oversized open-plan room with a soaring stone fireplace. This king had a fireplace that many a peasant would envy. The gas flames burning through the fake logs belted out the heat. Artwork graced the gallery-sized spaces. A grand piano stood in a corner of the room, its gloss patina covered with family photographs. Beyond the open-plan room an orangery furnished in colonial style had large windows on three sides that, come daylight, would give a view across the expanse of lawns to the trees; but now, the sheen of bare glass was a black mirror reflecting his image. A door off the room led through to a kitchen most top-of-the-line restaurants would envy.

'Are you armed?' said the genial host, pouring a whiskey from a cut-glass decanter.

'No,' Raglan answered, accepting the drink. The man seemed unconcerned about his safety with a stranger walking through his front door so that meant Raglan was being watched by others and they would be armed. The heat from the fire forced him to take a step back.

His host noticed, lifted a remote and took the gas flames down a few notches. 'The house is too big for me these days but I like to be warm.' He raised his glass. 'Cheers.'

They drank.

'Now, I ask myself why would a man driving Casey Zeller's vehicle come to my door? On a night like this. You'll appreciate I have a sense of foreboding.'

'I'm trying to find Zeller.'

'I see. And how did you find me?'

'His satnav had this place logged in.'

'Do you know who I am?'

'No. Do you know who I am?'

The older man smiled. 'Touché. I am Senator Mike Thomas. And you are?'

'Raglan.'

'Brief and to the point. You do not invite familiarity. An Englishman. Very well, now, you might not be aware of the fact, Mr Raglan, that senators do not have personal protection, unless of course they are running for president, which I am not, so personal safety and security is self-dependent, which is why...' He looked past Raglan to where a dark-suited man stepped into view. He wore a radio earpiece like any other bodyguard. He stood without threat, confident, hands clasped in front of him with a

9-mm semi-automatic clutched in his right hand. '... I have Wallace here for personal protection and...' He raised a finger to one side where a second man stepped into the room, similarly dressed, as big and efficient-looking. '... Roberts to work at his side. Would you mind?' he said.

Raglan knew the drill. He put down the glass and stood, hands clasped behind his neck. Roberts covered him with his Glock from the front as Williams did a professional pat-down. Wallace nodded that Raglan was clean and both men stepped back to their positions.

'Now that that unpleasant but necessary ritual has been attended to, I think you owe me an explanation. Uninvited guests might have friends lurking nearby, friends who are not as amenable as the one who has gained entry.' He gestured to one of the fireside chairs. 'Please, sit.'

'I'm alone, senator, and I came to the States to try and find Casey Zeller.'

'Then you have a connection.'

'We served together in the French Foreign Legion.'

'What unit?'

These were not idle questions. It was a test. He must have known Casey Zeller had served and in what unit. And if he did know then an imposter was unlikely to give the name of the regiment in French. 'Casey and I served in the Deuxième Régiment étranger de parachutistes and I went on to the regiment's commando unit – the Groupement des commandos parachutistes.'

'I've heard of those units,' the senator said. He sipped his drink, eyes on Raglan. 'Casey told me,' he added for emphasis, confirming Raglan's suspicions.

'Do you know where he is?' said Raglan.

'No.'

Raglan glanced at the armed heavies, who were hovering. 'Are you involved in his disappearance?'

'Quite the contrary, Mr Raglan.'

'This is a lot of house even for a senator,' said Raglan. 'The kind of house drug money buys.'

'With a modicum more taste, I hope,' the senator said with a smile. 'I spent the first twenty years after leaving Harvard setting up my law firm and then I went into politics. Yes, it's a big house for me to ramble around in on my own but my late wife loved it; we built it together, and when my four children and nine grandchildren arrive for Thanksgiving and Christmas it shrinks in size, I assure you. Casey Zeller brought me information, and I began my own investigation. I have served on the Senate Armed Services Committee and the Senate Select Committee on Intelligence. Do you know what Casey was investigating?'

'Yes. How much do you know?'

'Not enough.'

Raglan handed the senator Voss's calling card. 'Do you know this FBI agent? Have you had any contact with her?'

Mike Thomas shook his head. 'I have never heard of her.' He put the card on the side table. 'I'll look into her.'

'She has connections with the CIA. I'm not sure yet how big a connection that is. She's been following me since Florida, and I don't yet know why. What about a man called Luis Reyes?'

The senator nodded. 'The drug dealer. Once a pillar of the community and now a fugitive for killing a police officer.'

'I was there. I saw it. Someone has spirited Reyes away.'

'So, you will know there is a vein of corruption running

so deep through our system that it is difficult to know who to trust, and I am supposing you might feel that I am part of that cancer,' said the senator.

'Zeller came to see you on more than one occasion, didn't he?'

'He did. It was... our secret. Do you know how far he got with his investigation?'

Raglan did not want to give out any more than he had to until he was certain that this was the one man Zeller trusted. 'He discovered false shell companies buying arms.'

'He did and those bogus companies were hidden in a layer of other companies with retired senior intelligence officers on their letterhead.' He looked at Raglan as if to check his facts, leaning forwards to deliver his punchline. 'Those intelligence people died years ago. They don't exist. Their names were used to bolster confidence in the procurement process. Casey Zeller thought the corruption ran right through the intelligence community and it was backed by a group of powerful and influential people.'

'The Council.'

Senator Thomas slumped back. 'Then you know. And if you have got this far then you will realize that my hands are tied until I find out who those people are. That's what Zeller was going to deliver to me before he disappeared.'

Raglan held back a while longer. A senator with Thomas's background was well placed to know who the Council might be and not disclose it to the man who walked in out of a snowstorm.

'Whoever is behind this, they need Luis Reyes to ship the weapons down into Central America, but I don't know where yet,' Raglan said.

'And neither do I. We got so far and no further. I believe Zeller is dead,' said the senator.

'So do I. He's not the kind of man to go to ground without assuring his wife he's going off grid.'

'Is she safe?'

'I got her away.'

'Thank you. I could not reveal myself and offer help. Zeller insisted my name was kept out of everything.'

'If the CIA is running a covert operation can you subpoena their files?'

Senator Thomas nursed his drink. 'Mr Raglan, the CIA is like the Vatican. What goes on behind closed doors stays there.'

'You can't bring them up before a committee?'

'Oh, that's possible, of course – we did that when we learnt of the torture going on after Iraq. They made every pretence of co-operation. National security prohibited the examination of paper documents so they arranged for my committee to visit Langley and go through their digital files in a secure environment. What we did not know at the time was that they could see every paragraph we marked for questioning so that when they were brought before us at the hearing they had had plenty of time to prepare their answers.' He smiled. 'The Vatican on steroids.'

'Luis Reyes was spirited away by a team of men. I killed one of them in self-defence. He was an ex-Army Ranger. I used my contacts to trace them but they haven't shown up on anyone's radar.' He stared down the older man. 'Does the CIA still have a permanent assassination squad on standby?' He saw the man's hesitation. To admit such a unit existed compromised Congress. 'It was called ZR/Rifle back in the early days.'

'You are well informed. Yes, it was an executive-action programme, a concept resurrected from the sixties. I suspect you came across such people during your days in the Legion.'

'And afterwards.'

Realization dawned on the senator that someone with Raglan's skills would be at the sharp end of any conflict and would be used by trusted intelligence agencies as an asset. He knew too much to be otherwise. 'A regular commando unit was on standby for CIA covert operations and assassinations but they never disclosed it to Congress until ten years ago by the then director of the CIA. It was swiftly disbanded.'

'Or given over to private contractors,' Raglan said. 'That way they are unofficial and there is nothing on the record and you would not have to be informed of their existence. So, I ask myself, how far I should trust you, senator, because you must know more than I do.'

'I am gathering whatever evidence I can. I swore to Zeller that I would stop all of this. I gave him my word. I think he believed me when I helped him close those bogus companies. But there are others we have not yet discovered. My country lost close to a billion dollars in illicit arms dealing in one year alone. Military officers in positions of trust in the Pentagon have, over the years, been imprisoned for falsifying procurement deals.'

Senator Thomas's voice reflected the emotions of a man whose country had been betrayed by those in positions of authority and trust. 'I have spent my whole political career trying to stop malfeasance among the highest echelons of my nation's governance and security agencies. I will stop this, Mr Raglan, I assure you, and I will not let anyone stand in my way. My legacy is for my children and grandchildren and every decent-minded citizen of this country.'

The man's sincerity convinced Raglan. He recited the names on the list.

The man's face fell with shock. 'My God, I know most of them. I had dinner with one of them a week ago and four of them are on the same committees as me. How do you know this? Do you have proof?'

'I have the files on the Council.'

'Jesus. Where?'

'Casey hid them in his house. I found them.'

Mike Thomas put his glass down. 'Have you told Jack Swain?'

'No.' Raglan sensed something was wrong.

'Then don't. Not yet. Zeller was uncertain about him.'

'His own boss? The man who had him start this investigation?'

'Yes. The more Zeller dug the murkier connections became. Did you know Jack Swain was with the Agency and went over to the Pentagon when the DIA Clandestine Service was established?'

'I didn't. Swain offered to help. He wanted me to find Zeller.'

'I see.' The senator looked into the flickering firelight for a moment. 'Have you told Swain you have come here tonight?'

'No. He said he knew Zeller had made contact with a

senator but didn't know who that was. You're not involved as far as anyone else is concerned.'

'Those documents. You can get them? Tonight?' said the senator.

How long would it take to drive out to Stafford and back in a snowstorm? He looked across to the unlit orangery: its large windows allowed him to see that the snowstorm had passed; the clouds were edged with moonlight as they passed overhead, exposing a glittering crystal sky. The moon cast its glow on the open fields between the house and the trees and eight black-clad figures stark against the field of snow.

A silenced weapon's bullet punched a hole through the glass and tore open Wallace's head.

41

Raglan hauled the dumbstruck senator to his feet, snatched the dead Wallace's gun and pushed the stumbling politician ahead of him as Roberts expertly used the weight of the stone fireplace as cover and fired at the figures storming the house. Raglan brushed his hand against the light switch, throwing the room into darkness. The looming figures were silhouetted against the night sky and sparkling snowfield. Roberts killed two. Glass shattered. A stun grenade exploded. Senator Thomas reeled as Raglan shook his head clear of the blast. Roberts bellowed to get the senator to the safe room. He fired rapidly, giving Raglan and the senator time to reach a broad corridor as he edged back, covering his arc of fire.

'Safe room!' Raglan shouted at the dazed senator, who stumbled and was saved from falling by Raglan roughly grabbing him. The man nodded, comprehending that the nightmare he thought never possible was bearing down on him. Death was seconds away. He pointed. Raglan's strength barrelled him through the house. The damned place was too big for safety. They emerged into another sitting room, the glass shattered, a balaclava-faced gunman was half in the room, assault weapon in his shoulder. Raglan fired twice.

The man's face and throat a sudden bloodied mess. There was no telling how many were in the assault team.

Roberts was good. He backtracked after Raglan, laying down fire, keeping the attackers at bay, but his and Raglan's hand weapons were no match for assault rifles. Raglan pressed the senator down behind a corner, saw Roberts covering the corridor and quickly changing magazine. Roberts turned, checked the man he was paid to protect. Raglan shouted, 'Cover me!'

He ran for the dead man's assault rifle; hearing rapid fire behind him, he snatched the weapon and then a stun grenade from the man's combat vest. The size of the house gave the attackers the advantage. They had more than one entry point. Gunfire raked the wall above Raglan's head as he ran back to the corridor and the crouching senator. The unseen shooter had the advantage.

'Office door!' Roberts cried out, pointing to a recessed door out of sight that led from the room they were in. Raglan didn't have a clear shot. The angle was wrong and the shooter had the protection of the door's return wall. The gunfire eased. The killers from the orangery and main living room were creeping forwards, cautious now that the lights were down and the eerily moonlit rooms cast shadows where before there were none. Roberts gestured to Raglan to cover the passage as he crept behind a large walnut table to get a better shot at the hidden gunman.

Raglan watched him and the looming shadows in the great room. They would soon be caught in the crossfire from the advancing shooters, and the man in the doorway was in a perfect cut-off point. Killing the gunman was a two-man job. Raglan pressed the handgun into the senator's hand. 'They make a move along the corridor, shoot.' He hurried along the left-hand side of the room as Roberts stayed on the opposite wall behind the table. Roberts watched Raglan's progress, knowing what he would do next. He steadied himself for the shot. Raglan was going to offer himself as a target. Raglan saw the angle and stepped into the room. The shooter was right-handed, weapon in his shoulder, left hand extended, holding the grip, which meant he had to expose at least half his torso to get a clear shot. Roberts shot twice. The bullets struck the man's chest and he staggered back. Raglan saw the shots weren't fatal. The man's Kevlar vest saved him and he was tough and experienced enough to be already rolling from the hit. Another couple of seconds and Raglan and Roberts would be hit with full automatic fire. Raglan took two steps to his right and put a burst into him. His body shuddered. Raglan didn't need to check him, but was already halfway back to the senator, who fired four shots down the passage. Roberts got to the senator first, pushing him ahead, protecting the man with his own body. He mistimed his courageous action and rapid gunfire punched into his back, throwing him face forward. Two attackers had crept tactically into the far end of the corridor, unaware that Raglan was off to one side in the next room. Raglan killed them.

Senator Thomas looked as though he was about to vomit. The bullets and blood splattering the walls of his beloved home was a desecration of everything meaningful to him and his late wife. Bile caught at the back of his throat. Raglan, the stranger who had come seeking help,

shielded him. Raglan's lips were moving. He was saying
something but the senator's ears were ringing from the
confined gunshots.

'Roberts is dead,' said the senator, voice dulled, as if
Raglan hadn't noticed.

Raglan saw shock setting in. Fear, confusion, denial.
Emotions that would become a toxic mix, poisoning the
body and thought process. Raglan slapped him. Mike
Thomas gasped.

'Get a grip. We're winning this fight. There's not many of
them left standing. You understand? We get to the safe room
and then hit the panic button. This place will be swarming
with cops. Show me!'

Mike Thomas wiped an arm across his face. His mind
cleared. 'Two rooms along. A door into an airlock and then
the room.'

Raglan chivvied him along the corridor. Six of the
snowfield assault team were dead. There were only two
more. But if he had planned the assault on a building this
size he'd have had another team already flanking the house.
The backup would come in another way or act as backstop
for the assault. These shooters were pros but if whoever
sent them thought there was only one old man and two
bodyguards then maybe, just maybe, Raglan had got lucky.
Perhaps there *had* been only eight.

Raglan covered their retreat. They reached the safe-
room door. Senator Thomas fumbled with the entry code.
The door swung open as Raglan kept watch. He heard
nothing. There was no sign of the two remaining men. All
clear. He eased the handgun out of the senator's hand, slid
free the clip. Several bullets remained in the clip and one in

the chamber. He tucked the Glock into his waistband and pressed the assault rifle into the senator's hands.

'See that lever? I've put it on automatic fire. If for any reason the next person you see isn't a cop, press the trigger. They won't stand a chance. Understand?'

'You're not staying?' A note of panic and incredulity that someone would abandon a chance of safety.

'I'm going after them, senator. There was only one way for them to get here and that was upriver. I need one of them alive. We have to find out who's behind this.'

Mike Thomas nodded his understanding. 'There's a path down to the river and my boathouse and jetty.'

'Go inside. You'll be OK. I'll be back.'

'Mr Raglan... I... How can I thank you?'

'Do what you promised Casey Zeller and stop this thing, whatever it is.'

The senator nodded and went inside the panic room. Raglan closed the door, saw the electronic catch take hold. He looked up at the camera's eye that nestled in the doorframe. He nodded to the man who would be watching inside; then he turned to seek the remaining two killers. He took another magazine clip from the fallen bodyguard and skirted the killing ground. Stepping around and over the bodies, he reached the shattered orangery windows and saw two gunmen running for the trees. There was no backup team in place. The killers were beaten.

Raglan clambered through the window frames. The temperature had plummeted, the air freezing, the ground crunching underfoot. He ran steadily across the snowfield, following their footprints beneath the midnight moon.

42

It was half a mile to the forest and the way leading down to the senator's boathouse and jetty. Raglan swerved away from the path, evading any chance of ambush; he crouched, listened and heard the laboured breathing of the men ahead. They had taken longer to find the path back than they had on their approach to the house. Withdrawal from an attack always looked different to the approach. That suggested they were not local. That they didn't know their ground as well as they should. How long would they have had to plan the assault? How long had they known that Senator Thomas was the mystery contact that Casey Zeller had been in touch with? Everything pointed to a hasty attack. Had Raglan led the assassins there? He followed after them.

Less snow had penetrated the hardwood forest than what lay on the open ground. Raglan heard the men, but they were too far ahead to see. Quickening his pace, he took the twisting track more by instinct, what moonlight there was showing a curved break in the depleted undergrowth. The water glistened in the distance and a dark shape loomed three hundred yards ahead. The boathouse. There was a crash and a curse as one of the men ahead fell into the bushes. Raglan stopped, held his breath, listened beyond his heartbeat; the killers had remained silent. No voices called out except for the breathless curse. Silent attack dogs, well trained. He remembered the dead Army Ranger, one of the men on the security camera at Luis Reyes's house. Whoever protected the drug dealer wanted the senator dead, which meant they knew of his involvement. The question of how couldn't be answered. Not yet. Not now.

Raglan pushed on but a doubt began to nag. The fact that he was with the senator at the time of the attack had to be more than coincidence. His thoughts were interrupted as the boathouse came more clearly into view. Fifty yards before its dark shape, the broken outline of boulders offered jagged cover at the bend in the path. Raglan stopped, glanced around and saw one man running forward. The second man was nowhere in sight. If Raglan continued his descent along the path around the rocks then the hidden gunman would cut him down within a few more paces.

He clambered up and over the broken boulders, then kept low on the ridgeline, peering across towards the river. He saw the black patch in the trees twenty-five yards away, darker than the tree trunks, the wrong shape in the wrong place. The man waited while his partner ran clear, hoping to draw their pursuer around the path. Raglan had no approach to close in on him. Whichever way he moved he would be exposed; he couldn't rush the man and he couldn't sneak up. He held the Glock, crouched and called out.

'Here!'

The shadow lurched, turned and looked up.

Raglan fired three rapid shots. The man pitched backwards as his partner a further fifteen yards beyond shot instinctively towards the gunfire. Raglan heard the screeching whine of ricochets, then felt a hot tearing in his side. He ignored it. He had already leapt down from his vantage point and begun pushing through the low undergrowth towards the shooter. The gunman heard him, fired a rapid burst that was at first way off the mark but then clipped the bushes around Raglan who was saved as his foot caught a root, tumbling him headlong. The fall snatched the Glock from his grasp. His arm and shoulder glanced off a tree and slowed his descent. Ignoring the further stab of pain, he rolled and found his footing. He came up yards from the gunman, who levelled his weapon. Raglan charged forwards but knew the man couldn't miss from there. There was a dull click; the man's head dipped and his hand snatched at the empty magazine, yanked another from his belt. As he reloaded Raglan used the downwards slope to launch himself. He thudded into the thickset man. He was heavier than Raglan by thirty pounds but the force of Raglan barging him slammed him flat on his back and winded him, throwing his rifle clear. Raglan bunched his fist and hit him, but the man half blocked it and had the strength to roll clear. Despite his size the gunman was quickly on his feet. He snatched at his sidearm. Raglan was more than an arm's length away. He felt the man's empty assault rifle at his feet, bent, snatched and swung. It caught the man's arm; the semi-automatic pistol curled away into the undergrowth. Undeterred, the man pulled free a combat knife from his shoulder webbing. Moonlight caught the dull matte steel. A killing knife. The man's hand wrapped around the hilt, a finger ring giving a firmer grip for the combat-designed blade. Raglan, ignoring the seeping wound in his side, watched and moved as quickly as his adversary, who held the knife steady. The blade's single bevel cutting edge was like an arrowhead, its lethal sharpness accentuated by the serrated ridge on top of the blade above the chamfered blood channel. The man pulled free his face covering, easing the restrictive tightness on his skin, sucking in the cold night air. It would be a fight to the death.

He lunged but kept his balance; Raglan had nothing to block the strike. He twisted, threw his forearm out enough to deflect the man's wrist, stepped forwards like a boxer dancing in for a jab. The man's eyes never left Raglan's face. He took the punch into his biceps without a sound, twisted on his heels and struck a low jab towards Raglan's stomach. He was off balance, but the blade nicked Raglan's jacket. Raglan stepped inside the blow, half turned and slammed his elbow into the man's face. Blood spurted. It rocked the attacker but he held the knife steady despite his pain. Raglan snatched at the man's wrist with one hand, ready to punch with the other. The killer was too quick and deftly twisted his hand and the blade slashed Raglan's thigh. It caught flesh more than muscle. The man's weight was forwards. Raglan kicked him hard in the kneecap, heard it crack. The man gasped, but held in his pain. No cry or curse despite the stomach-churning injury. His leg gave way. He didn't fight it but used its sudden weakness to fall and roll. Raglan took four quick paces after him. By the time the assassin's tumble came to a halt he was only a few strides from the boathouse. He slammed his back against the timber wall for support, glaring at Raglan who drove home his assault.

There was nothing subtle about Raglan's attack. He went in like a cornered street fighter. Boots and fists, intent on inflicting as much violence as he could. The gunman took a hammering but still wouldn't go down. He grappled with his assailant. Raglan jammed his thumb into the man's face, found his gaping mouth as he sucked in air, and forced his thumb inside, ripping at the man's cheek while at the same repeatedly kneeing him between his legs. By the time the fourth blow landed, the gunman was gagging; head bent, he vomited, and then with a final effort launched a straight-armed fist at Raglan's chest with the knife. Raglan blocked it, grasped the man's wrist and forced it back. The killer's injured leg gave way again and his weight fell against Raglan who dropped down, dragging the man on top of him. The man's elbow slammed into the ground next to Raglan's face, but the finger hole in the knife's handle kept the knife clasped tightly in his hand – which was held in turn by Raglan's grip. Raglan twisted his fist, smothering the man's hand, turning the knife point towards the man's neck. Raglan slammed his right hand down in a hammer blow, plunging the blade into his throat. The man spasmed, choking on blood as Raglan heaved him away.

Raglan stood over the dying man. He could see his eyes staring wide at the flickering stars. Death took another minute. Raglan wiped the sweat from his own exertions and then pulled free his phone. Every one of these killers needed to be identified. He pulled free the knife from the man's throat and hovered the lens over his face. Raglan shut his eyes as the camera's flash lit the dead man's features, preserving his night vision. Then he placed the knife on the man's combat vest and took another picture. It was like no fighting knife he had seen before and he had served alongside most special forces. Identifying the weapon might help determine who these killers were. Raglan stepped around the sprawled body towards the jetty and the black boat, a RIB, tied up there. He was close to the boathouse doorway when the sudden chatter of gunfire ripped into the wooden building and splintered the jetty. He threw himself against the door, it gave way and he rolled inside, scrambling for cover as the gunfire swept the building. He leopard-crawled beneath a boat on a support trestle and turned to face the door and the gunman who might step inside to kill him. There was only the roar of the RIB's outboard engines. Raglan got to the open door and saw the shallow-hulled boat disappearing around the bend in the river. Raglan's instincts had been correct. One more killer had stayed out of sight at the house when he gave chase to the others. Raglan snatched up one of the fallen assault rifles and ran for the house.

The glittering field of snow revealed the darkened building as he had left it. He had expected flashing police lights and a cordoned-off crime scene. There was nothing. He found Senator Mike Thomas in the safe room. The door was wide open. The assault rifle lay across his lap. It had not been fired. The trademark killer had cut the senator's throat. Raglan examined the door. They were designed to resist explosives, and it was obvious that the intruder had not attempted to use them. He remembered the cleaning crew he suspected of gaining access to Casey Zeller's house and that an electronic lock disabling device had most likely been used. Which pointed again to intelligence services. Either that or for some reason the senator had voluntarily opened the door.

Raglan followed what he thought would be the alarm wiring route. Outside the house was a concealed armoured box. That's where the small explosive charge had been used. The blackened wiring told its own story. The senator had unknowingly pressed a disabled alarm button. The assassin had kept out of sight and had probably not taken part in the gun battle. And that told Raglan that the reason the two men had escaped from the house instead of pressing on with the attack was to draw a bodyguard, or Raglan himself, into pursuit. That's when the box had been blown and the senator killed.

The blood from his leg wound had congealed against his jeans. He was about to return inside and find a medicine cabinet when he heard the first distant sirens. Ignoring his leg, he clutched his side, ran limping to the Honda, tossed the assault rifle inside, fired the engine and sped for the turn in the road before the police drove down the narrow lane and boxed him in on the panhandle. The narrow road back to the highway gave little opportunity to pull over. The night sky caught the flashing red and blue in the distance. There was a bend in the road ahead. The lights grew brighter. The sirens louder. Raglan floored the accelerator and the 4 × 4's wheels gripped the compacted snow. He was twenty yards away from a blind bend when the SUV slewed as it hit black ice and slid on a sideways trajectory.

Raglan took his foot off the accelerator and his hands off the wheel, going against every human instinct to try and control the vehicle's sidelong plummet towards the trees. The impending crash would expose him to the approaching police cars. The black metal beast was hurtling at fifty miles an hour when one of the rear wheels bit into less compacted snow, twitching the rear end; the Honda slid forwards by ten yards and ploughed into a field at the edge of the forest. It hit deeper snow and slowed to a standstill.

Raglan killed the lights and kept his foot off the brake so as not to show the rear lights. He was out of sight of the road now. The police drivers would have their attention pinned to the bend in the road as their cars slewed. They recovered from the danger area successfully and sped off towards the house. Lights and sounds faded. Raglan reversed, turned the SUV and headed calmly towards the city.

Twenty minutes later, he was halfway to the motel when he saw the neon pharmacy sign. It was off the main road, the building in darkness. Raglan switched off the Honda's lights again and eased it along the narrow side alley into the building's shadow.

He lifted the tailgate and took the crowbar from the wheel well. The service entrance was another ten paces. His phone's torchlight on the door rim showed no wires. That meant a silent alarm. How long until the cops arrived once he triggered it? Five minutes? Less? He rammed the crowbar's lip into the door jamb and forced it open. The rear entrance led through a storage space into the counter and dispensing area. Raglan swept the light across the controlled medicines cabinet, broke the lock and rummaged inside until he found a vial of lignocaine and a couple of packs of Tramadol. The clock was ticking. A patrol car might already be in the area and alerted. He counted the minutes. Three so far. He needed an antibiotic. He found a container of flucloxacillin; then he picked up one of the pharmacy's shopping baskets and let the torchlight sweep the shelves. He found what he wanted. A tube of antiseptic cream, liquid iodine, a bottle of alcohol, a scalpel, a syringe, a few needles, some sterile gauze dressings, crêpe bandages, a packet of 3/0 catgut and a packet of 3/0 nylon already on a needle. Once his cuts were attended to, he'd have to dig out the bullet in his side and whatever he used to do that would need sterilizing. He grabbed a packet of latex surgical gloves. Basic field surgery meant improvisation. He dropped in a bottle of hydrogen peroxide. Four minutes. The basket held all he needed. Time to go. Raglan grabbed a couple of cans of isotonic drink loaded with glucose. He'd need that. Shock was setting in.

Raglan pulled into the motel with the medical dressings and a bottle of whiskey bought at twice the normal price from a reluctant barman at a roadside bar that was just about to close when he walked in. No sign of anyone in the motel's car park. All the rooms were in darkness.

He covered the assault rifle with a car rug and, using the shadows, headed for the gap between the two wings of the building and the ice machine in front of the locked office. He scooped a tub of ice and then went into his room, shoving a chair beneath the door handle. There was no time to lose if he was to stand any chance of keeping infection at bay. Sweat prickled his face. Cold and clammy. Couldn't be hypovolemic shock: he hadn't lost enough blood. Maybe neurogenic from the pain. He gulped the isotonic drink, stripped his clothes and, after washing and drying his hands, pulled on the surgical gloves. He cleansed the cut on his leg and the wound on his side with cool water and soap, and then poured liquid iodine into the gashed leg to sterilize it. It stung. After a final smear of antibiotic cream on the gash he closed the wound with butterfly strips, placed antiseptic gauze across the whole thing and taped it down.

The gunshot wound needed more time. He prodded his fingers along the tear on his flank. He felt the small piece of metal. He needed better light. He dragged the room's small table close to the bed and angled the reading lamp, then laid out everything he'd taken from the pharmacy on a clean towel. There was a shaving mirror on a concertina arm next to the mirror in the bathroom. He wrenched it free and turned it so the magnified lens was angled beneath the desk lamp.

Raglan drew 1 per cent of lignocaine into the syringe, tapped free the air and injected the anaesthetic around the wound. It was impossible to anaesthetize deep into the muscles where he had to probe. This was as much as he could do to deal with the pain to come. He repeated the same procedure as his leg and poured iodine into the wound, pushing it in deep with a sterile swab, making sure it saturated the tear and the surrounding skin. He winced. But what he was doing was no different than any surgeon would do prior to surgery. Once the iodine had seeped into the wound he poured in the clear alcohol and fought the wave of nausea threatening to engulf him. He peeled back the aluminium cover from the sterilized straight needle, and then tore open the surgical tweezers pack. The angled mirror and his fingertips told him where to probe. The serrated edges on the tweezers gouged the deep muscle. He

swore. Took a breath and punished himself again. He felt
the pincers scrape against the spent bullet and, ignoring the
searing pain, drew it out.

Sweat ran down his back. The inside of the wound had
to be stitched. If he didn't, that's where a clot would form
and then there would be no chance of avoiding infection.
He swilled the wound with iodine again. His free hand
manipulated the wound as the needle threaded with self-
dissolving catgut stitched the muscle wall together. Satisfied,
he cut the excess catgut. Sweat stung his eyes. He took a
breather, wiped his face with a towel and listened for any
unusual sounds outside. His concentration had been so
intense there was a risk he hadn't heard approaching danger.
Law enforcement or killers. If either discovered where he
was they would come for him. He needed to finish quickly.

Raglan gripped the needle with his bloodied fingers; the
attached nylon suture would hold the wound tighter than
any butterfly clip and there was no doubt more violence
was imminent. He needed the wound to stay closed.

He stitched neatly. An image from his early days in the
Legion when he was a fresh-faced kid darning his socks
flashed through his mind. He grimaced. He was better at
it now than then. Raglan closed the wound and taped on
a dry sterile dressing. He bandaged the stitching, got to his
feet, tested his flexibility. Everything held tight. The wound
hurt but the Tramadol would take the edge off. He took
two of the flucloxacillin and washed them down with a
mouthful of whiskey. The cuts inside his mouth stung from
the blows he had taken from the tenacious fighter but the
hard work was done. He was good to go. He put ice into
the plastic food bag and pressed the ice pack tightly against

his ribs. The marks on his torso left by the fight would soon bruise and the ice would aid the healing. The grazes on his knuckles and the cuts and contusions from the fight would fade in a few days. He poured another half-glass of whiskey and took it down in one gulp.

It did not soften the regret he felt at having to kill such a determined and courageous adversary. The man he'd fought was one of the best and in another time and place would likely have been the kind of man to fight at Raglan's side. A dependable, brave man who never gave up and who died without complaint. He sent the photographs of the dead man and the combat knife to 'Bird' Sokol, then climbed into bed, pulled up the covers and fell instantly asleep.

It had been a long day.

And a hard fight.

43

Jenna Voss held the Acura's two hundred horsepower in check as she navigated the treacherous snow-compacted road to the senator's house. The phone call had wrenched her from her sleep, and Kim Burton's none-too-friendly voice had told her to get to an address north of the city. Now.

A police car blocked the narrow road into the turning circle in front of the senator's gates. Armed officers guarded the entrance; black Suburbans and unmarked cars were parked at the front of the house. Light blazed through the windows and she could see hooded snowman figures moving around inside. Some half bent, a flash of light, another angle, another flash. A police search team moved carefully across a snowfield as torchlight beams danced in the distant trees. Whatever the hell had gone on here, this was a major crime scene. Feds and cops, coroner's vans. Killing on a grand scale.

She gave her name to the officer booking people in and out of the house, went up the steps to another uniform who handed her shoe covers. She pulled her own set of latex gloves from her pocket. The place looked like a slaughterhouse. Dozens of evidence markers were strewn across the floor; bodies lay where they had fallen. Four suits stood further down the corridor. One of them looked back. Detective Delaney. He spoke to the woman whose back was turned to Voss. Kim Burton swung round and looked Jenna up and down: hooded tracksuit and pink sneakers weren't the usual FBI dress code. Voss had no idea why someone with Kim Burton's seniority looked to be in charge.

Burton beckoned Voss to her. Jenna stepped around the evidence markers and the bodies in the corridor. Bullet-holes peppered the walls, artwork hung askew in splintered frames, ripped canvas flapped in a breeze that swept through the house from the shattered orangery windows.

'This a drug shootout?' she asked the gathered investigators.

Kim Burton glared at her. 'This way.'

The detectives stepped aside and fell in line behind the senior agent. Kim Burton led the way to the safe room. She stood aside and let Voss look at the dead man inside. She knew she'd seen him before but couldn't place him. What she did recognize was the way he had been killed.

'Who is this?' she asked.

'This is Senator Mike Thomas's house. He and two of his personal protection team were killed here tonight along with six attackers.'

'Any idea why?' said Voss.

'I was hoping you'd be able to tell me,' said Burton.

'Me? I recognize him now you've told me his name but how would I know?'

Burton nodded to Delaney. 'Show her.'

Delaney raised a plastic evidence bag. Inside was a card.

'Your card was found here,' Burton said. 'Like to tell me how?'

'No idea. I've never met the man.'

'And you've never been in this house?' said Delaney's partner, Medina.

'No.' She looked at the three inquisitors facing her. 'Why do I feel I'm being dragged into this?'

Medina wanted to get in Voss's face. She took a step forwards, her teeth bared in a barely concealed snarl. 'Because I think you had something to do with this and the other killing we're investigating.'

Voss rammed the palm of her hand into the belligerent woman's chest. 'Fuck you.'

Delaney stepped in front of his partner to stop her retaliation as Kim Burton snatched Voss's arm. 'For God's sake, what's wrong with you?' she snapped.

Voss shook herself free and pointed at Medina. 'Keep your attack dog on a leash, Delaney, or you'll have an expensive veterinary bill.'

The experienced detective played peacemaker. 'Things are heated because one of the dead men is an ex-cop who served with us.' He pointed to Roberts's covered body lying in the corridor. 'Besides, there's more evidence of you being connected to all of this.'

Voss's face creased. 'With what?'

'You came to a crime scene, said you were looking for someone.' Delaney beckoned to one of the crime-scene examiners. 'Evidence bag on the table,' he said, extending his hand. The snowman duly put the plastic bag in Delaney's hand. It had a cap inside. 'There's a name tag on the inside of the hat. TJ Jones. We checked his other hats.

He was fond of them all. Four more had his name in them. Whoever killed Jones killed the senator and these men. But this was a concerted attack. Military style. Those guys lying out there look as though they were ready to attack Fallujah again.'

Voss took the bag and felt the hat. Crumpling the plastic, she could see TJ's name tag. If Raglan had killed the Vietnam veteran and then come here, what was the connection? Did it go back to the CIA? She kept the thoughts to herself. Kim Burton was in bed with the CIA and the two detectives weren't in the loop. 'This isn't evidence connecting the man I was looking for. There is no connection.'

'Except for your card,' said Medina. 'You're in on this, somehow, I can smell it.'

Kim Burton turned Voss away from the two detectives and walked her to the entrance hall. 'Thank you, detectives, my agents will liaise with you on this.'

'Liaise?' said Medina. 'You Feds can have the senator's murder; we have the others.'

'They're linked, detective,' Burton said with no doubt in her voice as to who was in charge. 'We'll liaise.'

She heard Medina swear under her breath.

'You think you can recognize him?' Burton said to Voss. 'You say you followed him down in Florida.'

'Am I on this case?' said Voss.

'Why would you think that? You're expected back in Clarksburg.'

'I've been following Raglan.'

'You have been following a ghost. For all I know he doesn't exist. That man might be lying by a pool somewhere in Florida in a friend's house drinking pina coladas. Placing him in that man's apartment is circumstantial at best. But someone was there and that someone came here tonight. And a dead senator had your calling card. And you can't tell me how that came to be. Or you're lying to me. You look at these dead gunmen and tell me if there's any resemblance to the man you say you are chasing down. If he's not here, then there's enough blood splattered around to tell me he might be in a hospital's mortuary or ER. Find out. And then you get back on the highway and rejoin the geeks. If you play fast and loose with this and you're not back in Clarksburg in two days, you're on suspension and I'm instigating another psych evaluation on you. Check the bodies and then get out of here.'

Kim Burton turned on her heel and headed back to where Delaney and Medina waited. Voss swallowed the threat and her rising temper.

'You have a flashlight I can use?' she asked a snowman. He took one from his bag. 'Thanks.' She went to the first dead gunman, checked his face, and then did the same with the others. None of the dead men bore any resemblance to Raglan. She followed the lights outside and the tracks across the glistening field. The moonglow deepened the forest's shadows and the night air plumed her breath. Once in the forest the way ahead was silhouetted by the glare of crime-scene arc lamps illuminating a boat shed and jetty. She skirted the large outcrop and saw one man sprawled on his back. One of the examiners was still taking photographs, small lighting flashes bouncing off the rockface. He looked up.

'You looking for the victims?'

'More like the perps,' she said.

'You found them. One here; another over by the jetty where your Feds and cops are.'

'This one?' said Voss.

'Three in the chest. Nice grouping. Looks as though shots could've come from on top of those rocks. That's a guess at this stage.'

'Sure.' She stooped and played the beam over the dead man. 'Thanks,' she said and continued on to where the next group of cops and Federal agents were looking at the scene.

'Jenna, long time no see,' said one of the men studying the ground under the arc lamps.

'Ricky,' she said, acknowledging the special agent she'd known briefly when at the DC Field Office.

'You on this?' said the younger agent.

'No. Just a passing interest.'

'This one had a helluva fight by the look of it. He's busted up. Whoever did this to him must have been good at what he does.'

Voss crouched and looked at the man, whose fist was bunched close to his throat. 'Burton wants me to check his face.'

'Burton's pissed off, Jenna. Dead senators are bad for business. Pressure to get this solved will be high.'

'And the knife?' said Voss, pointing to the blade lying on the dead man's chest.

'Weird stuff,' said Ricky. 'It's what killed him. You can see the serrated tear in his throat. Found it like that. Maybe it's some kind of message or trophy. The senator's throat was cut.'

'Like the throat of another victim, another investigation.'

'Connected to this?'

'Dunno.' She stood, looked around the crime scene and gazed downriver. 'Anyone else?'

'No. Just these two and those at the house. Plus the two dead bodyguards and the senator.'

She nodded her thanks. 'Good to see you again, Ricky.' She turned back on to the approach path laid out by the snowmen.

The young agent called after her. 'You still on the Hostage Rescue Team?'

She turned and looked at him in case his comment was a deliberate jibe. He looked innocently at her.

'Just asking. I've been out in the Manassas office for a year. Got back to DC a week ago,' he said.

She took him at his word. 'No, not right now,' she said, and turned back towards the kill house. The path back felt trickier than the way down to the river, but as she picked her way along it, she knew with utter certainty that Raglan was involved here. Perhaps it had been a slip of the tongue from Kim Burton when she called Raglan a ghost. Perhaps that's exactly what he was: a ghost CIA killer.

And the body count was rising.

44

Raglan jerked awake when his phone vibrated, and groaned at the tug of the stitches.

It was Serge Sokol. It was still dark and the two hours since he'd closed his eyes felt like twelve.

'You can talk?'

'Go ahead, Bird, what do you have?'

'Not a lot but enough to make you look over your shoulder. I came up with nothing at first but I remembered Tomasz's brother fixing you up with those fake tattoos when you went into Russia. I spoke to him and tracked Tomasz down again.'

Raglan remembered his former legionnaire comrade being engaged in security work for the Israelis. 'Is he still doing what he was back then?'

'That's why I thought of him. When I came up with a blank he was my last chance. He's gone dark, working on a job who-knows-where. I sent him those photos of the people you lifted off the security camera and the dead man and the knife. *Mon ami*, you have bad people biting at your heels.'

'Do you have names?'

'One. So far. But first, those people from the security cameras: Tomasz didn't know the guy with the beard.'

'He was ex-Army Ranger. He's the guy I shot.'

'Then he was the least of your troubles. One other remains unidentified but the man up front in the photo: he's Mossad. Or was. Nothing confirmed. Name is Asher Elias.'

'Mossad? You sure? I asked Maguire and he didn't have him on file.'

'You know how it works. They have units no one knows about, but Tomasz recognized him. Said he was in a meeting three or four years ago before their people assassinated those two Iranian scientists in Morocco.'

'What the hell is Mossad doing operating in the States with a drug runner?'

'That's the connection Tomasz couldn't make. His work doesn't put him in the inner circle, but he has good contacts and from what he's picked up there's a problem that has people there slamming doors and huddling in smoke-filled rooms. It might have something to do with the knife I showed him. It's special forces, made especially for the Ya'ma'm.'

That's why it had been so hard to kill the man he faced at the boathouse. The Ya'ma'm, Israel's ultra-selective and highly secretive counter-terrorist and hostage-rescue unit. Serious contenders for the title of Best in the World. One in a thousand gets through their selection course and most of those applicants are already trained to special-ops standards. 'Operational?'

'I don't know. Personally, I doubt it. I would say all of these people are ex-service personnel. Who would put a legitimate team on the ground in a sovereign country? Danny, you never know with the Israelis, they're so damned sharp at this. If they are in the game then it's for a bigger reason than what you can see from where you are.'

'Anything else you can tell me, Bird?'

'Yes. There's an assassin in play. A woman.'

'A name?'

'Aram-banou.'

'She's Iranian?'

'One hundred per cent. Trained by the Pasdaran, and despite what you might think of their Revolutionary Guard, they are pretty damned good. You remember all those thousands of highly trained ninja-type women they recruited? She was one of them. Trained to bring death and destruction to the West and defend Iran against its enemies. Knocks seven kinds of bells out of some fighting corps we've seen, I can tell you.'

'Bird, it doesn't make sense. No Iranian is going to defect.'

'Two years back the Pasdaran arrested her father. He was tortured and then hanged in a public square. All false accusations. He was innocent. That did it for her. She killed the judge and his two bodyguards, and fled to the West. Into the open arms of the Americans. Watch your back and get out of there as soon as you can.'

Raglan kept the lights off and phoned Jack Swain's number.

'Yes?' said Swain's voice. He sounded as though Raglan's call had woken him. And he played his response cautiously. He made no mention of his rank or status when he answered. It could have been a wrong number.

'It's Raglan.'

There was a silence. Was Jack Swain taken by surprise, hearing Raglan's voice? He recovered quickly.

'You in trouble?' said Swain.

'Not any more. I found your senator.'

Once again Raglan heard a brief hesitation. 'My God. Wonderful. Now we might find Zeller.'

Hesitation meant one of two things to Raglan. If Swain was on the wrong side and knew about the assassination attempt, it would have surprised him to hear Raglan's voice. If he was clean, then discovering Zeller's contact was a giant leap forwards and the hesitation was one of relief or disbelief.

Which was it? Raglan wondered.

'Who was it?'

'Michael Thomas. I was there when a hit squad came through the door. Senator Thomas had two bodyguards. I saved him at first, but they're smart. They got to him.'

'Christ. They kidnapped him?'

'They killed him.'

Silence again. Raglan waited.

'Are you hurt?'

'A couple of scratches. The cops and most likely the Feds are at his house now.'

'Did you find out anything?'

'I think so. Enough to keep me here. I've a good idea where the documents are hidden,' said Raglan, deliberately evading the truth.

'Names?'

'Plenty.'

'Where?'

'I'm double-checking on that now. As soon as I have the documents Zeller hid we'll have everyone involved.'

'I'll send men.'

'No. I need some sleep and I'll head for where I think the files are tomorrow. I've done enough for one night.'

'Sure thing. Keep me in the loop.' Beat. Another pause. 'Like you said. Get the documents and we'll put this thing to bed.'

Raglan was about to hang up when Swain called out. 'Raglan? Did the senator have any copies? Did he share the information? We don't want the wrong people getting their hands on it.'

'He had nothing. Casey Zeller had shown him and then hidden them. The senator thought it better that Zeller stay in control. It had worried him that he hadn't heard from Zeller. I reassured him that there was nothing to worry about.'

'Did you mention you were working for me?' Doubt. An edge. Concern.

'Not a word, Jack. Told him Zeller had called me in before he went missing. Like you said, I'm on my own with this one.'

He hung up.

Raglan looked out of the window. The sky was clear; the snow looked as hard as concrete. Doubts about Swain persisted. Why hadn't he asked him where he was? You have a man on the ground working off the books. Injured. Why wouldn't you ask where he was holed up? In case he needed help? There could be no answer unless it was that Swain already knew. Stay focused, a voice told him, and trust no one.

And Voss? What about her? The dim lights exposed the car park. Voss's car was parked in a different bay now. She had been out somewhere. The house? Was she involved in the investigation? TJ, the blonde strands of hair clutched in his grip. Was she involved in the killing of his friend?

He stretched his arm, testing the wound on his side. It was tight, and the skin pinched, but not enough to impede him. There was no clear road ahead other than to go back to Jack Swain. But Mike Thomas had cast doubt on Swain's trustworthiness. The events since Casey Zeller's disappearance tumbled freely in his thoughts. Robert de Vere murdered so damned close to him leaving Orlando that it would be easy to implicate him in his killing when someone finally joined up all the dots. Something he was trying to do now. Had the FBI agent Voss followed him from Orlando, and had she killed TJ Jones? If so, why? Was it because she was associated with Kim Burton who had connections with the CIA? Was that the connection to what might be a Mossad kill team?

But why kill TJ? Most obvious answer was to lay the blame on him. Why? To force him to run? Then he had found the senator, thanks to Casey Zeller and his satnav. But assassins had arrived the same night. That was too much of a coincidence. He knew that Voss had not followed him there and could not have alerted them. And how could Voss have tracked him to TJ's? Raglan took a step back in his reasoning. There had seemed to be little love lost between Voss and Burton when he'd watched them at the museum. Maybe he had Voss all wrong.

Maybe it was time to confront her. But first, coffee.

Raglan dressed, pulled on the dark crew-neck sweater.

His jeans were slashed where the knife had scored across his thigh. No time for mending now. He slipped out of the room, boots crunching on the compacted snow, until he reached the covered entrance that fronted the locked reception. There was enough light from the outside walkway to show the food and drink dispensers offering high-calorie, sugar-loaded, multiple-choice snacks. He had just pumped in enough coins to get a paper cup of sweet coffee when the sound of slow-rolling tyres on the hardened parking area made him step behind a vending machine. Whoever had pulled into the bays had done so without headlights. A black-clad man got out of the passenger side. The driver stayed behind the wheel. Raglan edged around the wall to watch as the man stooped, crossed the parking area and made his way through the shrubbery. Raglan saw the dark shape of a gun in his hand. The man went straight to Raglan's room, listened outside for a moment and then kicked hard against the unlocked door. The unmistakable sound of suppressed gunfire spat out. Raglan dumped the coffee and ran towards his room. The driver saw the fast-moving shadow and hit the horn in a panicked blast.

Raglan reached the door as the shooter stepped out. He saw Raglan, and in the split second it took for him to recognize the man he had come to kill, he brought up the gun, half turned, lost his footing on the hard snow, grabbed the door frame to steady himself but had no chance to recover as Raglan barged him with his shoulder. The gun spun away, Raglan rolled clear and, as the winded gunman scrambled to his knees, punched him hard. The car horn blast had woken some of the guests whose room lights came on. Raglan hauled the downed man to his feet, drove a fist into his stomach, felt the man's toned muscle beneath his clothing and knew he must belong to the kill team. The man fell back; Raglan took a step forwards, but his feet went from under him on the frozen path. He rolled, avoided the man's lashing boot, caught it and twisted it; then, as both men slid on the tricky surface, his attacker found his footing, scrambled to his feet, grabbed the fallen gun, fired a couple of wild shots to keep Raglan's head down and ran for the car. Its engine turned.

A voice thirty yards down the walkway called out. 'FBI! Stop or I shoot!'

Raglan saw a barefoot Voss in sweatpants and vest, ignoring the cold, holding her badge high and levelling her Glock as the gunman reached the open passenger door. The driver leant out, fired rapidly. Voss ducked as the rounds splattered the wall next to her. She was quick to react, ran at a crouch as the car's tyres spun. She hadn't seen the shadow of the long-barrelled weapon pointing at her from the passenger side. Raglan was already in full stride, realized he couldn't reach the car and the shooter who was levelling the sub-machine gun towards Voss as she stood and shot twice. He shouted, 'Down!'

Caught unawares, she pivoted ready to shoot the man hurtling towards her. She hesitated that second too long because the car's headlights flashed on and illuminated the man she had last seen in Florida. Raglan tackled her as the machine-gun fire splattered through the bushes, caught the motel walls and ricocheted. Someone in a room screamed. The car's tyres found purchase and the kill team was gone.

Plunged back into half-light, Voss fought Raglan, striking out at the man she suspected of being a killer. He pinned her, his face close to hers. Her gun in his hand pressed beneath her jaw.

'Live or die. Your choice.'

45

It looked to anyone who dared glance into the dimly lit walkway as though Raglan was helping a woman get to her room; his actions concealed the gun in her lower back and firm grip on her arm. He pushed the door closed behind them and shoved her across the room. She looked cornered, ready to fight for her life, but the gun Raglan levelled at her kept her at bay. No one, no matter how well trained, could attack across that distance and survive.

'You have two minutes before the cops arrive to decide which way this is going to go. Why are you following me?'

She was reluctant to say anything. And being caught unawares meant she had to swallow her pride. 'I wasn't.'

'You're lying.'

'OK. Yes, at first. Straightforward surveillance. Two days tops.'

'And yet here you are.'

'They transferred me to north Virginia. I heard a man was murdered the night you left Vero Beach. You're a suspect. And for the DC killing as well.'

'The murdered man was my friend. He gave me a place to stay,' said Raglan, keeping the gun levelled at her.

'And now there's evidence putting you at a murdered senator's house.'

Raglan ignored her. 'Before my friend died, he grabbed a handful of his killer's blonde hair. I suspect it was you. You killed him.'

She gaped. 'Me? I'm an FBI agent.'

'Perfect cover. And you went back to the victim's apartment. That's a neat trick. It gave you a chance to contaminate the scene.'

'You were there?'

'Outside.'

'It wasn't me. I found his address from the video footage on the Greyhound. I tracked him looking for you.'

'I followed you.'

'Here?'

'After you met Kim Burton. You two looked as thick as thieves.'

'Jesus, how the hell do you know Kim Burton?'

'She's tight with the CIA.'

'So it's true you're their asset. Is that how you know her?"

'I'm not. And I don't know her. Think about it. Who put you on my tail in Florida? CIA, right?'

'So what? Burton called me to Senator Thomas's house a couple of hours ago. You're implicated. They found a cap belonging to the man you stayed with. Two murders, Raglan. Maybe three.'

Raglan didn't care about leaving the cap. It wasn't important. Had he known there was a name tag inside he might have thought otherwise, but given the circumstances at the time, a forgotten hat had hardly been forefront in his mind. 'I saved the senator. I put him in his safe room. Then

I went after two of the gunmen. They had another man. Or woman. Same execution style as the others. They drew me outside and one of them killed him. The cops will find a handgun down at the boathouse. It'll have my prints on it. The gun belonged to a dead bodyguard but it will give the Feds more evidence against me. It was a co-ordinated attack. The senator and I were going to work together.'

'On what?'

'I tell you, you tell Kim Burton, she tells the CIA.'

'You're wrong. She threatened me. She thinks I've gone rogue. I had a hunch about you and she knocked it into left field. Dammit, I'm supposed to be at my desk hours from here, but I went out on a limb to find you, and if I don't get back, then I'm suspended and up for a psych eval.'

Raglan studied her. Observe. Assess. Act. She hadn't flinched. There was an intelligent brightness in her eyes and enough evidence of her courage and skills for a credible claim to be in an FBI Hostage Rescue Team. And if what she said was a lie it was a damned good one. Sirens wailed in the distance. 'Let's see what happens when the cops get here. Tell them you tried to stop punk kids stealing a car. Tell them anything. It doesn't matter. You can bluff it out.'

She glanced at the Glock. 'Like I have a choice.'

The sirens were less than a block away.

Raglan kept the gun levelled at her. Without taking his eyes off her he released the magazine and thumbed the cartridges on to the floor. Then jacked the round in the chamber, deftly dismantled the slide action and tossed the pieces of the gun on her bed. 'I bet you can put that together faster than I stripped it. It's your call. I'll be in room five.'

He stepped out into the night as she lunged for the bed.

He was a few paces from the reception area when blue and white lights flickered across snow-laden branches. Headlight beams flooded the building. Three police cars: six armed officers piled out and crouched behind their car doors.

Raglan ignored them. Too damned late. The bad guys were gone.

Behind him he heard her call, 'FBI!' He turned and saw her raise her badge again. She hadn't called for him to stop and she wasn't pointing the Glock in his direction. She held the reassembled weapon at her side. The badge held high towards the cops.

She was still barefoot.

He liked that.

Raglan headed for the coffee machine again.

46

When the gunman had kicked open Raglan's door it had not been locked, so there was minimal damage. The police questioned those who were willing to sacrifice more sleep but having an FBI agent give a detailed statement was enough for the cops. It appeared she'd happened to be in the right place at the right time to stop some car thieves.

Raglan pushed the spindle-backed chair beneath the handle. If Voss changed her mind and wanted him in custody for questioning, then she and the police would come in hard. There was no point worrying about it. Worrying didn't help. Until that happened he didn't want to be questioned. They could knock on any of the doors and Raglan bet ten to one no more than a couple would open. Who wanted to be dragged into police business when they weren't involved? Who saw anything? Most were sleeping.

What interested him now was how the killers had found him. He kicked off his shoes and examined the soles. Then he fingertip-searched his jacket. The only time it had not been worn was going through security at the airport in London and then in Florida when he had taken Steve out for the day and contacted Robert de Vere. He felt the metallic touch of the tiny tracking device, as small as the stitching behind the collar where it had been pressed neatly in the seam. Thinking back, Raglan realized that if he was being tracked then there had been a period when no one knew his whereabouts, when Beth Ann was repairing it. When he had borrowed a coat from TJ. Same again when he went to the prison. So his pursuers would not have known how he had discovered the link from Zeller to Esposito and from him to Reyes.

His jacket had been at TJ's, but Raglan had not. What was the purpose of tagging him? To find and kill him, or his opponents' need to know where he was and who he was talking to? There was still no clear answer. He reckoned someone had gained access to Lisa Mayfield's house in Vero Beach and planted it when he was out with Steve. Easily done. He was being watched from the time he landed. If not the FBI, then who? It made no difference. Whoever it was they had seen everyone leave the house and they would have been in a repair van or some such thing and then got themselves through the gated community security. In, out. Device planted. Job done. And since then they had followed him everywhere and killed innocent people along the way.

There was a tap on the door. Undemanding. No threat. A secret lover's tap. Raglan saw headlights sweep across the window. He lifted the chair away and unlocked the door, then stepped back letting the visitor enter without further invitation. The door opened slowly.

'It's me,' said Voss. 'I'm alone. The police have gone.'

She stayed at the threshold, wary of walking into violence.

Raglan gave a mental nod to her professionalism. He stepped into view and saw she had pulled on a sweat top and sneakers. He held the door and gestured her inside, then checked beyond the door and closed it. She held the Glock at her side, still wary of the Englishman, uncertain whether he was a killer, official or otherwise.

'They believed you?' he said.

She nodded. 'I explained why I was staying here. If it gets back to the detectives investigating the senator's murder or to Kim Burton, then it will raise a red flag. They'll want to know if the shooting here is connected. Am I connected? Well, I am now.' She looked around the room. There was no sign of luggage. The bathroom door was closed. Raglan watched as she nudged it open and saw the blood-soaked dressings in the waste bin. She turned back into the room.

'You hurt bad?'

'No. A ricochet. The stitches will hold.'

She kept her gaze on him. If he had dug out a bullet and stitched himself up then he knew what he was doing. It told her more about him. Of what he was capable of.

He pointed towards the chair for her to sit as he perched on the edge of the bed. He lifted the bathroom's tooth glass, rattling the squashed bullet fragments. 'I dug these out of the mattress. No point asking you to get them to forensics. It'll be nine millimetre and untraceable.' He returned the glass back to the side table. 'Tell me again how you tracked me to DC.'

Voss went along with it and repeated everything she had told him earlier, but the Glock was still in her hand, resting on her lap.

'One of your people questioned my friend at Lisa Mayfield's house, asking about me.'

She nodded. 'My partner. You'd left already. Me too. We weren't that interested in you after we called off surveillance. We were doing the Agency a favour.' She shrugged. 'That's not unusual on home turf.'

'And you didn't have anyone go into the house before that?'

'There was no reason. What, you mean unofficially?'

'To plant a bug maybe?'

'Believe it or not, we need court orders for wiretaps and traces. You weren't on any kind of watchlist.' She checked herself. Raglan was probing for a reason. 'You've been tagged?'

'Tracking device. Nothing audible.' He turned the jacket's collar.

'Where?' she said.

'Run your finger along the stitches.'

Her eyebrows arched when her fingertips found it. 'We don't have anything that small. We're pretty sophisticated at putting a wire on somebody. Nothing like this, though.' She expected Raglan to question her further. He remained silent. Waiting her out. 'And so what do we do now?' she said.

'We? You go back to wherever it is you're supposed to be. There is no "we".'

'Raglan, you're a wanted man. My people and the police won't let a senator's murder slip away from them.'

'I'm involved in something.'

'Death and destruction are what you're involved with. I want to know what I'm letting myself in for here.'

'Agent Voss, you're not letting yourself into anything.'

'I lied to the police. I covered for you.'

'I saved your life. You owed me.'

'Not if I thought you had information that could help get me back in the field. I have a crap assignment to go to. Give me something.'

'I work alone. What I know I keep to myself.'

'I can help for at least another twenty-four hours. After that I'm up before a disciplinary committee and my career is over.'

Raglan sensed her determination. He suspected he knew what drove her. 'You lost people in a raid. You want a chance to redeem yourself. I'm not a priest. I don't absolve transgressions. You screwed up – you live with it.'

He saw the colour creep up her neck and knuckles whiten as she gripped the Glock. He'd hit a nerve. Deliberately. What was important now was her reaction. Was she in sufficient control to let the hurtful accusation pass?

'I don't know how you got that information,' she said, her throat tight, her voice controlled. 'Yes, I led a team and bad guys killed two of my people. They ambushed us.'

He saw her eyes moisten. Was it with anger or regret?

'I won't stop following you, Raglan. Not now. If I was a problem to you before, you wouldn't have saved my life.'

'I did it to find out if you were responsible for murdering my friends. If you were, then I'd have killed you.'

There was no doubt in her mind that the matter-of-fact answer was sincere. 'I have contacts. You're going to need all the help you can get.'

'I'm a suspect in a double homicide. Maybe three deaths. And you're willing to help a fugitive? You don't add up.'

'And you never follow your instincts? Mine got me into

trouble on that raid but that's the roll of the dice. You're trouble, Raglan, I can see that, but there's a part of me that thinks you're on to something bigger than you're telling me, and if the Bureau doesn't want me around this case then I'm volunteering.'

Raglan threw the spent bullets from the glass, blew out the dust fragments and tipped in a generous amount of whiskey. He offered it to her after taking a mouthful himelf. She took it and waited. Raglan let the liquor settle on the cuts in his mouth. He studied her a moment longer. He picked up his phone and ran his thumb along the slider until he came to the pictures of the men at Luis Reyes's house.

'These men are protecting a major drug dealer. I shot one of them who tried to kill me.' He handed her the phone.

She studied the image. 'I saw the news the day you killed him. So, it *was* you.' She looked up at him. 'Two cops shot in Georgetown. One dead. You helped the other.'

'Then went after the shooter. His name is—'

'Luis Reyes,' she said. 'I remember his name being mentioned.'

'He's long-gone. His minders have spirited him away. There are more pictures.'

She slid her thumb across the screen. She froze. Her head jerked. She dropped the glass as she clutched the phone with both hands. She raised her eyes to Raglan. She looked as though she had seen a ghost. She turned the phone and pointed at one of the men. 'His name is Lennie Elliot.'

'And that means what?' said Raglan.

'He was my informer. He led me to a major drug-money laundering operation. Me and my team went in. It was an ambush. That's what finished me at the Bureau. I'm reassigned a desk while the man responsible is this damned close. There's a connection, Raglan. Drugs, money laundering and murder. I was close to shutting down something major. I can see that now. And I had to be stopped.'

Raglan reached forwards and eased the phone from her grasp, then picked up her glass and poured in another double shot.

'Maybe,' he said. His mind raced. Luis Reyes had a drug-smuggling operation. Money was being laundered. Arms paid for. 'Maybe,' he said again. 'All right, this might tie in to why I am here. I came to find a man who's gone missing. Bob de Vere, the plane mechanic in Florida, was my first contact. He was killed the night I left. Then I hook up with a stranger who helps me and *he*'s murdered. In the middle of this is the missing man, who works for a government agency. He's left documents implicating other government officials but he was working secretly with the senator. You think it's a coincidence they attacked him the night I was there?'

She studied the whiskey for a moment. She was hot-wired into him now. Lennie Elliot joined her and Raglan at the hip. 'If they wanted to kill you, they could have done it at any time.'

Raglan's thoughts unfolded the past days. It was obvious he was a target. But he was a target who served a purpose. He didn't want to tell Voss about Casey Zeller. Not yet. It was obvious to him now that when the two men attacked Zeller's house before he got Anne Zeller to safety, they were there to kill her. Not him. He was being set up and her death would have taken its place with Bob de Vere's and TJ's in the mounting evidence against him.

'They needed me alive until tonight. I get pinned with three homicides because there's evidence I visited the victims. Then if they had killed me in the raid tonight, I would have been seen as one of the attackers. Case closed. No one asks any more questions. Whoever they are they wanted to find which senator the missing man was working with. I led them straight to him. They wanted him dead because he was the one man in authority who could expose and stop them. They had me tracked every step of the way. I'm the fall guy. Only I didn't die.'

She swallowed the whiskey and reached out the glass for a refill. As he tipped the bottle she said, 'When we followed you back in Florida you went to the Space Centre with the boy and then to the Warbird Museum.'

'That's right.'

'You knew we were following you.'

'That was the idea. You follow a tourist. You call off the tail.'

She nursed her drink.

'You weren't wearing your jacket then. So they couldn't have traced you. The killer knew where you were going to be. They must have already known the mechanic was your contact.'

'And tonight they came here to finish me off in case I had discovered anything.'

'And have you?'

'Enough to make them keep trying to kill me. Now I choose the ground and everything changes.'

'How?'

'I flush them out and kill them first.'

47

Voss readied herself for what they had planned. No matter how great the shock of seeing her informer alive, there was still the nagging doubt that she was about to betray the very organization she had been prepared to give her life for. Lying to the police and helping a suspect in a major homicide investigation contradicted everything she believed in.

She had always felt there was a daemon that sat on her shoulder, which had taken her through gun battles and assaults. Its whisper in her ear had saved her on numerous occasions: instincts honed, she had acted, and survived. And when it had gone wrong, when her team had died, she hadn't been able to comprehend why the spirit had deserted her. She just knew she was on her own now. And her choice tormented her. Raglan or the Bureau? Everything she believed about herself was on the line, so she decided she would trust herself, even if no one else did.

No, that wasn't true. Raglan did. He had taken a risk on her. And saved her life.

She showered and dressed for work. She clipped on her holster, checked the Glock, and let her palm brush the gold shield clipped to her belt. Too late now to change her mind.

She closed the door behind her. She couldn't help but smile. That old thrill of the chase was back.

Mindful of the registration-plate cameras, she had taken a hire car rather than her own. Voss pulled into the Pentagon parking lot. She wasn't obliged to go through the same procedure as Raglan had during his visit. Jack Swain was usually at his desk during lunch but today he was running late. His secretary told her he had an appointment in the city. She waited in the main reception area. It was too late for sightseeing tours for the public and there were only two senior officers waiting in the seating area. She glanced up at the large screen that listed waiting visitors and whom they were waiting for. One was a Marine Corps major waiting to see someone in logistics, the other an army colonel waiting to see DoDEA, the Department of Defense Education Activity. A part of her hoped he was there to offer some educational advice to those who had made some of the dumb decisions in recent years. Too many service personnel had died because of them. Her name was listed as 'Jenna Voss waiting for J. Swain'. No titles. No indication of what agency either served. She waited an hour and then another until she was summoned to his office.

'I'm usually advised by the DC Field Office about visits from the Bureau, Special Agent Voss,' said Swain after his secretary had accompanied Voss upstairs and delivered her to his office. He gestured for her to take a seat.

'Time isn't on our side, Deputy Director Swain. I'm grateful you agreed to fit me into your busy schedule.'

'What can I do for you?'

'I'm here about Senator Thomas.'

'Yes, of course. I had a call in the early hours giving me a heads up.' Jack Swain damned near bit his tongue. What the hell was wrong with him admitting that? It immediately gave the sharp-looking agent sitting opposite him a line of inquiry. Which she immediately picked up.

'Would that have been an official call?' said Voss.

He hesitated. 'It was someone who has been working for us.'

'Can you tell us who that individual is?'

'I can't.' He smiled apologetically. 'National security.'

'We are looking for one man who we believe is involved in these killings.'

'Do you have a name?'

She ignored the question. 'Why would anyone contact you about the senator? Were you involved in any investigation that would have interested him? And if there is someone you can't tell me about then we'd like to know what involvement that individual had with the senator prior to the killing.'

'I'm sorry, Special Agent Voss, I really cannot discuss this any further, other than to say we were watching the senator because he had taken the unprecedented step of hiring personal bodyguards.'

'Then you thought him under threat?'

'He had made no such report to the relevant authorities.'

'So why would you become involved?'

'Because we were concerned that he was in contact with one of our employees who has gone missing. And we didn't know if that event was connected in any way with the senator.'

'And is it?'

'We think not.' Swain could lay a smokescreen without a second thought.

'This man we are looking for is wanted in connection with two other murders and a killing in a shootout in downtown D.C. The man's name is Raglan. He is a foreign national. An Englishman.' She watched as he spread his hands in a small gesture of helplessness, of not knowing. He gave no sign of recognizing Raglan's name. 'We also believe he stole documents from the senator's safe and that these documents implicate high-level government officials. So, you can see that national security might well be compromised. We might both be looking for the same thing.'

Jack Swain's mind raced. Raglan had told him he knew where the documents were and Voss was telling him they believed Raglan already had them. Raglan had no reason to lie but an investigating FBI agent would have every reason to draw Swain out and add confusion. How had they linked him to the senator? He remained calm, seemingly disinterested.

'So why did you connect me to the senator and why would you think there are documents of a sensitive nature involved?' he asked.

Voss took her time. She kept her gaze firmly on Swain. Wanting him to think she knew more than she did. She shrugged. 'I thought you might have been working together on an investigation involving those documents. The senator gave the police your name before he died and said his safe had been raided and files of a secret nature taken.' She stood. 'But as you say, whatever information you have pertains to a national security issue, so I guess we'll take our investigation elsewhere.' She extended her hand. 'Thank you for your time, Director Swain.'

Swain held her firm grip a moment longer than necessary. 'Let me assure you that the person we had watching the senator had no involvement in events last night.'

'It's good to have that reassurance. Thank you. We have some leads on the man we are after and I think we'll soon have him in custody. Men like him leave a trail.' She smiled. 'Dead bodies mostly.'

Swain's secretary escorted Voss from the building, leaving the director to gaze out into the central courtyard. Raglan had told him that the senator did not have the documents but now the FBI said differently. Did the FBI woman buy his lie that he had someone shadowing the senator because of Casey's disappearance? It was one way of giving Raglan a cover if anyone discovered his involvement. He needed to check out the FBI interest and, more importantly, he needed to find Raglan.

How much time did Swain have left? His overdue return to the Pentagon had been the result of a meeting with his oncologist. He had known many effective killers but his pancreatic cancer was the most deadly assassin yet. Even more lethal than Raglan. And now the Englishman was being hunted. Which of them would die first?

48

Raglan departed soon after Voss left the motel. He left the tagged jacket in his room. It was doubtful another attack would be attempted so soon after the previous failed attempt and especially in daylight. They would track him when he was on the street before trying to kill him again. As far as those watching their monitors were concerned, Raglan was still bunked up in his room recovering from his wounds. There was an old windcheater in the Harley's panniers for the ride out to Stafford.

He and Voss had agreed on a plan of action for the afternoon and night. Raglan wanted to be back at Casey Zeller's house in Stafford soon after the construction crews left the site. It was up to Voss to question Jack Swain under the guise of being involved in the investigation into the senator's murder. There was no reason any of the genuine investigators would get in touch with Swain; they had no knowledge of him or of his involvement with Casey Zeller and Raglan. Jack Swain was a nobody as far as anyone in the Bureau's or police detectives' investigation was concerned. It was up to Voss to convince him otherwise. Raglan needed to shake the tree and see if Swain revealed anything about Zeller or Zeller's investigation into the illegal armament purchases, or if he acknowledged Raglan. And, most crucial of all, whether Swain would break cover if he was panicked by Voss's questions.

Though panic was the wrong word to apply to Swain. Rapid action was more appropriate. Raglan had been brought in to find Zeller. And the fear that lay behind that happening was the material Zeller had found and with whom he had shared it. Raglan went through every stage of his own involvement. He had been tagged in Florida and that's how the kill team followed him to DC. But before that, only Jack Swain and perhaps Zeller had known about Raglan getting in touch with Bob de Vere.

He checked to see if Zeller's back-door key was as he had left it, in a seashell with a small piece of leaf beneath. The leaf was gone. As he suspected, someone was going in and out of the house. And, like Raglan, the intruder knew how to get past the alarm. He reversed the Honda into the double garage and closed the doors, taking the assault rifle with him. He cleared the alarm, locked the door behind him and went through the house. The bookcase had not been disturbed. The books he left as markers were as he had left them. He bent down and double-checked. The hidden screws for the back panel were still concealed behind the shelving. Raglan went through the house and into the back yard, replaced the key in the shell, went back through the yard door, turned the latch to lock it, and then reset the alarm. Returning to Zeller's office he lifted down the books he had previously stacked, carefully making sure he could replace them again in the same order. If the intruder had been in the house since Raglan's last visit and checked the shelves he would have seen they had been moved. Raglan unscrewed the panel, lifted out the files and reassembled everything to how it had been.

All he had to do now was wait.

The first of the construction workers began to leave. Voices were raised in raucous banter. Power tools and hammering fell silent. His guess was the intruder would come across the back fence, around the side of the house and in through the back door. Raglan stretched out on the couch, giving the wound in his side as much rest as he could. He read one of the file's contents again. Thanks to Senator Thomas, he knew that the shell companies were fronted by ghosts. Behind them were the real perpetrators of the illegal arm shipments. He felt certain that those involved had a purpose beyond skimming money from the US government. That these men thought themselves to be patriots, which meant the arms were going somewhere they thought would benefit American interests. Now that he had a good idea of those known as the Council, he needed proof of their intent to commit conspiracy. Zeller had gathered evidence linking them to the illegal armament purchases but nothing that brought proof positive to the table. What Raglan needed was to find the arms cache. And if he did that, he might find the assassin who had slain two of his friends.

Raglan lowered the file and listened. A creak of a wooden fence and a dull thud as someone landed on the ground. Raglan checked the windows at front and back. He saw a man had dropped into the yard at the rear. He wore a thick canvas jacket, plaid shirt, work boots, a sweat top with the hood pulled over a woollen headwarmer. His face was obscured. Raglan heard the lock turn, the alarm beep and then fall silent. The man grunted with effort; then there was a clunk of boots hitting the ground and the whisper of unshod feet on the wooden floor along the passage. The man went into Zeller's study. Raglan moved quietly, listening to the sound of the unsuspecting intruder shift the office chair and drop books on to the desk's surface. Raglan edged towards the study door and then watched the hunched figure move the shelf to expose the screws to the hidden compartment.

'Hello, Casey,' he said.

49

Casey Zeller twisted in shock; his back slammed into the bookcase, books tumbled. But he was agile and quickly on his feet, shock turning to relief. 'Raglan! I thought you were dead! Dammit. I'm glad to see you.'

Zeller recovered his poise. He had broken cover and returned again, he told Raglan, because he thought Raglan had died in the shooting at the senator's house.

'It was close enough,' said Raglan.

'When did you realize it was me coming into the house?' Zeller said.

'It took a while. At first I thought the hit team had a clean-up detail in place and a means of bypassing the alarm. Then I figured the boot print in the garage was made after the Feds and Sheriff's department had been here after you disappeared and that it was deliberate. I hoped it was you and that you wanted me to see it. That's when you keyed the senator's address into the satnav. If it had been there beforehand then the Feds would have checked and questioned him. That information was for me.'

Zeller smiled. 'I hoped you'd figure it out, but when I saw the news I thought I'd signed your death warrant.'

'You weren't followed here?' said Raglan.

'No. I'm clean.'

Raglan ushered him through to the front room so that they could observe both sides of the house. His first question was about his wife.

'A long way from here. Pennsylvania.'

'There's no one there I know.'

'That was the idea. It's an old friend of hers. No one else knows about her either. Time for you to go, Casey. You need to get out of here until this blows over. It's a fourteen-hour train ride to Toronto from where she is, but if the weather holds she can drive there in six. She doesn't know it yet but I've already found a small hotel in the city for her. That was the next part of my plan to get her out of the States if I had to. This is over for you now. I've got a score to settle. As well as the attack on Senator Thomas, whoever's dogging my footsteps killed Bob de Vere and an innocent man who helped me.'

'I'm sorry to hear that. Dammit, this mess has caused good people to die.'

Raglan keyed in Anne Zeller's burner number and handed it to Zeller. 'Speak to your wife. She needs to know you're OK. Tell her to go to the Orchard Hotel in Toronto.' Raglan stood. 'I'll make the coffee.'

Raglan stayed out of the room long enough for the man's voice to subdue and quieten. When he returned he saw the tension had drained from Zeller's face. His eyes were moist and there was a slight tremble in his hand as he took the coffee mug from Raglan.

'I can't thank you enough.'

'You'll go?'

'I'd rather stay and see this thing through.'

'You can't. The moment you're seen, whatever's going on will end in one of two ways. You'll be shot on sight or they'll panic and shut down their plan for months. Maybe both. We'll have lost whatever momentum we've gained.'

Zeller nodded; there was a lot to go through before he left to join his wife. 'OK. But we need to put some pieces together now that you're still alive and kicking. There might still be a chance to unravel what I discovered.'

Raglan listened attentively as the man he had come to find explained the how and the why of his disappearance.

He had gone out that night and run his usual five-mile route. For days he had noticed he was being watched and knew damn well it was because he had got close to a powerful cartel of hawks, here and abroad, who were gathering an arsenal to wage a foreign war and put America in its midst. He had planned as far ahead as he could. His cache of clothing was a couple of miles from home. Had he left making a run for it much longer they would have moved on him, and that meant they would snatch Anne and use her as a bargaining chip. It was time to get out. He followed the track he knew so well through the trees – they would never follow him there – and retrieved his cache. Three hours later he had returned to the furnished room he had rented a month before where he kept a ten-year-old pickup. Everything bought and paid for using the false identity he had prepared in advance.

That first night away from his wife and his home the guilt he felt at abandoning her had seared him. It was assuaged only by the knowledge that he was protecting her the only way he knew how. He stayed away for two days, knowing the various agencies would descend and put her through the wringer. She was resilient and that would stand her in good stead, because once the Feds and the Pentagon cops each questioned her she'd be exhausted, but safe. Knowing her life was no longer in danger had eased the tightness he felt in his chest at her distress. When he thought the coast was clear he mingled with the construction crews, easily passing himself off as one of them as he moved from house to house wearing a construction worker's belt and hard hat.

Observing his own house wasn't difficult. He watched as the investigators flooded his home and questioned his wife. He had planned for this eventuality meticulously. It was a clandestine operation in all but official name. Everything hinged on bringing in an outsider who was an asset to the intelligence services, someone he trusted implicitly and who, as soon as they arrived, would get his wife to safety. He waited patiently every night in the forest until Raglan had appeared at the house. Zeller had stood by helplessly as he saw a man he recognized from his investigation go into the house. He was part of a kill team and he never came out. Soon after, his wife left with a suitcase, accompanied by Raglan. Once darkness fell Zeller recovered the dead man. He was now buried under the foundations of a nearby house.

'Did you know there were surveillance cameras here?' said Raglan.

Zeller nodded. 'I put them in so I could watch out for Anne on my phone link.'

'And I pulled the plug. Sorry. Thought it was the bad guys' set-up.'

'Did the senator tell you anything before they killed him?' said Zeller.

'He was on your side and was shocked when I told him the names in the dossier. I was about to return here and hand it over to him. I let you down on that, Casey. I didn't know they'd put a tracking device on me. They had a kill team ready and primed. It didn't take a genius to quickly check the address once they located me. Senator Thomas said there was a doubt in your mind about Jack Swain.'

Zeller slumped into a chair and tugged on his boots. 'I don't know.'

'He pulled you into the clandestine op to investigate the illegal arms deals.'

'Yeah, and maybe that was to see if the conspiracy could be exposed and whether it could implicate him.'

'Is he involved?'

Zeller shook his head. 'I can't pin it down. I left a flash drive hidden. The information in the files can be seized and destroyed. That's my backup. Did you find it?'

'The drive's safe. You didn't encrypt it.'

'Couldn't in case anything happened to me. It had to be accessible to read.'

'Well, I put a password on it: 26-9-7-26-1-7. A six-year-old could break it in an hour but for now it might help delay anyone if it's found.'

Casey logged the number in his memory. 'The drive?'

'It's hidden,' said Raglan.

A smile of relief creased Zeller's stubbled face. 'I knew you'd find it. The shit pit is deep,' he said. 'I don't know who's in on this. Senator Thomas was my one big hope of digging them out.'

Raglan hunched forwards. 'I'm going to give Swain a

chance to clear himself. I'm going to tell him that I know the documents are here.'

'You mean really give them to him?'

'Yes.'

'Raglan, then it's game over. If he's a part of it, he destroys the evidence. If he's not then we need to know he'll pursue the investigation before whatever's going to happen blows up in our face.'

'I think it's worth the risk. You shared your doubts about Swain with Senator Thomas. If it turns out he's involved, we can use the flash drive. Once we bring these people out of the shadows then the information goes straight to the Feds and the State Department. But not yet, not until we know who we can trust.'

'Swain won't take the bait.'

'Someone will. Can you take me through this investigation?'

Zeller reached for the bottle of whiskey on the coffee table. He gestured with the bottle. 'Pleased to see you made yourself at home.'

Raglan shrugged. 'I pretty much lived here for a couple of nights. You need a bigger sofa.' He let Zeller spice up their coffee.

'I reckon it started a few years back in Venezuela,' he said.

'When I did that job there a few years ago?' said Raglan.

'This was later. I was Defense Intelligence, and Swain was CIA and on his way up the greasy pole. I got wind of a big push by the Agency to get rid of Venezuela's president. You know how it works. DIA does military threat, the Agency does political.'

'President Maduro ran a drug cartel.'

Zeller checked the window for anything untoward outside. It was clear. He nodded. 'Cartel de los Soles. Ran it through Honduras and Belize, Mexico and into the US. Bought plenty of well-armed muscle to go with it. A lot of people ended up dead. Bad dead. Skinned alive, decapitated. Strung up from bridges. Gutted like fish. Very serious dead.'

'Luis Reyes,' said Raglan. One small piece in the jigsaw fitting into place.

'You found him?'

'Thanks to your wife remembering where you went on your days off.'

Zeller hunkered back down, eager to share his thoughts about his investigation. 'Reyes had the best trafficking route. And Maduro was supplying heavy weapons to FARC, the so-called revolutionary armed forces across the border in Colombia. They were little more than his personal militia, ready at the border to do his bidding and provide an escort for his drug shipments. The Colombian government was pissed, the US was pissed, but he turned the border into the Wild West. And if you create chaos you control the situation. But that was just the start of it. I thought I was following one trail at first, but then it got more complicated.'

Raglan listened without interruption as Casey Zeller recounted the start of his investigation when he was stationed in Venezuela. The country was on its knees. America was doing everything it could to get Maduro out of power. Venezuela's oil supplies were run right down. He was mining millions of tons of gold and using the revolutionaries to escort his gold for shipments to Iran. Iran took gold in exchange for oil supplies.

Raglan lifted the file. 'Then all of this has to do with the US secretly arming an insurrection in Venezuela against FARC? To help the Colombians secure their border with Venezuela? That doesn't make sense.'

'It's not that. That's not even the game plan. It's bigger. Before I made a run for it I was getting close to Luis Reyes and the people helping him. The Council, as I called them.'

'He's been lifted by whoever's bought him off. He's not here, I'm sure of it. He'll be back in the jungle. He has protection.'

Zeller rattled off what he knew. 'His network is being used to get the illegally purchased weapons from here to Central America. My guess is Honduras, that's his home turf, or maybe somewhere on the border with Guatemala. I kept asking myself: why do we need to get illegal armaments down there? I think Jack Swain knows. When they set up the Clandestine Service he came across from the Agency. An ex-CIA man running clandestine ops with a military angle. Now, he's either getting too near the heat and is wary of getting burnt, or he knows how close I got and wanted me out of the way. No matter what agency I thought might help, I had no idea who was involved. You were my best hope.'

Raglan tried to assimilate the fragments of information. 'They've got heavy hitters on my back. Some are ex-Mossad and Israeli special forces. The best. And I killed a former Army Ranger who was a Middle East specialist. There's a connection there somewhere to Iran.'

Zeller said nothing for a moment but Raglan saw that the information meant something. Zeller's eye widened.

'Back when I was stationed in Venezuela their strongman vice-president, Tareck El Aissami, set up links with the

Islamic Revolutionary Guard. The Venezuelans were doing deals with Hezbollah. They even had companies of them, fifty strong apiece, at the port where the gold was being shipped. There were a hundred and more Iranian tankers sailing from Iran to Venezuela in one year. That's a lot of gold heading for Iran and their Revolutionary Guard.'

Raglan shook his head. 'This is way beyond drug deals. Put the pieces together. Mossad, Israeli special forces, drug trafficking. Jump ahead a bit. What if the people you uncovered did a deal with rogue Mossad units? Their government would love to take out the Iranians – unofficially, that is. The DIA looks for military threats. What if someone in the DIA helped create one? Someone who had already been involved in trying to get rid of Maduro and knew the trafficking routes both to the States and then shipping and flights to Iran?'

'Swain?'

'He's a candidate. At least that. He ran ops for two agencies.'

Casey pointed to a folder. 'Who do we trust to use what's in there? If it's Swain behind this then we don't know who among his old pals at the Agency is backing him. Senator Thomas was my only hope. Before I left I tried to blow the thing wide apart. I got a copy of that file to a reporter at the *Washington Post*. The journalist was killed. The file was never mentioned, no mention of discovery, and no one at the *Post* knew anything about it. She was an investigative reporter and she played a tight game. No sooner had I got it to her than she was dead. We can try again, there are other journalists, but if these bastards get wind of it then more innocent people are going to die. I don't know how they got to her except that they were tapping my phone from the get-go. She phoned me here one night. Damned if I know how she got my number, but she did, and it killed her.'

'We have to deal with this. I have a contact in MI6 but they might not have any choice but to share it,' said Raglan. 'It could end up on CIA desks within hours. There won't be an intelligence agency that won't know about it. First, we need to get Jack Swain to show his hand, one way or the other.'

'How?'

'I have somebody already giving him a prod.' He swallowed the whiskey. 'Believe it or not, she's FBI.'

50

Jenna Voss left her meeting with Jack Swain, making certain she wasn't being followed from the Pentagon. Once she had returned the hire car and got back to the motel she checked out. She wanted to be one step ahead of anyone trying to link her presence with the shooting there. Word would have reached the DC Field Office, and someone might have joined up the dots. They needn't have bothered. Voss knew her visit to Jack Swain was as good as poking a stick into a hornet's nest. Voss's phone rang. Kim Burton was already in the loop. Voss answered.

'Yes, Kim,' she said.

Kim Burton's voice was measured. Patient. Like a teacher or a parent explaining to a naughty child. 'Jenna, I'm doing you a favour. I'm not your immediate supervisor but I'm telling you that you are digging a grave for your career.'

Voss felt a warm glow of satisfaction. If Kim Burton was going to try to persuade her one last time to go back to Clarksburg then Jack Swain had reached out and questioned the FBI team investigating the senator's killing as soon as she had left his office. And that call would have alerted Kim Burton.

'I'm pretty busy right now, Kim,' said Voss, politely defiant. How long would it take to crack the cool, seasoned diplomacy of the senior agent? Not long. About seven seconds.

'Fuck you, Jenna.'

'Having a bad day, Kim?'

'You listen to me, dammit. God knows what you are up to but you have no authority whatsoever to even approach Jack Swain at the Pentagon. As of now, you are officially suspended from duty.'

'You don't have that authority, Kim. We don't even share the same ladies' room. Your division is downtown. Mine is four hours' away.'

'Then why in God's name aren't you back there?'

'Because I think I have a lead in the senator's killing and I want to know what the Deputy Director of the Defense Clandestine Service has to do with it. I might not have hard evidence and you might think my instincts are blown but I have a gut feeling about him.'

Kim Burton took a deep breath. She needed to calm down. Voss heard her do it. Cage-rattling was fun.

'Your gut feelings have been lethal before, Jenna. I'm worried about you, for your mental health. You're armed and you might be dangerous. I am telling you now to present yourself to the DC Field Office and surrender your badge and your weapon.'

'The mental-health angle lies at the Bureau's door. Are you or they prepared to listen to me? Do you think it possible that the DC Field Office might have checked back and seen that there is a missing clandestine officer at the Pentagon? That they stripped out the computers from his house weeks ago? Have they and the Pentagon police and the Stafford County Sheriff's Department made any attempt to question Jack Swain before now? The missing man was one of his own. Their inquiry was cursory. They might as well have asked him what he had for dinner the night before his man went missing. All Swain will say is that whatever he does know is covered by national security. You need to lean on him.'

'If you have anything, turn it over.' Kim's voice was level, but tight.

'Why would Swain phone you if he wasn't rattled by me going to his office and questioning him? I didn't accuse him of anything.'

'Jenna… you're talking crazy talk. Come on now…' Kim's tone was soothing now. Cat-stroking. Calming. 'Let me help you. I will take any information you have and share it with Homicide and my investigators. We would never turn away from evidence.'

'I gave the Bureau evidence once before and it was ignored. I identified the man who betrayed me and my team in Miami and it was ignored. I won't be ignored again, Kim. I saw him again. He's involved in this whole mess.'

'Who is?'

'Lennie Elliot.'

'Who the hell is he?'

'My informer in Miami. The one who led us to the biggest money-laundering operation in years. Lennie Elliot, Kim. The bastard is alive, and he is involved in whatever is going on here.'

She ended the call. Kim Burton would be chewing razor blades. She would be so pissed off she might just reopen the failed Miami operation to see if there were any links between drug-money laundering, a missing intelligence officer and the death of a senator. It was a long shot. But then so were her chances of living long enough to hang out with the Englishman. She pressed a speed-dial button and pressed the phone to her ear.

'What happened?' said Raglan.

'Swain denied everything. Said he had no knowledge. Said national security was the reason he couldn't tell me more. I played it down but let him know his name had surfaced. And I have just had a call from Kim Burton telling me to back off. Swain must have called her the moment I left his office.'

'Could she be involved?' said Raglan.

The question jolted Voss. Kim Burton was an astute and ambitious woman. There was enough animosity between them now for them never to speak to each other again. 'No. She's not. I'd stake my life on it,' said Voss without hesitation.

'You might have to,' said Raglan. 'OK. Next. Phone the cops. Tell them you've been given a tip-off that the missing motorcycle taken from TJ Jones's apartment is located at an address in Stafford. Tell them to make a silent approach. There are armed men inside the house.'

She memorized the house number and street Raglan gave her. Voss couldn't second-guess what Raglan was planning. This was no time to ask. 'When?'

'One hour,' said Raglan. 'Get to Stafford. There's a late-night coffee shop near the mall. Wait there.' The phone went dead.

Voss gauged the time it would take for her to get out to

Stafford. If Raglan wanted her there, then he wanted a way out back to the city. She keyed in the number. The pace was quickening. The trap about to be sprung. Three thudding heartbeats later the call was answered.

'Detective Delaney, this is Special Agent Jenna Voss. I have a lead for you.'

'I'm listening.'

Voss gave Zeller's address. 'There's evidence hidden there pertinent to the TJ Jones murder and quite possibly the death of Senator Thomas. I'm giving you heads up until my people get their ducks in a row. Go in quietly and approach with caution, detective, there are armed men in the house.'

Delaney was not the kind of man to interrupt or question how the information came into Voss's possession. Those facts could be cleared up later. Delaney ended the call.

'You're welcome,' she said to the silent phone.

Raglan turned to Casey Zeller. 'Cops will be here in a little over an hour.' It was getting dark. Raglan checked the window. The street was deserted. The looming shadows of the half-built house opposite was the perfect place to be when the cops got there. Raglan pressed a speed dial on his phone. 'But we need more help if we're to move forwards with this.' It didn't take long for the call to be answered. 'Maguire, how long can you keep what I'm about to tell you from becoming official?'

'As long as it takes,' said Maguire. 'Or until I really have no choice.'

Raglan deliberated for all of thirty seconds. 'There's some

kind of link between rogue Mossad units and gold being shipped to Iran. What's going on in the big wide world?'

Raglan heard what he thought to be a sigh of exasperation. 'Jesus, Raglan, you're close to something big. It's been brewing for a couple of years. How the hell you picked up on it I don't know.'

'Mainly because they've been trying to kill me.'

'Good to hear they've failed. The Iranians are using gold from Venezuela to buy arms from China; China gets around any American sanctions or hard-nosed trade deals by having Iranian oil thrown in on the deal. China needs oil and Iran has sold what's left of its soul to China in a major trade deal. Now China has a firmer foothold in the region. The Iranians have new friends.'

Raglan saw the pieces fall into place. 'Maguire, find out what you can about Central America. Especially Honduras. Any of those hotspot countries. Heavy shipments going in by road or air from here. Small airstrips. Anything on satellite.'

'We don't have any overflights. We can ask the CIA.'

'Not yet. We have to make sure of what we're dealing with here. We don't know who the players are in the game.'

'What game is that?' said Maguire.

'Regime change pushes out China. Hawks here arm and equip Iranian opposition and insurgents. Do we know who that is?'

Maguire went silent.

'You know more than you're telling me, Maguire.'

'You're not cleared for what I know.'

'I need to know what I'm up against.'

There was another pause. In his mind's eye Raglan saw

Maguire sitting at his uncluttered desk, his pen tapping out a slow rhythm as he decided how much sensitive information to give out.

'Short version is this,' said Maguire. 'The USA has backed away from Iranian opposition groups. They still want a diplomatic solution.'

Raglan knew his instincts hadn't failed him. 'The hawks won't tolerate that. Who would benefit from being armed with US weapons?'

'The Mojahedin-e-Khalq. They supported Iraq in the Iran–Iraq war in the eighties. The US State Department had them flagged as a terrorist-supporting organization; that was until 2012. More recently there was behind-the-scenes contact made with them.'

'Officially?' said Raglan.

'No. But the Mojahedin-e-Khalq have connections with people of influence in the USA. There is absolutely no proof of any kind that it involves anyone in the administration.'

'Maguire, there are others deep in the shadows. That's what Casey Zeller discovered. It's going to kick off. Someone's going to start a war. A big one.'

51

Raglan instructed Zeller to put the dossier back behind the panelling. 'We need to give the cops time to get here and the visitors to find it,' he said. 'Can you fire up the router again? Get your inside cameras working?'

Zeller nodded and went through to his study as Raglan wiped down the assault rifle used at the senator's house and emptied its magazine. He followed Zeller into the study. 'Don't touch this. We need it here for when the scalphunters come.'

He left Zeller to replace the documents, went back to the sitting room window and checked the street. It was quiet. He keyed in Jack Swain's number. Swain answered:

'Raglan, I phoned twice.'

'My phone was off. My wound opened up; I had to deal with it.'

He heard Swain's hesitation. 'You said you weren't badly hurt.'

'I'm not, but the damn thing started bleeding again. I have to make sure it doesn't get infected. It's slowed me down. What do you have for me?'

'I had an FBI agent here. They have linked you to the senator and the missing file.'

'Not possible,' Raglan lied. 'There is no connection.'

'It was a female agent. She said you're the prime suspect in his killing and other deaths. She said Senator Thomas was alive when they got to the scene. That he told them you had raided his safe and taken the file.'

'She's lying. Check her out,' Raglan told him, knowing that's exactly what Swain had done, showing himself as being in Swain's corner.

'I did. No one knows anything about her being involved in the senator's investigation.'

'Then someone's playing you,' said Raglan, heaping further uncertainty on top of Swain's doubts. 'Listen to me, Jack, I've found where the documents are.' Before Swain could react Raglan threw out the baited hook. 'And I know where Casey Zeller is.'

He heard Swain gasp. 'Jesus, Raglan. Are you serious?'

'Long story cut short. Casey Zeller's body is buried under the foundations of a house being built near his own.'

'How the hell do you know that?'

'I got it out of one of the shooters before I killed him at the senator's.'

He heard the half-second moment of doubt in Swain's voice. As he had expected. 'You never mentioned it when we spoke.'

'I had to check it out and see if it added up. It was exactly as the guy described. Why would he lie?'

'Then who has the missing file?' Swain asked.

'It's still hidden in Zeller's house. The Feds and the cops did a lousy job of searching. It's behind a panel at the back of his bookcase in his study.'

'If you know then get it.'

'I can't. I don't know who's in play, Jack, and I'm in no condition to take them on. I have to get out of here. If I end up in hospital with this gunshot wound turned bad, the medics will call in the cops. If the cops and the Feds know my name and that I'm involved then I need to get out.'

'Raglan, this doesn't add up. How did you find out about the dossier?'

'Something his wife said when I first spoke to her. It didn't sound important; it went over my head. She complained about how much time he spent in his study and the mess he made when he put wall panelling in. I reckon that's where he hid the files, in a false wall.' Raglan sighed as if regretting his own stupidity. 'I should have checked, I'm sorry, Jack. I've let you down on this one, but I'm bleeding. I need to attend to this injury. I can't do any more than I've done. Zeller's wife didn't set the house alarm when she left in case it triggered and disturbed the neighbours. Can you deal with this?' Raglan waited. The lie had to be accepted. It took only a moment.

'I will, of course I will.'

Raglan could almost hear the gears clicking in Swain's mind.

Raglan's voice was weary, the voice of a hunted man, hurt and running out of time. 'If the Feds have put me in the frame then I'm going to hide out tonight. Mix in with a crowd somewhere. Find a bar. Stay off the streets.'

Swain's voice softened. No edge now. And he still hadn't expressed any grief over Zeller's supposed death. 'Raglan, I have to rely on your complete discretion. If you are questioned by the Feds...' He let the statement hang.

'You think I'd cut a deal? Not my way, Jack. Like you

said at the start, I'm in this on my own, I don't expect any help. Listen, better get someone down to Zeller's house right away.'

'Of course. And Raglan?'

'Yes.'

'Thank you.'

Casey Zeller led the way out of the house. Hoarding panels alongside the unfinished houses were perfect cover. Raglan followed, his memory noting the route in case anything went wrong in the unlit street and they needed a way out. Zeller slowed, pointed to where the light barely penetrated the shell of the building, showing obstacles for the man behind to avoid. He reached the centre of the house's shell and clambered up some scaffolding. Raglan followed. Zeller had chosen well. The scaffolding was an ideal observation post. They crouched below the building's gable end. Space for a window had been prepared in the timber-frame structure. They were far enough back from the street to see the house and the approach road. Zeller opened his phone.

'Whoever Swain sends we'll pick up their torchlight inside the house.'

'If they're the ones he sent to watch my back before, they're dumb enough to put all the lights on and throw a party. Recruitment in the service is in a bad way.'

Zeller sighed. 'You don't have to attend West Point to become a field officer on surveillance.'

'Getting through Junior High might be a start.'

Zeller's teeth showed in the darkness. 'You hear that?'

Raglan nodded. The deep rumble of a big-engined pickup approached. Raglan glanced out and recognized the vehicle. 'It's the Bozo twins. Same two who were watching me.'

'Let's hope they brought a screwdriver,' said Casey as Raglan watched Swain's two men park in the driveway and slip along the side passage. A minute later Zeller turned the phone, showing Raglan the torchlight entrance and the men's progress into his study. 'I should've rigged it for sound.'

'Silent movies are often more entertaining,' said Raglan. He checked his watch again. 'Cops from DC will have to bring in the Stafford Sheriff's Office. There'll be some convincing to do. Jurisdiction issues can depend on who's got the clout and who's got the rule book in their back pocket.'

Zeller showed Raglan the men inside the house. 'So far so good. They're unscrewing the panel.'

'Perfect timing,' said Raglan as he beckoned Zeller to the gap in the wall. Two Sheriff's cars glided silently up from the far end of the street, their headlights off. Another convoy led by an unmarked sedan came from the opposite end of the street. Whoever the detectives were from the capital they knew their silent approach routine. The hushed sound of car tyres was all that could be heard. A man and a woman detective got out of their car, split up as each beckoned uniformed officers to follow them. The man went up the side of the house. If the cops made a no-knock entry, Swain's men had better not come over all alpha male. Cops weren't required to announce themselves if they believed evidence of a crime could be destroyed by doing so. Zeller brought the phone closer. Disembodied voices came across the street from the house as the silent scenario on screen played out. Lightsabre beams danced across the room.

'Show me your hands!'

Blurred images of one of Swain's men reaching for his gun were thrown into startling clarity from the flare of gunfire.

The shots boomed across the street.

Cross-hatched torchlight showed the second man on his knees behind the desk. Arms raised. Shouts of 'Clear!' reached Raglan and Zeller as the police checked every room.

'Shit, Raglan, they're dumber than my dog and he's been dead five years.'

Lights came on in the house. The front door opened. A Stafford County police officer came out and spoke into his radio. Raglan and Zeller heard the word *ambulance*. The cop grabbed a first-aid box and ran back into the house.

Raglan and Zeller watched the small screen. They saw Swain's man handcuffed and disarmed; the female detective wearing latex gloves putting folders into a plastic evidence bag, sealing and signing it. Two uniformed officers attended to the second of Swain's men who was sprawled on the floor.

They peered across the street as the garage door swung open. Light flooded the garage as the male detective walked around the Harley.

'Yours?' said Zeller.

'A friend's.'

Zeller frowned. 'The cops look interested.'

'It's part of their murder investigation. Now the backup evidence is in the hands of the police and it will be impounded in their evidence yard because it belonged to a murdered man.'

Zeller's brow creased into deeper ridges. Raglan pointed. 'You had a short-barrelled Maglite flashlight in the garage.'

'Yeah, my dive light. Fits into my scuba webbing.'

'I took out the batteries, hid the flash drive inside and slipped it into the Harley's tank. Now, even if these unknown powers-that-be shut down the police investigation, seal off your house the flash drive is safe and sound in a police lockup.'

An ambulance turned into the street, its seesaw lights painting the houses. Residents from the occupied houses further along the street dared to peer from their windows as the Sheriff Department's officers taped off the block. Raglan waited long enough to see one man stretchered out, the other handcuffed and escorted into the detective's car.

'Time to go,' said Zeller.

Raglan remained watching the unfolding scene below. 'Not yet. Give it a few minutes.'

'There's nothing more we can do here, *mon ami.*'

'If I were Jack Swain and had sent two muscleheads to retrieve evidence, I'd sacrifice them first in case it was a trap. But if they went in and got what they were after, then I'd have backup in case they were followed. I'd have another team back there. Waiting.' Raglan looked to the forest and half-built houses. 'And I'd use them for interference, to block anyone after the retrieval team got what they came for.'

'Then why didn't we set that up for the authorities? All we've done now is knock out two of their team.'

'Two less gunmen to worry about and we have delivered your evidence into the hands of the cops,' said Raglan.

'They'll be jealous enough to want to keep it but if Swain is involved he'll soon snatch it back. These cops aren't hunting for a conspiracy theory; they're hunting me and anyone else they think might be helping me.' He nodded towards the arrest below. 'Now we have the upper hand. The material and the backup is safe.'

Raglan settled back, letting the minutes tick by.

He tapped Zeller's shoulder. 'Time to go.'

52

Raglan followed Zeller through the darkened building site, skirting street and construction vehicles, weaving this way and that to draw out anyone who might be following. Every fifty yards they stopped, found shadow and waited, checked and then moved on. Once they were through the trees Zeller pointed to an old pickup parked in an unfinished storm drain.

Raglan rode back into town with Zeller who remained quiet. Raglan sensed something wasn't right. 'Drop me a block from the motel. My contact is waiting. I'll use the trace on my jacket to bring in the next scalp-hunters. You OK?'

Zeller shrugged, hands gripping the wheel. 'Doesn't feel right. Me heading north, you staying back. This was my fight to start with.'

'I promised your wife to find you and get you back to her. The best thing you can do is get across the border to Canada and stay there until this ends.'

'And how does it end? You're not going to get to the people who are really behind all this. You saw how many layers of camouflage they've got. I say we should have handed the dossier over officially. You could have cleared your name.'

'That wouldn't be so easy. I'm an outside asset for intelligence agencies. They're not coming to help me get out of this; I have to do that myself. That's where we're at.'

'But it's risky enough leaving it in the hands of homicide detectives,' said Zeller. 'Give it a day and it'll be back with whoever's running the operation. Dammit, Raglan, I just don't see it, is all.'

'The cops will log it as evidence. Whoever wants it back will bring pressure to bear. If it's Jack Swain then he's been obliged to show his hand. Sure, he'll get the dossier, but if he cries national security in the middle of a murder investigation, he runs the risk of being dragged into that investigation. It flushes him out. If he is genuinely concerned about the contents of that file then he will work with the cops and the Feds. The file and the murder investigation are intrinsically linked now.'

Zeller seemed to accept the reasoning. But he was unhappy about it.

'Get home and be with Anne. Give her that much. You've kicked over a rattlesnake's nest, Casey. There's no way this is going to stay hidden for much longer.'

'And you're going out there, tagged so more of them come for you.'

'The more that come, the closer I get to whoever it is who set this whole thing in motion,' Raglan pointed out.

The city was busy enough, despite the late hour. There would be a concert on somewhere. Traffic would be heading uptown to the restaurants and clubs. It wasn't the time of year for tourists. This was just ordinary city living. Journeys in from the upmarket suburbs. Raglan saw the turning for TJ Jones's apartment. The red-zone map TJ'd drawn for his visitor warned of dangerous areas, but it had been Raglan's presence that had brought murder to a place of relative safety. The memory triggered a visceral response: this was why he was using himself as bait. He wanted the killers. This time around he was the scalp-hunter.

'Take a right at the lights and drop me off,' he said. 'I need my coat.'

Zeller peeled around the corner and pulled over, then eased into a parking zone. Zeller checked his mirrors. There had been no sign of anyone following them. He turned off the engine.

'Casey, she's waiting for you. I don't have anybody tearing themselves apart over me. You owe her. The I-70 on to the I-80. Pay the tolls. Seven hours' straight drive. Tell me you're heading north. Don't look back. You have another family beyond the one we shared.'

Zeller glanced at him. Domestic duty fought against his true nature. 'The mission is sacred, Raglan,' he said, repeating the Legion's often avowed determination to never stop until what they set out to do had been achieved.

'You have a new one now. Make sure you see it through.'

Zeller nodded grimly. They clasped hands. Raglan slammed the door, turned away and, by the time Zeller checked his wing mirrors, was gone. He eased the pickup from the parking zone into the traffic.

An hour later Zeller had driven free of the city and swung back towards his house. His sense of guilt at going against Raglan's advice gnawed at him. But this time Raglan was wrong. Handing the evidence to the police left his whole investigation wide open to being seized by those the dossier exposed. And what if the CSI people looked too closely at the Harley? Casey Zeller was convinced his decision was correct. This was a power game and Raglan was an outsider who didn't understand just how the rotten the swamp was. That's why he had done what he had done. The wiper blades sluiced away light rain. He had been reluctant to leave Raglan to face whatever opposition came his way. Old fighting skills lay only skin-deep but the warrior spirit was his breath of life. He had been deadly serious when he spoke of the Foreign Legion's credo that the mission was everything; that commitment might as well have been tattooed on his soul.

When he had sat with Raglan in his house and the Englishman had left the room allowing Zeller to speak to his wife, she had cried with relief at hearing his voice. He had promised her it wouldn't be long before they were together. He had ignored what Raglan had set up in Toronto. That could wait. He had told his wife to stay in Stroudsburg, that he would come to her – but not yet. He couldn't come right now; he had to help Raglan; the job wasn't finished. He'd said he was not in danger. That was a lie. That he loved her deeply was not. She had to be strong. He would be there. Soon. Soon as he could.

He had stayed in the shadows for a couple of weeks; he could do so again. This time he would back up Raglan. When Raglan had returned to the room he had made a play of accepting that he had to return to his wife. Raglan was right, of course. If the enemy, whoever they were, identified him then the whole operation could go down the pan. But they wouldn't. He had a new identity. How could they possibly find him?

53

The jazz club off Wisconsin Avenue was packed. Raglan's eye swept the room. There must have been a hundred people in there, with maybe room for another thirty. The saxophonist played a sweet rendition of 'Good Morning Heartache', a Billie Holiday classic. It was mood music. And this being a listening club, people listened. Couples nudged each other, whispered low. Mood music did that. The saxophonist was good enough for Raglan to think it might have been Scott Hamilton playing. It wasn't. But it was good. So many damned fine musicians playing gigs who would never hit the high note of international success.

Voss had booked ahead. Raglan paid for the thirty-dollar tickets. They ordered food and sat in a corner. The second show had started fifteen minutes before ten so the atmosphere was warmed up. Raglan had his back to the wall so he could see where the patrons would enter. No one was allowed in when the performance was in progress and that gave Raglan and Voss some downtime to eat. Any soldier knows to eat when you can because when the killing starts no one can be sure when the next meal is coming.

'Whoever Stanley Turrentine is, they named a great dish after him,' Voss said, forking in a mouthful of crab cake and Cajun red beans and rice. 'They'll know about the failed attack at the motel – you really think they'll track you here?'

Raglan had stuck with the steak and a cold beer. 'Swain knows I've gone to ground. Whether he's involved or not, someone's still got a trace on me.'

He kept his eyes on the crowd. The Billie Holiday ended. The audience applauded. The set was over. A half-dozen people edged their way in and were shown to their table. Two of the six people were singles. They weren't a couple. They looked as if they worked together. They took two of the bar stools vacated after the last number. One of them scanned the room, the other ordered drinks. Raglan lowered his head.

'Turrentine played tenor sax. All the food here is named after jazz players.'

'I don't know about jazz. I still like Abba. Makes me want to dance.'

But now wasn't the time to discuss musical preferences. 'They're here,' he said. 'Two at the bar.'

She swallowed, dropped her napkin, bent to retrieve it and sighted the two men through the diners. 'Do you recognize them?'

'No. If this thing is as important as I think it is, there'll be more than one team here. They look ex-military.' He peeled off dollars to cover the food and a tip and eased back his chair. 'We'll do it now. Before the next set starts,' he said and abandoned the table.

She watched him make his way to the stairs leading to the restrooms on the second floor. One of the men at the bar looked at his phone, and then nudged his partner, who checked what was obviously a tracking signal. They scanned the room and saw Raglan heading up the stairs. They abandoned their drinks and followed him. Voss waited until they were out of sight and ducked low as musicians moved forwards to the front of the stage. She would wait outside. If they were a professional crew then they would know Raglan was a difficult man to kill. There would be others waiting. And she would make certain that Raglan walked out safely.

She went through the main entrance and skirted the front of the building. Raglan would use the fire escape. She turned down the side alley. There was barely enough light to distinguish shapes so she criss-crossed the narrow passage, aiming instinctively for the rear delivery yard. She kept her Glock pointed to her front, crouched when she heard movement, but realized it came from the rear of another building further along the street. She edged around the corner that brought her into a dogleg at the rear of the jazz club. Once around the next corner she would have a clear sight of the fire-escape area. So far so good. There was no second team in place. If there were, they would be in a parked vehicle or waiting in the poorly lit yard. She drew breath, held it, let it go slowly. No sound. No movement. The way ahead was clear. Then pain coursed through her. A blinding sheet of light behind her eyes that put her on her knees. Something warm trickled from her hairline on to her face. She fought the engulfing darkness but fell forwards face first into the stench of the alley.

★

Inside the club, two gunmen reached the restrooms. One stood outside while the other went in, silenced semi-automatic raised in one hand, phone in the other. There was no one in sight; the patrons were trapped downstairs now the music had started again. All the cubicle doors were open except two; the gunman scanned the closed doors, and the silent blinking light on his phone increased its intensity until he identified which cubicle Raglan occupied. He stood back, levelled the weapon and aimed at a low angle. He fired a rapid six shots, the door splintered, he kicked it open and saw Raglan's jacket propped on the toilet pipe. By then his arms were extended into the cubicle. Raglan stepped out of its neighbour and aimed a vicious punch beneath the man's ear. An executioner's blow, breaking the second cervical vertebra, just as a hangman's knot does. The man dropped. Raglan picked up his weapon and took his phone. He retrieved his punctured jacket and stepped out to where the second man waited outside the door. He turned, his guard down, expecting his companion to come through the door. Raglan fired one close, silent shot. He dragged the body into the restroom and propped him in an undamaged cubicle with the other man sitting on his lap, arms embraced in a death hug. Raglan pressed each man's weapon into their hands, pulled the door closed, locked it and clambered over into the next empty cubicle. The music's dying notes faded. Applause followed as Raglan found the fire escape and stepped out into the cold fresh air.

He descended quickly into the darkened alley, street lights filtered along its walls picking up the dumpsters. As Raglan reached the alley a figure stepped out of the shadows.

'I told them you were too good,' said the man's voice. A voice he had heard ask for his help. Who had stood in the background as Raglan hunted for the missing Zeller and the secret documents.

Raglan froze. As Jack Swain stepped forwards, gun raised, the light caught his face. Raglan saw that the shadows made his face more gaunt.

'Jack, you should have let them kill me at the motel. You can't walk away from this tonight.'

'Oh, the motel shooting was a prize fuck-up. They thought you had the file. I knew you didn't, but I was too late to stop them. The others wanted you dead and blamed for the senator's killing.' He gestured with the pistol.

Raglan complied and went down on his knees.

'Lace your fingers behind your head, Raglan. You're too damned quick for me these days.'

Again, Raglan did as ordered.

'Your boys were arrested at Zeller's house, Jack. The cops have the file.'

'Nice try.'

'I'm telling you. I phoned it in. Zeller hid it behind the bookshelves like I told you.'

'You only guessed it was there because of some vague thing his wife said. My boys phoned me before the police arrived. The files were there but the documents were not. Now I have to tidy up another mess and explain to the police why we were there. National security is a neat catch-all phrase I like to use.'

Raglan winced. Zeller had not replaced the dossier. Hadn't trusted Raglan's judgement. Zeller hadn't had them on him when they escaped into the night. That meant he had left them somewhere in the house and would go back for them.

'If those papers are there, my people will wait for the cops to wrap up the crime scene and this time we'll tear the place apart.' Swain smiled. 'Time to get a bit more aggressive.' He was six feet away and kept his weapon aimed at Raglan's head. Even a lousy marksman could pull the trigger rapidly enough to kill a man on his knees and Swain was anything but a poor shot.

Raglan's mind raced. If Zeller had hidden the files then odds were he intended to go back to the house and he'd walk into a trap. Everything achieved would be lost. He needed Voss to step out of the shadows and end this now. Then warn Zeller. Why wasn't Voss here backing him up? Had he misjudged her as well? He needed to keep Swain talking.

'The evidence won't be in the house,' Raglan said, hoping the lie might at least sow doubt.

'But now it's worth doing a hard search.' Swain seemed to be in pain. He pressed a hand to his side. Then he sighed. 'So, when did you suspect me?' he said.

'Too late in the day to save innocent lives. It was when I found the tracking device. At first I was uncertain because the CIA had my address in Florida, but it was you who was close to Zeller. You're the one who put him out there to see how exposed the operation was. He did too good a job. I worked it backwards. How would the CIA have known about my connection with de Vere? Whereas you knew Zeller's wife used him to get to me. He had to die so you could build a case against me when the time came for me to root out the senator. You shouldn't have had the old man killed in DC.'

'He was convenient. How much longer did he have left anyway? Grim reaper and all that. Death does not show any respect.'

'He served his country, Jack.'

'We all did, Raglan. And we fought for nothing. Besides, killing him put you on the run. Forced the pace.'

'How far back does the killing go? France?'

'We traced the calls, Raglan. Had Zeller's phone bugged from the start. We sent local assets in Marseilles to stop your man from calling you in. We really didn't want you here but you arrived in time to kill them and find the message from Bob de Vere. Once that happened we changed the plan. You know how it is. Flexibility in the face of adversity. I decided to use you to track down Zeller and the dossier and the senator he'd found. A simple plan, Raglan, to build a case against you for murder. Step by step.' He coughed, pain creasing his face. 'We got there in the end.' Swain sighed again. 'I get so damned tired these days. I'm being eaten alive.' He saw Raglan's reaction and nodded. 'Pancreatic cancer. It's a bitch.'

Raglan twisted his head to look at his tormentor. Swain gave a none too gentle tap with the barrel across his cheek and then took a couple of strides back to sit on a packing crate. He still had a clear shot. He looked up. 'You know what, Raglan, I bet I haven't got a month left. Terminal cancer has a way of making you look a damned sight more closely at the night sky. With both of us dead it'll all be smoke on the wind.'

Swain leant forwards, arms crossed on his knees. His tone was conversational. Like old friends catching up on past times. 'Raglan, you've played a big part in this. Thanks to you being so damned efficient we have you as a scapegoat. And because of you we found the senator. And so' – he smiled – 'because of you we have won and we have ourselves a war.'

'There's a backup flash drive. I hid it.'

Swain didn't give a damn. 'So what? With you dead no one will ever find it.'

'Casey Zeller is alive. He's been in plain sight all this time. He knows about the backup.'

'You're bluffing.'

'OK. I'm bluffing. Is it worth the risk of killing me?'

'Here's my story. Zeller is a traitor. You worked with him, or he with you, either way it works for me. I apprehended you and shot the man involved in killing Senator Thomas. I'll roll the dice after that.'

'The dead are always with us, Jack. I'll remember the pain you unleashed on innocent people. I'll think of you and know that I should have let you die a lingering death rather than kill you.'

Swain stood up and stepped back behind Raglan. He pressed the muzzle into Raglan's scalp. Swain was more interested in processing Raglan's taunt than pulling the trigger right then.

'Jesus on the Cross. You damned bullshit frontline heroes spew such comic-book crap. I've seen it all before. Marines in Fallujah, special forces in Afghanistan. You people don't know when you're beat.'

Raglan felt the metal against his head. Hard. Meant to

hurt. Meant to tell him he was going to die. Meant to make him concentrate momentarily on the pain and not on the shot that would soon blow his head apart. A twisted act of compassion.

Raglan sucked in air. Death was a heartbeat away.

54

Every night sound reached out to him. Every shaved fraction of a second heralded his death. Yet within that compressed time Swain's finger had not taken up the slack on the trigger. Time to keep the ball rolling. 'Who killed my friends? One of your contractors?' said Raglan.

Swain hesitated. The pressure from the muzzle eased. Swain sat down again. Raglan had bought himself vital seconds. Maybe the dying man wanted to let Raglan know how damned efficient he had been.

'No. They're good but they're... they're rough. Y'know, all that macho stuff.'

'It was a woman; I know that much.'

'You do? I held her in check long enough not to kill you. We needed you alive until the attack on the senator's house. I don't know how you survived that.'

Raglan stared into the half-lit yard. Voss was out there somewhere and she was cutting it fine. He hoped she hadn't developed a sudden love of jazz and stayed for the next set. Jack Swain seemed content to talk. And Raglan encouraged him. He needed more time because wherever the Pentagon man positioned himself it would be impossible for Raglan to attack him or escape.

'A lot of innocent people are going to die when you and your war-lovers kick off an uprising in Iran. Let's stop this now, Jack. It's gone too far,' said Raglan. 'You and the Council did a deal with Mossad or people who used to work for them.' Raglan knew the lack of circulation in his legs would soon make it impossible for him to make any move at all against the man training his gun on him. 'You've got a mixed bag of contractors, Jack, ours, theirs and a few Central and South American terrorists, people who know how to initiate and lead an uprising. Face the facts. It's a non-starter. Iranian secret police will have every known member of the Mojahedin-e-Khalq written in their big black book. You'll throw this administration into the biggest international shitstorm.'

'So, you know about our friends in Iran. Our government will seize the opportunity. They'll see what we have started and they will commit. The Middle East has to be ours, Raglan. The Chinese and Russians are making us look like fools. They're already neck-deep in the region. And we do nothing. We talk, for Christ's sake!'

Swain stood and took a stride closer to Raglan. It was another potentially fatal moment. Raglan had no way of striking out. He saw the moves he could make. Dip and roll towards the man waiting to kill him. Hope the deflection was too shallow an angle for the gun to bear down. How many seconds? Three? Four at the most. That was already as many bullets as Swain would pump into him. He needed Swain to step closer. He did, but he knew the moves as well and stepped behind Raglan. Execution-style.

Buy time. Voss had to be close. 'I know about the Iranian, Jack. Aram-banou. Sounds like your kind of woman. You shacked up with her?'

Swain laughed. 'Are you kidding me? God knows how you found that out. I have some South African contractors down in Honduras and they call her the Praying Mantis. She devours men, Raglan. Likes to see them bleed.'

Honduras. Swain had confirmed where Raglan suspected the secret base to be. He took a breath. Every second counted. 'You'll be in the ground but the big plan will fall apart. You wasted your whole damned life for one lousy plan that doesn't have a chance,' said Raglan.

'I'm a patriot. Lives are lost in the pursuit of protecting my country. What would you know about that? Your allegiance is to a foreign army. The Legion is your home.'

Where the hell was Voss?

'Jack, I copied photos from Reyes's security cameras. You got careless. Your people were laundering drug money and a few months back you used one of the men we saw on the camera to sucker the FBI into an ambush. The Feds'll find the bank accounts of all those shell companies buying arms. They'll piece it all together.'

Raglan's explanation made Swain listen. Thirteen seconds. A distraction that held his attention before he pulled the trigger. It gave Jenna Voss time to finally step out of the darkness, weapon extended. She pulled back the Glock's hammer.

'FBI. Drop your weapon. Raise your hands. Slowly.'

Raglan heard Swain's breath catch. He saw the bloodstain down Voss's temple and face from a head wound.

'Agent Voss. You must have a tough head. I hit you hard. Wise up. This is the man the police and the Feds are looking for. You could be a hero.'

Voss remained silent. The Glock gripped and aimed. But

Raglan saw the blow to her head had made her unsteady. She swayed, blinking clear the wavering vision she must be experiencing.

'Except of course you aren't looking for Raglan, are you?' said Swain.

He was weighing the odds. Could he raise his gun quickly enough to kill Voss fifteen feet in front of him? If he could, did he then have time to shoot the man in front of him? The woman yes. The man no. Raglan knew the moves.

It was decision time. 'You won't make it, Jack,' said Raglan.

Swain hesitated.

'Shoot me, she shoots you. It has to be her first,' said Raglan. 'Then at least you have a chance at me. But I'll get you. Give it up. Help yourself by helping us. Information can buy you a deal.'

Still the man hesitated.

Raglan knew he wouldn't buy the offer. He was one of those warriors trained to give his all. To roll the dice when the last bet had been laid.

'Hands!' demanded Voss as Swain reached his free hand into his coat pocket.

'Easy,' said Swain. 'He's going to die anyway. When is up to you. See? My phone.' He raised his phone for her to see.

'She'll shoot you, Jack, no matter what.'

'No, no, Raglan. This is where I bring in the cavalry.' He kept his eyes on Voss without taking the gun from the back of Raglan's head. 'I'm in a win-win here. I might be dead in less than a minute but the operation in Iran will go ahead because Agent Voss will be a fugitive just like you are, Raglan.'

Raglan fixed his gaze on the wavering FBI agent. 'Take the shot, Voss. Head shot. It paralyses muscular reflex,' he said.

Swain had pressed a speed-dial number. Kim Burton's disembodied voice on speaker penetrated the night. 'Swain?'

'I have apprehended the Englishman you wanted for the murder of Senator Thomas but Special Agent Jenna Voss has a Glock pointed at my head. I suspect she has gone rogue on you.'

'Don't listen, Kim!' Voss called out. Her voice was uneven. 'He's part of the conspiracy. He's going to kill Raglan to cover his tracks. We have evidence!'

'Shoot him in the head. Do it. Now,' said Raglan calmly, urging her to concentrate on what needed to be done. 'Focus. Kill him.'

Kim Burton's voice reached her. 'Jenna, lower your weapon. You've gone too far. Do you hear me?'

Conflicting voices crossed between Voss and Swain who stood, a querulous look on his face, a half-smile.

'Evidence, Kim. Not a hunch. Hard evidence,' Voss insisted.

'Then we will address that when you bring in Raglan. Swain? Can you hear me?'

'I can. But your agent isn't listening.' Swain smiled and cocked his weapon. 'Time.'

The gunshot boomed in the confined yard.

Voss's shot went wide as she slumped to her knees and sprawled forward, her Glock skidding across the concrete. A breath of surprise from Swain, a slight shift in his defensive body position as he instinctively moved to shoot back. It gave Raglan his chance. He raised his right arm to block any movement of the weapon pointing at him. As he spun, his arm struck Swain's as he tried to bring his gun to bear. Raglan was the stronger and his blow numbed Swain's gun hand. Raglan threw himself clear from Swain's paralysed arm as the old pro took the gun into his left hand and fired.

A wild shot. And another. Raglan rolled, ignored the hot tear in his side from the strained wound, seized Voss's weapon, twisted and fired.

Swain's neck whipped back from the force of the 9-mm bullet punching a hole in his forehead.

Raglan got to his feet and hauled up a groggy Voss.

'Fuck,' she said.

'We need to clean your head up,' said Raglan.

She put a hand to the drying blood on her scalp, staggered a couple of paces and went down on one knee, dizzy from the pounding in her head. 'Does it need stitches?'

Raglan shook his head. 'It's a scratch. Looks worse than it is.' He wasn't going to give her the pleasure of claiming wounded-hero status and she knew it.

She looked at Raglan. 'I thought you were a dead man.'

'So did he,' said Raglan.

Raglan picked up Swain's phone. 'He should have killed me first. You made him react. Besides, he wasn't the kind of man to die in a hospital bed.' He checked the phone. The line to Kim Burton was disconnected. 'Now he's put you in the frame for his murder. They'll track his location. They'll match ballistics. There won't be any doubt in their mind you shot and killed him to save me.'

'I'll stay and explain.'

'How long do you think the Bureau will hold you for

questioning? She heard everything. The cops will be here soon enough. They can slug it out with the Feds. They'll be dealing with the men at Zeller's house, the assault rifle used in the senator's murder and a big question mark over the Clandestine Service's dead Deputy Director. It will take them time to start putting the pieces together.'

He pulled out the tracking device from his coat's collar and crushed it under his heel. He needed to get back to Zeller's house and this time he didn't want the killers knowing.

Voss took one last look at the sprawled body. 'And now I'm a fugitive.'

'You wanted in,' said Raglan, handing back her weapon.

She holstered it, shook her head in quiet despair at what had gone down. 'Have been ever since I saw Lennie Elliot smiling at me from your phone,' she said, resigned.

55

The morning heralded a grey pre-dawn, the weather stubbornly refusing to yield to the clear sky behind the clouds. A cold, pellet-hard rain stung their faces as Raglan led the way through the trees, taking the route that Zeller had used the previous night. When they stopped to check for any movement in the skeletal buildings, steam seeped from their bodies from the extra half-mile Raglan had made them walk. He had pushed hard and Voss had kept up the pace a few strides behind him, as aware of danger as the man leading her. She squinted in the rain when Raglan stopped again, shivering as water dribbled down her neck. She brushed her soaked hair from her face, keeping her eyes on the intended route that Raglan indicated with a brief chop of his hand. Three hundred yards more and they were in the building he and Zeller had used as an observation post. They clambered up the scaffolding, the gable end protecting them from the driving rain. They peered across to Zeller's house. It was deserted. The police had taped off the house and the approach to it either side of the building's perimeter. There was no sign of Zeller or anyone else having intruded past the police tape across the door and garage.

'Stay here,' said Raglan. 'If Zeller got back into the

house it'll be from the rear.' Raglan was about to turn away when his phone vibrated. He took it out and stared at the screen. It showed a bound and beaten Casey Zeller. An unseen figure stepped behind him, grabbed his face and lifted it towards the lens. He was barely conscious. Raglan and Voss heard a woman's accented voice, foreign but with an American inflection, tell someone to bring the papers. A man's hands showed the documents that Raglan had spent so much time studying.

'Do it,' said the woman's voice.

The shaky image showed a man's hands toss the papers into a waste bin, squirt lighter fluid and throw in a lit match. The papers flared.

The phone's lens turned on a self-image of a blonde woman. Her almond eyes stared straight into the camera. Her dark eyebrows and olive skin told Raglan she was no natural blonde. Before she could speak Raglan butted in.

'You murdered two friends of mine. I'll find you and kill you for that.'

Her voice was stilted, its cadence not that of a natural English speaker. 'Your ambition is understandable but futile because you will be dead before you can raise a hand to me. Because my employer Jack Swain's phone is answered by a police officer we assume he is dead. That is why I called you. Of course he shared your number. We have known about you from the beginning and now you can be of service to us more than we had anticipated.'

'You inflict more hurt on Zeller and you will get nothing from me, Aram-banou,' Raglan said, already knowing what her demands would be. Her eyes flared at the mention of her name.

'So, now we both know who we are dealing with,' she said.

'I'm dealing with an assassin. You're of no importance to the operation. There are others who have the authority to negotiate. Jack Swain said as much before he died,' said Raglan, hoping to goad her into revealing who might now be controlling events.

She smiled. She was attractive and Raglan could see how her looks might distract someone long enough for her to kill. 'I am in a position to offer an exchange,' she said.

'I don't know where it is,' said Raglan, wanting her to know he was one step ahead of her.

'I think you do. And if you do not then I have no reason to keep your friend alive.'

Raglan remained silent for a moment. Better to let her think she had put him under pressure. 'Was it you at the senator's house?'

'Of course.'

'The shooters drew me into the woods down by the river but you stayed behind and killed him.'

'I confess I did not expect you to survive the attack. It upset our plans.'

'And made me a fugitive from the FBI and the police.'

'That is not my problem. The evidence is destroyed except for the backup. We want it. You will not be able to trace this number. I will phone later this morning and arrange the exchange. Make sure you have what we need.' She smiled, eyebrows raised. At any other time, an enticing invitation. She ended the call.

Raglan fell silent. Why wait to arrange the exchange? It told him that she was on the move. And if his suspicion was correct, out of the country. He had stared into the face of the woman responsible for killing two of his friends, and a senator who stood in the conspirators' way. He felt neither anger nor rage. He had held her gaze with his own. And she had not blinked. She was steadfast. Two killers. Neither backing down. One determined to kill as many as stood in her way. The other intent on killing her. Raglan's gaze was as accurate as a radar-painted target for a drone strike. He would seek her out.

'Blonde Iranian. I'll bet she has an expensive hairdresser. Her roots weren't showing,' said Voss.

'Then you'd better pull a comb through yours and dress for the part because you're going to retrieve the backup flash drive.'

Voss sat on her haunches, back pressed against the wall, shoulders hunched against the rain, trying to stop the water dribbling down her neck. 'If you told me where it was hidden I might have an opinion on how to retrieve it.'

'Where do the cops take a vehicle suspected of being involved in a murder?'

'The Evidence Control compound. It's hidden in a vehicle?'

'A Harley motorcycle.'

'Well... I dunno, first get to the main building and then the compound. They're across the river, south of the city. I'll need to look the part.'

'How long from here?'

'About an hour, and I need a quarter-hour to get changed.'

'Do you have your clothes here or at the motel?'

'Back of the car.'

'You think you can get inside the compound?'

She thought about it. Saw the scenario unfold in her mind's eye. 'They open at eight, we need to get in and out before the news channels flag our pictures. My people won't waste time before posting us as Most Wanted. A dead senator and now a director of the DIA Clandestine Service. We're hot property.'

Raglan checked his watch. 'Construction workers will be here in a couple of hours. Time for breakfast.'

He got to his feet. She looked in disbelief. 'You're thinking of food at a time like this?'

'I'm thinking of fuel to keep us going. It'll be a long day and I don't know when we'll next get to eat.'

Raglan had Voss park the car across the street from the diner. They would see it from inside and its position did not immediately flag where they were. They were both soaked from the cold rain, and the mouth-watering smell of hot coffee, ham and eggs stabbed at their hunger. The diner was empty except for one lone man at the far end reading an early-morning edition. Head down, scooping food, his attention was on the newsprint. The newspapers wouldn't yet have the story. What occurred outside the jazz club had happened after the press had gone to print. It would be in that evening's newspapers and flashed across the DC television channels. The same waitress approached with the coffee jug.

'Hey, English, you're up early.'

'It's been a long night, Roz.'

She poured. 'Uh-huh. I won't ask,' she said, glancing at Voss. 'What'll it be?'

'Two specials with extra ham and toast,' said Raglan.

'All righty,' said Roz. She glanced at Voss. 'Lady, you happy having English here ordering for you? Plenty of gals don't like it.'

Voss smiled. 'He's done all right so far. My independence and femininity aren't threatened.'

'Well, good for you, lady. Two specials it is.' She winked at Raglan and walked away.

Voss's expression questioned him. Raglan smiled. 'She's old school. We hit it off last time I came in. She had my back when two of Swain's men were following me.'

'You suspected him from the start?'

He shook his head. 'Later. OK. How do we do this? Do you just walk into this compound area and get to the Harley?'

'Main administrative offices first, make sure we know where it is.'

'Why not phone and use your shield number?'

'Better face to face. No being put on hold. No one phoning around and checking on me. I get in, I get out. I know enough of what's gone on to sound convincing. Where's the flash drive hidden?'

Raglan told her. And then added, 'There's a thin piece of garden wire wrapped around the gas tank lid holding the flashlight.'

'OK. What do we do with the flash drive when we get it?'

'Exchange it for Zeller.'

'Then it's all been for nothing.'

'It's been to save Zeller.'

'But you're handing them the last piece of evidence.'

'I know, but I have it backed up in cyberspace with an encrypted password in case we don't make it. I have to stretch this out as far as I can.'

'Then I think you've reached the end of the rope because as of now every law-enforcement officer from a park ranger to a traffic cop will be looking for us.' She yawned. 'Damn, it's been a while since I slept.'

He pushed a couple of sachets of sugar towards her. 'Take a hit. It'll give you a boost.'

'I haven't taken sugar in years.'

'You need it today. It's short-lived. It can help. Eases the stress.' He let her toy with the sachet. 'How long before the Feds put a trace on your car?'

'We're going somewhere?'

'We can't fly or take public transport.'

'To where?'

'Your car? How long?' he said, not yet prepared to tell her his plan.

'Well, it should be OK for a while. It's my dad's car. It's old but still registered to him.'

'Is he still alive?'

She shook her head. 'Died a few months back. He always wanted me to have the car.' She shrugged. 'So I did as he asked. I haven't changed the plates and the tags are all up to date.' She realized it could be advantageous. 'I doubt they'll put two and two together for a while. They'll be looking at flights and rail. Buses as well. That's if they think we're going to make a run for it. Which, from what you're saying, we are.' She grimaced at the coffee she had absentmindedly tipped sugar into.

The food arrived. 'There you go, hon. Enjoy.'

Voss squirted ketchup. He looked up with a hint of a smile.

'What?' she said.

'Food tastes better without it. You should try it first.'

'I know what I like. Mind your own business.'

'OK. I'll remember not to take you to any good eateries if you ever come to France.'

'France?' said Voss, suddenly ravenous as she shovelled food into her mouth. 'Raglan, we'll be lucky to get out of DC alive.'

56

Raglan waited in the car across the road from the Evidence Control building where Voss presented her credentials. It was 8.05 a.m. and with luck those early-morning news channels would have been missed by the evidence clerks on their way to work. Time was tight. They still had to drive down to the impounded vehicle yard. Back at the diner Voss had taken her sports bag into the restroom and changed into her business suit. Roz, the waitress, had brought Raglan's change to the table.

'No, that's it,' said Raglan.

'That's generous, my Brit friend.'

Raglan smiled. 'Roz, you're going to read and hear things about me but I want you to know none of it is true.'

'Uh-huh,' she said. 'And you think paying me off is gonna keep me quiet?'

'I don't want to make life difficult for you, so if cops or Feds come around asking questions, tell them I was here. I'll be long-gone.'

'Oh yeah?'

'Yes.'

'OK. You don't need to pay me to keep my mouth shut.

Thing is, I don't see too well without my glasses and my hearing is bad on the best of days.'

'That wasn't what the tip was for.'

She smiled. 'I know.' She pointed at Raglan's jacket. 'That tells its own story. Those aren't moth holes.'

Raglan said nothing.

'OK, you can't walk around looking like a deadbeat panhandler.'

'I'm fond of that jacket, Roz.'

'Fondness isn't love. Time for a parting of the ways. There's a closet back here. We had a big fella come in a month or so back. Got all het up on his phone, left without paying, drove off in a hurry. Never saw him again. It's an old trick guys use to get a freebie meal, but he left his coat. He was about your size.'

Raglan had followed her to the staff area where she pulled out a workman's thick canvas coat. It zipped and buttoned to his waist. It was a good fit. Roz took his bullet-torn coat and tossed it in the dumpster out the back. When she returned, she made a fuss of wiping down the counter. 'You could do worse,' she said, cocking her head towards the smartly dressed Voss as she came back into the diner.

Raglan glanced at Voss. 'I'm not her type.'

Roz had smiled. 'Oh yeah? I told you, we serve it hot in here.'

Raglan kept an eye on the building opposite as he answered his phone.

'Raglan.'

'Maguire, you're up late.'

'There are some very worried people here and in Israel. There is no pre-emptive plan to strike Iran. Mossad have their balls in a vice but I tightened it. They say there are disaffected people from their special forces and intelligence agencies. It's been brewing for a while. Their hawks believed American sanctions were too weak, and once China did the deal with Iran, that pushed them into preparing for an insurrection.'

'I'm screwed if Mossad bleats to the Americans.'

'I've got the Israelis in check, for now at least. They don't want this any more than us. They don't know who's involved in the States either. They can't blow the whistle. Not yet. But if they have people on the ground then diplomatically it all goes up in smoke.'

'Why are you telling me this, Maguire?'

Maguire's voice was calm and the information he passed on was concise. 'Back in the eighties the CIA set up a training camp in Honduras for the Nicaraguan Contras. They trained insurgents and death squads. It went tits up when Reagan left office and the Senate shut it down. Fifteen years ago an American security company bought the site for a knock-down price.' Maguire rattled off names of the company CEOs.

'They're dead,' said Raglan. 'They were listed on the shell companies. They're a cover. Zeller and Senator Thomas discovered as much.'

'The site is active, Raglan. The contractors are Executive Decision Management.'

Raglan felt the big piece slot into place. EDM was the group behind everything.

'During the Iraq war they had a US government deal to send Honduran and Venezuelan mercenaries to Iraq and Afghanistan. But it went quiet two or three years ago. I think I know where their base is and where the weapons are stored,' said Maguire. 'You can't go in there alone.'

'I'm on the clock and Casey Zeller's life is hanging by a thread. Give me a location.'

'Send me the information Zeller found.'

'You're trading a man's life.'

'I'm obtaining insurance against you ending up as crocodile bait. I need that dossier as evidence.'

'I need your word you won't share it.'

'Until you're dead or you ask for help.'

'Until I'm dead,' said Raglan. 'Or I give you the go.'

'Agreed. Coordinates on their way.'

A moment later his phone showed a series of longitude and latitude coordinates.

'You got them?' said Maguire.

'Yes.' He sent the encrypted link.

Moments later Maguire said, 'Just numbers?'

'I kept it simple for your intelligence boys. Keep your word on this. It's evidence. Don't let it get into the wrong hands.'

'As agreed, Raglan.'

'One thing, Maguire.'

'What?'

'Jack Swain was behind it.'

'I see. Anyone else we know of?'

'Not yet. Doubtful anyway. He had all the connections. Venezuela, Central America, Pentagon. All cloak-and-dagger stuff.'

'The Pentagon will be pissed off, and the DIA. Can you contain him?'

'You might say that. I killed him.'

He ended the call before Maguire reacted.

Voss stepped briskly out of the building. Raglan shifted back to the passenger side as Voss reached the car. She slammed the door, fired the engine and swung the Acura across the street.

'So far so good.'

'What did you tell them?'

'That I needed to check the odometer reading on the vehicles as part of the ongoing investigation.'

'How far to the yard?'

'Five minutes. One block east of here. I'll drive in alone because they'll check who's going through the gate.'

She drove in a long curving loop through a bleak, windswept semi-industrial area and pulled up outside a yard with silo towers and heavy plant machinery. The sign said it was an asphalt contractor. 'The impound yard is down that slip road. There's nowhere for you to wait. Stay here; I'll text when I'm on my way out. You can make out you're looking for a job inside the yard.' She checked her mirrors. There was no one else around at this time of day but the workmen operating the asphalt machinery. 'You look as though you could do with one.'

He watched her drive down to the main gate, present her ID to the guard and the documents granting her access. The guard pointed. She drove off into the vast compound housing thousands of vehicles. There was a small public parking area across the road from where Raglan waited. Vehicles were parked rear end to the steel-mesh fence. Raglan killed time. He walked fifty yards one way, turned and walked back. Movement was less suspicious than loitering. He extended the fifty by another twenty after the fourth turn, checked his watch as if he was waiting for someone. Took a few minutes' break. He checked the yard. The few men who were there paid no attention to him as they attended to their work. Raglan checked the length of the road. There was no traffic. This area was unlikely to be known to anyone who didn't have an interest in construction materials or impounded vehicles. Twenty-seven minutes passed. He saw a dark sedan approach from the distance. He walked into the yard's entrance, hid behind the main gate's pillar and watched the car slow before turning. He recognized the two detectives who had been part of the raid on Zeller's house.

Raglan pressed Voss's phone number. There was no answer. He keyed in a warning text.

The tall African-American detective got out of his car and spoke to the guard at the gate. Had the machinery behind Raglan not been so loud he might have heard the voices drift on the breeze. As it was, the guard pointed into the yard and the detective reacted, climbed into the car and drove off at speed into the yard's depths. It was obvious the guard at the gate had told the detective the FBI were already logged in to inspect Zeller's vehicles. Raglan sprinted across the road towards a small haulage truck with its tailgate pressed against the four-yard-high fence. He pounded on to its hood, up on to its roof and vaulted over the sturdy fence. He landed, legs tucked together, and rolled. Raglan ran hard out of sight of the guard's building, ducking and weaving through the rows of vehicles, keeping the detective's car in sight. Three hundred yards into the pound it turned away down a gap in a row of cars. The rain started again, light at first and then stiffening as the breeze brought in the clouds across the Potomac, hurling the front-line raindrops into his face. Ignoring the stinging rain, Raglan caught sight of the Acura. Voss had thought it through. She was parked fifty yards beyond the Honda and the Harley. It was tucked out of sight, merged with the thousands of other vehicles. He saw her blonde hair bob as she was making her way back to her car. The detectives' sedan turned, found the way ahead blocked by cars. The man and woman piled out. They split up, each running to cut off Voss.

The woman shouted Voss's name. Voss hadn't heard her approach through the rain drumming on the car roofs. She spun around, saw that she was caught and raised her hands. The rain had served Detective Medina but it also smothered Raglan's approach. Raglan pounded towards Delaney who was concentrating on reaching Voss and his partner. He did not see or hear Raglan on his flank. When he did, it was too late. He grunted in surprise as Raglan drove him into the ground. He twisted, finding the strength to strike a blow against Raglan. It wasn't enough. Raglan had his knee in the man's back and a choke hold on his throat. He pressed the detective's weapon against his head, still holding the man on his knees with his arm around his neck.

'Drop it!' he called.

Medina was between Raglan holding her partner and Voss who, the moment Medina glanced back, had her Glock aimed at her.

'Do as he says, Medina,' said Voss. Calm. Unhurried. Meaningful.

Medina was in a crossfire. At best she could shoot and duck but the Englishman would kill her partner. She surrendered.

She cursed in Spanish as Voss roughly pushed her against a car, made her spread, pulled free Medina's handcuffs and snapped one over her wrist and the other through an old Chevy's door handle and on to her other wrist.

Raglan reached for the detective's handcuffs and did the same to him.

'You're crazy,' Delaney said to Voss. 'You're a damned Fed.'

Voss ignored him and stripped Medina of her shoes, tossing them into the metal wilderness.

Raglan made certain the handcuffs bit hard enough for Delaney to grimace. It got his attention. He pulled the man's tie free and gagged him.

'Listen to me,' Raglan said calmly as he thumbed the bullets from the Glock's clip. 'I'm going to tell you what's gone down. I'll only say it once. You're a cop so you can judge it for yourself. Jack Swain was running a black op. He tried to shoot me and was killed in self-defence.' He stripped the Glock and let it fall into Delaney's lap. 'I had uncovered documents that named who was behind a massive conspiracy. We're talking serving senators and former intelligence chiefs. Senator Mike Thomas was going to bring it down. Swain organized the hit on him. I'm being framed. A woman assassin killed the senator, a man in Florida and TJ Jones. Check the hair strands you found in his hand. Check your police logs. The shooting at the motel downtown targeted me. I have shown Agent Voss evidence. She's sided with me. We can't trust Kim Burton, the CIA or anyone else in the intelligence community. Not until we know who the players are. So, Mr Detective. Shake down the two men arrested at the house. Check their assault rifle ballistics because it was used in the senator's attack. Then, when you've put the pieces together, you – no one else – *you* make the case, once you think you know who to trust.' He stared at Delaney. 'If I'm the man you and the Feds are after, then why don't I kill you both now? I'm chasing down the real killers. That, my friend, is the truth.'

Cold rain dripped from their faces. Delaney shook free the droplets, glaring through the rain at Raglan. He mouthed something unintelligible but Raglan ignored him. He found Delaney's phone, raised it for Voss to see so she would do the same with Medina's, then cracked the phone beneath his heel. He dangled the handcuff and car keys and dropped them just about close enough for Delaney to stretch out his foot and drag them to him. Raglan looked concerned and tweaked the gag. 'Your tie's not straight.'

Raglan stooped inside the unmarked car and tore out the handset for their receiver. He joined Voss as she waited with a bound Medina. The detective was barefoot, her weapon stripped, a sock stuffed in her mouth, her belt used to hold the gag in place. Raglan looked from her to Voss.

'That woman's got a foul mouth on her,' said Voss.

'She has now,' said Raglan. He ushered her towards her car. Neither Delaney nor Medina could see where it was parked so would not be able to identify it. 'Did you get the flash drive?'

'Got it,' she said, patting her inside breast pocket.

Raglan smiled and extended his hand.

'You don't trust me after all of this?'

'Don't go all prima donna on me.'

Voss knew damned well it belonged to Raglan and tossed the flashlight to him. He unscrewed it and tapped out the military-grade USB drive. It was as dry and undamaged as when he had first hidden it.

They reached the car. 'I'll go in the trunk until we're through the gate. Then we wait for the exchange and get Casey Zeller back alive.'

'And what happens then?'

'We go somewhere warm. Away from this lousy weather.'

57

Raglan had Voss drive to a mall where there was a sports shop. She didn't question him when he told her what to buy. Using a side entrance, she kept her head low, avoiding security cameras. It was an easy purchase. Cash. No ID. No credit card. Fifteen minutes later Raglan and Voss waited at a multi-storey parking garage on the northern edge of DC. They looked out across the city. The Capitol building curved above rooftops in the distance. Voss was edgy. Raglan glanced at her finger tapping on the steering wheel.

She shrugged. 'This is my city. It feels small. I worked here for years. I know every back alley and squalid drug den there is. I've had running gunfights with drug crews: Barrio-18, MS-13, the Tiny Rascals. These gangs...' She shook her head, still looking out at the city, perhaps, Raglan thought, seeing the images and remembering the adrenaline-fuelled times. '... Black, Hispanic, Cambodian, Chinese, Korean. They were ready to kill or be killed. Killing was as simple as breathing in and out for them. And we obliged them when we had to. That was what it was. Them or us. We all knew what side of the fence we were on, but what Swain and his people did to my team? That ambush murdered two of my people. Good family men. And I took the heat. Lennie Elliot was a paid FBI informer and he played me, and my people paid the price.' She took a deep breath. 'And Swain was in on it from the beginning because he was helping launder money so others could buy weapons.'

'Swain is done with. Wipe that slate clean. The others we'll get to. You want the informer; I want the blonde.'

She glanced at him. 'Do you always get what you want?'

'So far,' he said.

'Do you really think they'll let Zeller live?'

'If we play our cards right.' He checked his watch. 'My guess is they'll want Zeller and me dead the moment they have the flash drive. Luckily they don't know about you. At least as far as we know. She made no mention of you when she called and that means Swain hadn't raised his suspicions about you to her.'

'But you're handing them the evidence.'

'It doesn't matter. Not now. I've got it in the right hands.'

Before she questioned him further Raglan's phone pinged with a text message.

'We're on,' he said.

He texted back demanding proof of life.

The killer had obviously been expecting the demand and Raglan's screen flared into a photo of Casey Zeller, looking the worse for wear with a morning edition of a Washington newspaper showing the day's date held next to his battered face.

Voss started the car as Raglan read the text.

'An hour for the handover. There's an urban renewal project north of the city.' He showed her the photograph that appeared soon after Zeller's. The vast building had car parking for at least fifty cars but the parking lot was empty. The sign on the building had letters missing but enough remained to tell them it was the Maryland County Industrial Laundry Company.

'That off the I-27?'

Raglan scrolled down the message. 'Yes.'

'I know it,' she said. 'It'll take forty-five minutes to get there if we're lucky. It's been for sale for years. The city planners have been in a wrangle over it with developers. The company went bust.' She pulled out her own phone and keyed in the address. She showed the picture to Raglan. 'It's fenced front, side and back. The rear opens on to an industrial estate. She pulled her fingers across the screen and enlarged the image showing the site plan. 'Abandoned buildings on the right beyond the fence, but they'll give me cover.'

'They'll be watching and waiting.'

'For you, not me. I'll drive to the industrial estate, then you take the car through the front. That's what they'll expect. One man. One car. No foot soldiers.'

'No. If this goes down the way we want then we need the car afterwards. If I drive in they'll disable the car. You drop me a block away and get into position.'

She nodded. Raglan was correct. Voss pressed the accelerator, sweeping the Acura so close to the curved concrete walls down the exit ramps that Raglan thought she would lose a door panel at any moment. She was good. She glanced at Raglan and smiled. She knew it.

Four minutes shy of the hour, Raglan walked up to the front fence of the abandoned factory. The mesh gate was padlocked. The weed-cracked, concrete parking lot looked as ragged and forlorn as the building's flaking paintwork. Raglan waited. A man with stubble for hair, wearing a leather jacket, appeared from a side entrance, strode across the parking area and, with a keen eye on passing traffic, opened the padlocked gate. He signalled Raglan inside and then padlocked the gate again.

'Walk ten feet forwards, stop, hands where I can see them.'

Raglan obeyed. The gatekeeper was American through and through. The surplus combat boots, the broad belt beneath his denim jacket, which would hold a weapon. He frisked Raglan. He knew what he was doing. Raglan had no weapon. The American pointed to the dark side of the building from where he had emerged.

'Over there.'

Raglan walked across the forlorn concrete and alongside the building where he saw a Suburban parked out of sight of the road. A metal door led inside. Raglan could have dealt with his escort but it served no purpose and the man knew it. He smiled congenially as he opened the door and ushered in the assassin's prey. Raglan knew that if Voss was not in place inside the building then he and Zeller would soon be dead.

The cavernous building was so vast it could have housed a football pitch and more. Oversized machinery lined both sides of the building except for a hundred square yards. Evidence suggested that other machines had once been bolted to the floor by large metal plates but they had long-since been removed. A welcoming committee of four men and the blonde assassin stood in a half-circle at the far wall, facing the length of the building. The side door brought Raglan within fifty yards of them. The blonde was tall. A lithe, athletic-looking woman, something the close-up clip on the phone hadn't shown. She wore cross training shoes, slim-fitting Lycra pants, a tight-fitting sweat top that was probably a high-spec manmade fibre and a loose weatherproof jacket. She looked as though she could function in any terrain in any weather. The perfect killer.

'You have it?'

'I want to see Zeller.'

'Of course you do.'

She half turned her head and nodded. In the background a door opened and two men dragged Zeller into view. He couldn't walk on one leg. It looked broken.

'He's a tough man,' said the blonde.

'You broke his leg?'

She shrugged. 'We needed information. Only then did he tell us there was a backup and that you had it.'

'Casey?' Raglan called.

There was no response.

'He's alive,' said the woman.

'Casey?' Raglan called again.

One of the men holding Zeller slapped him back to consciousness. Zeller raised his face and focused on Raglan.

Zeller nodded. 'Raglan. Sorry. Had to tell them.'

Zeller was hurt but staying on script. He and Raglan had known it might come to this.

'Bring him to me,' said Raglan.

Once again the woman nodded her consent. The men

dragged the lame Zeller and eased him down so that his back rested against old machinery. For a moment it looked as though the two men might tackle Raglan.

'No need,' said the woman. 'Raglan will surrender the flash drive without violence.'

Raglan handed it to one of the men who returned to the woman who was obviously in charge of this crew. One of her men stepped forwards with a laptop and plugged in the drive.

A moment later he shook his head. 'It's encrypted.'

The woman's expression did not change but her eyes offered an immediate threat. 'Raglan?'

'I don't know the passcode. If I did I would have copied the drive. Only Zeller knows the code to unlock it.'

'Then it's time we completed our business.'

Her tone of voice conveyed a simple message that their time had run out.

'Tell her,' said Raglan to Zeller who played the game again and shook his head. 'Tell her, Casey. You know how this'll play out.'

'No!' Zeller insisted.

Raglan knelt next to him. 'Tell them the code. Then we get out of here.'

'Then they'll kill us,' Zeller gasped, the pain from his beating evident in his voice.

Raglan glanced from Zeller to the woman. It looked convincing. A man who had stepped into a trap. A man not clever enough to have an exit plan except to go through with the exchange.

'Give it to them, then we have a chance to get out of here. I promise you.'

'You make rash promises, Raglan,' said Aram-banou.

'I made a trade; you won't kill us.'

For a second the assassin looked uncertain. Her eyes tracked around the building, seeking out any backup Raglan might have. She smiled. 'Raglan, you're alone. You're a fugitive. You have no way out.'

'Let me worry about that,' said Raglan. He eased Zeller up into a more comfortable position. 'Tell her.'

Zeller should have been in the movies. His face screwed up with anguish, stretching out those final moments before making the decision. Finally, he nodded. 'It's 26-9-7-26-1-7.'

The laptop holder keyed in the numbers, waited a couple of seconds. 'Got it.'

Aram-banou smiled. 'Our business is concluded.'

It was a signal to the men with her and as they began to raise their weapons Raglan hoped that Voss was in place.

She was.

A red laser dot appeared on the assassin's chest.

'I have friends, said Raglan. 'You have what you wanted. Try anything now and the high-powered rifle will kill you first. Your men might get to me and Zeller but you will be dead before you hit the floor. See it as a fair trade. Now it's just you and me and unfinished business.'

The Iranian looked at the unwavering dot on her chest and then to where the shooter might be. She was weighing the odds,

'Clear line of sight,' said Raglan. 'Turn away now and you'll live long enough for me to find you.'

'You will never find me and if you were ever that

unfortunate you would die. I am finished with this country now. I have what I want. And you must be grateful that you and you friend are alive.'

Raglan held her gaze. 'You murdered two good men. Innocent men. Like I said, one night I'll come and kill you, and it will be a slow death. Count your days. They are few.'

It was decision time. Aram-banou was a skilful operator but even she knew the risk of killing Raglan there and then was too great. She glanced down again at the unwavering red dot on her chest. She backed off with her men, eyes still searching the factory's vastness for the hidden sniper. It was a slow retreat with the laser staying on the woman. And then they were gone. Raglan heard the Suburban's tyres squeal.

Voss's voice carried from somewhere in the cavernous room. 'Raglan?'

'Clear!' he shouted. He bent down to Zeller. 'I should break your other leg.'

Zeller nodded. 'I didn't want to lose control of the dossier. Now they've got everything. Tell me you got the information to whoever.

'It's in safe hands and we still have time to get to the blonde and find where they have the weapons.'

'We?' said Zeller, forcing himself up from the floor with Raglan's help.

Voss appeared.

'Special Agent Jenna Voss, meet Casey Zeller, the man who started all this.'

Zeller looked Voss up and down and saw that all she

carried was her service weapon on her hip and a rangefinder laser sight. 'Jesus, no rifle?'

'Just the sight. It's all we needed.'

'Damn,' said Zeller. 'Remind me never to play poker with you.'

58

Nine hours and forty-six minutes after leaving the car impound, Jenna Voss pulled off Interstate 95 into a small town in South Carolina. She had kept to the speed limit, not wishing to give cause to any Highway Patrol officer to pull them over.

They had taken Zeller to hospital for treatment, being careful that they were not followed in case the Iranian killer decided Raglan and Zeller still posed a threat. Realistically she had no cause. She had secured the backup drive and Raglan was a fugitive. Why draw attention to herself and those with her? By the time Raglan had phoned Zeller's wife and arranged a private ambulance to take him to Pennsylvania, he guessed the assassin would be long-gone. And Zeller knew his part in it all was over.

'You get to Stroudsburg, you bring in a criminal lawyer and make a sworn statement of everything you know and what's gone down,' Raglan had told him. 'Then you get that in front of a judge. It's out of state so you'll be dealing with local jurisdiction. Give him the name of Detectives Delaney and Medina of the DC Metropolitan PD. Then you get out of there and into Canada until all the loose ends are tied up. I need your word, Casey.'

Zeller had agreed.

'I told Anne I'd get you home. Don't make me come and find you again. It's too much like hard work.'

Raglan and Voss had waited until the ambulance arrived, the private company paid by Anne Zeller on her credit card over the phone, and then they watched it leave. He and Voss headed south.

Raglan had said little during the journey other than to brief her on what he had learnt from Maguire.

'And how do we get to Central America?' she asked. 'Airports will have us flagged by now.'

'I don't know yet. One thing's for sure: we can't drive.'

They were a long way from DC now and although any news about them would surely have been shown on national television news channels, Raglan reckoned that in a small town local news would be of more interest to viewers. The odds were on their side. Voss and Raglan had taken cash from an ATM before leaving the city. If the authorities traced Voss's withdrawal, it might keep their search for her in the area for the next few hours at least. Raglan wondered if Delaney had taken what he'd been told seriously. He remembered Voss telling him one of Delaney's former colleagues had been a victim at the senator's house. That was motivation enough to pursue a lead and in forty-eight hours a judge in Pennsylvania would be asking the DC detectives questions.

Ever since they had rescued Casey Zeller, Voss had noticed Raglan favouring his wounded side. It was obvious that scaling the impound fence, along with everything else Raglan had been through, had caused some damage.

'I reckon we need to take a break, Raglan. There's less traffic at night and we're more easily noticed. Besides, that wound needs attention. I've got a medical kit in the trunk.'

He scowled. 'We can push on.'

'You're no good to anyone if we don't see to it,' she insisted. 'All we need is a Highway Patrol cop on night shift looking to break his boredom by pulling over a lone car travelling in the early hours.'

She was right. He had felt a couple of stitches tear the moment he had vaulted the fence. 'OK.'

Raglan told Voss to find the cheapest motel. The Acura was old enough to fit right in. Anything more expensive meant the car would look out of place. There was a motel opposite a shopping mall. It was cheap, it was clean and it had a half-dozen small trucks, U-Haul and delivery vans parked outside for the night. A convenient stopover for people driving long distances.

Raglan had Voss book her room first and then he followed twenty minutes later to book his own, making sure their rooms were not close to each other just in case things went wrong and either of them were identified. The night clerk didn't look twice at them.

Reglan stripped down to his underwear and looked at the ugly wound in his side. The gash on his leg needed a fresh dressing as well. There was a knock on the door.

Voss stepped quickly through the half-opened door, carrying a compact medical pack. She barely stopped herself looking for a moment too long at his near-naked torso.

'Couple of stitches have torn,' he said. 'I've washed it, but I need antiseptic.'

She nodded, rested the pack on the small table while he sat on the edge of the bed. He twisted to look at the wound in his side, ready to swab it.

'I'll do it,' she said. 'Easier.'

He nodded. She cleaned her hands and gently swabbed the skin around the ugly scar. The antiseptic stung, but he didn't flinch. Her face was close to his as she leant in to apply a fresh dressing, tape it and then rebandage. She knelt as she attended to the cut across his thigh, tugging a couple of butterfly clips across the wound.

'I can put the dressing on that,' he said without much conviction.

Her hand lingered. 'I can do it.' Her voice was a whisper. The pulse in her neck beating more rapidly.

She finished the dressing as he cupped her hair and lowered his head to kiss her. She didn't move. It was a slow, unhurried kiss. She sighed. They both knew it couldn't go any further.

'You'd tear open those wounds again,' she said.

He nodded. 'Worth a try, though.'

Voss eased back. 'Bad timing, Raglan. You have to rest up. We've a way to go.'

There could be no argument. The wound hurt like hell. His body needed a few hours to recover.

The television claimed their attention – CNN was covering the story. He flipped the channel. Fox had it as well. Voss and Raglan's photos were on screen. There was no mention of Delaney and his partner. No mention of the car they were thought to be driving. Just a basic news filler.

Two minutes tops. The death by shooting of a Pentagon official. Nothing more.

Raglan hoped it was all the FBI had, and they weren't hiding the fact that they knew about the Acura. He ran the odds. If Voss had been stationed in Virginia, would her car have been logged as belonging to an employee for the car park? If so, then the Feds would have checked back and already have the registration.

'Where you worked, would they have your car's registration?

'No.' A shrug. 'You needed to be supervisor level and above to warrant a parking bay. I used the main parking area.'

'We still need another car,' he said. 'Someone will remember. We've got another seven hours before we get to Miami. That's too long to be driving it now. It's dark. Move the car. Take it to the furthest point in the motel. Wipe it down. Park it at the back. Next to extractor fans or dumpsters. We need to get rid of it.'

'OK,' she said, and left. What had passed between them was for another day, perhaps.

Raglan checked outside and then locked the door behind her. He phoned for pizza, using the number on a card stuck next to the telephone. Twenty minutes, he was told. Raglan hung up and dialled Sokol in France on his mobile. The call was answered quickly.

'Bird, I need to get to Honduras in a hurry. I can't go commercial. I'm heading for Florida as a jump-off point. Do we know anyone?'

'You're still alive, then?'

'A couple of stitches and a stiff drink pulled body and soul together.'

'Danny, there's no one else in the States I know about. Not from our time in the Legion. I can start reaching out, but it will take days to find anyone. And unless we can find a hot-shot pilot or a drug smuggler with a high-speed boat, you won't be going anywhere.'

'There has to be a way. Anyone in Central America we can bring in? Belize? Guatemala?'

'Who we can trust? That's the Wild West, and can you imagine any of those cartel boys serving with us? Use fake ID and get on a plane in Miami.'

'I'm a fugitive, Bird; they'll pick me up. I'm on national news already. Being wanted by the FBI makes life difficult.'

'Zeller?'

'I got him. He's on his way home.'

'Good. But your trip to Honduras? We need to find a fast boat or a plane. I'll keep looking.'

Raglan finished the call. Getting out of the States was going to be a problem. Until the even bigger problem of the Honduran jungle and what he'd find there. But one step at a time. First he had to steal a car.

There was a knock on his door. Raglan glanced through the window and let Voss back in.

'Dad's car is hidden around the back. I let two of the tyres down just to dissuade anyone from stealing it. I want it there when we get back.'

Raglan gave the minimum tip to the pizza-delivery boy. Anything more would be conspicuous. Now Raglan would be invisible. Unkempt, unshaven, insignificant. One of many drop-offs made that night.

'We need a way out,' said Raglan as they shared the food. 'I've got no connections here. You know anyone?'

She shook her head. 'I'm going to be as hot as you are.' She lifted another slice of pizza. 'Maybe,' she said. 'Yeah, maybe.' She didn't say anything more. Raglan waited. She winced. 'It's a long shot.'

'We're lucky to have even that.'

She wiped her hands and pulled free her phone. 'I have a friend and he has a boat.'

'It'd need to be a big and fast boat. It's a long way.'

She shook her head dismissively. 'He'll have *the* boat we need. Guaranteed. He goes deep-sea fishing.'

'Ask him. I'll write a list of things we need. We'll pay him.'

She swallowed a mouthful of food, unfolded her legs and went for the door. 'Give me what you need. I have to check a couple of things out first.'

59

At 4.17 a.m. Raglan slipped out of bed, pulled on his jeans and felt the raw skin around the stitches in his side continue to complain. Not as bad as before Voss cleaned and dressed it. You take any bonus offered.

He skirted the motel's shadows, heading for the late-night bar several hundred yards away, one that he had noticed on their way into town. It had looked to be a noisy, fun-filled place with twenty cars or more parked up beneath the beckoning neon lights. Those lights had flickered off a couple of hours before and Raglan's instinct told him it was a watering hole for local barflies, some of whom would stagger out at two in the morning. Potentially too drunk to drive.

Three vehicles remained. A six-year-old Audi, a two-year-old pickup that defiantly sported a Confederate sticker and a Chevy Impala that looked to be at least twenty years old. Its paintwork, such as it was, looked as though it had been in a sandstorm, rubbed down to bare metal in places. The seats were ripped and there were abandoned fast-food packets in the rear footwell. A car no one would steal, which is why its owner would never lock it. It would be worth more on a scrap heap than for sale.

Raglan tugged the creaking door open, sank into the driver's seat and rammed the flat-head screwdriver he'd taken from the Acura's tool-kit into the ignition switch. Surprisingly, the engine sounded sweet. Clearly its owner cared more for the mechanics than the interior decor. He drove slowly down the back access road from the bar until he reached a turning that took him back on to the main road and within a hundred yards into the quiet of the motel. Raglan parked it near the Acura, with the commercial dumpsters between the two cars. He stripped out the detritus and then put the Acura's licence plates on to the Impala. If anyone found the Acura and wanted to trace it they would need to use the engine number to find its provenance. By then Raglan reckoned they would be a long way from South Carolina.

He rang her room when he got back. There was no answer. Then a knock on the door. She bore a cardboard tray with rich-smelling coffee cups and blueberry muffins. She smiled, tossed aside her peaked cap and settled the offering on the small table.

'Found the all-nighter on the next block. Figured we can get an early start.' She checked him out. He was dressed and looked ready to go. 'How's the side?'

'Good to go. Your friend with the boat?'

'No answer. I'll keep trying.'

It was another eight hours to Miami. The radio crackled; the Chevy had no CD player and the aircon and heater had long-since given up the ghost, if it had ever existed in the first place. But the engine purred and if Raglan tapped the accelerator it gave a tentative cough: a clearing of the pipes that said it was ready to go; the road was straight, and soon the sun would shine. It wasn't all bad. Only uncomfortable.

She phoned Ronnie Diaz again. This time she got through. 'Ronnie, it's Jenna. I've been trying to reach you.'

'I know,' said the retired FBI agent.

'You didn't pick up.'

'Because you are a fugitive and I am retired and I do not wish to be arrested. Mother of God, Jenna, you're wanted for murder.'

'I didn't kill anyone and I need help,' she said.

'Why else would you phone? Not to ask about the fishing, I bet.'

'Ronnie, Lennie Elliot is alive. He's not only mixed up in money laundering and drug smuggling, but a major armaments conspiracy. I have a lead. I want him. Can you help me?'

Ronnie Diaz fell silent. She waited. Raglan glanced at her. She continued to wait, hoping that the chance of catching the man responsible for leading her and her men into an ambush would provoke Diaz's sense of injustice.

'You're certain of this?'

'I saw his photo. The Defense Clandestine Service Deputy Director Jack Swain was running a black op in Central America. Big players. Senators and private contractors. Check out a company called EDM – Executive Decision Management. They're huge, and are funnelling hundreds of millions of drug-money dollars through shell companies to buy arms. When Lennie Elliot set my team up it was small change compared to what he was protecting. We must have been breathing down their necks, we just didn't know it.

Our own people killed us, Ronnie. There's more but if that's not enough to convince you then I'll understand.'

She heard him sigh. Forty years of law enforcement would never let him off the hook. 'We'll talk. How long will it take you to get to Pelican Harbor?'

'Seven hours, maybe eight.'

'Text me what you need. Leave whatever you're driving in the parking lot then walk to the end of the long dock. I'll wait there. Mine's a thirty-four-foot Sea Ray. It's old like me, but damned if we still don't have some juice left in us.'

He hung up.

Voss looked uncertain as she gazed at the dead phone in her hands.

'Can you trust him?'

She nodded. 'But he's putting himself on the line. He's just retired. He could lose everything. I shouldn't have asked him but I don't know where else to turn.'

'We turn to our friends when we have to. He thinks highly of you. It's his decision.'

She nodded and gazed through the light rain at the dull road ahead. In that moment Raglan sensed her own vulnerability. She had taken the same decision to put her life and career on the line to trust him.

'We'll be OK,' he said.

'Raglan, I want the bastard who killed my men.'

'Then let's get to it,' said Raglan and pressed the accelerator. The engine growled; the car surged. They both needed more than OK.

60

Hours later the I-95 took them close to Vero Beach.

Voss remembered her surveillance of Raglan and his time spent with a young teenager. This was where her relationship with Raglan had started and her instincts that Raglan was more than a tourist were proven correct.

'Your family is here.'

'They're going back tomorrow.'

'We're close. You could see them.'

'No. Feds will be crawling through the bushes. You know that.'

'The boy?'

'He's been through a lot.'

'Then why don't we pull over and phone? Your burner won't be traced.'

Raglan shook his head. 'Don't let emotion get in the way, Voss. I need to focus and so do you. We haven't even got close to the people we're after and we might never, but until we know we've done everything we could then we don't need distraction.'

★

They drove into the outer city limits and Voss guided Raglan to the Pelican Harbor Marina.

'Left on the JFK Causeway,' she said, gesturing him off the long boulevard. 'Halfway along, turn across at the traffic lights.' Raglan pulled the Chevy across the double-lane road into the broad open space. The glittering water beckoned them. She pointed for him to park. The glare from the sunlight bounced off the hard concrete surfaces.

Raglan wrenched free the Acura's licence plates. She looked as though he had torn a sticking plaster from a wound. 'No need to give the cops a gift,' he said. 'They see these plates here on a stolen car and the Feds will know who to look for in the marina. Your friend. I'll bet no one here is going to give a second thought to a battered old Chevy without plates. It'll get towed to a pound and crushed.'

She nodded. Raglan was right. He tossed the plates into the ocean. 'I hope you can trust this guy,' said Raglan, 'because we are as exposed here as a pimple on a nudist's backside.'

'I'd trust him with my life,' she said, and grabbed her small rucksack from the car. 'This way.'

He stepped alongside her. 'It's not *your* life I'm worried about.'

They made their way along the harbour wall that jutted out beyond the marina moorings. A motorboat was tied up. There was no sign of anyone on board. If Voss's friend had decided to protect his pension and the Miami FBI wanted to spring a surprise on their rogue agent and the fugitive she was with, this is where, in Raglan's view, they would do it. Armed men from the boat suddenly appearing and a vehicle boxing them in on the breakwater. Game over.

Voss called out. 'Ronnie?'

The man Raglan had deliberately confronted at the space centre when he had first arrived appeared from below decks.

'Jenna,' he said, with a weary look. 'Come on down. I don't want you two felons in sight.'

They clambered down and entered the cabin's cool interior. The leather seats and cherry-wood laminate fittings shared the space with a small but well-fitted galley. Raglan could see ahead to the forecabin sporting a double bed. A chart table and rack with folded charts were on one side of the saloon next to bench seats but there was enough electronic equipment not to need them.

Ronnie Diaz saw Raglan take it all in.

'I'm old-fashioned and I don't believe in putting my life into the hands of a damned GPS system that gets switched off for maintenance. It's there if I really need it. Sit.'

They pressed next to each other on the bench seat as Diaz took a jug of iced water from the refrigerator. He poured three glasses. Raglan could smell the mint floating in the ice.

'Ronnie, thank you for—' Voss started.

He held up a hand to stop her before she had barely begun. 'Don't thank me, Jenna. I can't help you the way I would like.'

She couldn't hide her disappointment.

'This boat could never get us get to Honduras,' Raglan explained to her. 'It's got a range of, what, a hundred and fifty miles plus?' he said, looking for confirmation to Diaz, who nodded. 'We'd need a boat a damned sight bigger than this.'

'And it'd take a long time to get there by sea. Longer than you folks have got,' added Diaz.

Raglan drank the refreshing water. Voss looked at her former partner. 'Ronnie, everything we need to finish this is in Honduras. Every airport will have us red-flagged. How long to get us down to Key West?'

'If I watch my speed and fuel we'll be there in five or six hours but that's the nation's appendix. There's nothing down there except sea, sand and a tourist industry based around Hemingway having lived there.'

Voss shook her head. 'More than that, Ronnie. There's a flying boat. A Grumman Mallard. It has a flying range of two thousand miles. With a bit of careful manoeuvring past Cuba she'll get us there below the radar.'

Diaz looked from her to Raglan, who was as nonplussed as him. 'We don't have the money,' said Diaz.

'I know, but what I have is persuasion and leverage.' She raised her hand to stop any further interrogation. 'Trust me. I'll explain later but now we have to get going.'

He shrugged and turned the key in the saloon's ignition switch; then he stepped on to the companionway leading to the cockpit. 'Head's in there; it's a vacu-flush toilet so when you're puking don't put your head too far down.' He grinned. She grimaced. 'And I've made up a bed for'ard. That's up front to you. The sharp end.' He looked at Raglan. 'She gets seasick in a hot tub.'

Raglan eased out of the bench seat to follow Diaz. He turned to her. 'And you thought this was a good idea?'

'You can throw me around in a helicopter and I can handle it. But not these vomit buckets. You've no idea how badly I want to catch these people, Raglan, and if I have to puke all the way to Central America, I'll do it.'

The boat's powerful twin five-litre engines throbbed; the boat swayed.

They were under way.

61

Raglan sat topside as Diaz piloted the boat away from the confines of harbour and city. Once in the open sea he opened the throttle, the bow parted the calm waters, the powerful wake pluming behind them. Raglan relished the buffeting salt-laden air. It had been years since he had sped across water in a high-speed RIB as part of a commando attack. Now the speed and tang of the sea blew away the creeping fatigue his wounded body felt.

'Nice boat,' said Raglan. 'The FBI must have a great pension plan.'

Ronnie Diaz glanced from the wheel at the man who, to his way of thinking, had caused all the trouble. 'I took a bribe.'

For a moment his comment caught Raglan by surprise. Then he saw the older man's shoulders rumble with laughter. Diaz looked back with a grin on his face. 'That always gets them. Back in the day this was a quarter-million-dollar boat. Twenty years later it's a thirty-thousand-dollar boat. I sold up what I had. Wasn't much. If I get homesick for a hot bath and cable I'll book a week in a motel.' He fell silent, concentrating on the distant horizon.

They were soon clear of land and Diaz kept the throttle

at a fixed position. Raglan was content at the lack of conversation. By now Maguire would have digested everything he had been sent in the dossier. He would hold the information close to himself until all the pieces made sense and it was clear whom to trust. He heard Voss retching below deck. Diaz shook his head, but kept his eyes on the open sea. 'Since day one she figured you were more than a tourist. She's a good agent. And she was the fall guy for an operation that had been cleared by the suits. She took it hard. They threw her career down the pan. This informant was a set-up, but you know that, right?'

'I know,' said Raglan.

'If she ever finds him I hope she doesn't kill him. She needs him back here. He'll make a deal, clear her name, get her back on the HRT.'

'Why are you telling me this?'

'No reason. Just passing the time. And to let you know that if things go bad, which they will, she'll have your back.' He glanced at Raglan. 'I can only do so much and then the Bureau will put two and two together. I'll be dragged into this whether I like it or not. And I don't.'

'But here you are.'

'I made a choice. She got a raw deal, and this case is worth pursuing. I don't like bad guys and I hate those who betray what we stand for. I'll do what I can.' He pointed to one of the lockers. 'What you asked for is in there.'

Raglan steadied himself against the buffeting power and opened the locker. There was a large black nylon valise in the roomy locker. He pulled it out, settled his back against the bench seat and unzipped it.

'I left it all loose. There are a couple of daysacks in there.

Figured you'd want to pack your gear the way you want it. Sorry, but I forgot the compass you wanted.'

'No problem,' said Raglan. 'This is all good. Thanks.'

Diaz watched Raglan finger a grubby roll of dollar bills held with an elastic band. 'There's five hundred in used notes. Groundsheets and tie cord. Got you a Glock each with silencers; they're untraceable. Two full clips apiece. And maybe three days of cold rations if you eke them out. The two satellite phones might be your last chance to get out but you know how useless they are under the tree canopy. Need to find a clearing for them to be of any use. There's a couple of emergency flares and two decent combat knives. Last time I looked, Honduras had the highest murder rate in the Americas. Gangs, drug dealers, kidnapping, smuggling. You're going into a shitstorm. You do know that, right?'

'Doubt it'll be anything other,' said Raglan.

'Uh-huh.' Diaz settled himself deeper into the pilot seat. 'Don't get her killed.' He looked at Raglan. 'I'd be mighty pissed if she didn't get back in one piece.'

'I'll do my best.'

'I made sure to throw in the insect-repellent sprays. Mosquitoes will eat you alive in the jungle. But I figure you might know that already which is why you asked for them.' He looked at Raglan who didn't need to answer the obvious. 'Of course you know,' said Diaz. 'Damned bugs and their viruses can kill you just as soon as a bullet.'

Voss retched so loudly both men looked at each other again. Voss wouldn't be in any fit state to tempt mosquito bites if she didn't get past the seasickness. Raglan remembered when he had first volunteered for the Legion's paratroopers. Crammed together in the confined space of a transport plane, overladen with equipment as the aircraft hurtled through the sky buffeted by cross winds, flying low at a combat height of five hundred feet, hardened men vomiting on to the steel floor. The stench bringing the gorge to the back of the throat. Nervous recruits desperate for the door to open and the rush of cold air, wind and noise to relieve them of their misery.

Raglan steadied his gait against the sea swell and went below. Voss was wretched. He leant down and hauled her away from the toilet bowl. Too weak to offer any resistance, she allowed him to manhandle her on to the deck. He braced her back against the bench seat bulkhead, facing the stinging spray from the bow wave, reached into the cold box and pulled the tab on a club soda. 'This'll help,' he said.

She gripped the cold can with both hands, her body trembling from the nausea. She guzzled, shook her head, and belched.

Raglan smiled. 'Only four more hours.'

Voss crushed the can and smiled bravely.

And then leant over the side and vomited again.

62

Detectives Delaney and Medina's humiliation soon waned when Delaney convinced his aggressive partner that they should investigate Raglan's claims quickly and with all the departmental backing they could get. A murdered senator was a federal investigation aided by the police; a murdered African-American veteran was strictly police and now, with a deputy director from the Defense Clandestine Service being gunned down in their jurisdiction, they had just cause to insist on taking the lead in the investigation. What they both knew was that the Pentagon Force Protection Agency and their own internal investigation division would vie with the FBI to seize control, so it was no surprise when they were refused entry to Jack Swain's office. The Feds already had their feet under the table, the door firmly locked and inter-agency rivalry clearly marked out. They and the DIA and Pentagon police had slammed doors in their faces. Which Delaney thought was good.

'Good?' said Medina as they walked back to their car. 'The Feds should stick to kidnappers and child porn,' she added.

Delaney shrugged. They were going through the motions.

Letting the federal authorities pull rank on them. So they behaved like the chided underlings the Feds thought them to be, which was, as Delaney repeated, good. The Feds would be at each other's throats while he and Medina got on with the job of pulling Jack Swain's life apart. When Raglan had not put a bullet in them at the car pound and told Delaney what had gone down, the cynical disbelief that every cop has buried in their DNA was momentarily suspended. He and Medina had opened a case file on Jack Swain and so far no one was talking. The only thing they heard were alarm bells.

'We knew it was a non-starter at the Pentagon,' he said as they settled back into the Ford Taurus. 'Jack Swain's office will have been cleared out minutes after they learnt of his death. And if Kim Burton is now counter-intelligence she'll have intelligence agency contacts we will never know about. Maybe the Englishman was right about her. He convinced Voss.'

'I would like to put that bitch in jail,' said Medina as she fired up their car.

Delaney pulled the seat belt across him and sniffed the air. 'Did you put clean socks on this morning?'

'Fuck you, Delaney.' She floored the accelerator.

Delaney sighed and smiled. 'Still got the bad mouth.'

In less than forty minutes they swung into the apartment block where Jack Swain had lived. On the tenth floor, police tape stretched across the door where an MPD uniformed officer stood. Further along the corridor a man in a suit and tie whirled around at their approach.

'Any trouble?' said Medina to the cop on the door, seeing the fast-approaching younger man.

'Nah. This guy says he's from the FBI Field Office, said he's here—'

The FBI agent interrupted the cop. 'You don't need to ask the flatfoot why I'm here. I've been told to check Swain's apartment.'

Delaney winced; the cop on the door smiled. The young FBI agent was out of his depth. He just didn't know it.

'Flatfoot?' said Medina. She had that smile which told Delaney and the cop that in less than a minute he would not be standing in the same place and if he was he would probably have both hands covering his genitals. 'Son, you've been working too many graveyard shifts. I bet you spend most of that time watching old *Columbo* reruns. We don't call MPD uniformed officers flatfoots. We have respect for the men and women who serve the nation's capital.'

'Like I give a shit? I'm investigating the death of a federal employee. You and the MPD are obstructing that investigation. This involves national security.'

'You don't have a court order, do you, son?' said Medina.

'What?'

'You see, the District of Columbia Attorney's Office has wide, sweeping authority. It's the federal prosecutor for the capital. We have the authority. Mr Swain was murdered on our patch as were two other men in the nightclub where Swain was found.'

'I don't have the authority?' he said incredulously.

'Did you shave this morning, Agent' – she glanced at his open wallet bearing his badge and identification –'Monroe?'

'What?' said the frustrated Fed.

'I didn't think so,' Medina said. 'When you're old enough to wield a safety razor without hurting yourself then you can come and join the grown-ups' club.' She smiled. 'Until then, fuck off.'

She ducked beneath the police tape. Delaney paused long enough to offer a consoling smile. 'I'd do what she says. She had a sock put in her mouth by one of yours. She's still upset. The FBI is currently Public Enemy Number One in her book. Oh, and she's correct. This is a homicide we're investigating.'

Delaney stepped into the apartment.

Special Agent Monroe was flummoxed. He shook his head and turned away.

'Have a nice day,' said the cop at the door. And with a smile added, 'Asshole.'

Once inside the apartment, Delaney followed Medina's example and pulled on shoe covers and gloves; then he made his way along the apartment's passage into the main living area. It was a spacious apartment. Two bedrooms, a study and views across the city. It had been elegantly furnished, probably by one of the city's designer shops, thought Medina as she stood and gazed at the wrecked apartment. She smiled. The white-suited crime-scene examiners had torn the place apart.

Delaney stepped around the upturned furniture, nosing through what remained. He stopped at a side table with a telephone and its integrated recorder. He paused. 'Why have an old analogue phone in a digital age?' he said to no one in particular.

'Some people like to hold a proper phone to their ear,' said Medina as she joined him.

Delaney flipped the message recorder's compartment. He pressed the button. The tape was silent. 'No welcome message,' he said.

'Maybe he wasn't a welcoming kind of guy,' said Medina.

'Unlike me,' said Delaney.

'Just like you,' she said. 'I dunno, maybe he liked to phone for hookers and didn't want to use his cell. No location finder on an analogue phone.'

'If these spooks want to use a phone out of hours they'll have burners.'

'You speak from experience?' she said.

He smiled and raised his hand showing his wedding band. 'I'm a good boy.'

She sighed. 'I know. I'll never have anything to blackmail my way out of trouble when the time comes.' She saw the senior crime-scene examiner enter the room from one of the bedrooms. 'Hey, Garcia. Anything?' she said.

The senior examiner stepped forwards and tugged down his face mask. 'Found meds in his bathroom. He was a sick man. Cancer.'

'Then he had a quick way out,' said Medina.

'You know, you can be a heartless bitch at times,' said Delaney without it sounding like a criticism.

'Bitch yes, heartless no. What would you rather have: the Big C or a nine millimetre?'

'What else?' said Delaney to Garcia.

The man pulled up his mask. 'You're gonna like this.'

The detectives followed him across the room to the gas fireplace. The glass-fronted fire was a yard wide with ceramic wood logs. There was an inspection panel in the side of the chimney breast. The examiner bent down and opened the panel. 'For the fire to work it needs to be plugged into the mains electricity. That's how you get the spark for the gas. This isn't plugged in.'

'The weather's cold,' said Delaney. 'I'd want extra heating. If only for the comfort of seeing the flames.'

'Especially for a sick man,' said Medina.

'Exactly. And there are big windows in these apartments so the glass holds the cold air. So, yeah, you'd think he'd want to light the fire. And before you ask, no, it's not broken. So we dusted for prints on the glass and found Swain's.' He pointed. 'Here and here,' he said, showing the blackened smudges on each side of the glass panel. 'You want to clean the inside of the glass you unhinge it and drop it down just like his prints show.'

'But there's no need to clean it if the fire isn't being used,' said Medina.

'Correct,' said the examiner and eased down the fire's glass front. 'Reach in and up to the front of the fire. There's a ledge. I saw it when I went in with a mirror light. Thought you should do the honours.'

Delaney obliged. His gloved fingers found a metal box and eased it down. It was several inches long and four wide. It looked like a child's pencil box. He prised the lid open. Inside, neatly stacked, were thirty micro cassettes, the kind used in an analogue answering machine.

Delaney smiled. 'Whatever Swain was doing he had an insurance policy.'

63

Ronnie Diaz had kept the Sea Ray at a steady speed, the rev counter always hovering just below 4,000, which gave the boat a comfortable twenty-nine knots. By the time the sun started to drop towards the horizon they had followed the Keys' coastline for more than an hour. It was almost dusk when Diaz pointed out the irregular-shaped harbour nestling between two of the low-lying land masses.

'Stock Island Marina. We're almost there.'

Voss had weathered the journey better than she thought possible. Raglan had kept her close, supporting her when she threw up, used an ice-pack compress on her forehead and made sure she had plenty of fresh water to drink. He had a quiet word with Diaz, asking him to talk to her as often as possible, forcing her to concentrate on something other than the oscillating horizon. By the time Diaz slowed the boat for the last half-hour she was looking stronger and ventured below decks for a cold shower. When she emerged she had changed into slim-fitting running clothing – leggings and top – from her backpack. Raglan noticed she now wore a pair of sturdy cross training shoes. One step removed from being a decent-enough jungle boot.

Ronnie Diaz smiled at her. 'Y'see, not so bad after all, eh?'

She grimaced as she stood next to Raglan and gripped the handrail looking towards the landfall. 'I'll never complain about flying the red-eye in coach again,' she said.

Diaz eased back the throttles; the boat slowed and glided more elegantly through the offshore waters. 'Now that you resemble a human being again and can take in what I'm telling you; I gave Raglan the equipment. Everything you need for a couple of days in that valise. Everything except a few pounds of common sense, that is.' He shrugged. 'No point telling you not to do this, I suppose? This is your last chance to bail.'

Voss gave him her best glare of disapproval.

'OK,' he said, surrendering to the inevitable.

She pointed. 'See that grey flying boat on the mooring pontoon? That's the *Grey Goose.*'

Raglan and Diaz stared towards the twin-engined old flying boat which barely moved in the sea swell. The fuselage sported faded paintwork of a flying goose, its head thrust forwards on to the front of the aircraft, its extended wings climbing up across the bodywork to the underside of the plane's wings. 'That's an old plane,' said Raglan.

'Grumman Mallard. Like an old Volkswagen Beetle of the air. Those things just keep on keeping on. That one's circa 1950. And it's called *Goose*?' said Diaz.

'The pilot's a contrary SOB. He used to fly a Grumman Goose that crashed. He hates the idea of flying a plane named after a duck,' said Voss, focusing on the plane.

Diaz shut down the throttles and let the boat drift. They were a couple of hundred yards off the anchored Grumman.

'I busted a smuggling operation. It was run by the Chicago mob,' said Voss. 'One of the couriers was a hotshot Australian pilot, Marty Webster. I turned him. We put two Chicago mob families away for a long time. I gave him witness protection and a new name, Harry Briscoe. I set him up with a legit commercial business down here. He runs supplies to the islands, occasionally takes passengers. He lives on board the plane. He's our man. Get us alongside, Ronnie.'

Diaz started the engines and edged closer to the fat-bellied aircraft. The plane's above-water side hatch was open. Diaz brought his boat alongside, reversed the engines so the boat steadied, then let the boat drift gently to nudge against the aircraft's fuselage, aft of the wings.

A distinctly Australian accent called out. 'Hey, whoever you are, piss off out of it. I'm not a bloody mooring buoy!'

'Harry Briscoe! Get you Aussie ass out here,' said Voss in response.

A moment later, a lean, tanned, shaven-headed man of indeterminate age wearing tattered shorts and vest bent down to peer through the hatch.

'Aw jeez, mate, don't tell me. You're bringing trouble to my door.'

'It's a matter of life and death, Harry,' said Voss.

Briscoe looked at Diaz and Raglan. 'They look healthy enough to me.'

'Not their lives, Harry. Yours.'

Twenty minutes later an unhappy Briscoe sat in one of the metal-framed seats bolted to the floor, nursing a cold bottle of beer. A makeshift cot straddled the aisle at the rear of the aircraft. Harry Briscoe was one step away from being a beach bum: the main difference being he didn't drive a battered van strapped down with surfboards. Raglan saw the official-looking uniform hanging next to the bed. Pressed blue Bermuda shorts, crisp white shirt with wings over the breast pocket. Briscoe might look rough and ready on his down time, but he knew how to behave and dress for his public role when dealing with clients.

Briscoe's head drooped after Voss told him what was needed. 'I never thought you'd blackmail me, Special Agent Voss. That's a helluva long way. Bloody Honduras. Look, I'd love to help you out, I really would, but it's a no-go, love. My co-pilot is off with his bird for a few days. I've no idea where he is.'

'You can fly this single-handed,' said Voss. 'Don't BS me, *Marty*.'

Briscoe's face dropped at the mention of his real name, and the implication it carried. How difficult would it be for his new identity to be leaked to those who would take revenge?

'I'll take the right-hand seat. I'm rated on twin engines,' said Raglan.

Briscoe looked at Raglan. 'You bloody well would be, wouldn't you?' There was little doubt in Briscoe's mind that the man sitting opposite him was more than capable of doing most anything he was asked to do. And the woman hadn't even raised a smile in his direction.

'It's an easy run,' said Raglan. 'We go in below radar, land, you turn around, find a place to refuel and you're home and dry.'

Briscoe looked from one deadpan face to the other. 'Easy? Hang on, what do you know I don't? There's a US Naval Air Station at Key West.'

'You file a flight plan for somewhere remote and close enough to fly low and land. Tell ATC you're doing an instrument check and when you're about to touch down you switch off your transponder. They think you've landed. You open the throttle and away we go,' Raglan told him.

Harry Briscoe seldom had cause to not slug beer from a bottle. He was a connoisseur. But the bottle only got halfway to his lips. 'Away we go to bloody jail if we get nicked. You're making me a criminal.'

'You're already one,' said Voss. 'You were reprieved and given a second chance.'

'And I've got a clean slate. Jeez, now you want me to do this?'

'If it goes pear-shaped I will make sure you are not prosecuted.'

'Oh yeah? I reckon you're up to no bloody good and this bloke here,' – he nodded at Diaz – 'hasn't said a word since he came aboard.'

'I'm a retired FBI agent. She's my old partner. We'll cover for you, Briscoe,' said Diaz.

'What, a retired Fed has clout?'

'Enough to guarantee you'll be out in the cold if you don't play along,' said Voss.

Briscoe looked decidedly unhappy.

Voss nodded towards Raglan. 'He's worked for British intelligence. We're pursuing dangerous men, Harry, and we have to do it off the books with someone we trust, someone who has the skill and the nerve to see it through. If for any reason you run into any kind of difficulty with the authorities I will vouch for you and my superiors will give you blanket immunity. And I wouldn't be surprised if the government didn't reward you for your co-operation.'

Neither Raglan nor Ronnie Diaz showed their surprise as Voss lied through her teeth.

Harry Briscoe took a swig, looked at the three supplicants and shrugged. 'Why didn't you say so from the off? I'll get my charts.'

The moment Briscoe had agreed his persona changed. No longer the beer-swilling beach bum, he chose the appropriate chart, settled a makeshift table across the seats and drew a line from their position at Key West.

'We can't fly at night. That'll bring the authorities down on us before I even get airborne. So, let's see... first light we tell air traffic control I'm out on a local VFR flight to Dry Tortugas National Park, which is... here,' he said, indicating a small group of islands beyond Key West. 'Lots of boats and sea planes do the trip. It's a short hop. Raglan here is right. We put a flight plan in and just before landing turn off the transponder, go south for Honduras avoiding Cuban and Mexican airspace.' He looked at Raglan. 'You're a devious bastard, mate. I don't know how you know this stuff.'

'I have friends like you, Harry,' said Raglan.

'Do we have the range?' said Voss.

Briscoe nodded without taking his eyes and finger off the chart. 'I have a couple of thousand Ks, but where in Honduras do you want to land?'

Raglan studied the route, tracing a line along the Central

American Yucatán Peninsula, past Belize and Guatemala, and then pressed his finger on the tip of the Honduran land mass.

'There,' said Raglan. 'Put us down in that lagoon. It's a big one.'

Briscoe hummed and hawed, appeared to weigh the odds and then nodded. 'Yeah, could do. There's an airport just south of Jericó at Trujillo, so they'll pick us up if we fly too close. I'll take the long way in, stay out at sea then come in low, further north... here. I'll get out the same way.'

'You won't have enough fuel to get back,' said Raglan.

'I'll manage.' He tapped the map. 'I'll refuel in Mexico, at Laguna Chunyaxché, just south of Cancún.' He glanced up at the others, as if by way of apology. 'I know a girl there.'

64

Ronnie Diaz headed for the shore. A mooring for the night at the local marina and then he would go back to Miami.

Briscoe threw a couple of sleeping bags at his uninvited guests, told them to bed down as best they could on the stripped-out metal fuselage. Showed them where he kept cold rations for hot nights and then clambered into the co-pilot's seat and crawled beneath the instrument panel through a narrow space into the forward hatch, wedged himself in, and fell asleep.

Voss winced as the plane's rivets dug into her ribs. It was humid inside the aircraft. She watched Raglan clamber outside and slip into the water. She looked out of the hatch and saw he had swum to the mooring pontoon where he clambered aboard and settled himself for the night. The stardust-sprinkled water looked inviting. She slipped into the inky warm water and swam over to him. He hauled her up. They lay side by side gazing at the firmament. The warm air settled over them.

'You don't mind sharks, then?'

'They'd choke on me,' she said, smiling.

He remained silent for a minute because so far she hadn't

asked what might lie ahead. Raglan wanted to make sure she understood.

'Once we get there, we make our way inland. We'll establish a fallback position. An RV.'

She nodded. Tactical logistics were second nature. 'Understood.'

'We have satellite phones and we might need help at some point.'

'From?'

'I dunno yet. But my guess is the Feds.'

She gawped. 'Say what?'

'Listen to me. We're going into a situation where we are likely to be overwhelmed. Getting in is one thing, getting out another. If we stop these people—'

'You mean if you kill the Iranian,' she interrupted.

'And I'm supposed to believe you're not here for anyone but yourself? This is no flag-waving jaunt, Voss. You want the man who led your team into an ambush, I want what I want, but when it comes to staring down too many barrels we might need help. Suicide missions are overrated.'

'And how do I call in the cavalry?'

'You call it in to the Miami Field Office. You tell them you've been abducted.'

'By you?'

'Take your pick, there'll be plenty to choose from. If a US citizen is abducted by a foreign power then the FBI has the right to put a task force together. They didn't teach you that at the academy? I thought you led a Hostage Rescue Team?'

'On my home turf.'

'You're the key to bringing in the cavalry when we need it.'

'They couldn't get to us in time.'

'There's a US task force based at Soto Cano Air Base in Honduras. Been there for years, providing medical assistance, disaster response and military training. They'd love a punch-up. They can have choppers with us in thirty minutes. All I am saying is the time might come when we can't get out on our own.'

She nodded. The way ahead beckoned. In a few hours she would arm herself and follow the Englishman into a hostile arena. The projected scenario of fighting in an unfamiliar environment clearly worried her.

Raglan caught the brief shadow of concern. She had the courage to go into a firefight with an FBI Hostage Rescue Team but he didn't know how reliable she'd be in an unknown environment like the jungle. The one thing Raglan did not want was for her to freeze on him once they started wading through snake- and crocodile-infested mangrove swamps. Best to get the reality into the open.

'Listen,' he said gently. 'We'll be going through some tough terrain. Mangrove swamps and jungle rivers can be brutal.' He paused to let her imagine the hostile environment. 'And there'll be crocodiles.' He saw her features harden.

'I see. Obviously I thought there would be.'

'Yeah. Obviously. Voss, you've come this far, but I travel best alone.'

'No. I go with you.'

'Stay at the RV and bring in the cavalry when I need them.'

'I'll dog your footsteps, Raglan, so don't even think about me staying behind.'

'All right. Thought it worth mentioning.'

'Thank you.'

There was nothing more to be said. The following days would be hazardous; their thoughts now needed to be focused on reaching their objective. They knew so little – but it had to be enough. Raglan glanced at her. Like a soothing waterbed, the pontoon bobbed gently on the tide. There was no denying his desire for her. And he was damned sure she felt the same for him. She turned, knees bent. He extended his arm and she folded into him.

He listened to her breathing. She had fallen asleep.

He sighed. There was nothing like a good night's rest.

65

Soon after dawn Briscoe had called air traffic control and told them he was heading for a VFR test flight to Marco Island. After an hour he skimmed the surface as if landing, switched off his transponder so he could not be tracked and turned for the north-west coast of Cuba. For three hours he remained at low level, avoiding Cuban and Mexican radar. Raglan had done the pre-flight checks with him, and let himself be seen in the co-pilot's seat on take-off by anyone observant enough and who might have thought it suspicious that the Grumman was airborne with only the pilot on board.

The route was as planned. The Grumman had older instruments on the panel above Raglan's head, and a modern multifunction navigation display on the flight console that Briscoe asked Raglan to tick off as they went through their pre-flight checks. The focus and attention to detail reminded Raglan how good it was to be in a plane's cockpit. Briscoe was clinically efficient. And once airborne gave Raglan the nod.

'All right, mate, I'll take it from here. You get back with the lovely lady. You two need to have a conversation about what's down there. Bloody jamboree of trouble as far as

I remember. Not the friendliest of places. She knows that, does she?'

'I mentioned it.'

Briscoe grinned. 'Yeah, I bet you did. You won't catch me wading through mangrove swamps. Like to keep my feet dry and my balls intact.'

Raglan clawed his way out of the small cockpit back to where Voss had checked the contents of Diaz's bag. She pulled back her hair and tied it in a ponytail. To Raglan's eye she looked to be a different woman than the one he had spent the last few days with. As if this was what she was cut out to do.

'You have any idea where we're heading once we land?'

Raglan unfolded the chart and settled into the seat on the opposite side of the aisle. He traced his finger from the estuary at the end of the lagoon. 'There's a road on the fringe of the lagoon that comes down from the small airport. Briscoe is going to come in far enough away and low enough to avoid their radar. That estuary is forty metres wide. He'll get us as far upriver as he can. We'll strike out for this small settlement here.'

'If this is drug-lord territory they won't help us.'

'If the old CIA training camp is where I think it is then Luis Reyes's haunt will be close by. He had a distribution base where Jack Swain's people wanted to store the weapons. They'll transport them to a northern port and then load them on to a ship for Iran.'

'They must have flown the cargo down here. You can fill a C130 with enough cargo to make the move clean and simple.'

'No, I don't think so. A Herc needs five thousand feet of

runway. There's nothing on any map. And if there was, the jungle would swallow it in months if it wasn't kept clear. No, what they needed was road transport and then a place to store the weapons.'

'If they had hangars, those kind of structures would be seen from the air. Raglan, we can't do this on our own.'

'We'll make that determination when we find them.'

'And then?'

'Make a noise, create a diversion and get inside their compound.'

'This is not the most well-planned incursion I've been involved in.'

'We've all made plans for attacks in the past and when it goes down it usually goes pear-shaped. Adapt or die, Voss.'

'My name's Jenna.'

'I know.' He shoved the chart back where it belonged. 'But this is business, so let's not get too cosy.'

'After the other night?'

'If you get injured or go down with a snake-bite, I leave you. Same goes for me. The mission is everything. Once that's done, whoever's left standing goes back to get the other out.'

'Jesus, Raglan, you're a cold-hearted bastard. My team always came first.'

He stretched out across two seats. 'Then you got it wrong, Voss. The target comes first.'

Thoughts flooded her mind as she imagined being left to rot in a jungle far from home. 'You'd leave me to die?'

'Yes.' He raised himself up one elbow. 'Don't let your imagination run riot. You've had hard contacts before. You've had people die.'

'I'm not as matter-of-fact about going operational, Raglan. I try to cover every eventuality.'

'And in this case you can't. We have a way in, up river and then jungle, and a way out if we survive. Someone's trying to start a war and we have a chance to stop it. And the bonus is we get to find the people we both want to kill.'

'I don't intend to kill Lennie Elliot. I want him alive. He's my ticket back to the Bureau and what I did before he screwed my mission.'

'Wrong thought,' said Raglan.

'What?'

'You're going into a firefight trying to capture someone who set you up, who got your people killed. That means you're not thinking straight. You will do whatever it takes to take him alive and that puts my life in jeopardy. Don't hesitate if you get the chance. Kill him. Take his damned picture and show your boss.'

'I led a Hostage Rescue Team. We were there to save people, Raglan. We weren't a hit team.'

Raglan lay back down. 'You are now.'

66

About the time Harry Briscoe began dropping the nose of the Grumman Mallard down to wave-hopping height, Detectives Delaney and Medina stood in front of the United States Attorney for the District of Columbia. The department was the largest US Attorney's office in the country because of its breadth of responsibilities and its location in the seat of the federal government, which meant it had responsibility for cases of national importance and for the prosecution of all federal crimes and serious local crime committed by adults in DC. The evidence discovered on Jack Swain's tapes exceeded the criteria required for DC Attorney William Frank's office to act.

For twelve years he had prosecuted members of Congress for everything from tax evasion to benefitting from insider trading using sensitive information they had gained while in office. He had brought down illegal trade deals with North Korea and had wide-sweeping success against Venezuelan drug lords and high-level businessmen associated with the cartels. He was a die-hard patriot who some said would be the last man standing when the barbarians were at the gates. And he would be draped in his beloved flag when that time came. When the telephone tapes found in Jack Swain's city apartment had been played and the shock waves had rippled around those present in the closed-door meeting, William Frank's hand trembled with anger and despair at the conspiracy the tapes revealed. He placed his hands palm-down on the desk, focused his mind and let the anger subside.

'You have my full authority. Arrest warrants will be issued by the time you leave this office.'

'Thank you, sir,' said Delaney.

'Proceed with due care, detective. There must be no infringement of protocol.'

'And what about Special Agent Kim Burton, sir?' said Medina. 'She's about to become Deputy Assistant Director of the FBI's Intelligence Operations Branch. She's tight with the Agency.'

'I will deal with that matter. You and the MPD will carry out the arrests here.'

The two detectives quickened their pace down the Justice Department steps. A dozen MPD officers with backup had been primed. Corrupt government officials were already targeted in their various administrative offices. The corruption was more widespread among lower echelon officials than even Casey Zeller had discovered. He had found the big fish, and Delaney and Medina were about to reel them in. They drove to Capitol Hill. Blue-uniformed Capitol Police officers under an inspector's command waited. They confirmed the arrest warrant for the Tennessee Senator Rufus Billingham and the Florida Senator Margaret Hillsum. The Metropolitan Police Department did not have the authority to enter and arrest members of Congress. As the blues made their way through to each senator's office, Delaney and Medina waited in the crisp wintery sunshine.

Delaney felt the warmth of the sun on his back and the growing sense of satisfaction that a rotten core of government had been cut out.

'Damned if that bitch Voss wasn't playing straight after all,' said Medina.

Delaney turned his face to the sun. 'Do me a favour. When they bring these senators out, don't indulge your acerbic desire to humiliate, belittle and insult them. They'll have plenty of that coming their way.'

Medina shrugged and wrinkled her nose. 'I know.'

'Thank you.'

'But I'd like to get in first.'

Kim Burton's long, open raincoat swept across her legs. Her five-inch heels clattered noisily as she made her way through the CIA building at Langley, Virginia, across the river from FBI Headquarters. Her department learnt that the two DC detectives who had been investigating the murder of Senator Mike Thomas – before she had pulled rank and made it an exclusively FBI investigation – had found evidence from the murdered Jack Swain. Her people couldn't even get through the door of his apartment because the DC Attorney's office deemed it first and foremost a homicide on the MPD's home turf. And then it had all unravelled.

'Ma'am,' said the escorting security officer who had led her through to Lewis Culver's office waiting area. 'Would you please wait here for Task Force Director Culver?'

She nodded. The man went through a door marked

Authorized Personnel Only. She glanced at the photographs on the wall showing the previous Deputy Directors of Operations since the CIA was formed after World War Two. Names she had read about, legends; there were a couple of men she had met as she worked her way up through the Bureau, one of whom had made life hell for everyone, playing the blame game after 9/11. That was always the problem. Boys and their toys. All those men and not one woman until now. A sense of satisfaction swept over her. The times were changing. Three women now ran top departments in the Agency. Her attention was broken as another figure strode down the corridor towards her. He was a long way off. She knew him to be part of the OCA, the Office of Congressional Affairs, advisers to members of Congress. Kim Burton did not need an administrative wrangle right now.

Her escort stepped back into the area and said, 'Director Culver is not available right now, ma'am.'

She gave a withering look and sidestepped the startled aide. Ignoring his demand for her to stop, she went through the door leading to another corridor with rows of doors. Culver's was straight ahead. She barged in, ignoring the protestations from his secretary who reached for the phone. Kim Burton might as well have pointed a loaded weapon at the startled woman as she stabbed her finger at her. 'Don't bother. I'm not staying long.' Burton pushed through Culver's door. He sat in his shirtsleeves, going through a report.

'Kim! What the fuck?' he said.

'Reading about Luis Reyes and Jack Swain and Casey Zeller and one of my people, Jenna Voss?' she snapped.

'I'll have your ass thrown out of here.'

The OCA and security officer were right behind her but they stopped in their tracks when she threw a folded warrant at him. He fumbled the catch. 'Keep your hands where I can see them unless you want to check your balls before I cut them off. You're under arrest.'

67

The Grumman Mallard bucked in the cross wind, throwing
Voss against the bulkhead. She regained her balance.
'Briscoe! We're not crates of cargo back here!'

'Be better if you were. You might want to strap in,' he
yelled.

She steadied herself and then slumped into a seat and
buckled up. Raglan ignored Briscoe's suggestion and
clambered into the cockpit. 'What's happening?'

Briscoe pointed ahead and to the port wing. A grey
swirling mass was approaching rapidly. 'Squall,' said
Briscoe. 'It'll hit us in a couple of minutes. We can't avoid it.'

'This time of year?' said Raglan.

'Weather's screwed, mate, doesn't know if it's Arthur or
Martha.'

'How far out are we?'

'About a hundred miles. I was going down low until that
bugger popped up out of nowhere.'

'Use it,' said Raglan. 'Can you fly in that?'

'I can fly a bloody washing machine through its spin
cycle if I have to.'

'Then get in the squall, fly as low as you can and no one'll
see us from the ground. It's ideal cover.'

Briscoe's face broke into a wide grin. 'The old *Grey Goose* won't let you down, I promise you that, but the landing might be a bit hit or miss.'

'You want me in the seat?'

Briscoe shook his head. 'I got it.' And immediately began to ready the aircraft for the squall. Raglan saw him make efficient, quick adjustments to the trim. The engines' pitch altered; the plane bucked. Raglan rock-and-rolled back to the sparse cabin.

'You need a bucket?' he asked Voss.

'I told you. Choppers and planes are no problem. It's the sea that makes me puke. These boneshakers are my bread and butter.'

Raglan strapped in. A surge of power from the turboprop engines and the plane dropped like a stone; then it steadied, engines alternating in their demands against the squall. A sudden clattering against the fuselage told them the rain had hit. It was loud. Echoing around the empty cabin. The plane shuddered. It felt more than a squall. Briscoe was cursing. The plane swooped and dropped again. Raglan and Voss were lifted out their seats, their bodies following the lurch from their stomach.

'Change of plan, Raglan! Take the seat!'

Briscoe's urgent instruction, no longer as confident as before, made Raglan unbuckle and stagger his way through the bulkhead's archway into the cockpit. He slumped into the co-pilot's seat and strapped in. The windscreen wipers were working flat out. They made no difference. The sheet rain obscured everything. Raglan placed his hands on the controls. The shared Y-shaped control column from the centre of the cockpit gave each pilot hands-on manoeuvrability. The radar showed the squall had a heart of darkness.

'Sneaky bitch, this one, mate. All the energy's right there,' Briscoe said, pointing to the dark-green-infused blue patch. 'Not so much a bloody spin cycle, more like a full tumble wash.'

The aircraft lurched again. Raglan steadied his hands on the controls, felt the aircraft's energy shudder into his arms. Briscoe's right hand reached for the overhead throttle lever. Raglan immediately placed his left hand over Briscoe's right as he eased the throttles forwards. The engines increased their power. Briscoe was flying blind, depending solely on instruments. It reassured Raglan to see that the man who had looked like an outback bush pilot lived up to the image and knew what he was doing. When flying blind, the mind and body conflict. Many a pilot, even experienced ones, listen to their instincts instead of obeying their instruments, and they die because of it. The Grumman ploughed belligerently into the squall. It might have been an old aircraft, but it was like a tank ploughing through a cornfield.

The windscreen cleared. The coastline loomed. Briscoe grunted with satisfaction. He had brought the lumbering plane across the treetops at full throttle and timed it perfectly. Fifty feet lower and the aircraft would be in the dense forest. 'There!' said Briscoe, nodding to the front. There was no need for him to draw Raglan's attention to the shimmering lake, vast enough to imitate an inland sea: Raglan was already scanning the surrounding forests. Briscoe turned and grinned at Raglan. 'You have arrived at your destination,' he said in his best imitation of a satnav. 'But you're gonna get wet, mate. That squall's right behind us.'

'My skin's waterproof,' said Raglan. He pointed to the farthest point of the lake. 'There's the estuary. Get us in as far as you can. Still need me here?'

Briscoe shook his head, his eyes now on his approach. They were already skimming the water as he expertly kept the amphibious plane's hull metres above the surface. Raglan squeezed out of the co-pilot's seat, tapped Briscoe's shoulder in thanks and bent through the hatch to Voss.

'Came close to collecting a few souvenir branches back there,' she said. 'Didn't he check the weather radar before we left Key West?'

'There was no sign of anything and there shouldn't be rain squalls at this time of year. It's warm rain. Given the time we've spent in this sweat box, we'll need it.'

The engines slowed; the airframe creaked. 'Landing!' said Briscoe.

Raglan grabbed the bulkhead. Vapour-like spray covered the windows as Briscoe touched down. The plane's cleft-faced hull sliced across the surface in a perfect landing. Unlike a boat, the aircraft had no rudder, and the only way it could be steered was by using the throttle to manoeuvre it into position. Raglan opened the side hatch. The sun was still high in the sky. He glanced to where the squall was fast approaching the coast. It had been good camouflage on their approach and soon it would serve the same purpose when Briscoe nosed the stubby aircraft into the mangroves.

'How far can you get us up the estuary?' said Raglan.

'Fair way along. Soon as I see it narrowing I'll turn and let the tide nudge me beneath the overhanging tree canopy.'

Voss checked the Glock once more. Habit. Do it once, be satisfied. Twice, be certain. Now the engines were purring, slowing as Briscoe found the spot he wanted. It didn't take long for him to throttle up the port engine and turn the aircraft. He nudged his *Grey Goose* into the perfect spot and then cut the engines. The silence was a relief, and was disturbed only by the gentle lapping of the lake's slow-moving water, urged along by an onshore breeze that was already stiffening ahead of the approaching squall. Briscoe ducked beneath the flight-deck console into the forward hatch, and balanced and moored the plane by tying it off on a stout overhanging tree trunk. If anyone looked across the lake or searched from the air, the *Grey Goose* would be out of sight.

'Leave your FBI identification behind,' Raglan told Voss. It would be natural for her not to think of parting with it. 'Not the best way to meet any unfriendlies.'

She nodded and stripped wallet and badge away. She handed it to Briscoe.

'Does this make me an honorary Fed?'

'Makes you in deep shit if you try anything with it,' she said.

Raglan peered out of the hatch. 'What are we in? Mud?'

'Soft silt beneath us,' said Briscoe. 'Shallow enough. You want the inflatable?'

Voss peered out at the uninviting, brackish water. 'Good idea.'

'No. We'll wade and swim,' said Raglan. 'We'd have to ditch it once we find dry land anyway.'

'No one would see it in these mangroves,' said Voss. 'We can sink it when we're finished.'

'Makes sense, mate,' said Briscoe.

'There are dozens of these inlets off the lake. Locals will fish in them. I want to get to the road through the swamp and then find this village,' he said, pointing at the map. 'We don't need the inflatable.' He cast an eye at the sun's position in the sky. 'I know where I'm going. Two hours' hard slog and we'll be on dry land.'

'Unless the crocs get you,' said Briscoe, glancing at a concerned Voss.

'Or the snakes,' said Raglan, ignoring the plea Briscoe had made trying to ingratiate himself with Voss – obviously trying to get her to stay at the aircraft.

'What kind of snakes?' she said.

'Nasty little buggers,' said Briscoe. 'Fer de lance is the worst, couple of metres long, strike the same distance as their body length and spew venom that'll blind you. If the venom goes on your skin it blisters and eats the flesh. And if they get their fangs into you, that's goodnight-and-good-luck time.'

Voss looked aghast at Raglan.

'Ignore him,' he said. 'He's exaggerating.' Raglan tightened his backpack straps. 'There are plenty more deadly snakes besides the fer de lance.' His smile told her he wasn't going to be swayed about wading into the mangrove swamp.

Briscoe shrugged helplessly. 'Sorry, love. I tried. Don't you worry none. The girl in Mexico can wait. I'll stay for as long as I can and get you home safe and sound.' He delivered his best smile. He hoped he'd see her again. She was, after all, eye candy with a gun. That made an interesting combination in Briscoe's mind.

68

They were wading waist-deep. Minutes later the squall hit. Stinging rain pockmarked the river. Shadows leapt through the canopy as monkeys sought shelter beneath umbrella branches. Within moments Raglan and Voss were drenched, the warm rain sluicing away the sweat from their endeavours as they moved through the stultifying air. Their clothes sucked close to their flesh as the humidity and rain enveloped them. More sweat dripped down their faces.

Raglan turned. Grim determination was etched on Voss's features. She was fit and strong and had endured the rigorous training at the FBI Quantico facility and had then volunteered for the Hostage Rescue Team. Raglan guessed there would have been a hundred applicants and maybe only a handful passing the testing ordeal of selection – something he was familiar with from his time in the Legion – so he knew Voss would have what it took in a firefight. But clambering through mangrove swamp was punishing. He had briefed her how to get over the arm-thick roots and keep her head below any low-lying branches, the undersides of which hosted biting insects and burrs and thorns that cut into skin that would quickly become infected. Raglan waited for her to catch up with him. The water became shallower.

'There's a reed bank twenty yards ahead. I'm going forwards to check it out.'

'For what?' she said, looking across the waist-deep black-water pool they had to cross before reaching it. Raglan had warned her places like this concealed snakes and leeches; to her it looked to be the kind of place where a crocodile would drag its prey.

'Can't you smell it?' said Raglan.

She faced the drifting breeze. Her nose wrinkled. 'Everything stinks here. The water's fetid; the jungle's nothing but rotting vegetation.' Then she swallowed hard and spat out the foul taste she had suddenly caught. 'Jesus, what is that?' She knew what it was the moment she asked the question. 'That's a body.'

'Stay here. It might be a crocodile's kill.'

She gritted her teeth. She had lived in Florida long enough to know how fast a crocodile could move and strike on dry land. She pulled free the Glock. 'To hell with this, Raglan.'

'No shooting. Not unless we have to.' Raglan's low voice was a warning. 'Plenty of creatures around, upright and otherwise, that might hear us.'

Did crocodiles have good hearing? she asked herself. Dumbfounded, she watched as Raglan pressed ahead through the slimy pool of water, gripping his knife. She looked nervously left and right and behind, from where they had travelled. Was this the perfect place for a crocodile to have its lair? Did crocodiles have lairs? She shook her head to clear the stupid questions her mind persisted in asking.

Raglan pressed through the water. He examined the

rising beach of vegetation and debris drawn in through the inlet. The ground bore no sign of claw marks, or anything having been dragged ashore. He clambered up, wary of the dense bush five metres away. He threw a rock into the undergrowth. Nothing moved. He tried again. Still nothing. Satisfied that the narrow bank was safe, he signalled Voss to follow. He followed the stench, hacking the leaf stems with the jungle knife. Jaguars hunted here and if they were successful there was one place they would stash their kill: the fork of a tree. He looked up but there was no sign of an animal kill. What remained of three men hung from a tall bough. Their lower limbs were shredded by animals, probably a big cat or a crocodile, leaping up as far as they could and tearing the flesh from their bones. One of the men looked like a mannequin with torn ribbons dangling below his knees: his entrails had been torn from his stomach cavity.

'Fuck,' said Voss quietly as she reached him. 'Those bodies haven't been here that long.'

'Hanged high enough to stop them being dragged into the bush or the water. The rope's hemp, man-made. No sign of it rotting. You're right: it's recent.' Raglan strode three or four metres in each direction, looking for clues as to who had been there. He pointed. 'Something's been dragged ashore.'

She followed him, giving a wide berth to the grotesque carcasses being consumed by a ravenous forest's creatures. Raglan moved cautiously along a narrow animal track. He stopped, raised a hand and knelt. Voss followed his example by going down on one knee as Raglan peered beneath the low overhanging branches. Satisfied, he stood and pushed on ahead. She followed. She heard water lapping. Raglan beckoned her, his gaze constantly checking their surroundings. Another small inlet pierced the mangroves. They could just make out the twisting route the boat would have taken as it was hauled from the river to where it now lay hidden beneath an old military camouflage net and cut ferns and branches. Raglan tugged aside vegetation. The boat was no more than six metres long and the big outboard engine that would have been on the transom was missing.

'That looks like a fast boat,' said Voss. 'The lagoon and river have access to the sea. We must be close to a drug-smuggling route.'

Raglan nodded. 'And those men hanging belong to it.' He pulled the camouflage back over the boat. 'And whoever killed those men wanted to return here and use their boat.'

'Rival drug gangs, do you think?' Voss said.

'Possible. But out here, far from any base? If that was the case they'd be decapitated and hung upside down in true cartel fashion. These are delivery boys running drug shipments to coastal ships at the mouth of the lagoon. They have nothing to do with the arms shipments.'

'Maybe there are other cartels operating down here. Other drug-processing plants,' Voss suggested.

Raglan shook his head. 'Reyes is still in the game. He's keeping the drug money coming in as well as being in the pay of the people we're after. Let's push on – it'll be dark soon enough.'

Voss looked up through the canopy. The forest light had dimmed noticeably. Sweat trickled down her back. She itched. Unseen bugs were already pinpricking her skin. Raglan seemed immune to the tropical forest. She noticed he still kept the hefty knife blade in his hand. To her way of thinking he was going to kill any intruders he confronted silently. Her mouth dried. She knew she didn't have the stomach for that kind of fighting. One desire drove her to follow in Raglan's footsteps: to overcome the inherent fear she felt from the suffocating rainforest and the threat of unseen creatures. She was determined not to let him down and be the liability he thought her to be. Urban warfare was a skill set she understood and had mastered, but this alien world played on her fears. She dreaded spending the night there, sharing the jungle floor with poisonous spiders, flesh-biting ants and lethal snakes.

Leaves rustled.

Invisible creatures moved.

The jungle was alive.

69

Raglan found a small clearing and dropped his pack. Fallen trees covered in lichen and moss lay shoulder-height. The gentle knocking of thick bamboo nudging each other in the breeze from their high canopy sounded like an offbeat marimba. He pulled aside a couple of fallen split bamboo, each a couple of metres long. Voss dropped her gear and waited for his instructions. He beckoned her to him and lifted her arm. 'OK, don't get alarmed.'

She was about to pull back but he showed her his neck just below his short collar. 'See that?'

'Oh crap!'

'Take it easy, it's just a leech. They don't hurt; they're not poisonous. If I left this long enough it would drop off when it's full of blood.'

'Oh, God, Raglan. Don't tell me...' She winced. 'Have I got one?'

'Let me show you how to get rid of them.' He ran his fingers alongside the bloodsucker. The gentle pressure released the leech.

She checked her limbs but the long sleeves and leggings had protected her. Raglan waited, his eyes telling her where to put her fingers. She grimaced and reached up to her neck and felt the gelatinous creature. It felt like one of the slugs she used to see eating her father's vegetable patch; now this was eating her.

'Let me,' he said and reached forwards and eased three of them from her neck.

She peeked down her shirt front and saw one suckling between her breasts. 'Oh God,' she said again.

'Shall I get that one as well?' he said with a smile.

She reached in, felt the spongy slime and did as Raglan had instructed. It came away leaving a speck of blood. She tossed it.

He nodded. 'OK, see, you just have to understand the environment you're in. Become a part of it. Don't worry, it's a learning process. So far so good?'

She nodded.

'Good. Let's get a fire going and rig up somewhere to sleep.'

From what she could see there was nothing dry enough to make a fire or create a shelter.

Raglan placed the split bamboo on a fallen log. 'Here,' he said, 'grab this. We need to work fast before nightfall.' He leant into the bigger length and began drawing the smaller piece back and forth, shredding the fibres. He handed it to her. 'We need dry kindling. Get a couple of big handfuls. See that small hole I cut in the piece you're sawing? That'll give the kindling air and the friction will create enough heat to ignite it. Keep going until it smoulders. Got it?'

'Raglan, this is all Boy Scout stuff. All we needed was a Zippo and firelighters.'

'Lose the lighter and we'd have to do this anyway; besides, you'd be surprised how far away a jungle fighter could smell it.'

She did as he asked without further question. Raglan hacked down another bamboo. Tipping it horizontally, he punched a slit into it and held his water bottle beneath it. The bamboo pole was full of fresh water. He topped up Voss's bottle and then unfurled her nylon hammock from its small sack. It expanded as he tied off one end and then the other. All he had to do then was slide across the mosquito net. He repeated the operation with his own hammock. Cicadas announced the closing darkness. By the time their two sleeping hammocks were tested, Voss had scraped away a bundle of bamboo fibres. Raglan nodded, took the smouldering bundle, blew on it until fingers of flame crept out of the mass and laid the kindling between rocks. After he'd laid dried leaves on the fire, it caught. Within minutes he had a fire going and had added twigs and lichen. The heat was kept inside the stacked fire and the breeze wafted the smudge-smoke over them.

She blinked tears and handed him a can of something that looked vaguely edible. He nodded his thanks and squatted by the fire.

'Is that it?' she said.

'You were expecting silver service and a waiter? Grab some food, then get off the ground. The insect repellent never lasts long enough when you sweat this much. The smudge fire will help and the mosquito nets will keep the worst offenders away.'

'Aren't we cooking something to eat? We could make coffee. Ronnie put sachets in the field rations.'

Raglan looked relaxed. He tore back a tab and spooned the food into his mouth with a square of off cut bamboo. Voss stared at him. Raglan was as much at home in the jungle as the city streets. 'The smell of cooked food will carry. Same with coffee. Water is all we need. The more we sweat the better. Gets rid of soap smells on us.' He glanced around the small clearing. 'Indigenous people will smell us a mile away. Our body odour is different as well.' He relished the food, keeping his gaze moving across the dense jungle all the time while he ate. 'They'll know we're here. They won't come at night though.'

'Why not?' said Voss. 'The fire's bright enough.'

He shook his head and picked food from his teeth. 'Twenty yards from here the forest will have shut it out. Anyway, no one likes being out here at night, it's when the big cats hunt. So stay in your hammock. You need to pee? Don't. Urine attracts jaguars. We relieve ourselves tomorrow before we head out.'

She remained silent. The night was already on them. Even now she heard different sounds coming from the jungle.

He noticed a cut on her hand. 'Let me see that.'

'It's nothing. The bamboo's sharp. It's a paper cut is all.'

'I know,' he said, unconcerned. He reached out and pulled a handful of what looked like bindweed, its forked leaf bigger than his hand. He crushed it and squeezed the sap into the wound. 'That'll stop any infection.'

'We could have used the antiseptic in the medical pack. Oh, wait, you're telling me you can smell chemicals all the way back to the Keys, aren't you?'

He smiled. 'We can look after ourselves out here.'

She abandoned the tin of cold food and slapped her arm against whatever bug had found her blood attractive. 'Raglan, this is crazy. We don't know where we are. We can't see the sky to navigate our way out. The men who strung up those drug runners, if that's what they were, could be anywhere near. We should call this off and get back to the plane. I'll get in touch with Kim Burton and ask her for help.'

'Sure, if that's what you want. I thought the guy you're after was important.'

'He is, but we're never going to find Luis Reyes's compound. You can see that, can't you?'

Raglan got to his feet and wiped his hands on his trousers. 'First light I'll show you the way back to the plane. You can wait for me there, but now we both need sleep.'

Voss scrambled to her feet. The blackness enveloped everything except the fireglow. The shadows clawed up to Raglan's face. He stood his ground, facing her; the fire lit his eyes as fingers of darkness gripped his hardened features.

'You would do that? Send me back? Alone?'

'Voss, you're a liability. It's better for both of us. It's a straightforward way back. Stay with Briscoe, and when I call you, bring in the cavalry. You can lead the charge and save the day.'

He placed a bundle of dry palm leaves on the fire. They flared, and then he threw on damp branches. The mixture of flames and smoke served the dual purpose of keeping wild animals at bay and stopping bugs from trying to invade their hammocks, despite the netting. Raglan climbed under and tucked it around him. He placed the wicked-looking blade across his chest. Easy to grab. The Glock at his side. Close to hand. There was nothing more to do.

He fell asleep. .

70

Voss's back ached from the sagging hammock. Eyes open, she pressed her hand against the mosquito netting suspended over her face. The night was pitch black but the fireglow gave enough light for her to realize that the net was swarming. She squeezed her eyes tight. Claustrophobia threatened to crush her breath, but she fought against it: this was a case of mind over matter. She knew damned well she was vulnerable. Leading a rescue team tested her in an urban environment where a target assessment could be formulated. The team would advance tactically in a well-rehearsed manoeuvre. But this? Every step through this jungle could have a killer barely steps away. Animal or human. Sleep had abandoned her. How much longer until daylight? She squinted at her watch whose dull luminous fingers told her it was either ten after four or twenty after two. She prayed it was the former because Raglan had told her that dawn was soon after five.

A blood-curdling scream made her catch her breath. The pitiful wailing was so close it was deafening. Instinctively she rolled in the hammock and fought the confines of the mosquito netting. The Glock was in her hand. The shrieks tore through the night. She cursed, kicking and snatching at the netting. The back of her neck had ice-water running down to her spine. Heart pounding, she finally fell to the ground, half crouched, ready for an attack. Raglan had beaten her to it and held a flaming branch in one hand and his flashlight in the other.

'Stay there!' he commanded.

She froze. Her eyes followed the beam of light. It settled on a black patch in the bushes a dozen paces from their camp. Yellow eyes glared back, ivory fangs smothered in blood. A black jaguar gripped a paca, a rodent the size of a medium-sized dog. The jaguar shook it violently, snapped its neck and turned with the lifeless creature firmly clamped in its jaws and disappeared into the forest. Voss snapped out of the mesmerizing few seconds and fired two shots.

'Don't!' Raglan yelled.

There was no sign of her having hit the big cat. Raglan ventured closer to the kill site, flashlight and burning branch sweeping ahead of him.

'Did I get it?' Voss cried.

Raglan turned back. 'No, you didn't.' His temper flared; he tossed the branch back into the fire. 'What the hell is wrong with you?'

'What the fuck, Raglan? It could have taken either of us.'

'You're a damned idiot. You behave like a rookie on their first patrol. If the jaguar had wanted to kill us, it would have done.'

'What? I'm supposed to be a goddamned mind-reader of a jungle cat?'

Raglan stabbed the air. 'It had its kill.'

'I reacted to a dangerous situation,' she insisted.

'You overreacted. You don't belong here, Voss. Get back

to your inner-city drug dens and street-smarts. This is not the place for you.'

'It's a wild animal!'

Raglan loosed the quick release ties on his hammock. He shook out the mosquito net. 'Jack Swain thought the FBI was a dumb bunch of suits. Now I know what he meant.' He turned to face her. Colour seeped up her neck into her face and it wasn't from the firelight. 'Those gunshots will have alerted anyone in the area.'

She hadn't moved. 'I'm going back, Raglan. Enough of this bullshit.'

He folded the hammock and squared it away in his backpack; then he tightened the straps. 'I wish. But the crocs will have you in less than an hour. I don't want them choking on your stupidity.' He put out the fire. 'They're on the endangered list as well.'

Anger fuelled her urgency. She had packed badly, stuffing everything into the backpack, and then, torn between her desire to get out of the jungle and the knowledge that Raglan was 100 per cent correct about her chances of survival, followed him. The dawn chorus of howler monkeys raced across the canopy; their bellowing shrieks and barking sounded like they were hurling abuse at her. Being mocked by Raglan was bad enough, but when the wildlife got in on the act she was sorely tempted to empty her Glock at them. Raglan seemed to know where he was going. He kept looking at his watch and finding what light there was in the treetops. After two hours of meandering along a narrow animal track and wading through waist-deep mangrove pools, she was filthy, sweating, scratched and exhausted. Raglan reached down the muddy embankment; she took his hand and let him haul her up.

'You're doing well,' he said.

'Don't patronize me, Raglan. I did HRT selection.'

'So you did. I apologize. We're almost there.'

'Where is there?'

'If we are in the right place, there's a road a mile from here. It cuts through the jungle and swamps going east to west.'

'And you know this how?' she said.

'I get a glimpse of the sunlight through the trees, use my watch as a compass.'

'Jesus, more Boy Scout stuff?'

'Soldiers use it when they have to and we have to because Diaz forgot to get us a compass. It's rough and ready but we'll be close enough.' He smiled. 'It's a long road. We'll hit it somewhere; all we needed was a sense of direction.'

She wiped a muddy hand across her face and pushed past him. 'Good to know. I didn't see you as a Boy Scout.'

'Don't be alarmed but we're being followed. Have been for more than an hour.'

She spun around, checking the forest. The small clearing they were in merged back into the rainforest without any sign of movement or shadow.

'You won't see them until they want to be seen. My guess is they're locals. Hunters maybe.'

Her hand went to the holster. He reached out and stopped her drawing her weapon. 'We'd already be dead if that's what they wanted.'

'We ignore it?'

He nodded. 'We reach the road and see if they show themselves.'

The news they were being watched pumped a sharp edge of adrenaline through her. Fatigue was banished and she concentrated on every step of the way, not only following Raglan as he wound his way through the forest, but also trying to peer through the congested undergrowth. It was an impossible task. Despite herself, she felt grateful. Ego aside, he was the expert and she was the tourist. Her life was in his hands. Rollercoaster emotions took her back to when she waded away from the *Grey Goose* and the determination not to let herself down. She got a grip on the fear and uncertainty. Focus was everything now.

Raglan raised a hand. He stood unmoving. Head turning left and right. Listening. He went down on one knee. Stayed silent a moment longer and then stood.

'The road's ahead. They're there. Don't do anything stupid.'

She nodded her understanding and followed him. Barely twenty metres later they emerged on to the forest edge. A single-track road cut through the jungle. Where two beaten pickup trucks were parked. Doors open. Six leather-featured men waited, rifles aimed at them.

71

They were covered by the rifles as their weapons were taken. No one leered at the beautiful woman and no attempt was made to touch her until a woman climbed from behind the wheel of a truck and frisked her. Raglan had already been checked by the men. No further invitation was needed other than being prodded with the rifles to climb into the back of one of the pickups. A bumpy ride on a dirt road followed and twenty minutes later the men drove off the road into a hamlet. Raglan saw it was a one-way-in, one-way-out settlement. Chickens roamed and pecked, pigs snuffled in a pen and a couple of horses grazed in the clearing behind stockade fencing. The forest had been cleared a generation before and now crops grew in neat rows. As they drove deeper into the hamlet they passed drying sheds where gutted fish hung. Generators hummed outside the small houses with tin roofs. Scrawny cats and dogs lolled in the shade. The trucks pulled up outside one of the bigger houses. They were herded inside to a cool room where an elderly man, white-whiskered, sat in dungarees and undershirt. A fan circulated the air.

'These are the ones, *patrón*,' said one of the men in Spanish.

The old man looked like the others. Dirt farmers had little chance of changing out of dungarees and frayed shirts. It was almost a universal uniform for those who battled to survive scratching a living close to subsistence. A pack of cigarettes and glass of amber liquid rested on a side table next to him.

'Please sit,' said the old man, gesturing to the chairs opposite him. 'We sometimes see *Yanquis* come from Trujillo airport. They come to sightsee at the lagoon near the airport. They get lost. They are confused because there are no road signs. This is considered by many to be a hostile environment so they are guided to where they will be safe. But we do not see *Yanquis* come through the mangrove swamps from the lagoon further around the coast. Especially those who are armed.' The *patrón*'s English was perfect. Raglan glanced around the room. A small bookshelf with a dozen dog-eared books was squeezed in next to an old-fashioned television set, and two of the shelves were packed tightly with audio tapes. The books had English titles. The old man saw Raglan's gaze.

'We sometimes take vegetables to the hotel at the coast. We are poor; the tourists are rich. They leave those behind. I like reading and listening.'

'You speak good English,' said Raglan.

The man shrugged. 'There was a time I worked on a fishing boat owned by an American. That was before the drug boats came – thirty years ago. More. And now you have come ashore in a dangerous place. Perhaps you have seen things you should not have seen.'

Before Raglan could answer, a woman appeared with a tray of glasses of chilled water.

'Please, you must be thirsty,' said the old man.

Rivulets of water glistened on the glass surface. Voss gulped; Raglan sipped. Ice-cold water hitting the stomach in a hot climate could cause cramps. The old man's eyes hadn't left Raglan. Every gesture was being assessed. He nodded. Raglan was a pro. Knew what he was doing. The woman? Well, she was strong and showed no sign of fear but she was clearly not used to the sweltering jungle, yet here she was.

'And now you will tell me what you are doing here? You,' he said, looking at Raglan again, 'your accent is not *yanqui*. I have heard it spoken by tourists at the coast. You are not a tourist though. You are an Englishman?'

'I am. Did your people hang those drug runners?' said Raglan. His comment put him on the offensive. This was no time to be evasive or to try and talk their way out of trouble. Raglan had staked his claim. He was unafraid and now the old man knew it.

The old man gave an imperceptible sigh. 'Perhaps you have seen too much, and that is bad for all of us.'

'If you did kill them then that makes you no friend of Luis Reyes and the people he works for.'

One of the two armed guards who stood at the door muttered an exclamation.

'You have mentioned a name that is known to us. What is your association with this man?'

'Reyes is being paid by people in power in America. His drug route into the United States is being used to ship weapons down here and from here to another country to start a war. There are other foreigners here who stand shoulder to shoulder with American mercenaries. They have killed my friends. I am going to kill them.'

There was a brief moment of surprise on the old man's face. Then one of the guards at the door laughed. The *patrón* smiled. 'You are a fool. No one can get into their compound. We know about these people. You think we are deaf and blind? We are the ones who take them food; we see how many men there are with guns.'

'And yet you choose to kill them without fear of retribution,' said Voss.

'We are not at war with the Reyes cartel,' said the old man.

'But still you kill them,' insisted Raglan. 'There is a reason.'

'There is always a reason for killing. We have ours. When their men have delivered their drugs to ships out at sea through the lagoon, sometimes, when they return late at night, we kill them. When we can. The drug people do not come looking. We are not suspect. Why would we be? We get paid by them so they can eat fresh food. And not one of them would venture into the jungle forty miles from their compound to search for three or four missing men who were probably drunk, fell overboard and taken by *los cocodrilos*.'

The old man studied them a moment longer. He shrugged and paused to light a cigarette and sip whatever it was in the glass. 'Anyone in any village who has a business, a taxi, a bus, who sells fruit or has a store: they pay the gangs a war tax. If we do not, we die. That is how life works here.'

'And that is a strong enough reason to kill the smugglers?' said Raglan.

The old man coughed from the cigarettes that must have clogged his lungs over the past sixty years. '*Sí*, we have reasons. Years ago they caused us harm. Hurt some of our people to keep us in line, to make sure we knew who it was we were dealing with.' He stared at Raglan. 'You are serious about this business?'

'I am. Why else would we be here?' said Raglan.

'And the woman?'

'The woman can speak for herself,' Raglan answered.

The *patrón* looked at her. Voss did not flinch. 'I am a fugitive.'

The old man's face beamed. He looked to where the guards joined him, laughing. 'From?'

'The FBI,' said Voss. 'Him too.'

The old man spread his hands. 'Two fugitives from the FBI and I have brought them to my village. If the FBI have spoken to the Honduran authorities this can cause more trouble than Luis Reyes's people.'

'They don't know we are here, *señor*,' said Raglan.

'My men found satellite phones in your packs.'

'Because cell phones do not work in the jungle,' said Voss.

'Or perhaps to speak to people in America, eh?'

'There is no one in America I wish to speak to,' Voss answered.

The *patrón* leant forwards. 'Let me tell you something, I believe these people with Luis Reyes are protected by people in our government. So this is a dangerous situation for us. What is in it for us if we help you?'

'Nothing except to know that I can kill those who need to be killed to stop them ever causing you harm.'

'You kill enough of them and we are poor again. Remember what I said? We sell them food.'

'How much money do you think they have in that compound?'

'A lot.'

'Then you will have no need to worry about money again and no blame will rest on you or your people here. I am an outsider. All I need from you is information.'

The offer clearly made an impression on the old man. 'And what of the weapons?'

'The Americans will be told when they are found,' said Raglan.

'So there *is* someone you wish to speak to in America with the satellite phones.'

'I will tell them,' said Raglan.

'And the drugs?'

'I don't deal in drugs. Do you?'

'We do not.'

'Then if there are drugs there they will be destroyed.'

The *patrón* exhaled a plume of smoke. He looked over their heads to the guards at the door. 'Fetch my grandson.' He chain-smoked another cigarette. 'Luis Reyes's compound is near enough forty miles by road. A mile from his gates he has guards watching the road. There is never any trouble. On rare occasions a tourist gets lost on the dirt roads from the coast, and they are given directions. No outsider gets hurt. That is how Reyes has stayed safe for so long in the jungle. He gives the police no cause to call on him even though he owns them. The compound is almost surrounded by water. There are many *cocodrilos*. They capture you: they feed you to them. These people are cruel savages; they take pleasure inflicting pain. These others you speak about, these foreigners, there is one who was here months ago. Then she disappeared and returned a few days ago.'

'She is a tall woman with dark eyes and blonde hair,' said Raglan.

The glass was at the old man's lips but he failed to drink. His eyes met Raglan's. '*Dios mío*, she is the one you are going to kill.'

'Why would you think that?'

'She is one who is protected here by the Americans. She has no heart. A snake has more warmth.'

'What do you know about her?' said Raglan.

The old man grunted. His face contorted in disgust. 'This woman, she found a servant girl stealing food. In front of the girl's mother she let the girl know what was to happen to her.' He shook his head at the thought. 'Then she cut her here,' he said, slicing the edge of his hand across his groin. 'And tossed her down the riverbank to the creatures. She was still alive when she was taken.'

It was the same lethal cut TJ Jones had suffered.

The *patrón*'s teeth clamped together as if his words should not escape. 'She made her mother watch.' He shook his head. 'The mother, she killed herself later. The horror was too much to bear. My men, they are tough, they know hardship and danger hunting in the jungle, but some of them saw this happen and were sickened to their stomachs. The woman watched. She did not smile. She watched as if... as if it was something that needed to be studied.' The old man shook his head. 'Cartel murders are brutal. They cut off the head and hang you by the ankles, and your blood stains the ground, but to do what she did to a girl? That is something different and...' He crossed himself. 'Something God will never forgive. She is a godless woman. If you are here to kill that one, then we will help you. But you must promise me one thing.'

'Which is what?'

'You deliver Luis Reyes to us.'

'I don't see how I can.'

'We will make certain you have the opportunity. You will know it when you see it.'

Raglan nodded his agreement. 'If he lives then I will.'

'We accept it might be a request you cannot deliver.'

'Why?' said Raglan.

'There is one great obstacle for you to overcome. If you get inside the compound, then how will you ever get out?'

Before Raglan could question him further about the compound the old man raised his head and smiled. 'Ah, here is my grandson, Carlos.'

One of the men carried in a young man in his late teens while another guard pulled up a chair to settle the boy next to his grandfather. He was a strong-looking youth with tousled black hair and, like many teenagers in Central America, bore tattoos on his upper arms and shoulders. Unlike many other teenagers, his legs were amputated at the knee.

His grandfather spoke rapidly in Spanish. The boy listened attentively, glancing occasionally at the two people who sat opposite. He nodded frequently, acknowledging his grandfather. Raglan knew enough Spanish to understand that the old man had explained what had been discussed.

'Seven years ago, Luis Reyes came back to Honduras to check that everything was under control with his smuggling routes. My grandson was eleven years old then. We had delivered food while our children went in search of wild orchids for the tourists. Orchids are our national flower and we make good money selling them at the hotels on the coast. He found some deep caves. Inside one of the caves there is a narrow tunnel leading inside Reyes's compound. The tunnel is where Reyes stores his cocaine. Carlos ran but Reyes's men caught him. They called us back into the compound. I begged for the boy's life. I went on my knees in the dirt and swore the boy saw nothing and would never speak of it to anyone. I offered myself in place of the child.'

Raglan saw tears well in the old man's eyes.

'Luis Reyes said he would make certain the boy would never trespass again. They used a machete on his legs.' He blinked away the tears.

Voss stared in disbelief. She looked at Raglan who showed no sign of emotion at the telling. In that moment she knew that if anyone could get inside and bring justice to his slain friends and these people, it would be the Englishman.

The old man continued. 'Then, when Reyes returned to America, we began killing them. If we found three or four in a boat, we ambushed them. We left them in the forests for the beasts. And we carried on our daily lives.' He reached out a comforting hand to the smiling boy. 'Carlos knows where the cave is. With help he will guide you.'

Raglan faced the boy. 'I need to go in without being seen. Explain to me how I can do that and I will be in your debt.'

The *patrón* squeezed the boy's hand and kissed it. The boy smiled. 'He cannot tell anyone. When they took his legs they also cut out his tongue.'

72

Raglan and Voss sat with the old *patrón* and a dozen of his armed men. Their attitude had changed once they knew of Raglan's intentions. What Raglan needed was a model of the compound and the location of the cave. Carlos's grandfather related his knowledge of the area, his men adding their experience of jungle tracks, tributaries and swamps. The men settled stones into the dirt and drew the shape of the compound as the old man questioned the boy whether their model was accurate relative to the cave's location. As the mutilated boy nodded or shook his head at the queries, the *patrón* would lean forwards and change the model's shape. The river seeped into mangrove, forest and then deep pools where crocodiles took their prey. The cave entrance was difficult to get to. Since the boy had trespassed, Reyes and the men who controlled him had had guards patrolling the jungle. There were small, scattered outposts beyond the compound, huts where a handful of men were housed and fed. Reyes's house was a two-storey villa in the middle of a jungle clearing, surrounded by gardens. There was a low perimeter wall with guards at the main entrance and men who patrolled the compound. There were staff quarters and accommodation for the foreigners.

The old man placed a stone to one side of the compound beyond the broken twigs and grass that represented the gardens. 'That is the woman's quarters. She is treated like royalty. She is untouchable. She is guarded.'

'Who else is in there?' said Voss.

'Americans would come here and speak to Reyes. He was away for a long time but he came recently with some of these Americans. He did not look well. My men think he is using his own drugs.'

One of the men pointed out parts of the crude model with a stick. 'The house is large. They have guest quarters, here and here,' he said. 'I have taken food into the kitchens here.' He pointed again. 'And upstairs I have seen men on this balcony. They drink and smoke and they look to be important men. One, I have seen a photograph of in the newspaper.'

The old man nodded to him. 'You still have it?'

'*Sí, patrón.*'

'Fetch it.'

Raglan took out his phone and showed the pictures of the men at Reyes's house in Washington. 'Any of these here?'

Each of the men nodded in turn as they passed the phone between them. Raglan looked at Voss. The man she knew as Lennie Elliot, who had drawn her and her men into a fatal ambush, was at the compound. He saw the flash of anticipation cross her face.

The man sent to fetch the newspaper returned with a two-month-old copy of *La Prensa*. It showed Tennessee State Senator Rufus Billingham being greeted by government officials. The headline stated he was in Honduras to offer co-operation with the Minister of Infrastructure and to agree financing the expansion of the country's airports.

Raglan passed the newspaper to Voss. 'Now we know for sure. He's one of the names Casey Zeller uncovered. Let's hope I don't end up killing an American senator here.' He turned to the *patrón*. 'Is this man here now? With Luis Reyes?'

The old man asked his men. None of them knew.

'Then we'll face that problem when we come to it,' Raglan told Voss. He looked at the weapons the men carried. 'Are these all the weapons you have?'

'We hunt for food. We are not equipped for war.'

'Then we go with what we've got,' said Raglan.

'That's not enough,' said Voss.

He smiled. 'It never is.'

Four pickups that had seen better days drove fast along the dirt road. Raglan and Voss sat in the back of the lead vehicle, shoulders pressed against the cab's bulkhead. Voss tugged her sweat-soaked shirt from her skin. The humidity wrapped her in its warm blanket. Sweat prickled her skin. Itching. The debilitating heat made it difficult to think straight, and what she needed in the following hours was a clear head. She wiped her face with the palm of her hand.

'It gets hotter in the swamp,' said Raglan.

'You're not getting rid of me, Raglan, so don't try.'

'You have to let the jungle become your friend. Become a part of it. Don't fight it.'

She was too hot to argue. Fatigue was already setting in,

the sucking air robbing her of energy. Before they had left, Raglan had attended to his wounds. The stitches had held, so he had dried the sweat off his skin and applied a dry, waterproof field dressing across the ugly-looking tear in his side; then he had cleaned and dressed the slash across his thigh. Now he showed no sign of discomfort from the heat or his injuries as the truck bounced along the unmade road. She offered an unspoken prayer that she could keep up with him.

The old man sat at the passenger window with Carlos wedged between him and the driver. Dust swirled behind, half obscuring the three vehicles that followed, loaded with crates of fresh food and vegetables. Forty-five minutes later the old man brought the small convoy to a halt, climbed out and gestured for Raglan and Voss to join him. Dense jungle pressed either side of the road.

'We go no further until we believe you have reached the cave. Then we do nothing different than usual. We deliver our food, we get paid and we return home. You understand this? We are not involved.'

'I understand,' said Raglan.

The old man turned his gaze to the road that disappeared into the jungle. He was hesitating about something. Finally he turned back to Raglan. 'What if the weapons are not there? Will you still go into the compound and do what you came to do?'

Raglan sensed there was more to the question.

'What do you know about the weapons?'

'Nothing.'

'Then why ask?'

'Two nights ago a convoy of trucks left the compound.'

Raglan guessed the old man had kept back the vital information because Raglan was the means to an end: the capture of Luis Reyes.

The old man shrugged. 'It is an opportunity that will not come again for us.'

'How many trucks?' said Voss.

'Several.'

'How long before they reach a port?' Raglan asked the old man.

'Twelve hours, maybe more. The roads are bad for much of the way. They go to the furthest harbour, which is Puerto Cortés.'

Raglan walked away from Voss and the gathered men. She strode after him.

'What do we do now?'

Raglan knew that if the convoy had carried the armaments then he was too late to stop them being shipped. There was only one person who could. Raglan had the satellite phone to his ear. 'Your people jump through hoops to get anything done. I have someone who doesn't.'

Maguire watched as the gloom-laden rain lashed the large plate-glass windows of the MI6 building at Vauxhall Cross. The Thames looked particularly malevolent as its surface coiled and fought the underlying current. All in all, the weather's mood matched the disturbing news from the United States that had landed on his desk from the US National Intelligence Agency. The murky undercurrents of the intelligence world had spewed out detritus. It looked as though Raglan had kicked the hornets' nest all the way down the road, and so far, he was one of the few not being stung.

'Sir?' said Jenny Armstrong.

He turned. His secretary's face betrayed no emotion but her voice had a lilt of expectation. 'Raglan. Line one.'

Maguire nodded his thanks. She closed the door behind her as he picked up the handset.

'Maguire, I need your help.'

'Where are you?'

'Honduras.'

Maguire knew better than to begin asking questions. If Raglan was there, it was for a reason. 'What do you need?'

'The arms shipment from the States is already on its way to a ship at Puerto Cortés. Don't know any more than that but best bet is the ship will be registered under a flag of convenience. Crates will be boxed as something like farm equipment. What can you do to stop it?'

'We have a Royal Navy vessel working with the US Coast Guard in Caribbean waters on anti-drug-smuggling duties. Right now they are off the coast of Belize.'

'Get them. They're a spit away. If the ship hasn't finished loading then they can stop it after it leaves.'

'Raglan, the FBI arrested Lewis Culver. He and Swain worked hand in hand on this. And they have also arrested two senators. It seems Jack Swain covered his back. There's enough evidence for more arrests. The job's done, Raglan.'

Maguire took the receiver from his ear as the line went dead. Raglan was no longer listening.

⋆

Raglan told Voss the information Maguire had given him. 'Two senators and Lewis Culver were arrested by the Feds. One of them might be Rufus Billingham.'

'CIA are involved in this as well as Defense?' she said. The conspiracy had just become a lot more serious.

'Not the Agency, just Culver is my guess. He and Swain go back to the old days when they worked together in the CIA.'

'And Kim Burton? Was she part of it?'

'No word on that. If we're lucky the Feds shut down the key players in the States before word got to these people down here, otherwise they'll be expecting trouble.'

The old man beckoned them. 'We leave it too late and they will start asking questions about what has kept us from our regular delivery. *Señor*, please? You are ready? My grandson will show you the route.'

Raglan gave the old man his satellite phone. 'You know how to use this?'

'I have a cell phone for when I go to town.'

'Same thing, except this works out here. Need an open sky. No tree cover. We get into real trouble, we're going to need someone on this road. Leave a truck here with someone on the other end of this. We might need a way out in a hurry.'

The old man nodded and looked to where Carlos was borne on the back of the hulking man who had shown them the newspaper. 'Gerardo will carry him as far as necessary and then you are on your own. Do you understand that there are men in the forest who patrol? They are as wild as the animals. They will have your scent before you see or hear them. *Señor*, I will ask you again if you are certain this is what you are determined to do.'

Raglan smiled. 'By the time they get close enough I'll stink like a swamp rat.'

The old man nodded. It was decided. 'My grandson's name is Carlos Alvarado. The woman whose daughter was murdered: her name was Gabriela Mejía. You will find women who work for Reyes in the house sympathetic. They might be prepared to help you.' He shrugged. 'They live in fear so the risk is great.' The *patrón* nodded to Gerardo, who strode into the jungle. Raglan and Voss followed.

Gerardo moved effortlessly, as if he bore nothing but a shirt on his back. By a rough estimate it seemed they had travelled for an hour before Gerardo stopped at the boy's command. Raglan joined them. The boy pointed. At first Raglan could not make out anything different than the trees and undergrowth but then, as he took his eyes from one tree to another, penetrating his gaze deeper into the forest, a shape took form. A tall structure, the gable end of a ruined building covered with vines and lichen, stood in the forest. It looked like the front wall of an old church, its bell-shaped pediment reaching for the light.

Raglan's guess was correct.

'It is an old church built by missionaries before even the *patrón*'s father was born. The cave is another mile, maybe more. We don't go any further. The swamp is half a mile beyond the ruin.' Gerardo kept his voice low. A warning that they were close to where Reyes's men patrolled.

'Is there a track beyond the swamp?' Raglan asked. Hacking through dense undergrowth would take a day.

Gerardo shrugged. Carlos pointed and grunted his malformed words. Raglan sensed that since his mutilation he had been able to make himself understood. Gerardo nodded. 'There is an animal track on the other side of the swamp. Two hundred metres along, maybe more. You will have to get on to the bank to find it. The track is used by the men who patrol the forest. If you miss the track then you will have to stay in the water and that takes you very close to where those men camp. The track is better. It gives you a better chance. The river, it has dangers of its own. You understand?'

'I understand,' said Raglan.

Carlos smiled at Raglan and uttered more unintelligible sounds. Gerardo nodded. 'He says he will pray you are given courage to face the evil men who keep our village in fear and who kill for pleasure.'

Raglan grasped the boy's outstretched hand and nodded, then strode ahead towards the edifice that even God had abandoned.

73

Voss followed Raglan into the stinking water without complaint. They eased down the slimy bank into chest-deep grey water. She fought her imagination as to what unseen threat lurked below the surface. Raglan waded close to the mangroves. The silt beneath his feet gave way and he sank lower still. Stepping clear, he extended his hand and guided her around the sinkhole. Two hundred metres further along, the vegetation gave way to a muddy bank. Raglan clambered up, then put out his hand again to help give Voss some purchase. They crouched, catching their breath. Raglan gestured her to stay put and ducked along the bank. Moments later he returned.

'The track's there. It's well-worn. There'll be patrols.'

She nodded and checked her Glock, tugging it free from between her waistband and skin. She pointed the barrel downwards, letting the water drain from the firing pin channel and barrel; then she slid free the magazine clip and drained what water was there. She raised her head. Raglan had already checked his. She attached the silencer and followed him as he led the way along the animal track. It meandered, curving around broad trees; they were obliged to step across raised roots that had a claw-like grip on the forest floor. They were barely twenty minutes from the swamp and Voss's boots still squelched with water. Her mind was distracted, moving her toes trying to accommodate her bunching socks, wishing she had followed Raglan's lead when they left the plane and he had peeled away his socks and then pulled on his boots barefoot. He had reduced his dependence on comfort to the bare minimum. As she lifted her foot across the roots, she lost her footing.

It saved her life.

A man stepped out of the undergrowth, slashing down with a machete, an AK-47 in his free hand. His impetus carried him forwards off balance. Voss fell badly, side on across the iron-hard roots, her left arm caught beneath the weight of her body. She cried out as the bone broke, and cursed as pain from her ribs streaked through her lungs when she gulped air. The agony did not stop her lashing out with her boot. It caught the man's jaw as he scrambled to his feet. He was close enough for her to kick again and connect with his groin. The AK-47 clattered to the ground but he still gripped the hacking blade. Voss couldn't move. The raised roots stopped her from rolling clear and she wouldn't have been able to even if they had not impeded her. Pain nearly blinded her.

What happened next was so quick she barely saw Raglan's killing blow. He was suddenly there, with a vicious punch behind the man's ear and then a stranglehold. She heard the faint click of his neck breaking. Voss attempted to raise herself but knew she must have broken a couple of ribs. Raglan remained silent, unmoving, letting her struggle. Listening for any other approach. He stepped into the jungle. Voss's agony bit deeply but she forced herself on to her knees, sucked in air, held it, used the pain to lever herself to her feet and used the tree trunk for support. Where the hell was Raglan? He was nowhere in sight.

Jungle predators lie in wait. Movement and sound reveals their prey. And so it was with the second man who suddenly stepped on to the path from the dense undergrowth. Muscle clung to his lean frame; a sheen of sweat ran across his shoulders. His old sweat-stained T-shirt was big enough to flap loosely, a bandanna covered his hair and a scar on his face ran from ear to jawline: his badge of honour as a knife fighter. He levelled the AK-47 he carried and snarled a challenge in Spanish at Voss who pressed back harder against the tree. A rapidly moving figure was little more than a blur in the green undergrowth. The hunter spun around but met Raglan's fist which drove a knife hard into the man's sternum. Pain wreaked havoc in his brain. Blood filled his chest cavity. His eyes widened. His legs folded. He dropped to the ground. Raglan pulled him clear of the path as a burst of gunfire shattered the silence. Birds squawked; monkeys screeched. Raglan half rolled and saw Voss with the silenced Glock raised. He looked to where the barrel pointed. Fifteen metres away, sprawling on the track, lay another man whose death throes had squeezed the trigger on his AK-47.

Raglan ran to him. Two holes punctured his shirt front. He was dead. Raglan pulled him into the undergrowth and threw his weapon after him; then he strode back to Voss, who, with gritted teeth, pressed her broken arm against her body.

She shook her head. 'He came out of nowhere.'

Raglan scanned the forest. There was no movement.

'Men work in groups. These three will be missed and others will have heard the firing. OK, let's take a look.'

She winced as he tested her broken arm and tenderly ran his hand along her ribs.

Ever watchful of the path in both directions, he eased her down into a sitting position, dropped his pack and pulled out the first-aid bag. He unwound a broad bandage and gently tucked it beneath her arm to cradle its weight; then he tied off the sling on her uninjured side.

'Oh crap,' she muttered.

'Sit up as much as you can. You've got bruised ribs or you've busted one. Nothing we can do about that.' He smiled. 'No ice packs in this neck of the woods.'

She winced again.

'Deep breaths – keep the lungs working. Do it every hour, you understand? Pain or no pain, a dozen deep breaths every hour.'

She bit her lip and nodded. 'Those shots will bring others.'

'I know,' said Raglan, spilling out a couple of hefty painkillers from the first-aid kit. He offered them to her with his water bottle. She gulped and swallowed. 'But if you hadn't killed him, then we'd have bigger problems than a broken arm and ribs. It is what it is. When does anything go the way we planned?'

'Christ, Raglan, you told me what would happen if either of us got hurt. You have to leave me.'

'I know,' he said, easing her on to her feet. The sling supporting her broken arm held firmly across her body as Raglan pulled her satellite phone from her backpack and tossed the bag into the bushes. 'You won't be needing that.'

She looked perplexed but before she could question him

he eased his arm around her waist. 'We'll get you back to the church.'

She did what she could to match his stride. She was strong and fit enough to press on hard but had it not been for Raglan's strength bearing her weight she knew there would have been no choice but to await death in the jungle. When they reached the swamp he slid down the muddy bank, then took the weight of her boots as she eased herself into the water. She gasped in pain as her arm jolted and her ribs pressed against the bank.

'OK, I know it hurts like hell, but suck it up. Use it. Focus. Understand?' He cradled her again. 'Not far to go.'

'Raglan, you're a terrible liar,' she said through gritted teeth.

They had gone fifty metres along the riverbank and reached the edge of the mangroves when they heard the voices of men scouring the ground above them. Ducking below the entwining mangrove roots, Raglan pulled her deeper into the water. She snatched a lungful of air as he placed his hand firmly across her mouth. She convulsed, her body racked with pain. He pulled her close to him, careful not to crush her arm or ribs, offering safety. She held him with her free arm. The men would have to skirt the mangroves by staying on firm ground. Raglan and Voss remained motionless. Insects bit and the current beneath the surface tugged their legs. The silt shifted. Raglan steadied them both. The voices faded. He nodded and guided her back out into the main swamp. When they crossed to the other side they would be exposed to anyone on the near bank but Raglan sensed the men had gone deeper into the jungle. He pressed on along the nearside bank until he felt they had the best chance to reach the far side. As he eased her into mid-stream he stopped.

'Keep still,' he whispered.

She clung to him, looked behind them, saw no one on the bank. The danger was in the water. She scanned the surface. She couldn't see anything that posed a threat. And then the tell-tale ripple showed her the crocodile, snout and eyes barely breaking the surface.

'Oh my God,' she whispered.

'Don't move,' he said calmly. 'It's not us he's after. But let's not get in the way.' He felt her go rigid with fear.

Crocodiles have multi-sensory organs in the skin, sensitive to vibration, touch, heat and cold, and the chemicals in their surrounding environment. Something had made the water ripple. Thirty metres away a troop of spider monkeys sat in the branches; fruit they gathered had dropped from the overhanging branches into the water. The fruit of temptation brought one monkey to the lower branches. A shock wave of water surged as the crocodile propelled itself out of the river. Its vertical strike took its body length out of the water; its jaws snatched at the monkey. The strike failed, but the monkey fell. For several seconds it had a chance as it struck out for the riverbank. It paddled furiously. The crocodile had submerged after its failed attempt. The soaked monkey was halfway up the riverbank urged on by the chattering troop when the crocodile launched itself, front legs clawing at the muddy shale. This time the lunge was successful. The monkey shrieked. Voss had survived shoot-outs and had men die around her but the terror-stricken screams of a small monkey sounded like a child being taken. The water settled. The monkey drowned; the crocodile feasted.

Raglan seized the opportunity to strike out for the far bank. To Voss it felt like the longest fifteen yards she had ever endured. Raglan ignored her cry of pain as he hauled her up the riverbank on to dry land. She slumped.

'Get up,' he demanded. 'You can rest when we get there.'

'My God, Raglan, after what we've just been through, you're pulling rank? I need a breather. I'm in agony.'

'You can get up or I can leave you.' Raglan stood back.

Voss glared back at him and forced herself through her pain to get to her feet.

It was what Raglan needed from her. 'Now you have a chance to survive.'

'Screw you, Raglan.'

'Maybe later.' He smiled.

By the time he helped her to the old church the sun was already edging its way across the high canopy. He'd be lucky to reach the cave by nightfall. The best-case scenario was to get there before dark and then he could move silently in the night. He propped Voss up, gave her his water bottle and the painkillers. 'Drink as much as you want. The Tramadol will kick in. Keep taking them every four hours.' He pressed the speed-dial button on the satellite phone. Someone answered.

'*Necesito ayuda en la vieja iglesia. La mujer está herida,*' said Raglan. He listened to the response to his request for help from the men at the road. He nodded, ended the call and gave the phone back to Voss. He crouched, gently lifting a strand of muddied hair from her face.

'Gerardo will come for you.'

'You can't go back there, Raglan. Let's call it in,' she said as he stripped out the groundsheet and mosquito net and then draped it around the edge of the old stonework in front of her. It would prove good camouflage should anyone other than Gerardo come looking. He propped his backpack against her side to offer her injured side support.

'That's your decision but give me till first light.'

There was no point trying to persuade him to do other than what he intended. 'I need Lennie Elliot alive,' she said.

He nodded and put her Glock into her hand.

Moments later he was out of sight.

The feeling that welled in her chest shocked her. The feeling that she would never see him again. Alive at least.

74

Raglan retraced his steps but stayed in the river moving upstream. He had lost too much time and now needed to reach the cave and the quickest way was to do what Carlos had told him not to do. Follow the river. Marsh gas bubbled beneath the mangrove's rotting vegetation. He made good time staying close to the slimy roots and by the time he reached another riverbank he realized the manhunters were scouring the ground as only those who lived in the rainforest could. He listened. They were close. Twenty, thirty metres? Their voices were muted by the dense bush but clear enough to reach each other. By now they might have found their dead comrades. The water bellied out into a deep pool. On the far bank were signs of crocodiles, the bank scarred where they clambered out of the water. For now the still water rippled only from him moving cautiously forwards. If the men came closer to the riverbank they would see the movement. He stopped, checked behind him in case a silent predator glided just below the surface. All was still. He eased forwards, his feet finding the shifting silt, careful not to flounder and fall. If he splashed into the water, keen hearing would soon bring the hunters on to him.

Another fifty metres and he would climb ashore and belly crawl into cover. The wound in his side tugged at the stitches. He realized he must have torn a couple when he fought the men attacking Voss. Ignoring the wound's insistence, he clung to the last of the mangroves until he reached the riverbank rising several feet above the water. The darkened shape of a rockface peaked above some lower trees in the distance. It rose three hundred metres distant from where he stood in the foul-smelling water. There would soon be no choice other than to get ashore and find the cave. He listened, breath held, head turning this way and that. The men were still there. Difficult to say how close. For a moment he thought he could make a few extra metres and use the cover of an overhang but the ruffled water ahead stopped him. The snake was as long as Raglan was tall, its body wrist-thick. Its venom would paralyse him. If the gunmen were as close as he thought then any movement would alert them. There was little choice. He waited as it twisted through the water, its head raised above the surface, the cold black eyes staring, the forked tongue flicking. Seeking him out.

Two lethal creatures facing each other.

The reptile gathered itself to strike. Raglan half turned in the water and snatched it behind its head and in one fluid movement tossed its writhing body into the undergrowth before it could entwine itself around his arm. He heard it crash into the bushes and moments later came the staccato chatter of gunfire as bullets tore the low-hanging canopy, a swarm of locusts gnawing leaves, shredding them above him. The sudden harsh gunfire reverberated through the forest. Birds' wings beat the air. Shadows hurtled across the canopy. Howler monkeys bellowed and shrieked. They were beyond the bullet strikes and none were hurt but panic had set in. Raglan used the cacophony to cover the sound of him splashing ahead and then scrambling up the bank to lie unmoving. Caked in slime and mud, he was barely distinguishable from the glutinous bush-pig wallow in which he lay. Knife in hand, he saw one of the men emerge from the trees ten long strides away. He moved with the slow, deliberate gait of a hunter. He stopped. Stared hard at the river. Saw nothing to alarm him and then turned his back to where Raglan lay and disappeared again. A voice called. Another answered. Raglan saw a man wearing a bandanna further along the bank staring into the water. Rifle in his shoulder. Satisfied, he too moved back into the jungle. Raglan waited. By the sound of their voices they had moved closer to each other and were heading away from Raglan's position. The male howler monkeys barked their guttural warnings to their troop and led them away through the treetops.

Raglan picked up his pace along a track, little more than a scar in the forest floor, an edge between undergrowth and river. Twenty minutes later, as darkness swallowed the last remaining vestige of daylight, he saw firelight in the distance and the white glow of a gas canister lantern through the trees. He smelt cooking and bread being baked. He crouched and sought out the campfire and those who lived there. The smell of the bread flashed an image through his mind of walking down the backstreet of Marseilles to the place where the killing had started.

Women's voices carried. Laughter and squeals at a shared comment. Creeping closer, he saw it was a settlement of six huts, wicker-built with palm-leaf roofs and a communal fire burning in the centre of the ring of dwellings, a couple of scrawny dogs stretched out alongside it. Smaller fires bore cooking pots and earthen ovens. A woman pulled out a tray of bread, called to another who laughed and went back to her own cooking. If there were six huts it suggested there had been at least six men before Raglan and Voss had killed three of them. If the women were cooking it meant they expected their menfolk home. They seemed unperturbed by the earlier gunfire. Perhaps they had been calling to each other wondering if their men had shot some game. Raglan checked the smoke from the fires. What little breeze there was funnelled up the river pushing the smoke towards him. He was downwind. The firelight played on the surrounding trees and the rising black mass beyond the huts, blacker than the night, was the mountain he sought. He skirted the settlement as the women's voices quietened. Beams of light cut through the jungle from headlamps as their men returned. Time had run out. Raglan stumbled in the dark, but was saved as his shoulder caught the rock face. Further along, fireflies prickled the slab of rock. He edged along the path next to the cliff face; the voices from the settlement were raised now. A woman wailed. And another. Men shouted them down. Those who had died at Raglan and Voss's hand had not come home and their women now knew of their deaths, but their grief was being stifled by the other men's anger.

Raglan reached the entrance to the cave. They were not fireflies but pinpricks of reflected light from quartz rock, spreading light inside and then disappearing into the tunnel beyond. The opening was where the hunters stored their meat. Gutted carcasses hung from hooks beneath the saw-tooth rock formations on the cave's roof.

Raglan stepped into the belly of the beast.

75

There was no such thing as an innocent death in the pursuit
of overthrowing the Iranian regime. Those who died serving
that purpose were useful deaths. The attempt to frame the
Englishman by killing those known to him had almost
worked. Now it made no difference. The first shipment of
arms stored in the jungle had left for the coast along with
fifty contractors. The second and final shipment of six trucks
would leave the following day along with the remaining
twenty fighters whose expertise would train those in the
Mojahedin-e-Khalq.

Aram-banou's work was done. She had subdued her
feelings about working with Israeli Mossad dissidents and
former special forces but soon they would be gone from
her life when they immersed themselves among those on
the ground in Iran. She stretched on her exercise mat in
the open-plan room of the quarters reserved solely for her
comfort. Her strength and agility were a result of discipline
instilled since childhood and enforced when she had been
trained by the Islamic Revolutionary Guard to become a
resistance fighter against the West. She was far from her
homeland but always close to its embedded memories. Her
mother had died of cancer when she was fourteen and she

had then been lovingly raised by her gentle father. Years later, the man she idolized more than any other had expressed his misgivings when she volunteered for the female fighting unit and his doubt had wounded her. That wound was cauterized when her father, an academic, had been publicly executed after his continued outspoken opposition to the abuse of human rights and use of state torture. A prison sentence was mandatory in the Revolutionary Courts but a state official brought trumped-up evidence against him from a junior lecturer at her father's university, a young man who had been arrested and tortured on false charges. His confession condemned her father to death. He was paraded through the streets of Teheran and hanged from a construction crane. This was no execution where the hangman's noose breaks the condemned man's neck: it was a slow strangulation that took twenty minutes to complete.

There was an innocent death, just one. Her father's.

The ugly sight of him choking and writhing at the end of the thick nylon rope was the only thing she regretted. The question she asked herself now was whether this Englishman would pursue her. Was it possible he had discovered this jungle base? What purpose would it serve to even try and reach her? She looked across the low-walled compound, the beautiful old house sitting in its tropical garden. It reminded her of the walled garden she had known as a child. The walls were her safety, her father her protector. She sighed. She was driven by revenge and a sense of duty. So was the Englishman.

Sooner or later. Here or somewhere else. He would come.

★

Raglan made his way through the cave. The pinpricks of quartz cast barely enough light for anyone to traverse from one end of the cave to the other. The cave narrowed and then twisted and Raglan reasoned that the creeping illumination at the far end came from the generator in Luis Reyes's compound because those living at the mouth of the cave had no electricity. Kill the power, and darkness would serve him. He reached a point where the cave walls and roof closed in, the sudden narrowing caused him to crouch. The rockface walls were worn smooth, probably from men passing through over the years. The lighting came to an end. This narrow, twisting umbilical cord separated the jungle hunters who guarded the entrance from the compound at the far end where Reyes and his masters lived. Raglan stopped. The cave blanketed sound but he had heard a murmur. If the narrow darkness was soon to widen, it was likely men were on the compound side. Raglan's inherent instinct for tunnel fighting brushed aside the claustrophobic thought of what might lie ahead.

Memory took him to the tunnels in West Africa. The attack then had been against terrorists. The killing had been to save others. An assailant had loomed out of the darkness and Raglan killed him. Only when he advanced further into the tunnel had he realized it was a boy, probably no more than ten or eleven years old. Sent to kill by an adult. A Salafist who thought no sacrifice too great. Even the life of a child. The child's eyes had locked wide in disbelief, staring at Raglan. The gaze of that dead child had never left him. Now his passage through the darkness was to seek a killer with a twisted mind and heartless disregard for anyone in her way, and to find a drug dealer who had mutilated another boy in another time and place. The cold-hearted and the brutal. A price to be paid.

Raglan gave a mental nod to the old tunnel rat TJ Jones. Perhaps the old Airborne veteran's spirit was with him now as he crept, knife in hand, towards what he knew to be men's voices. His silenced semi-automatic would kill effectively but there was no telling if the bullets would pass through the men and ricochet across the rockface. That sound alone would echo and alert the men in the compound. Killing these men had to be done the hard way.

Raglan thought there must be some kind of antechamber that barrelled their voices around the walls and then muted them further down the tunnel where he edged along. The closer he got the stronger the stench of human waste. The men were using the place as a latrine. He peered around the next corner, left hand guiding him along the rockface, knife held low, eyes closed momentarily, hearing where the men were and how close. He opened his eyes. Artificial light seeped into a smaller cave, revealing two packing crates serving as a seat to one man ten strides away; his back to Raglan, he was cutting something with a knife and eating. A second man stepped out of the hewn rockface area which was obviously the latrine. He was walking back towards his companion. They were speaking Spanish, their animated conversation rising and falling as they talked about opposing football teams. Their weapons lay propped out of reach. They had no need to be alert. Along the wall on hooks were stencils stained with red spray paint. Each stencil told a lie. *Manifolds. Transmission Gears. Tractor Parts.*

He saw their hands. They were dyed red. They were there to stencil the arms crates in the cave. It was gloomy enough for Raglan to edge forwards. Latrine Man was still approaching his companion when Raglan drove his knife into his neck. Making no attempt to withdraw the blade, he was already past the falling body as the eating man turned, uncertain what he had heard. His jaw dropped and eyes widened at the mud-caked apparition looming out of the dimly lit cave, whose rigid fingers aimed for his throat. The knife he'd used for cutting the piece of meat was forgotten, but he would have had no time to use it before his larynx cracked. He dropped the scrap of meat and the knife as both hands went to his ruptured throat. Pain blurred his eyes, blinding him to the temple blow that felled him. His knees buckled, head cracking against the rockface so hard it broke his neck. Raglan retrieved his killing knife and picked up one of the AK-47s. Some rapid gunfire in the right direction might prove the diversion he needed when he reached the compound. He muted the dead man's two-way radio and tucked it into his waistband.

He went forwards. The cave broadened; arc lamps flooded inside now. Crates were stacked ten high; at a rough guess he thought there were a couple of hundred of them. Marks on the floor showed where others had been stored. There were not only armaments crates being stored in the cave; pallets of Reyes's drugs were piled there too. The closer he got to the cave's entrance, the clearer he could see the outside. Several transport wagons were parked nose to tail. Their tailgates were down, their canvas flaps tied up. A dozen men, who looked to be locals, stood smoking on the blind side from where Raglan watched. Crates were stacked ready for loading. Military hardware usually required specialist transport but illegal arms shipments were a more rough-and-ready affair and that meant the more stringent safety procedures were unlikely to have been followed.

The main house was three hundred metres away, nestled behind low walls and tended gardens. It was an old-style Spanish hacienda built probably a century ago by a rich man who traded downriver. And then drug lords had moved in, and recent history had gifted it to Luis Reyes: the boy from Honduras who had gone to the city and found a route from jungle to concrete and rags to riches. The disgraced high-society gangster had overstepped the mark and then heaven-sent protection had arrived in the form of corrupt American government officials, and with their influence he had returned to his own private paradise.

Raglan took in the compound's layout. The balcony was where the mute boy had indicated; the long veranda and windows on the ground floor ran the length of the house. Warm light seeped from the spacious rooms behind the glass. Two armed guards, one each end of the veranda. It looked as though they patrolled the house perimeter and the front of the house was where they turned. Two hundred metres beyond the house, on the right, was a long low building, a more modern take on an indigenous village longhouse. It was raised on low stilts, like the other ancillary buildings, with a few steps leading up to a front veranda. From what he had been shown on the crude model of the compound, it served as the dormitory for Reyes's men who helped run his drug routes. Ten metres beyond their hut was another house. Raglan counted fourteen men; unmistakably contractors, they were loitering around an open fire and grill from where the smell of meat wafted across to where Raglan waited. The burly men were in good spirits, bottles of beer in hand; all looked to be American or Latino former special forces. Raglan guessed these were the core element who trained and led the insurgents and who guarded the Iranian assassin. Everyone appeared to be relaxed, which told him that word of the arrests in America had not reached them. The house showed activity inside; no sign yet of Reyes but Raglan identified one of the men from the security cameras at Reyes's DC house: it was the ex-Mossad man, Elias. That meant he and the others were still embedded with Reyes, and if the Israeli was here then Aram-banou might be also.

Raglan skirted the trucks, crouched along the low wall, ducked when one of the patrolling guards stooped to light a cigarette and call out to another. It gave Raglan the other man's location. Raglan saw the glow of a cigarette thirty metres towards the main gate. The narrow bridge beyond the gates spanned another forty metres across swamp and narrow river. It gave Reyes's house the perfect defence, just as the old *patrón* had explained. There were no lights generated beyond those at the gate, where another two men stood guard. Raglan could not have gauged the length of the bridge were it not for the headlights from a battered-looking pickup that blocked the far end of the narrow wooden structure. It was the old man's. Its bonnet was raised and the *patrón* and three of his men hunched over the engine using torches to examine the fault. There was no fault. The food delivery had been made on schedule as expected, and the breakdown was the old man creating the opportunity for Raglan to deliver Luis Reyes to face justice. For a brief, almost imperceptible moment Raglan entertained the thought that it would be an act of mercy to kill Reyes outright rather than hand him over to the villagers. The moment passed. Mercy was not on Raglan's mind.

Using the shadows, he darted across the approach track that led from the gates to the side of the house. Halfway across, he stopped and let his eyesight adjust to the darkness that lay beyond. The heavy blackness absorbed the night. A structure loomed in the background. At first he thought it another rock formation and then a sudden burst of light filled the void. Men whooped and cheered as one of the mercenaries let off a flare. It illuminated the tall edifice of a Mayan ruin, its stepped structure rising above the jungle canopy. Raglan reasoned this was once an ancient settlement, swallowed by time and jungle, but the tower had survived. That remarkable civilization had succumbed to starvation and illness but there, still extant, was their defiant edifice. If that tower had been any kind of sacrificial temple then it was well placed for what would happen before sunlight touched its peak.

76

Raglan now had a good idea of the lie of the land and where the guards patrolled. If he was to get inside the main house then he needed an outside distraction. Not easy. He squatted, concealed behind the wall and bushes near the kitchen door. Gaining entry and assaulting a house where armed men could be in every room was a foolhardy proposition. Better perhaps to ignore the main house and seek out the woman and kill her? He checked his watch. Men slept deeply in the small hours before daylight. That's when he would have the advantage. If all went well, that is. And one thing Raglan knew from experience: it seldom did. Time to reduce the odds of anything going wrong by controlling the situation. If there was going to be chaos better to be its instigator. Waiting until first light increased the risk of discovery. The time to act was now.

Raglan crouched and ran, ignoring the protesting wound in his side. The generator shed was a wooden structure, with a single door and no guard. Checking he was in the clear, he tested the door. It opened. There was no one inside. The hefty generator was a thirsty beast and there were fifty or more fuel cans stacked along the one side. Raglan lifted one. It was full. He checked outside. No sign of patrolling guards.

Raglan considered his options. Destroy the generator or rig a device to destroy the armaments awaiting shipment in the cave? The first would knock out all power and light. The second option would bring down the cave's roof. The cave walls would confine the explosion and the blast would blow outward and hit the parked lorries. It was a difficult choice. He decided to destroy both.

A bandanna sweat rag used by someone to wipe his greasy hands was draped over one of the fuel pipes. Raglan tied it around his head, which would, at first glance, give the impression of him being one of the locals used for labouring and guard duties. He slung the AK-47 across his shoulder and hefted a full twenty-litre jerry can in each hand. There was no chance of running to the cave undetected carrying that weight. He'd have to walk.

Raglan stepped out into the night. There was a route across the compound that gave him some cover. Trees and bushes skirted a winding path on the edge of the gardens. The house was beyond them to his left; the parked lorries and the men who now busied themselves loading were a hundred metres to one side. He followed the path. Dim lights dotted around the gardens showed him the way and the temporary arc lamps directed at the men loading the lorries shone stark white light across them. He hoped that if anyone should casually glance in his direction that it would look as though he belonged there. Would anyone question why one of the men was carrying fuel cans towards the cave? The poor light disguised his mud-caked clothing. He glanced left and right as he walked confidently towards the gaping hole in the mountainside 150 metres away. He only needed a few more minutes.

A voice called out. One of the men bending to load an ammunition crate. He hadn't stopped what he was doing. The shout was some kind of gibe. Raglan looked his way and nodded in the man's direction.

'*Púdrete!*' he cursed back. A bluff so he wouldn't be obliged to stop. The man laughed.

The path snaked through the bushes and as he reached the next bend he saw the gap in the low garden wall; beyond that it was another eighty metres to the cave. Almost there. As the path turned, low palm branches dragged across his shoulder, he ducked and in that instant saw one of the patrolling guards two metres away staring intently at the cave entrance. Raglan's footfall behind him broke his concentration. He turned and gaped for a moment as his brain tried to compute if he knew the man. Raglan smiled. It caused a vital moment of further uncertainty. Raglan lowered the fuel cans. '*Necesito un cigarrillo,*' he said, smiling again. By then the guard was in no man's land, that place where instinct was making him begin to swing his weapon to bear but his thought process was telling him the poor guy humping heavy fuel cans needed a smoke. Hands and brain never connected. Raglan jabbed his throat, strangling any chance for him to cry out. The man staggered back, dropping his weapon. He fell, eyes wide. He lashed out with his boot. It caught Raglan's hand that held his knife and then his leg, a lucky kick on to the wound. Raglan lost momentum, the knife fell from his grasp; he staggered as the man squirmed, trying to escape. Raglan fell on him, using his weight to smother him. The guard writhed and thrashed but Raglan pressed both hands over his mouth and nose and his weight on the man's chest compressed his lungs. The bones in his throat were already damaged. Raglan kept the pressure on him. The rank stench of the man's stale sweat caught Raglan's nostrils. It was nothing compared to the swamp mud Raglan had crawled through but the clawing stink added to the foul manner of the man's death.

It took several minutes for the man to die. Raglan drew breath, peered beneath the undergrowth and dragged him into the bushes, tossing his weapon after him. Raglan was hurting. The stitches in his side felt torn and the leg wound had opened up. He ignored it. Retrieving his fallen knife, he grabbed the fuel cans and limped towards the cave.

The two dead men lay where he had left them. Raglan ran a hand along the crates, using the outside arc-lamp lights to search the contents stencilled on their sides. Ammunition, grenades and mortars were the lifeblood of men who fought on foot and the crates were laden. He found the pallets he was looking for, cut one of the crate's holding straps and prised open the lid. He pulled away the heavy-duty cardboard packing. The light shone on packed US Army M67 fragmentation grenades. Raglan knew it would take only a few seconds to insert their fuses and arm one. In a couple of minutes he would have a handful of grenades ready for use. But there was no need. One method of shipping live grenades safely in transit was to cushion them inside empty plastic water bottles. And that's what Raglan was staring at. Hundreds of them.

He pulled out half a dozen. He checked the entrance, making sure no one had found the guard's body in the bushes. He would be missed before long. The men loading the lorries had almost completed their task. The convoy would soon head for the coast. Blood seeped from Raglan's leg. He pulled the bandanna free and tied it over the wound. Then he hauled the cans of fuel further back into the cave, released the caps and poured the petrol over the crates. When the first can was empty he spilt fuel from the second along the side of the crates and then hoisted the can up so that its contents ran down between the stacks. He went further back and pulled the pin on a grenade and balanced the spring lever beneath the prised-open lid. He did the same with three more grenades under another four crates. The best bet to rig a booby trap would be to put a live grenade under the body of one of the dead men. Raglan had seen terrorists apply the same method of killing, but having witnessed legionnaires mutilated in this manner he had a distaste for using the dead to kill others. He turned over the wooden box the man had used as a seat and blocked the passage into the cave. He pulled the grenade's pin and wedged it beneath the upturned crate. That would be the first thing to be moved out of the way and the explosion would trigger what would follow.

He checked his watch. He could see the convoy was now loaded, the tailgates secured, the men heading off towards the far side of the compound. Raglan waited. They were going to a different building than those used by the mercenary contractors, which meant they were being kept separate from the former special-forces fighters. A hierarchy was in place. He watched the men shuffle to the door of their quarters. A beer-swilling contractor shouted a derogatory remark. It sounded like a South African accent and Raglan remembered what Jack Swain had told him. There were men from different countries being paid for their expertise. One of them threw a bottle at the Hondurans. The men who had loaded the lorries dodged the projectile and shouted abuse but, even though they looked as though they were familiar with violence, they did not dare react against the tough fighters jeering at them.

Raglan waited until the local men had gone inside. Two women appeared, each carrying an urn of food. Raglan traced their route back to the kitchen. The contractors were in high spirits; some bowed and swept their arms in front of the women who ignored their comedic routine. The beer drinkers appeared to agree to grab the steaks off the grill and follow the women inside now their supper had been delivered. The coast was clear.

Raglan ran back towards the generator shed, ignoring the increasing pain in his side and leg. He concealed himself behind the low wall and watched the compound. Stragglers from the loading team shouted across the bridge to where the *patrón* still appeared to be attending to his engine. Any closer examination would have revealed he and his men were doing little more than biding their time. The men veered off to their quarters fifty metres from that of the contractors. The compound was settling down for the night. Raglan was between the main house and the men's quarters but he had a clear sight of the Mayan tower and the small house below it. It was dark. No lights showed. Was the woman still inside? He checked the silenced Glock and was about to head towards her quarters when he saw the Mossad man and Luis Reyes in the hacienda's large sitting room. Raised voices alerted the outside guards. They strode quickly to the veranda's glass doors but were waved away by a third man in the room. He too had been in the video clip Raglan had seen at Reyes's house in DC. Probably a second bodyguard. Raglan had shot and killed the other when he was pursuing Reyes through the side streets of DC after the cop shooting.

Reyes looked cowed; he poured a drink and swallowed it in one. The muted voices gave no hint of what was being said but clearly Reyes was being controlled by the Mossad man who turned to the bodyguard and nodded. It seemed whatever the argument was about had been settled. Mossad man and the bodyguard left the room. Reyes bent his face to the coffee table and snorted some cocaine. He would be high with energy and dangerous. A light went on upstairs. Mossad man walked across the window. Where was the bodyguard? He would be close. Reyes switched on the television. It was loud. Reducing the odds; snatching Reyes was now an opportunity. There was no sign of the mysterious Lennie Elliot who Voss wanted so badly to clear her name. But as far as Raglan was concerned, he wasn't a priority.

Raglan glanced over to the Iranian assassin's quarters. Still dark. He thought he saw a shadow move near the small house. He waited. There was nothing more to indicate she had slipped out. Raglan propped the AK-47 out of sight and skirted the wall towards the kitchen of Reyes's hacienda. A drainpipe led up to the balcony. It looked flimsy. Age and humidity had eaten into its fabric. The kitchen door opened. One of the serving women said something to another over her shoulder as she emptied a bowl of scraps into a pig pen a few strides away from the kitchen door. Light spilt out from the kitchen. It was Raglan's way in. The woman had her back to him, still talking to the unseen person in the kitchen. Raglan edged forwards and then stopped in the open. If she turned and saw him without warning then there was every possibility she would scream, so: 'Gabriela Mejía,' he said gently.

The woman whirled; the bowl fell from her hands as she smothered her cry. Raglan did not move: he knew the apparition of a swamp creature standing in front of her was a shock. The woman took a deep breath, one hand still on her lips, the other across her heart.

'Gabriela?' the woman whispered and crossed herself. She saw the gun in Raglan's hand, the knife in its scabbard and the bloodstained bandanna.

'Gabriela and Carlos Alvarado,' Raglan added.

She understood. She raised a hand to keep him there, glanced nervously left and right, and returned to the kitchen. Moments later the second woman appeared. Stared at Raglan and then beckoned him inside. The women stood aside. The first pointed to a passage, fear creasing her face. 'Reyes,' she whispered.

'The woman?' he asked. '¿La mujer?'

They shook their head. Looked at each other. 'She is not here,' said one and pointed in the general direction of Aram-banou's house. 'She is protected. By the men. She is... *importante.*'

Raglan nodded his understanding and then pointed upwards and wiggled his first two fingers to indicate stairs. They both nodded. One beckoned him to follow her and after several paces along the corridor stopped to let him pass. A narrow winding staircase, used by servants, curved up to the first floor.

'You have finished your duties for the night?' Raglan said quietly.

'Soon.'

'Finish now. Do not go outside. Is there somewhere to hide?'

'The pantry?'

'Stay there. You will know when to come out. Understand? Other men will come in daylight. You will hear them when they come,' he emphasized, hoping she understood that more help was on its way.

She nodded nervously. 'I understand. Soldiers?'

'Yes. How many people in the house? Upstairs.'

'Three men,' the woman said.

Raglan stepped towards the staircase.

'God bless you,' she whispered and returned to her companion in the kitchen.

Raglan climbed the stairs.

77

Jenna Voss had felt oddly spaced out from the drink the villagers had given her for her broken arm. Now the pain was biting back and her head was clear. There had been no sound of conflict from the jungle after the initial sounds of gunfire soon after Raglan had left. Had he been killed? If so, would his body have been taken to Reyes's compound? But if it had, then the *patrón* would have returned and told her. He hadn't. The uncertainty as to whether Raglan had failed and the attempt to snatch Reyes and kill the woman had gone down the pan gnawed at her. They knew that at least one arms shipment had left for the coast, but what if there was another? The men who remained in the village were alert and looked as though they might be expecting trouble. The risk they were taking was huge if Reyes suspected their involvement. If it went wrong, their village would be destroyed and the men killed. It was still nearly three hours until first light.

Her ribs hurt. She limped into the clearing and checked the signal on the satellite phone. The sky was clear. No storms loomed. She lowered it, undecided, and looked in the direction of where the village *patrón* and Raglan would be. The Black Hawks could be here in under an hour. Act too soon and they could blow the whole operation; act too late and Reyes, the Iranian and Lennie Elliot could be long-gone. Raglan had broken his golden rule and abandoned the mission to get her back to safety. Raglan broke rules.

She pressed Kim Burton's speed-dial button.

Raglan eased into the upstairs corridor. Brass ceiling lamps cast a dim glow along its length. Rooms led off it either side, front and back. Seven left, seven right. A larger door – wood-panelled, ornate, hefty frame – signalled a master suite. The television boomed from below, the noise echoing up the main staircase at the far end of the passage. The wooden floor had a strip of carpet running down its centre. The old hardwood floors would creak under his weight. He pressed his foot close to the edge of the wall, the strongest point. If the boards creaked, he hoped the noise from the television would muffle the sound. He put his ear against the first door on the left. It was unlocked. He eased it open. The room was large. A substantial double bed. Well furnished. Empty. He stepped across the hall and repeated his cautious entry with the same result. The more desirable rooms were obviously further from the kitchen end of the house. There were three men somewhere. Mossad man, the muscle, and one other. Third time lucky. Raglan eased open a door on the left and saw the crumpled figure of a man sleeping. The room was in darkness. Hard liquor and drugs were visible. The bathroom door showed a crack of light. Did the comatose man have company? Raglan nudged at the door. The bathroom was empty. Raglan crept forwards, levelled the Glock. The man was belly down; spittle dribbled from his mouth. He grunted but did not wake as Raglan switched on the bedside lamp to identify him. The elusive Lennie Elliot.

Raglan tugged the tie cords from the thick curtains. He pulled aside the silk sheets and wrapped the cord around one of the man's ankles. Still he didn't wake. The second tight knot on the other ankle made him groan and try to come back from dreamland. Raglan tied off both cords on the bed end and then pressed his knee into the man's back and bound his hands. Sudden grunts of alarm spewed from Lennie Elliot's mouth. Raglan pressed his face into the pillow and rammed a handful of sheet into his mouth. Now Elliot's eyes widened. Raglan tore a strip of pillowcase and gagged him. The naked man writhed. Raglan hog-tied him and put him back to sleep with a short sharp punch.

The next room was empty. Raglan waited in the corridor. The television station changed. He pictured the window where he'd seen Luis Reyes's ex-Mossad controller. Centre of the passage. Front facing. Dangerous if Raglan entered and it went wrong, because any of the guards patrolling along the front veranda below the bedrooms would be alerted. There was no light showing beneath the door. Raglan stepped forwards, eased the door handle. The room too was unlit, except for the dim glow from the outside lights in the garden. The shutters hadn't been closed. As Raglan stepped into the room a silhouetted figure lurched upright. Old skills, embedded deep in the Mossad man's DNA. Raglan fired once. The silenced bullet struck him in the forehead. He fell back; the head shot's impact splattered the half-open window. Raglan eased the door closed behind him. There was enough light for Raglan to examine the man's features. The neat puncture above his eyes had turned the man's death gaze upwards. The small automatic pistol had fallen from his grasp. He had slept prepared. Silk sheets can resist blood for only so long: the stain began to spread through the weave. Raglan searched the man's clothes on the stand, found his identification in his wallet. He had not tried to hide his Israeli citizenship. Beyond that there was no indication he had once worked for one of the most formidable intelligence agencies in the world.

Raglan found a briefcase in the bottom of the wardrobe. It was crammed with paperwork. Too much to carry loose. He flipped it open on the bed, saw the passport, checked it. There was a second one buried in the side pocket. Whoever he was, he had been a key player. Raglan closed the briefcase and turned for the door, briefcase in hand. A shadow fell beneath the doorframe, right to left. Raglan froze. He moved to the side of the room that gave him a clear shot for anyone attempting to enter. The shadow beneath the door had not moved. Raglan had nowhere to go. He would have no chance of going back out into the corridor. Anyone with even basic training would shoot him dead.

He crouched, ignoring the strain on his leg wound. Levelling the Glock, he drew a deep breath and began a vigorous coughing. He rasped for breath, the coughing sounding as though someone was choking. The door opened, and the light behind the man who stood there illuminated his big frame and the gun in his hand. It was the bodyguard, dressed in boxer shorts. He queried his charge as he stepped into the doorframe: 'Mr Elias, sir?'

Raglan fired twice. One bullet struck the big man beneath the chin, the second tore into his chest. The thud as his big frame slammed into the corridor must have been heard, but the television still blared. Raglan stepped over him and strode quickly back the way he had come, down the stairs and into the kitchen. He opened one door and then another. The second door was the pantry. The terrified women were crouched on the floor, arms locked for comfort. Raglan put the briefcase down.

'Soldiers will come. Give them this. Tell them the Englishman said it's important.'

They nodded; one hugged the briefcase to her side. 'When will they come?'

'Soon,' said Raglan. 'There is nothing to be afraid of,' he assured them.

They nodded, but they didn't believe him.

Raglan turned back along the ground-floor passage. He quickened his pace. The sound of the television grew louder. He opened a door into the vast sitting room. He could see the back of Reyes's head. He was watching an African wildlife film showing a lion kill. The female pride was cornering a big buffalo. Luis Reyes whooped as the killers closed in. Raglan looked out of the windows. The garden lights cast shadows but there was no sign of the guards. Reyes drank deeply from his whiskey glass. Then he cheered as the lions finally brought down their prey. Raglan pressed the silencer's muzzle into Reyes's neck. He started, dropped the glass, extended his arms.

'Don't shoot,' he said. The reaction of a man thinking he was about to die.

'Turn off the TV,' said Raglan as he killed the side lamps

either side of the sofa. Reyes pressed the remote. The garden lights threw spikey shadows across the glass from the plants. 'Look at me,' said Raglan.

The man's mind was on another plane, his sense of awareness heightened as he twisted his head, wide-eyed, searching Raglan's face in the low light. 'I know you, man,' he said.

'You don't want to know me.' Raglan tossed the two-way taken from the cave on to the table. 'Pick up the radio,' he said.

Reyes's hand brushed through the generous amount of cocaine on the tabletop and picked up the radio. He looked at Raglan. 'What is this? You're not one of my people.' He stared hard. 'Did Swain send you down here? I mean, look, things got out of control, I know that. I see the problem. But we're good, man. It's all good. Shipments are running exactly as Swain wanted.'

Raglan gestured with the Glock. 'On your feet.'

Reyes did as he was told. The lights outside caught the crazy look in his eyes. Not quite spaced. Not quite down. Ready to try something. He smiled. 'You're in a bad place, my friend. This place is crawling.' As if seeing Raglan's filthy state for the first time, his nose wrinkled. 'You stink. I've got expensive carpets here, y'know. I don't want any of your shit on my carpets.'

'How would you like your brains all over your carpets?' said Raglan.

'OK, OK, we're cool,' said Reyes, edging around the sofa. He glanced at the stairs.

'They're not coming,' said Raglan.

Reyes's face dropped. If he had hoped to keep the intruder

talking long enough for help to arrive, that possibility had been snatched away.

'The woman? Is she in the house? The one below the tower?'

'The woman?' Reyes acted dumb, hands spread innocently.

Raglan slapped him hard.

'*Jesús, Madre de Dios,*' Reyes spat. His lip was split.

Raglan levelled the gun against his forehead.

'All right, all right. The house. Yes, she's in that house,' Reyes said.

'And the men guard her? Protect her? The contractors?'

'The foreigners, *sí.*'

'Why?'

'Why?'

'Why is she so important?'

'Because.'

Raglan eased back the hammer. Once again Reyes raised his hands in surrender. 'She is the contact for the group over there.'

'Iran?

'Iran,' Reyes confirmed. 'She is valuable in more ways than one. She is an assassin, did you know that? Eh? I bet you didn't know that.'

'I knew,' said Raglan.

'Shit, who *are* you?'

'I'm a tourist,' said Raglan and grabbed his collar, keeping the Glock pressed firmly into Reyes's neck. 'Where's the money?'

'The money? You can have it. Sure. You can take it. Take the money and run,' said Reyes. If that's all this gunman wanted then Reyes had a chance to live. He pointed to a cupboard. Raglan made him open it. Floor to ceiling was stacked with oversized black zipper bags. Reyes unzipped one of the bags to show willing. It was full of shrink-wrapped bundles of high-denomination dollars.

'Zip it and bring it,' said Raglan.

'Take what you want. I can get more. Take it.'

Raglan slapped the silenced Glock across the back of his head. Reyes winced, bent and slung the bag over his shoulder. Raglan marched him down the corridor. They went through the kitchen and then Raglan pulled him back into the building's shadow and turned him through the garden route that Raglan had reconnoitred. Raglan retrieved the assault rifle and kept pushing the complaining Reyes forwards until they reached the garden wall that ran along the near side of the truck-loaders' quarters. The contractors' building was beyond them.

'How many contractors here?'

'I dunno. They were brought in.'

'Ten, twenty?'

'Yeah.'

'Which?'

'A dozen or more? I dunno.'

'Use the radio. Tell your guards in the compound to get into the cave. Tell them it's an emergency. That there's an intruder. Make it real.'

'The cave?' he said, his mind dancing around, searching for the gunman's reason.

Raglan jabbed him with the Glock. Reyes stooped, a hand half-raised in supplication. 'OK, OK.'

'I speak Spanish,' said Raglan. '*Sin trucos. ¿Entiendes?* No tricks.'

Raglan was impressed by the way Reyes ordered his men. His voice was raised, denoting convincing panic. Having a Glock pressed behind his ear helped. Beyond the house they heard guards shouting to each other. Raglan peered through the garden as shadows flitted through the trees and along tracks. Men dipped in and out of the lit grounds. There were probably no more than six or seven men patrolling the grounds but now they concentrated together as they raced for the cave.'

'You're a stupid man, my friend,' said Reyes.

'I'm the one with the gun,' said Raglan.

'For now, but you cannot hope to get out of here alive.'

Raglan watched the men reach the cave's entrance. Reyes had a point.

Jenna Voss listened to the familiar voice on the end of the satellite phone.

'I'm in Miami,' said Kim Burton. 'We're investigating how far the rot goes. We've arrested Lewis Culver. You have to come in, Jenna. I can't help you if you don't.'

'The only way you can help me is to get a team here. There's a US Army task force at Soto Cano Air Base. It's part of our southern command.'

'You know I can't authorize that.'

'I'm an American citizen and I've been brought here against my will. I'm in danger. My life is threatened and the man running the arms shipments is a forty-minute drive from where I am, so don't tell me you can't do anything.'

The explosion lit the night sky. The roar thundered across the jungle canopy; flames soared in the distance.

'What was that?' said a concerned Kim Burton.

'All hell breaking loose,' said Voss.

78

Luis Reyes's jaw dropped. The blast ricocheted inside the cave's confined space and moments later sucked oxygen in and spat out a roaring fireball that engulfed the loaded vehicles. The ground shook and the shockwave bent the tops of nearby trees. Raglan dragged Reyes behind the garden wall and pushed him down. Reyes struggled in Raglan's grip, cocaine and whiskey giving him strength and determination, and making him more stupid than when he was sober. The man was becoming a burden and getting between Raglan and his main target: the woman. Raglan restrained him with a knee in his chest and hit him hard. Reyes went down. Half-dressed men stormed out of their quarters. The sustained blastwave forced them down to seek shelter. The loaded trucks exploded. Raglan felt the heat strike him. Still crouching behind the wall, he saw that despite the chaos the contractors were alert; weapons in hand, momentarily shielding themselves from flying debris, they were looking towards the inferno. As more explosions followed, they ducked, taking cover.

The men who had loaded the trucks were in disarray as firecracker ammunition spat free of the burning crates. Both groups of men protected themselves as best they could from the lethal explosions. Raglan levelled the AK-47 and fired three long bursts into the contractors – they were the bigger threat of the two groups – and then quickly changed his arc of fire to shoot into Reyes's men. Four contractors went down, followed by as many of Reyes's men. Shouts of alarm barrelled between the local men as the contractors were quick to respond, half turning, searching for the unseen gunmen behind them. Raglan's angle of fire made them turn towards Reyes's men. They wasted no time in returning fire at the hapless locals. It was not a time to ask why men from the same compound were shooting at them.

Shrieks of pain mingled with cries of panic as the two groups exchanged gunfire. Raglan turned Reyes on to his back, lifted his torso to lean against the wall and, using the wall as leverage, hauled him on to his shoulders. Despite the weight of the man and the bag of money, Raglan managed to make for the bridge, the *patrón*'s gift on his back and his bought silence in the bag. If anyone saw him, they would see only a man carrying someone to safety from the ravages of the fire. Behind him the gunfire increased. The stench of burnt fuel, seared metal and weapon propellant flooded the air. Monkeys' screams overwhelmed screeching birds. Raglan was halfway across the bridge when the *patrón*'s pickup's headlights flared into life. The old man and two of his men appeared at the front of the pickup. Raglan pounded towards them, his wounds complaining all the way. He faltered as the *patrón* raised his rifle and fired. Raglan instinctively hunched. The *patrón* beckoned him, shouting something that Raglan could not hear. Raglan half turned and saw the sprawled body of one of the compound's guards whose post had previously been at the end of the bridge. Either he had survived the blast or had not responded to Reyes's order to go to the cave. It was obvious he had intended to shoot Raglan.

Raglan dumped the unconscious Reyes and the heavy black bag at the villagers' feet. The *patrón*'s men lifted Reyes into the back of the pickup. The old man slammed down the truck's bonnet, grabbed the bag and, with a curt nod to Raglan, climbed into the cab. The window was down.

'You live long enough, there's a fast boat at a jetty below the bridge,' he shouted.

The engine fired, the tyres found purchase and the pickup bumped on to the road leading back to the village. Raglan turned. He stopped for a moment to draw breath and gaze at the image of hell on earth. The tree canopy had caught fire, sparks flying high into the night sky; the trucks still burnt and the blast had caught men and slammed their charred remains against the scorched metal. Smoke billowed through the still flaming weapons containers and in the compound shooting continued, but only sporadically, telling Raglan that the firefight was all but over. Electric lights still burnt in the main house, garden and men's quarters. Raglan ran back across the bridge into the compound and then through the gardens, skirting where the contractors now stood, and walked among the dead. Several of them had survived Raglan's attack and then the return fire from Reyes's Honduran gunmen. They were in no mood to help the wounded locals. If one was found alive, they shot him. Raglan made his way around the buildings towards the generator shed; its hum continued unabated.

He checked his watch. If Voss had done as he had asked then the helicopters should be at the jungle compound in less than two hours. Intermittent explosions shattered the night as more armaments yielded to the intense heat.

As he turned down the side of one building a man, as broad and as tall as Raglan, came the other way. It was one of the contractors. Israeli, American, South African: it made no difference; he was quick to react. The stranger two metres in front of him did not belong there. He raised his assault rifle. Raglan lunged, smacked down the barrel with one hand and drove the heel of his hand beneath the bridge of the man's nose. The contractor whipped his head aside, took the half-landed hit, spat blood and was already reaching for the combat knife strapped to the webbing belt at his shoulder. Raglan smothered it with one hand and hit him again and again with hard damaging blows. Vital areas. Ears, eyes, throat, carotid artery, heart, ribs and kidneys. Blows were parried and returned. Raglan lashed out with his boot between the man's legs. Pain could be ignored but a sudden excruciating blow caused a moment's hesitation. The man sucked air. Raglan pummelled him back against the building and hurt him again. The man slithered down, tried to roll and escape the blows. He could not. Raglan gripped his wrist, twisted it, heard it snap; the man grunted as Raglan pushed his boot into his neck. The pressure on his throat was as unyielding as an iron bar. He kicked and squirmed but was held fast. A minute later he was dead.

Raglan released his grip. He winced. It hurt when he breathed heavily. His ribs were bruised and stitches in the wound in his side had parted company with the tender flesh. His nose was bleeding and he could feel the split in his cheekbone trickling blood on to his neck. Raglan limped on, holding the silenced Glock, and checked the dead man's friends weren't close by.

He didn't wait to see the result of the grenade he threw into the generator shed. When it detonated he was halfway around the protected woman's house. Two contractors guarding the front of the house whirled around at the sudden explosion. Raglan shot them with the Glock. Beyond the garden three 4 × 4s roared away from the rear of the compound. He ran to intercept them in case Arambanou was making her escape, but it was the remaining few contractors calling it a day, aware that if unknown forces had caused this amount of destruction then a bigger attack was likely coming their way. Raglan let them go. The killer he sought was not with them.

She was still here.

79

Aram-banou remained in darkness inside her house. When the flames leapt into the night sky they had forced her back from the window. The sudden burst of gunfire seemed to come from where Reyes's men were housed. Had the drug smuggler betrayed them? They had shot those paid to protect her; she saw three of them fall. From the screams of pain she knew others must have been hit as well. She retreated further back into the room and waited. She felt no sense of panic. Fate was unfolding in front of her, and fear played no part in her reaction to what she witnessed or her certainty about what was going to happen. The killing outside heralded the man coming to kill her. She would let Raglan fight his way through the cordon of men. When a predator has escaped its cage it is foolish to step out into its hunting ground.

She had abandoned western dress and clothed herself in her martial-arts black jacket and trousers, wrapping a black hijab over her head and covering all but her eyes. She had watched as explosions roared and then she saw the crouched figure of a man weaving through the compound with another on his shoulders. The buildings blocked her view and she lost sight of him when he reached the bridge.

Why the bridge? Why take an injured man there? One false move near the riverbank and the terrifying creatures who lay below the surface would strike. There was no answer. There was nothing to do but wait. The reason would soon reveal itself.

And then there was another explosion and the lights in the compound died. Only the flames cast any illumination, making shadows indistinct and wavering, casting uncertainty as to who or what caused them. It suited her. In the darkness she would be all but invisible to an intruder.

She held the blade low at her side.

Raglan circled the house. There was no movement. Only the dead lay nearby. He peered beneath the stilts. At the far side, one of the contractors he had killed lay face down, head turned his way. The dead man's eyes flickered in the flames, staring at Raglan. Bewildered and accusing. They would join all the others whose image would never fade from Raglan's mind.

The windows were closed and mostly shuttered, except for the one main window in the front of the house. If the interior was that airtight then whoever was inside was in a humid box. That might play to Raglan's advantage if it slowed their reactions. The risk was that a gunman was inside with the killer. He backed off from the house and hurled a rock through the front window. There was no replying gunfire. In the shimmering firelight, he moved quickly up the couple of steps to the front door. It was outwards opening so there was no chance of kicking it free of its lock. An old wooden chair nestled in the corner of the veranda. He heaved it through the remaining glass in the window. As the shards fell, he stepped across the frame's low threshold. The closed shutters and doors inside the house made it pitch black. How far did the room he stood in extend? He crouched. The flames helped him determine that the sparsely furnished room was the main living area and did not conceal the killer. He guessed the closed door on the opposite wall would lead to the bedrooms. His feet crunched broken glass; his hand turned the door handle. Raglan was flung back by the impact of the door being kicked in from the other side. The Glock flew from his hand as he fell on to the glass-littered floor and felt the sting of shards cutting through his shirt. Ignoring the flesh wounds, he rolled on to more glass to avoid the shadow that leapt at him.

Instinct made him cross his arms over his chest. His locked forearms stopped the sudden impact of the knife's downward lunge. He whipped his head to one side, avoiding the glimmering blade, felt Aram-banou's breath on his face but caught only a glimpse of her dark eyes close to his own. He kicked out; his boot connected. She made no sound as she fell back, despite the force of his kick, but he heard an intake of breath as the broken glass bit into her.

Raglan was on his feet, as was the shadow who danced to one side; flames caught the crouch and martial-arts kick that struck out at his face. He ducked, shifted his weight and punched hard to where her face would be. He was too late. She had pivoted and arced the blade through the darkness. Raglan's missed punch had turned his shoulder exposing his back. The searing cut went through shirt and skin. It was a maiming strike which, had it been successful, would have separated muscle from bone. A butcher's filleting cut. The rapid, indistinct movements of the black-clad woman gave her the advantage. Raglan parried another blow in the near darkness; she kicked his thigh. Once again the wound complained. Raglan took two fast strides backwards, pressing his back against the wall to help support the sudden dead leg and to draw her into the light of the flames from outside. She was intent on the follow-through. She stepped forwards and directed a swift upwards curving strike towards his groin. It was predictable. Her signature killing blow.

The blade found empty space. Raglan had sidestepped, turned on his heel and jabbed his knife into her left arm. She cried out. He snatched at her but all he grabbed was her head covering. She retreated, leaving him with a handful of black cloth as her blonde hair fell free. She ran for the door.

Raglan followed her into the firelit night.

He stepped over the bodies littering the compound. He saw Aram-banou's blonde hair as she jogged towards the bridge and turned to see if he was following. He saw that she was cradling her left arm where his knife had hit. Raglan doubted his cut had hurt her that badly. Was she showing him that she was vulnerable? Drawing him in? Hoping he would lower his guard? She still held her knife. She quickened her pace, turning off the road on the other side of the low wall. There was an SUV there, painted in disruptive camouflage pattern, easily concealed beneath the low palm trees. Raglan had not seen it when he delivered Luis Reyes to the villagers. If she reached it and there were keys in the ignition she would escape and people in power would protect her.

He ran hard for the bridge, desperate to block her route.
Pieces of metal from the destroyed trucks lay here and
there. Raglan grabbed a large, twisted side panel that had
been torn into sharp claws on one side. The tortured metal
was enough to stop a vehicle. It took all his strength to drag
it to the mouth of the bridge. Blood ran down his leg. His
wounded side had finally torn free of its sutures. The brutal
hand-to-hand fighting had taken its toll. He grunted with
effort, fell, got to his feet again and hauled the dead weight
closer to the bridge. The SUV's engine started.

Aram-banou floored the accelerator and spun the steering
wheel. The wound in her arm felt like scalded skin but
she could still use the limb and, ignoring the muscle
spasm, snatched the wheel to swing out and get on to the
road facing the bridge. She lost control as the back end
slid and caught the edge of the low wall. The vehicle's
weight slewed it forwards and it hurtled free. The high-
beam headlights caught the chunk of metal across the
bridge. Raglan waited beyond it. She stamped her foot
on the brake, holding the powerful engine back. But the
bridge was her only way out. The SUV might be snared
by the ragged metal, but perhaps it would push aside the
obstacle. She moved her foot from brake to accelerator.
Raglan retreated a half-dozen paces. The SUV slammed
into the metal. It reared, the four-wheel drive powering it
over. Elated, she kept her foot pressed down. And then the
sound of the undersides being ripped out tore away the
momentary feeling of success. The SUV stalled and died.
She put her shoulder to the door and scrambled free as

Raglan ran towards her in the headlight beams.

She ran for the river. A four-metre bank sloped down and levelled on to a mud lip at the water's edge. She hesitated, heard the sound of the pounding Englishman giving chase. Something moved in the water. She slithered down a couple of metres, grabbed a handful of grass to slow her descent, and then dug her heels in. Eyes glinted in the middle of the stream just below the surface. She gasped. Breath short, fearful of the death that awaited her at the water's edge if she tried to get below the bridge to the boat she knew to be moored there.

'Your choice,' said Raglan, standing on top of the bank. 'I hope you're feeling something of what that girl did when you cut her and let her be taken. I'll give you the same chance.'

Keeping her eyes on Raglan, she tried to climb back up but the rains had made the bank too muddy. Raglan watched as she slipped, grabbed vegetation and found purchase. 'Get past me and the road is open,' he said, taking a few steps back, giving her the chance to reach the top.

Whatever weakness she felt from her efforts vanished as she crested the bank. The Englishman looked to be in a bad way. His body language showed her that his side and leg were causing him a problem. Gore from the fight with the men and cuts from the glass in the house smothered his hands. His knife hand was empty and dripped blood. The caked dirt and slime on his clothes looked to weigh heavily on him. His head hung wearily, chin almost on his chest. She knew Raglan was finished. The punishing assault on the compound had finally pushed him to the limit of his endurance. She leapt forwards, catching Raglan flat-footed, feinted with the knife and then pivoted in a fast move that would bring the blade into his stomach.

Her knife arm was blocked in a bone-crushing grip. Raglan's shoulder slammed into her face. Blood filled her mouth. Training and instinct made her throw a jab for his throat. She heard and felt her elbow snap. Lightning pain flashed behind her eyes. Raglan had somehow avoided both blows and retaliated hard and fast. He was no longer the defeated-looking man. She read it in his eyes as their faces came close. He had drawn her in.

Her left arm was useless; bile surged into her throat. Raglan held her knife hand, his body pressed against hers, his strength holding hers, turning the blade, yanking it upwards. A burning sensation scored across her thigh and into her groin. Raglan released his grip. She staggered back, spat blood, dropped the knife and pressed her palm against the bloodied mess. Warmth flooded down her leg.

She couldn't comprehend it. She mouthed disbelief.

'Things have to be made right,' Raglan said.

She sank to her knees, shook her head, trying to free her thoughts from the weakness flooding her body. She looked up at Raglan. She slipped an arm's length down the bank. She reached out, grasping his boot to stop herself sliding any further. 'No... this is not possible... All I... All I wanted was justice,' she murmured.

He eased his foot back. She lost her grip and began to slide slowly towards the sound of the creature clawing itself from the water. A mask of terror distorted her features.

'Me too,' said Raglan.

80

Two Black Hawks, their rotors silent, squatted in the compound as the task force conducted their search of the house, grounds and houses. Kim Burton had flown in, an hour after they had landed. Voss handed her the briefcase.

'Two women who worked in the main house said it was from an Englishman. I checked inside. There's even more evidence for a special prosecutor. This was one hell of a conspiracy and I got dragged into it right at the start. Back then I had no idea I was so close to all of this. Raglan had the full dossier on a flash drive. Every damned thing. Who, where, and how.'

'And that information is in with these documents?'

'My guess? It's with British intelligence.'

Burton sighed. 'At least they'll share the information. It gives them skin in the game. They'll want in on everything. Fair trade.'

Burton and Voss walked through the compound's devastation. The soldiers had laid out all the bodies that could be found. Acrid smoke still drifted. Voss's face was smudged with sweat and soot.

'You were here?' said Kim Burton.

Voss shook her head. 'I took a pickup from the village when the men returned. I got here minutes before the choppers. It was all over.'

'It looks like a damned napalm attack here. How many bodies so far?' said Burton.

Voss shook her head. 'Enough.'

'It's a damned butcher's yard. Any sign of Luis Reyes?' said Burton.

Voss turned away in case the senior FBI agent saw her lie because she had seen Reyes being taken back to the village in the *patrón*'s pickup. 'No idea. He's not among the dead here.' She dared to face Burton again. 'Somewhere else maybe.'

'Our Coast Guard and a Royal Navy frigate stopped a ship carrying a cargo of weapons from here. Coast Guard said the British had alerted them. We had word there was a woman involved in all of this. A foreign national. Iranian.'

'She's dead. Over there. By the riverbank. Knife wound. She bled out. What's left of her. Looks like she ran into someone who knew how to inflict violence more effectively than she could. Before the croc got her, that is. She's mentioned in the documents in the briefcase. It's all there, Kim. The Agency and the DIA will hurt after this.'

Burton nodded, her nose scrunched against the stench that was undoubtedly charred flesh. 'The Bureau will come out of it well. You're already reinstated, by the way.'

'I never left,' said Voss. She pointed to where a man, naked except for a towel wrapped around his waist, was being frogmarched over to a chopper. 'Lennie Elliot. He'll fill in any blanks. The team found him tied to a bedstead.

That had to be Raglan's doing. Like all of this.' She smiled. 'A parting gift.'

Burton took the whole scene in again. Eyes searching out the missing Englishman. 'Where is Raglan?'

Jenna Voss shrugged without revealing her feelings. 'He's gone.'

ACKNOWLEDGEMENTS

Much of this book would not have been completed, or even started, had it not been for the beginning of a correspondence between the author and an American reader, Mike Thyrring, who had read my books and my bio on the website, and discovered we shared common elements in our lives. Our correspondence resulted in his generous offer for me to visit his place of work, the Pentagon, where he would arrange for me to have a private tour. Little did I know at the time that he was a retired lieutenant colonel in the United States Marine Corps. Mike and his charming wife, Gayle, acted as generous hosts during my stay in Washington DC. He shared his knowledge of the city and where not to go to avoid getting into dangerous situations, all of which, of course, fed into the narrative of this book. During my research thereafter he continued to offer invaluable advice on a broad number of what must have often seemed unimportant queries.

I would also like to extend my gratitude to Lieutenant Colonel Randy Odom, USA (Ret.), who took a great deal of time to lead me through the Pentagon complex on a fascinating and illuminating private tour. He was the perfect guide with a wealth of personal military experience that embellished much of the exhibits and background of the Pentagon's history.

Photographs are forbidden inside the Pentagon for obvious reasons. During my tour, we turned a corner and bumped into Major General Garrett S. Yee, US Army, who enquired who was the Englishman being escorted. Without a second thought, he suggested a commemorative photograph be taken to mark the occasion. A generous offer gratefully acknowledged. (You can see the photograph at www.davidgilman.com.)

There are different law-enforcement agencies operating in Washington DC, and to confirm my research on the various police procedures in the capital regarding the securing of evidence in a murder investigation, I contacted the Metropolitan Police Department, Evidence Control Branch, where the departmental manager Mr Roger Sutton kindly addressed my enquiry.

My thanks to Desmond and Aleta Gibson who graciously hosted my stay at Vero Beach during my research. Des was the perfect guide who drove me around the area described in this novel.

Dr Grenville Major kindly advised me on surgery techniques and Keith Chiazzari helped me choose the aircraft and how to avoid air traffic control at Key West. I am extremely grateful to them both for their unstinting aid.

Any errors made in the novel, or changes to the advice provided by those generous enough to have given it, are entirely mine.

My thanks to Ian McLean in Australia for his eagle eye. This is the tenth novel of mine that Richenda Todd has read and meticulously edited. Her tireless patience and skill go above and beyond the call of duty. So too the efforts of my publisher Nic Cheetham and the whole team at Head of Zeus.

To my wonderful and insightful literary agent, Isobel Dixon, at Blake Friedmann Literary Agency: thank you for your ceaseless enthusiasm and encouragement. We have come a long way since I submitted my first manuscript in 2006. And a big thank you to everyone at BFLA who beaver away behind the scenes.

None of my books could have been started, let alone completed, without my wonderful wife, Suzy Chiazzari, who has shared our home with me and so many of my characters with abiding love and forbearance. At times the dinner table has been overcrowded with phantom guests but, incredibly, she continues to tolerate us all.

David Gilman
Devonshire

ABOUT THE AUTHOR

David Gilman enjoyed many careers – including firefighter, paratrooper and photographer – before turning to writing full time. He is an award-winning author and screenwriter. You can follow him on his website: www.davidgilman.com; on Facebook: www.facebook.com/davidgilman.author; and on Twitter: @davidgilmanuk.